The Witch Diggers

Books by Jessamyn West
THE FRIENDLY PERSUASION
A MIRROR FOR THE SKY
THE WITCH DIGGERS

The Witch Diggers

JESSAMYN WEST

Harcourt, Brace and Company
New York

COPYRIGHT, 1951, BY

JESSAMYN WEST

*All rights reserved, including
the right to reproduce this book
or portions thereof in any form.*

PRINTED IN THE UNITED STATES OF AMERICA
BY H. WOLFF, NEW YORK

for Max

The Witch Diggers

1

CHRISTIE FRASER first visited Cate Conboy on December 24, 1899. Christie was twenty-two at that time and Cate four years younger. Never a very methodical person, Christie had to run for the train which was to take him to the Conboys'. He leaped onto the steps of the final car just as its wheels started turning and flung himself and his shiny new Gladstone bag down on the next to the last seat with so much force that he could feel the prickle of the stiff upholstery material right through his soft serge trousers. He felt considerably superior to his car-mates who had wasted a part of the day and their lives by arriving too early, and after he had disposed of his bag and while he was catching his breath, he looked them over.

The train, running south out of Indianapolis, carried two kinds of passengers: city-dwellers bound for the farms and small towns of the countryside to spend the Christmas holidays and those off the small farms and out of the small towns returning to their homes after a day of Christmas buying in the city. The nearness of Christmas altered the appearance of the passengers; like love, it had the power of transfiguration. The occupants of the car—ordinarily farmers, farmers' wives, lady clerks, train-dispatchers, pharmacists' assistants, windmill salesmen—had broken through these limitations into something less specific, and more endearing: they were the hopeful, the homeward bound. Christmas, like love, was a mystery. Time and again it might disappoint, but like love only the promises of the Christmas to come, never the disappointments of those past, seemed real. And the nearness of Christmas was a mesh: it held the passengers together, closer than blood relationships, almost as close as the beginnings of love.

Two hours outside the city snow began to fall. It wove a fine white web which the train easily broke and which the storm, once the train had passed, easily mended. It was a lodging snow, clinging to all it touched, building up snow-trees, snow-fences, snow-stumps and whitening the distant hills so that they merged indistinguishably with the colorless sky. Although it was only a little after four o'clock, the day was ending. It was already possible to say that Christmas Eve had arrived. The white surfaces of the snow-covered fields of stubble which lined the tracks held more light than the sky overhead and, from the final car, occasional stars could be seen, blue-white and uncertain, but still the stars of Christmas Eve.

Then the conductor, red-faced and genial, like a host entering his parlor, appeared to light the lamps. Their substantial domestic glow dimmed the outside world, put out the stars, and drew the passengers still closer together. Christmas had held them, the common journey, the chance of having taken the same car. Now the yellow lights looped them about in an even closer circle and inside this circle the conductor moved with assured familiarity. He knew many of the passengers and many knew him: Mr. Jefferson Ames who had risen from chancy farming to certain railroading.

Mr. Ames' communication with his passengers was not, this evening, on the level of his knowledge of their lives. Like a preacher speaking from a pulpit, he transcended the workaday world. He spoke from the eminence of the time of year it was and the time of day. Christmas had elevated Mr. Ames, and dusk. Knowledge of his passengers' marriages, failures to marry, gains, losses, children, lack of children, sins, repentances, and final fallings from grace (which he had in full) were unimportant to him. Tonight only the journey together was important and the destination.

Mr. Ames prodded bundles, shook packages, stroked fur collars, chucked chins, pinched cheeks, tweaked ears, pulled noses, patted arms, slapped shoulders, appraised, commented, questioned, applauded, congratulated, and no one took it amiss or turned from him. Mr. Ames was Christmas made visible. He was no caroling angel; he did not sing, "I bring you glad tidings," but his big nodding head, his plump, chapped hands managed to convey this sentiment to the passengers in the last car of the southbound train.

He plucked a long, bottle-shaped package from a basket, shook it, and cried, "The spirits within speak to my spirit." He lifted the gold locket which Carrie Samms had carefully hung outside her coat, snapped it open, and peered at the picture inside. "Not bad for a starter, Carrie," he said, "but never think of stopping there." He trailed his fingers across a hat's drooping feathers and whistled bird notes as if expecting the feathers to reset themselves in wings, the wings to fan the air, and the hat to fly off, echoing his whistle. He took a piece of hard candy from a child's paper bag, snapped open the thin jaws at the end of a woman's fur neckpiece and set the candy between them saying, "Merry Christmas, kitty." "Fox," the woman told him, taking the candy out and putting it into her own mouth; but Mr. Ames was already down the aisle and beyond correcting, scaring himself with a child's jack-in-the-box for the child's pleasure.

Christie, noting Mr. Ames' progress, put the letter he had been reading back into his pocket; but he was not quick enough for Mr. Ames who sank down somewhat winded into the seat beside him. "Does she still love you, boy?" he wheezed.

"Letter from my grandmother," Christie said, "advising me to keep my feet dry."

"Hah!" said Mr. Ames. "And are you doing it?"

Christie pulled his feet into sight from under the seat in front of him. Mr. Ames inspected them. "Dry ain't the word," he said.

"Cherished," Christie told him.

"That's going to be a surprise to them," Mr. Ames said and nodded outward to the snowy earth.

By putting his face close to the window Christie could still make out the nature of the country through which they were passing. Woodlots, gaunt and bare of leaves, alternated with cleared fields, and the cleared fields were either saw-toothed with corn stubble or scraggly with leafless orchards. The land was broken by abrupt hills and sudden ravines so that the train was forever curving around some out-thrust shoulder of earth or rumbling across a trestle beneath which black water carried a spattering of newly fallen snow. It was a countryside neither rugged nor savage. Only ragged, desolate, unkempt, cold. Sorrowful, too, Christie felt, as a land is which is neither one thing nor another; neither completely wild nor completely cultivated; forests half-deadened; earth half-farmed; orchards loosely rooted in the rocky soil with nothing more than a snake fence to protect them from the dark woods which everywhere seemed to be threatening to slide down from the hills and overwhelm them.

Approaching a crossing the train whistled, the quavering long, short, short, to which Christie had listened many nights in his room in Indianapolis and which, there, had sounded remote and mournful. Heard from inside the train the tooting was matter-of-fact and cheerful: the difference in feeling paralleling that of the stay-at-home uttering a tearful farewell and the traveler who, intent on new worlds, has scarcely time to wave in reply. The train passed a farm house so closely that Christie saw women bustling about the lighted kitchen tending stove and tables. He imagined them, at the sound of the long-drawn whistle, feeling pity for the train's passengers traveling on Christmas Eve, ringed about by falling snow, bound no one knew where. Well, let them pity us, he thought. It would make them feel snugger as he felt snugger, hearing in his bed at night the muted cries of the trains pulling out from the Union Station.

"Looks like big doings at the Dunphys' tonight," said Mr. Ames, at his elbow.

Christie turned away from the window. "You know all the houses along the tracks?" he asked.

"Houses, outbuildings, haystacks, hen-roosts!" Mr. Ames declared. "Why, I even know the dogs and cattle and the ticks on them. Dunphys have two cows and one dog. The cows are half Jersey, and the dog's pure nothing. His name's Pedro. Don't know where he was tonight. You're not from these parts, are you?"

"No," said Christie, who would not have cared to have been thought so.

"Indianapolis?"

Christie nodded.

"Getting off at The Junction, aren't you?"

"If the train'll stop long enough."

"It'll stop. Where next?"

"The Poor Farm," Christie was pleased to say, expecting a start of surprise from Mr. Ames.

Mr. Ames apparently was never surprised. "Permanent or visiting?"

"Visiting," Christie said, surprised himself at this question. "For the present."

"Got an invitation or just chancing in on them?"

"Got an invitation," Christie said, moving his finger around the outline of the letter in his pocket.

"Link, or one of the children?"

To this man, Christie supposed, Cate was one of the children so he said, "One of the children."

"Cate or brother Dandie?"

"Cate," Christie answered, beginning to understand the means by which Mr. Ames kept himself so well informed.

Mr. Ames nodded in approval. "Pretty girl. Clever and biddable too, from all I hear. How you figure on getting out there?"

"Walk," Christie said. "It's only three miles, isn't it?"

"Five. And in them shoes"—Mr. Ames looked at Christie's feet as if the elegance of their patent leather negated their existence—"it would feel like fifty. I'll fix you up a ride. I know a fellow going your way." As he rose to leave he added, "You ain't going to make a hit with anybody if you go in sorefooted and bedraggled."

As Christie watched the conductor's bulky, accustomed lurch down the aisle and out the door he thought, What makes him think I want to make a hit with anybody? He shoved his pointed patent-leathers, spangled with reflections of the lights overhead, under the seat in front of him and watched the snowy earth slip past the window.

II

HE HAD met Cate Conboy for the first time six months before at Stony Creek. He had gone down there in August, a month after his mother's death, to visit Uncle Wesley Cope. He had gone, partly because Uncle Wes had taken for granted that he would, partly because he himself wanted an interlude in which he could think about the past and about his mother. He felt that he needed a little time in which to remember, to gather up out of the past what he wanted to keep. His college days were over. In another month he would begin work. He considered himself to be standing on some kind of a dividing line, on the horizon of a new world.

Uncle Wes and Uncle Wes' daughter, Carmen Sylva, had met him at the depot in the buckboard. Christie at that time was able to see his Uncle Wes only partially. In the beginning of life there is so much to be seen and so much that needs to be learned quickly that nature, in an effort to protect the young from being overwhelmed, presents many objects to them in outline only: seemingly flat surfaces which the eyes can take in at a glance. The middle-aged are so presented, and Wesley Cope, being not only middle-aged but Christie's uncle, appeared to Christie as a very meager outline, indeed. Though not an unpleasant one.

His cousin Carmen Sylva, called Sylvy, was no outline, however. She had dimensions Christie could only imagine, perspectives stretching away into the unknowable. She was twenty-seven, five years older than Christie and had been named first Carmen, then later Carmen Sylva after the Queen of Romania, a beautiful woman; and a poet also, Christie understood. Christie did not know whether his cousin wrote poetry or not and he was unable to decide whether or not she was beautiful. She had at least the effect of beauty upon him. He wanted always to be looking at her and he followed her about from room to room as she did her work.

On the afternoon of the second day of his visit at Stony Creek, his cousin asked Christie if he didn't think that a pitcher of lemonade would be refreshing. Christie did. The morning had been hot and muggy, and now at midafternoon under a livid mushroom-colored sky the air was heavy and motionless. Christie squeezed the lemons and his cousin did the measuring, stirring and tasting. Then, just as Christie thought the mixture ready to drink, Sylvy thumped the yellow crockery pitcher down on to the kitchen table.

"Where is my mind?" she demanded of Christie. "What am I thinking of?"

Sylvy's voice was naturally low. Now, speaking with intensity, Christie thought she sounded rather theatrical. But he thought, too, that since she was tall, dark-haired, and dark-eyed, it suited her to sound so.

"Where *is* your mind, Sylvy?" he asked, imitating her manner. "What *are* you thinking of?"

"I'm a natural-born fool," Sylvy said shortly. "This is a special occasion. Why don't I use the cut-glass pitcher?"

She went into the dining-room where the best china and glassware were kept, and Christie followed her. The dining-room was on the north side of the house, long, narrow, and papered in green. With the blinds drawn, as they were, Christie felt as if they had entered the weedy, shadowed backwash of some little creek, a stream not cool but restful and remote. He sat down astride one of the heavy dining-room chairs, folded his arms across its back, then rested his face on his arms. While his cousin shifted tumblers and jelly dishes in the china-closet trying to reach the pitcher she wanted, he watched her and thought about the matter of her appearance. It seemed unlikely to him that anyone born with a harelip, however neatly it had been repaired, could be beautiful. The scar on his cousin's lip though small and only faintly pink was, nevertheless, clearly visible. Nor did his mind stay away from imagining how the lip would have been had the disfigurement not been cared for. And Sylvy, whether because of the surgery or because her two eye-teeth slanted a little outward, often seemed to be making an effort to bring her lips together. And this also, which should have been unpleasant, was not. Instead, it suggested that his cousin, breathless and eager, needed always to be reminding herself that the world would last and to be calm.

After Sylvy got the pitcher from the china-closet, the two of them began to talk. Sylvy stood, the pitcher glistening like a shaft of ice in her hand, while Christie continued to ride his chair as if it had been a broad-backed plow horse. Neither was comfortable; but neither made any motion to leave the room. They lingered in its green darkness like swimmers entangled in weeds, too weary to struggle and reconciled to drowning.

"Everything's so quiet here," Christie said. "And soft," he added in a low voice.

"Soft?" Sylvy asked in a perplexed voice.

"After the city, I mean," Christie explained. "Haystacks instead of office buildings. Your dress instead of a city dress."

"My dress!" Sylvy looked down at it.

In the weedy gloom it reminded Christie of a water-lily. There was white lace about the hem of its full frothy skirt, white lace formed the high collar and edged the short puffy sleeves. Looking at his cousin's arms—they were cream-colored, though somewhat shadowed with dark hairs—while his cheek lay against his own arm was, in a way, like touching her flesh instead of his own.

"It's so soft and flouncy-looking," Christie said.

A thousand other examples of country softness came to his mind. Sycamores, like leafy bosoms, curving aloft; in the bedrooms, arched feather beds instead of city mattresses; and outside, equally arched and springy, beds of late larkspur and early China asters. Stony Creek itself, above its stones, appeared as pliable and sinuous as a fat summer snake, and the two cows who spent the afternoon in its shallows looked soft enough to be dented with a finger.

"You miss your mother, don't you, Christie?" his cousin asked, as if that explained something to her.

Christie nodded. "Yes, I do. Before she died I didn't believe in death."

Sylvy lifted her head sharply. "Didn't believe in it?"

"I supposed I believed in it," Christie amended himself. "But it was like the Sahara Desert. Away off and for other people."

"It's right here, I guess. And for all of us." Sylvy smiled a little, as if she would ease the news for him.

"I know that now. The wonder to me now is that any of us are able to hang on as long as we do."

"Why, the human race is pretty lasty," Sylvy said. "We're most of us put together pretty solid."

"No," Christie insisted. "We're rickety. One good tap in the right place and we're done for."

Since the accident in which his mother had died, Christie had seen mortality all about him, in any horse's hoof, any spark of fire, any chance misalignment of a buggy wheel. Everyone he met looked lucky to him—and doomed. Lucky to be momentarily intact, but invitations to death and wreckage nevertheless.

"Take our blood now," he explained earnestly. "Nothing but a thin layer of skin to keep it from pouring out. And without blood," he raised his head to watch the movements of a wasp trapped between glass and screen and outlined against the drawn curtain, "you'd be no better off than a dried-up wasp's nest."

"But it doesn't pour out. That's the point," Sylvy said matter-of-factly. She lifted her free arm and looked at the blue veins branching down its white inside. "What would you want us to be covered with, Christie? Leather?"

Christie paid no attention to this. He believed what he was saying and at the same time knew he was exaggerating. But it was all right, he felt, to exaggerate concerning death. Nothing he could say would equal it for strangeness or finality. Besides, he wanted to say something which would impress his cousin, make her wonder about what was going on in his head as she stood there calmly regarding him, the cut-glass pitcher gleaming in her hand.

"Take our hearts, now," he said. "The ribs should be closer together. No need for anybody to take aim as it is. Any blunt knife will slide past them, anywhere."

"I don't think we could breathe," Sylvy said reasonably, "if they were closer together. Or bend. Could we, Christie?"

"Well, we couldn't be stabbed so easy, anyway."

"Stabbed!" Sylvy exclaimed. "You don't go around worrying about being stabbed, do you, Christie?"

Christie didn't, but he went on determinedly. "Take our entrails," he said. "Look at them! What protection have *they* got?" He cupped one hand protectively about the nonexistent bulge of his own entrails. "Completely exposed," he declared. "A jab from any cow horn or broken fence paling will spill *them* out!"

"Entrails!" Uncle Wes exclaimed from the doorway and Christie looked up, abashed, afraid his Uncle Wes would think him a loose talker, an unsuitable companion for his daughter. "What's all this talk about entrails?"

"Christie thinks they aren't well enough protected," Sylvy explained.

"Depends upon whose entrails you're talking about," said Uncle Wes, slapping his own which were well covered. "City boy like you, Christie, I'm surprised to hear you even know about such things."

"They've got 'em in Indianapolis too," Christie replied. "Just like the country."

"Lord, yes," his uncle agreed. "But not just like the country. You've got a lot more of them up there in Indianapolis. I never see so many pot-guts in my life as when I go up there." Then recalling himself, he turned back to Sylvy. "Any objections if Lafe rides into town with me?" Lafe was the hired man.

"Tell him to go right ahead," Sylvy said.

"You'll have to take care of the feeding and milking, if he goes," Uncle Wes reminded her.

"That's all right. Christie will feed for me."

At this Uncle Wes turned to leave but noticing the pitcher in Sylvy's hand, asked, "Did you have some plan in mind for that?"

Sylvy lifted the pitcher and stared at it. "Lemonade!" she cried. "There's lemonade in the kitchen. Could you drink some, Papa?"

"I could," Uncle Wes said. "This lodge supper won't get started until late and some lemon juice in my craw will be that much better than nothing."

He walked into the kitchen, breaking the spell which had kept Christie and Sylvy in the dining-room. "A couple of jumbles," he said, "if you can rustle them up, wouldn't be bad either."

The kitchen, which was on the west side of the house, was filled with yellow light from the low sun. Entering it Christie felt as if he had stepped from water to dry air, from night to day. He saw that his cousin was also aware of the change for she moved about excitedly, swinging her skirts this way and that, flinging open the door to the safe as if she were defying someone.

"Here you are, Papa," she said. The lemonade, though less cool than it had been, was good and the jumbles were sweet and crusty. The three of them stood about the table eating and talking as if at a planned party, and no one made a move to go until both platter and pitcher were empty.

Uncle Wes brushed the crumbs from his sprawling mustache. "That ought to hold me, I guess."

"Hold you, Papa!" Sylvy exclaimed. "You won't be able to eat a bite of the banquet."

"Don't you fash yourself about me, daughter. I can play a good knife and fork any time, anywhere." He shook a few more drops of lemonade from the bottom of his glass into his mouth and with them a seed which he spat back. "Got to go slick myself up. Got three men riding the goat tonight, an important occasion," he said and was off up the back stairs to dress.

No sooner had he left than Sylvy exclaimed at what she had done: forgotten, after all, to use the cut-glass pitcher. There it stood, just as it had come from the china-closet, flashing crimson and blue and green as the sun struck its carved constellations, its sprays of crystal fern.

"And I was determined to use it," she lamented.

Christie curved his hand about the squat crockery pitcher. "It couldn't possibly have tasted better," he told her, "in anything else."

III

CHRISTIE held the lantern while his cousin milked. The milking should have been done long before dark, and Christie was the one responsible for the lateness. He had talked and talked, and his cousin had been reluctant to interrupt him with reminders of how much there was to be done. At last she *had* told him, and Christie had then managed to get himself down to the pasture. But there he had stuck, loitering until dusk and after beside Stony Creek. And it was the cows, finally, who brought him to the house, he treading along behind them, bemused and reluctant.

The day had first darkened, then lightened as he stood by Stony Creek. Just before sundown the clouds along the western horizon broke open exposing a rim of light, orange-yellow like the yolks of spring eggs. This light, pouring down on to the waters of Stony Creek, gilded gnats and midges and lined the tracks of scooting water-bugs with bright gold. Sycamore leaves drifted downstream as he watched. The water passing through a riffle spoke la, la, la. Birds sang wheezily as if hoarsened by their long day's trilling.

Christie felt both happy and unhappy, cold and feverish, hurried and with the whole of time before him. His mother was dead. Death awaited him. Yet out of this sorrowful and forbidding knowledge, even because of it, he was experiencing happiness and exultation. Now, *he* was not dead. Now, the whole area of his

[13]

body, and inside his body unnumbered miles of nerves and veins, were his with which to experience the world.

On a sudden impulse he stepped out of his clothes and into the creek. To experience *it* with the whole area of his body he had to lie flat upon its pebbles. The two cows bent their large mild eyes upon him in such ladylike astonishment and interest that Christie laughed aloud. He let his head sink beneath the water, pillowed it, as Jacob had done, upon a stone. But no angels came down to him from heaven. Instead, the sky itself from beneath Stony Creek became watery, and the dry summer foliage appeared damp and glistening.

Christie rose, and a beetle slowly circling, slowly drowning, was carried safely ashore on his shoulder. He shook the beetle off and said loudly, "I am Christian J. Fraser," as if that were a promise to cling to. The cows, startled by this declaration, turned homeward. Damp and buttoning himself as he went, Christie followed them.

It was the cessation of the rhythmical hiss of milk into the bucket, rather than his cousin's voice, which brought Christie back to himself.

"Christie," Sylvy said, "why don't you hang the lantern on that peg? That's what it's for."

Christie saw then that while his mind had been elsewhere, he had let the lantern droop until his cousin was milking in darkness.

"You hold the lantern," he ordered, "and let me milk."

"You don't know how, do you?"

"Squeeze, pull, squeeze, pull," said Christie, who had been watching the casual rise and fall of his cousin's wrists. "That's about all there is to it, isn't it?"

Without a word Sylvy arose from the milking-stool and took the lantern from Christie. "Try it," she said.

Something in her voice made Christie defend himself. "I may be a city boy, Cousin Sylvy, but I'm strong in the hands. Maybe I never milked a cow before but you ought to see me on the parallel bars."

This made Sylvy laugh and, feeling witty as well as capable, Christie moved the stool a few inches away from the cow.

"Like a player addressing a piano," Sylvy scoffed.

"Now for the music," Christie said, admitting the likeness and ready to demonstrate his technique.

"You better not use that back teat," Sylvy warned him. "It's cracked and Elizabeth objects if you don't handle it just right."

"Elizabeth!" Christie said. "Is this animal named Elizabeth?"

"Yes, she is," Sylvy told him. "Is there anything wrong with that?"

"Not if you like it," Christie said.

But *he* didn't. It was too human. It brought back a long forgotten, disquieting memory, a lost and unhappy imagining of his childhood, a fantasy which had occupied his sixth, or was it his seventh year? A fantasy which had sickened him and which he had been unable to put from him. When, finally, he had been able to rid himself of it, Christie didn't know. But he remembered, as if it were a minute ago, the night when it had first occurred to him. He had been homeward bound from the country, sitting half-asleep between his father and mother on the front seat of the surrey. Then, suddenly, there had been revealed to him the nature of the bad thing for which men wanted women and about which he had long wondered: they wanted to use them as cattle, to imprison them in barns, chain them to stanchions, feed them more than they wanted, exercise them little—and milk them! And they would be valued for the amount of milk they produced, as a cow was valued. All the images connected with this horrible practice had crowded into his mind that night so that he was at once fascinated and repelled. No wonder grown-ups lowered their voices when talking of such things! Silently, that night, he had assured his mother, "You need never, never worry about me, Mama. I will never be a bad man with women."

Now, as if Sylvy were able to detect in his mind the shadow left by these imaginings and because, strangely enough, their childish viciousness still had power to disturb him, he said boisterously, "A person who would call a cow Elizabeth would call a horse Percy. Or a dog Edwin. Or a cat Gladys."

"Well," said Sylvy, "this cow is named Elizabeth. Are you going to milk her or not?"

"Certainly I'm going to milk her," Christie said. "She's not responsible for her name. I'm not responsible for her name. Squeeze, pull, squeeze, pull," he instructed himself and practised these motions for a second or two. Then he gingerly grasped the two teats nearest him and energetically carried out his own instructions. Except that Elizabeth swung her head about to see what was going on, nothing whatever happened. No ping of milk against the side of the bucket, no creamy hiss of milk into the foam already there.

"You have to squeeze and pull at the same time, Christie," Sylvy told him.

"All right," Christie said. "Squeeze *and* pull." He did this vigorously. Elizabeth gave a short moo like a dog's bark. There was no accompanying flow of milk, however.

"Be easy, Christie," Sylvy said. "Elizabeth wants to be milked as much as you want to milk her."

"She don't act like it!" Christie said. "She surely don't act like it. She acts stubborn and uncoöperative to me. But if there's milk there I'm going to get it," he declared, combining the squeeze-pull in such a way as to elongate not only the two teats he held but the entire udder. Elizabeth's response to this was to lift a hind foot and with it the milk bucket so that he was thoroughly drenched.

"Why, the damned awkward, stubborn old heifer!" he sputtered, backing away and wiping the milk off his face and out of his eyes. Except for Sylvy he would have returned the cow's kick with interest. "I wouldn't have an animal like that on the place."

Suddenly he realized that Sylvy was laughing; had, in fact, hung the lantern on the peg so that she could laugh more easily. She was leaning backwards, hands pressed to her sides, eyes almost closed.

"What's so funny?" Christie asked.

Sylvy continued to laugh for a time without saying anything. Then she managed to gasp, "You, Christie. You look so queer. Like a big glass of milk. A big glass of spilt milk." This set her off again. "Spilt milk. That's what you are."

Christie stopped wiping milk from his face and gazed at his cousin. The light shining on her dark hair picked up reddish strands, and her full lips, with the tiny pink scar plainly visible, were widely parted.

He stepped angrily toward her, then stopped. "Spilt milk!" he said. "All right you can have some of it too, Cousin Sylvy." Without regard for her white dress and almost as if he were punishing her he put his arms about her, kissed her, held her so close that the milk on his face and shirt was transferred to her cheeks and dress.

"Now," he said, as if that had been his whole purpose, "if there's any spilt milk, it's on you too."

Afterwards, on his way to the house to get into clean clothes, he could not remember whether Sylvy had said anything or not. Or whether she had made any movement away from him. The memory in his arms was that she had not.

While he washed off the milk Christie looked inward for contrition. That was no cousinly kiss, he admitted to himself, slapping water on to his face and chest. But he could find no contrition, nothing but a kind of sober well-being which was both startling and disappointing: as if a man after a successful robbery should feel no more excitement than the honest recipient of an unexpected bequest.

When he had finished washing he went upstairs and stood at the open window of his room: somewhere far to the east, perhaps clear across the Ohio, there were sudden spidery tracings, lightning which spread and trembled about the horizon like the outline of a sick and uncertain hand. But it was still too distant for the accompanying thunderclaps to be heard.

Christie buttoned his clean shirt thinking that if he felt no contrition, the least he could do was to be a little confused as to what he would say when next he saw his cousin. What was he, anyway? A young and bereft cousin making a visit and receiving kindness and sympathy? A possible suitor? A seducer laying his plans? Ordinarily he would have wanted answers to such questions before he could feel comfortable. He would have needed, before going downstairs, a label for his own guidance. Now, it did not seem to matter. He was himself, unlabeled, and whatever he did next, that was what he was. He would not be separated from the coming event by a layer of analysis.

When he did go downstairs he saw that his cousin had either been acting before or was now acting. She was quite different. His own mother had never been so maternal. Nor so sunk into the abyss of years which separated them. Sylvy gave him his supper with the solicitude of an elderly aunt concerned lest a small nephew had become overtired—and perhaps overwrought—with the day's visiting. He half expected her to hold his teacup for him and cut his meat.

After supper she took him into the sitting-room and sat with him there, she on the ladder-back chair by the open window, he across from her on the leather-covered sofa. She talked of their common ancestors, speaking of the two grandparents they shared and whose pictures hung on either side of the organ, as if she were their contemporary but not he.

"There are two things I've always heard about Grandpa Sharp," she told him. "First that he—"

Christie interrupted her. "First that he was the greatest cusser hereabouts."

Sylvy laughed. It was pleasant to see her laugh, Christie thought, because the act was so spontaneous, so plainly against her intention of holding her scarred lip quite still. "How did you know?" she asked. "Did Aunt Therese tell you?" Aunt Therese was Christie's mother.

Christie nodded. "And the second thing was that Jackie Sharp had the whitest skin, for a man, anybody had ever seen."

At this, as if she considered a man's skin, even their own grandfather's, an unsuitable subject for them to be discussing, and as if, too, she blamed herself for having introduced the subject in the first place, Sylvy put an end to the conversation by going over to the organ and playing a few firm chords.

"Father always enjoys hearing a hymn or two before bedtime."

"Is it bedtime?" Christie asked. The clock on the mantel had not yet struck nine.

"It is for me," said Sylvy.

"Don't play any hell-fire tunes," Christie advised her. "It would sound too much like an invitation." He nodded toward the window where thunder could be heard growling steadily nearer. "It's creeping up on us as it is."

Sylvy swung around on the stool so that she could see the sulphurous flickerings. "I like lightning," she said.

"At a certain distance, I suppose," Christie told her.

"Near enough to smell the sulphur, anyway," she said and began to play.

Christie tried not to listen, to hear instead the night insects trilling outside the window, the distant thunder, the occasional rustle of leaves in the June-berry tree. He didn't like hymn tunes. They made him feel dolorous and uneasy; he understood why they made dogs howl. And though he enjoyed watching his cousin, seeing her arched wrists and noting the rhythmical rise and fall of her knees beneath her white skirts as she pumped, he was glad when she rose and said, "Good night, Christie. If you go to bed before Papa comes, see that all the downstairs windows are closed, will you? It's going to storm."

Christie followed her out into the hall where the bedroom lamps, after being washed and newly filled, stood ready for their trips upstairs.

"Do you remember which is yours?" she asked him.

Christie touched a tall plain lamp with a leaf-shaped handle.

"It doesn't matter, really, except that Papa likes his own."

Sylvy lit her lamp, took it from the table and turned to go. As she stood beside Christie, the two of them were reflected in the big walnut-framed hall mirror; rather shadowily, as in a picture painted with somber colors in the first place and with those colors now long since faded. Sylvy lifted her lamp and the picture became more clear.

"We look like brother and sister, don't we?" she observed, and Christie felt that in saying this she was attempting to minimize the kiss in the barn.

There *was* a family likeness, Christie saw, which he had not before realized existed, a common tallness and darkness; but nothing pronounced enough to make anyone think them brother and sister.

"Grandpa Jackie and his white skin lost out before we came along, didn't they?" Christie said.

"The cussing too, I hope."

"I can still cuss," Christie boasted, peering deep into the glass.

Sylvy's dark eyes, also deep in the mirror, met his. And, as if in another land (the two of them searching—for what?—something they had lost anyway), they drew together, touched, and each watching as though the two who kissed were strangers, kissed until Christie felt the throb of his heart deep in the muscles of his throat and along the quivering nerves of his eyelids.

"Put down the lamp," he whispered urgently; for though he wanted to clasp his cousin, to find beneath laces and flounces more than the outlines of the stranger he had seen himself kiss, still he did not want to do so at the price of setting the house on fire. "Put it down, Sylvy."

Sylvy, recalled by his voice from the mirror, turned her eyes from Christie's reflection to Christie himself. "Oh, no!" she said. "I couldn't do that," turned about, and holding the lamp carefully, walked quickly upstairs beyond his reach.

The storm Sylvy had predicted arrived about eleven: first the silence, then the gusty, sweeping wind, next the flash followed by the instantaneous cannonading of thunder, and finally the slow drops sounding on the dry roof like splashings of molten lead. Christie looked up from *Darkest Africa* which he was reading, from the silent monkeys suspended like festoons of wild grapes across a chasm, from the motionless rumps of hippopotamuses, black islands in the great rivers, to the clamor and motion outside. The white curtains were sometimes in the room, sometimes out. The more they were lashed about, the more Christie liked it. He did not want an imitation storm.

At midnight Uncle Wes came in, ruddy and rain-splashed, and banged down the opened windows. "Raining pitchfolks with saw logs for handles," he said with satisfaction, sat down, then bounced to his feet again. "Got something for you." He brought forth a paper-covered wedge. Christie unwrapped it, a battered, coffee-colored section of cake.

"I remembered you when this came along, Christie. The young are always hungry, I told myself. That's a mocha cake with hazelnut icing. Got a fine grain, you'll notice."

Christie picked a hazelnut from the cracked icing and nibbled at it. The grain didn't interest him.

"Ain't you hungry, boy?"

"We had a good supper here, Uncle Wes."

Uncle Wes took the wedge from him, sat in the Boston rocker, rocked and ate. "No use throwing pearls before swine."

The rain had settled to a steady drumming; the thunder boomed at a distance, like an echo of its earlier self and the lamp on the center table was brighter, now, than the lightning outside. Through the closed windows the rank, fresh smell of the soaked earth seeped in to join the fusty smell of burning coal-oil. Upstairs, Lafe dropped first one shoe then the other onto the uncarpeted floor. Upstairs Sylvy, Christie supposed, slept.

Uncle Wes finished his cake, wadded the paper into a ball, and flipped it into the hand-painted china jardiniere which held a maidenhair fern. Then, grunting, he rose and retrieved it.

"Sylvy," he explained.

"Sylvy?" Christie repeated for conversation's sake, understanding his uncle's meaning perfectly.

"A dainty housekeeper. Fine-haired. A place for everything and everything in its place. Looks nice though, don't it?" Uncle Wes gazed about with satisfaction.

Christie was no judge of rooms. He could tell dirt from cleanliness, confusion from order, drabness from color. This room was clean, orderly and had plenty of color. There was something else in the room and Christie searched for a word to describe this quality so that he could hand it to his uncle, a gift in return for his uncle's thoughtfulness about the cake. The room's contents fitted and filled the room in the way an egg fits and fills its shell: suitably, without undue crowding, curve matching curve. He would no more have cared to see things shifted in any way than he would care to have an egg's yolk moved off center, nearer to one or the other ends of the shell.

"It looks like Sylvy," he said, not finding any single word.

"That's what I'm telling you."

Christie felt they were mincing the room up pretty fine in their thinking. Running down the seams of the curtains and around the rungs of the rockers. He watched his uncle still adding up the room's contents. The chief difference, in so far as he could tell—appearances apart—between youth and age was that age liked "things." All their precious flims and flams, all their treasured chips and whetstones. Certainly his mother had done so. If I had to choose between this room with everything in it and Stony Creek—nothing but stones and water—I'd take Stony Creek, he thought. Uncle Wes would take this room. It's the difference between having and being. He regarded his uncle with pity: the prideful possessor of maidenhair ferns, red velveteen footstools, and Boston rockers; the relisher of *Darkest Africa*; a midnight eater of mocha cake and attender of lodge banquets.

"Did you have a nice meeting, Uncle Wes?" he asked kindly.

Uncle Wes answered kindly. "It was pleasurable. We initiated three candidates. Gave them a real ride. Their tails aren't going to be serviceable for sitting for some little time."

Uncle Wes shifted luxuriously about upon his own serviceable member. "Christie, I worry sometimes about the line of work you're taking up. It don't seem manly to me."

"Manly!" Christie exclaimed. Had the two of them been sitting there, each feeling sorry for the other? "How's it unmanly?"

"Working for premiums. There's girls come by here selling *Youth's Companion* subscriptions for the premium of a Turkish rocker. There's women whose husbands have made a poor out-of-it, selling Lion coffee for the premium of a sewing-machine."

"What's that got to do with me?" Christie asked.

"That's what you get for selling insurance, isn't it? Premiums?"

Christie was amazed. "You'd just as well call it a salary. It's an income. No different from what you make here on the farm."

"I'm a farmer," Uncle Wes said. "I grow things, but I don't peddle them. I don't go from door to door with a bushel of corn saying, 'Lady, please buy a bushel of corn.' "

"Peddling! Is that the way selling insurance strikes you, Uncle Wes?"

"How in flinderation else?"

"People come to me to buy, too," Christie said. "Insurance is a commodity like anything else, like corn and apples. It's a thing people want."

"Corn and apples are real. What's insurance? Fact of the business, it's no more than a tricky idea, is it, Christie? You betting a fellow on the matter of whether he'll live or die? Ain't that about the size of it? Kind of legalized gambling?"

Christie was too amazed to speak. This ignorance or prejudice or crankiness, whichever it was! He opened his mouth, closed it, got up from the sofa and began to walk about the room.

"Uncle Wes," he said finally, "you just don't know what you're talking about. Insurance is a way of planning ahead for what nobody can be sure doesn't lie ahead, accidents and sickness. And for what everybody knows *is* ahead, death. It's—"

Uncle Wes interrupted him. "If I take your word for all that, Christie, still we don't get away from the fact you peddle it, do we? Knock on doors, a drummer! That's the big and little of it, ain't it?"

"That's the big and little of it," Christie admitted, irritated.

"Honest work, maybe, but not dignified."

"What's dignified?"

"Farming, doctoring, teaching, preaching . . ."

"Farming!" Christie sputtered. "Spending all spring on a hillside with a pair of balky mules. Doctoring! Telling a woman she's got six months to live. Teaching! Telling kids an old story in baby words. Preaching! Saying, 'Brethren, let me be an example to you.' Thanks, no. Not for me, Uncle Wes."

"No use acting like an Arab, Christie, just because we don't see eye to eye. What's there about selling insurance that's got such a hold on you anyhow?"

It was a lot easier to say what he hated than what he loved. One was protection, putting on a steel jacket, the other was taking off his shirt and his skin with it. He liked people, wanted to be with them and talk to them but he couldn't do this without the justification of some reasonable business. He was interested in the way each man wore his hat and whistled to his dog, but he had to have a passport for watching and listening. He wondered what went on behind every door, but he couldn't knock on any door simply to pass the time of day. With his insurance portfolio in his hand he could knock and enter, for he was always bidden enter, and in ten minutes became a part of the life beyond the threshold he had stepped across.

"Maybe you're a born salesman," his uncle speculated in the same depressed voice in which he might have said, Maybe you're a born drunkard. "I hear there are such. Men born with an itchy foot. Men wanting to exercise their gift of gab. Drummers, they call them. Skimming the cream off the girls and taking all the copper that ain't nailed down."

Well, a drummer, then. Tonight in this town, tomorrow in another. Moving on, which he wanted to do, seeing people which he wanted to do, and justified in doing so because of the value which he sold. Peddled, then.

"Admitting you got drummer blood in your veins, Christie, though where you got it I don't know, how'd you happen to hit on insurance to sell instead of something solid?"

"Solid?" Christie asked doubtfully.

"Buggies," his uncle explained, "headstones, lightning-rods, churns. So's a customer could tell what he was getting."

"Headstones!" Christie realized that he was very near to yelling and lowered his voice. "Lightning-rods! Churns! I'd rather peddle the *Youth's Companion* for Turkish rockers. I'd rather sell Lion coffee for sewing-machines." His voice was going up again. "I'd rather—"

"Now you've gone and yelled Sylvy awake," Uncle Wes said.

Christie turned about. Sylvy stood in the doorway behind him wearing what appeared to be a flowered cape over her night-dress.

"*Did* I wake you, Sylvy?" he asked. She didn't look as if she had been asleep. Her face was as bright, her eyes as brilliant as if her flowered cape were an evening wrap and she had just stepped into a ballroom.

"No," she admitted. "I wasn't asleep. But I could hear you arguing."

"We weren't arguing, Sylvy," Uncle Wes protested. "We were discussing." He got up and yawning, moved over to Christie and laid an arm across his shoulders. "Isn't that right, Christie?" Christie nodded.

"What were you discussing, Papa?" Sylvy asked anxiously.

"Insurance." Uncle Wes slid the wad of cake paper he had been holding into Christie's hip pocket.

Sylvy looked unbelievingly at Christie. "Were you talking about insurance, Christie?"

"Yes," Christie said. "I'm going to sell Uncle Wes a policy."

Uncle Wes who had been bending over the lamp on the center table, his cheeks already puffed to blow out the light, straightened up and wasted his indrawn breath to say, "It'll be a long day before you sell *me* any insurance, boy." Then he blew out the light and from the dusk of the hallway Sylvy said, "You never told me anything about your selling insurance, Christie."

"Tomorrow," Christie promised, "I'll tell you all about it."

IV

ON THE next day Christie had told his cousin nothing. Neither about insurance nor any other of the subjects which interested him: Sylvy was never in one place long enough to listen to him. The needs of her household appeared to have multiplied a hundredfold overnight. She was upstairs, down cellar, out in the spring-house. She was busy at her sewing-machine, busy picking beans, picking China asters, kneading bread, thrusting a straw into a baking marble cake. If she had been motherly the night before, now she was housewifely. Christie followed her about until midmorning, then gave up, went outside, and proffered his services to his uncle. Uncle Wes put a hoe into his hand, evidently forgetful of his nephew's lack of manliness and told him to get the purslane and pigweed out from between the corn rows. The air after the rain of the night before was muggy and warm but Christie worked with pleasure. She's running away from me, he decided. It was a flattering thought.

At supper that evening while Uncle Wes lingered over his second helping of peach cobbler and dip, Sylvy said, "Christie, I was supposed to have a sociable this Saturday evening."

Since the word emphasized was "supposed," Christie echoed it. "Supposed?" he asked. "Aren't you going to?"

"It's my turn but I was going to put it off. Because of Aunt Therese," she explained.

"Don't put it off because of Mother," Christie said. "That's the last thing she'd want you to do."

Sylvy, who had finished eating, had one elbow on the table and her chin on her hand. She was looking out into the summer twilight across the driveway to where the lawn swing stood under a clump of maples. On either seat of the swing, facing each other like companionable gossips, sat two plump birds—sparrows, Christie supposed. They sat quite still, only ruffling their feathers occasionally. Sylvy made a little motion in their direction and her father, looking up, said, "More rain coming, them birds squatting like that so early in the evening."

Sylvy turned away from the window. "It wasn't really because of Aunt Therese I was going to put it off, Christie. It was because of you. I thought you might not have the heart for it. But now I

[25]

think perhaps I should go ahead with it, that it would be good for you. You'd like a sociable, wouldn't you?"

"I'm not so sure I know what sociable is," Christie said. "A dance?"

Uncle Wes, who had been pouring another wash of dip across the last bit of his cobbler, put the pitcher down with a thump. "What ever gave you the idea I'd tolerate dancing here, Christie?"

Christie was considerably taken back. "I don't know," he answered, then defended himself. "What else can you do at a party? If a sociable *is* a party?"

"There are plenty of innocent things to be done at a party," Uncle Wes said severely, "without any holding of first one woman then another in your arms all evening."

"Could hold just one, I suppose," Christie said, trying to hide his embarrassment by joking, "not do any switching about."

Uncle Wes didn't laugh. "Men have certainly changed since my day. In my day there was no need to whip up the blood with dancing."

Sylvy broke in hastily. "It's a play-party, Christie. Games with singing. And for refreshments I thought cocoanut cake and banana ice-cream. They're both tropical and August is as near tropical as we get, so I thought they'd be suitable. What do you think, Christie?"

"I'd like them if it was December," Christie said, glad for the change in subject.

Uncle Wes got up and went to the dining-room window. "Them two birds sitting there as if magnetized," he said morosely. "They surely denote rain."

Magnetized or not, sparrows or not, the two birds, as Uncle Wes said, denoted rain. There were thunder-showers every morning until Saturday. Saturday was clear but opal-colored, as if the thought of autumn had just occurred to summer. The day was far from tropical but by noon the tropical cakes were baked and iced. Christie regarded them with mixed feeling. Not only had he grated the cocoanut for their icing, but there was a good part of his right thumb in the cocoanut. He held it up for Sylvy to see. "I've worked myself to the bone for you, Cousin Sylvy."

Sylvy tore soft strips from an old pillow-sham and wrapped his thumb skilfully; but when Christie started to thank her, she said, "It's not you I'm interested in, Christie. It's the ice-cream. I don't want you to have any excuse for not turning the freezer."

By five the cream was frozen, a strange mixture to look at, between gray and yellow, but delicious to eat. Christie licked a dasher while his cousin packed the two freezers with additional ice and salt. A party, Christie saw, was a different event here in the country from what it was in the city; or perhaps a different event, wherever it was, for women; or different perhaps for the planner, man or woman. This party, he saw, existed already in his cousin's mind. Anticipating its various movements and turnings, she went from room to room, shifting a chair, pushing a vase of lobelia to the back of a table, shoving a footstool into a corner. The house was burnished and polished, decked with flowers, sweet-smelling, the scent of blossoms and tropical foods mingling. It was over-orderly, every tassel on every fringed coverlet hanging plumb, every lampwick cut to an exact horizontal. There were special ribbons tying back the parlor curtains; tomorrow they would be untied, pressed, and put back into a bottom bureau drawer. The coffee boiler, not used since threshing time, was scalded and waiting; the best silver teaspoons made a glittering fan on the dining-room table.

Rising above all this preparation and above the waiting house was the imagined party: a great dome capable of housing all the unequaled felicity and enormous merriment of which Christie saw his cousin dreamed. He watched her pause on the threshold of the parlor, head tilted as if already able to hear the sounds of that merriment.

The day which had dawned sullen, though lovely, had become regal at its close; the regality, however, of an old king and a second-rate kingdom, monarchial colors but faded: dingy golds and rusty saffrons. By the time these colors had seeped into the parlor they were less regal than churchly, and Sylvy, wiping the dust from a begonia leaf and taking the lurch out of a postcard askew in the wire postcard rack, reminded Christie of a clergyman preparing his church for a service. He had a feeling that for her sake the party should be over; that time should stop and what she had imagined be, to her, the reality. For the reality of the sociable, he was sure, was never going to measure up to her dream, inside which one speck of dust on a begonia leaf would be a stumbling-block to happiness.

Sylvy finished her tour of inspection and stopped to rest in the hall.

"Everything's ready, I hope," she said anxiously.

"What else you could do, short of tearing down the house and building a new one, I don't know," Christie told her.

"I did make myself a new dress, Christie. The kind you said you liked."

"I liked?"

"Soft. Flounces and frills, you know. But not white. Gold of Ophir is what the color's called though it's really nothing but yellow."

"I expect it's pretty," Christie said. He felt as if their two reflected figures—he could see them from the corner of his eye in the mirror—were eavesdropping. They made him self-conscious.

"I hope so. You can tell me after the party."

"I can tell you now. It'll be the prettiest here."

"Don't be too sure. You might have to take it back. This neighborhood has plenty of fancy dressers. And there's a visitor coming—Cate Conboy. They say she's a fashion-plate."

"I've never cared for fashion-plates."

"Maybe they're wrong about her. Maybe that's just gossip."

Together they turned toward the mirror. It, too, held all the kingly colors and among them, they met and kissed again, not once but many times.

"Either way," Christie asked, "gossip or not gossip, what do we care?" Then once again, kissing doubled, sight adding to touch, they clung together mouth pressed to mouth.

v

THE PARTY started at seven. At first there was time for Sylvy to introduce the guests to Christie and at first he could keep in mind which name belonged to which face.

"Astra Bell Duke, I want to make you acquainted with my cousin from Indianapolis, Mr. Christian Fraser." (Miss Duke was less than royal to look at, in Christie's opinion.)

"I'm pleased to meet you, I'm sure, Miss Duke."

"Ormond and Oral Ami Fruit, my cousin from Indianapolis."
(Mr. Fruit's a lemon, Mrs. Fruit's a peach.) "I'm happy to know you, Mr. and Mrs. Fruit."

"Mister and Miss."

"Mister and Miss." (That's more like it.)

"Septimus and Zerelda Pearl."

(Awful big pearls: perhaps pearls make oysters here, not the other way about.) "I'm happy to make your acquaintance, I'm sure."

"Miss Ice Rita Addis, my cousin, Christie Fraser."

(Warm ice.) "Happy to—"

"Indiana Rose Cavanaugh, my cousin, Mr. Christian Fraser."

(Thorns, thorns.) "I'm glad to meet you, Miss Cavanaugh."

"John and Mary Funk, may I present my cousin, Christie Fraser?"

(They look like mother and father. I could be their child.) "It's a great pleasure, Mr. and Mrs. Funk."

Then the names and the faces came too fast, and he lost all track, only knowing that there were more names and more faces, and that faces he did not know called to each other across the room.

"Hi, there, Tassie!"

"Hi, Walt! You're looking live as a hot coal tonight!!"

"Seen you down by the spring branch bridge, Pascal. You and Ashba. What you doing there?"

"Making a wish over running water."

"Think it'll prove out?"

"We think so, Chad," and after this answer, laughter from all over the room.

"Yeh, we think there's a strong chance of it, Chad."

As the party grew, Christie stood against the wall in the sitting-room watching his cousin greet her guests. She is really happy to see them, he thought. If there is any difference between this party and the party she imagined, she will never know it. She will keep right on believing in the face of things.

Though he knew none of the guests, Christie, because he felt himself to be in some part one of the hosts, was at ease. At a signal from Sylvy he was to put all the furniture against the wall and roll up the parlor carpet (the rag rug in the sitting-room was tacked down and would have to stay where it was). At another signal he was to bring in lemonade (the cut-glass pitcher this time and no mistake about it). These tasks justified him. They were as useful as the insurance portfolio. He was born to be a host, not a guest. It was easier for him to say, "May I fetch you a chair?" than, "Thank you kindly, I'd appreciate that." But while being one of the hosts put him at his ease, Sylvy's presence made him self-conscious. He felt that she was watching him and he wanted her to approve him: he found himself shaking hands gracefully for her benefit and lifting his voice so that she would overhear him. But as the number of guests increased his awareness of Sylvy began to leave him, and he was able to look about with less thought of himself.

He began to understand what Sylvy had meant by "fancy dressers." The room was a-rustle with extravagantly full skirts, a-quiver with trembling ten-inch pompadours. Puffed sleeves doubled a girl's breadth at the shoulders and gathers extended her below the waist, he knew not how far, beyond reality in that location. A half-dozen naked females, he judged, could easily be packed into the space one of them, wired and padded, ratted and flounced, required. But they were a pretty sight, in spite of their size, and the sitting-room was large enough to accommodate them, together with their embellishments.

"Nice to have a room big enough to cuss a cat in without getting hair in your teeth," somebody declared appreciatively.

Someone else cried, "Crowd right up close to me, Ice Rita. I've never been a tetchious man, and I'm willing to hold my breath now to make room for you."

Outside, wheels continued to crunch on the gravel of the driveway, and riding horses to nicker as sporty young men wheeled their mounts in sharply to the upping-block. Inside, Sylvy continued to ask guests to lay their wraps in the parlor-bedroom, and young ladies who had arrived horseback left the room, austere as nuns in their long dusters or black calico riding-skirts, and returned outdone by no one in the confusion of their colors and the numbers of their furbelows.

At fifteen of eight Sylvy gave Christie the signal to push back the furniture and before the clock struck the hour half the guests were engaged in play-party games and all of them were singing:

>   "I'll step her up to your weevily wheat,
>   I'll step her up to your barley,
>   I'll step her up to your weevily wheat,
>   To bake a cake for Charlie."

The whole house quivered like a joggling board as the dancers promenaded, curtsied, bowed, and swung. It *was* dancing, Christie thought, and why Uncle Wes bothered to call it anything else, he didn't know. If, as a general rule, the participants clasped hands rather than embraced, there was enough energetic rule-breaking to put a waltz to shame. And if there were no fiddles crying and sighing, who needed them when the low-pitched voices sang,

>   "Take a lady by the hand,
>   Lead her like a pigeon;
>   Make her dance the weevily wheat
>   Till she loses her religion."

At the close of this dance, while partners were changing, Sylvy, who had been dancing with a little round man, the color of an underdone corn-pone, came up to Christie and asked, "Aren't you going to dance, Christie?"

"I'd better watch a while first, see if I can get the hang of it. This isn't like waltzing, the same thing over and over again."

Already the next dance was beginning, the guests singing,

>   "The cat's in the buttermilk,
>   Skip to my Lou,
>   Skip to my Lou, my darling."

Mr. Funk pulled Sylvy out into the double line, and Christie was left alone. He edged around the crowded floor and into the dining-room where those who did not dance, or wanted to talk, sat visiting. Standing inside the dining-room and gazing outward at the dancers was a girl who still wore her dark riding-cape.

"Hasn't anyone asked you to lay off your wraps?" Christie asked politely.

"I've only just come."

"Someone should have seen to your cape anyway."

"I came in the back way," the girl explained. "I was so late I didn't want to disturb the dancing."

"Let me take it."

The girl untied her cape and handed it to Christie. "I'm much obliged to you," she said stiffly.

"Not at all," Christie replied. He hung the cape over the back of one chair, pulled up another, and said, "Let's sit here by the door where we can watch."

"Thank you very much," the girl said and gazed into the sitting-room with a look of absorbed interest, as if watching play-parties were her life's one pleasure. Whenever there was a burst of laughter in the sitting-room she smiled, too, although she could not possibly have heard, above the general uproar, the remark which caused the laughter; and though she held herself unusually erect, her foot, in a black kid slipper with a jet buckle, tapped and countertapped to the music.

Christie thought she was very young, no more than sixteen; though her short, curly hair, in the midst of the billowing pompadours about her, made her seem, perhaps, younger than she was. Her curls also gave her a somewhat boyish appearance, as did her short, rather square face, level eyebrows, and mouth which, while pretty, was no cupid's bow. But there was nothing boyish about her figure. Or her dress. It was green and with its ornamental buttons, ruchings, and bows, was the most intricate he had yet seen; and it was belted about a figure a little more agreeably and abruptly curving than that, even, of any of the older girls.

Somewhat embarrassed to discover himself watched in this inventory-taking, Christie hastily asked, "Are you a great play-party dancer like everyone else hereabouts?"

"In what sense are you using the word great? Do you mean skilful?"

This school-teacherish question from the youthful, over-dressed, boyish girl was too much for Christie. He couldn't help laughing.

"Is it funny to want to be sure what question I'm answering?"

Christie saw that the eyes under the level eyebrows were hazel. "No—it's not. I meant, do you go to play-parties a lot and dance a lot as the rest of the people down here seem to do?"

"No. But I don't live here. I'm visiting the Cavanaughs."

"Indiana Rose Cavanaugh?"

The girl nodded. "We went to Normal together. This summer."

"I saw her come in but I didn't see you."

[32]

"I came with her brother Bert."

Christie looked about wondering why young Cavanaugh wasn't dancing with the girl he had brought.

"There's no use looking for him. After he got here he changed his mind and went home." The girl glanced sidewise at Christie, as if daring him to ask her any more questions, and though she did not lose her brilliant party smile, Christie thought she was not far from crying and changed the subject.

"So you're going to be a teacher?"

"No."

"I thought that was what Normal was for."

"I was going to be—now I'm going to help my father." Once again she looked sidewise at Christie. Christie said not a word. "He's the head of an institution," she added with hauteur. "The superintendent."

Must be a prison, Christie decided, she's so touchy about it. I wonder what she does to help her father? Probably sits outside the gate with a shot-gun and shoots escaping prisoners.

"In Indiana?" he ventured, hoping she wouldn't resent geography.

"Rock County."

"Way down South. I bet I know who you are. You're Miss Kate Conboy."

"Yes, I am. If you're spelling my name right."

"Kate or Conboy?"

"Cate."

"K-a-t-e?"

"No, with a C."

"Why with a C?"

"Because I'm Catherine with a C not with a K. I don't like Kate with a K. It sounds sharp to me, like knife."

"Knife with a K?" Christie asked.

"All right, laugh."

"How does Cate with a C sound to you?"

"I know, but I don't care to tell. I don't enjoy being laughed at."

"I heard something about you before I saw you," Christie said. If Miss Cate Conboy was interested in this she did not show it. She sat very straight and clapped her hands with the others, as if her entire attention were centered in the dance which was ending.

"I heard you were a fashion-plate and that all the girls in Stony Creek were jealous of you."

Miss Cate Conboy flashed about upon her chair. Facing Christie she cried, "I knew it! I knew this was too dressy!" Without another word she bent and ripped three moss-colored velvet bows from the lighter green of her skirt and two more from her bodice, one bow from each shoulder. Then she ran over to the dining-room fireplace and threw the five bows in amongst the hydrangea blossoms with which the fireplace was filled. If she had planned to make herself the center of attention in the dining-room she could not have done better. They were not accustomed, at Stony Creek, to seeing girls at parties throw any part of their dresses into the grate. But evidently she had not so planned for she sat down shamefaced, and gazed at the toes of her slippers. "I would purely hate to be a fashion-plate," she said in a low voice.

Christie felt sorry for her. In a minute she was going to purely hate being a girl who pulled the bows off of her dress in public.

"Do you know how to dance this?" he asked.

In the next room they were beginning to sing,

>   "Coffee grows on a white-oak tree,
>   The river flows sweet brandy-o."

"Yes."

"Would you mind trying to teach me?"

"No," she said. "Thanks."

She was a very good teacher. Promenading, swinging, casting off, she explained in quick exact words and illustrated with quick sure movements. She was like Christie himself, at ease in doing. Dancing, she lost all of her sharp, self-conscious poses. The brilliant smiles which, when she was sitting still she had bestowed upon the dancers, were gone now that she too was dancing. Gravely she whirled and curtsied, gravely and firmly drew Christie to his proper place and gravely and firmly passed him on to the next in line.

>   "Coffee grows on a white-oak tree,
>   The river flows sweet brandy-o."

Momentarily Sylvy was Christie's partner, and he was surprised to find how small her hand was in his, much smaller than Cate's, who was not so large.

"Are you learning to dance, Christie?"

"Too soon to say, Cousin Sylvy. I'm learning something."

"Are you happy?"

"Too soon to say, Cousin Sylvy."

"You don't look sad."

"No, I'm not sad."

    "Now choose the one to roam with you [the voices sang],
      As sweet as sugar in the candy-o—"

and the dance returned him to Cate.

"Circle now," Cate said, "with me."

They circled, wide.

"Do you like it?"

"Best in the world."

"I should have told you my father's the head of a poor-house."

"I can't see it matters."

"It matters that I don't like to say it, and Father's—," but the circle was completed and Cate said, "Take this girl, now."

Christie lost track of the dances, shed his coat, danced with Fruits, Pearls, Funks, lost track of them too, sang songs he'd never heard and words he didn't know: "Here come four dukes a-riding, Tis a ma tas a ma tee." He came in strong on the "Tis a ma tas a ma tee." He cast up, cast down, whirled his partner, whirled the contrary girl, knelt, bowed, promenaded and at one point on an inspiration of his own flapped his arms and crowed like a rooster.

They were singing,

      "King William was King James' son,
        Up from the royal race did come,"

when Uncle Wes beckoned to him from the kitchen.

"Time to begin dishing up, boy," he said, and Christie got out a big iron spoon and hacked away at the banana ice-cream, now frozen harder than a donnicker.

"Any objection if I borrow Charlie and the buggy after the party, Uncle Wes?"

"Want to take a girl home?"

"Cate Conboy. Bert Cavanaugh brought her over, then went off and left her."

"You won't need to do a thing but drive her straight home, then. If she come over with Bert she's had her fill of spooning for one night."

"It never entered my head to do anything else, Uncle Wes," Christie said.

An hour after he left the house with Cate, Christie was back in the sitting-room. Except for a few shreds of cocoanut on the carpet and a forgotten case-knife on the mantel (a girl who had been dancing in her stocking feet and couldn't get her slippers on when it came time to go home had used it for a shoehorn), there were no signs of the party left in the room. The party had gone back to where it came from, the mind; and was not, Christie guessed, any longer even in Uncle Wes' mind, for he sat in the Boston rocker eating a bowl of light bread and milk as if it were nine in the evening instead of two in the morning.

"All that rich food made me kind of dauncy," he explained.

He finished eating, rose, took the case-knife off the mantel, and put it in the bowl with his spoon.

"You and that Conboy girl make out all right?"

"I guess so," Christie said.

"You got home in a hurry," Uncle Wes said, turning toward the kitchen. Far off, in the summer night, a cock shrilled. "Crowding sun-up," he observed. "I'll feel like a biled owl tomorrow if I don't get to bed."

"Mr. Conboy runs the Poor Farm down in Rock County," Christie said unaccountably.

"Only kind of a farm *anybody* runs down there. Land down there's too poor to breed a scab."

"Mournful way to make a living. . . ."

"You ain't so choosy yourself, dealing in death and destruction the way you do, Christie."

"Oh, choosy!" Christie exclaimed, repudiating the word.

"He don't have to do any going from door to door, anyway. No peddling."

A cricket, shiny as fresh tobacco juice, came out of the kitchen's darkness into the lighted sitting-room. "When bugs take over it's time for men to be in bed," Uncle Wes said, went into the kitchen, where Christie heard him first put down his bowl, then begin his climb up the back stairs to his room.

In half an hour Christie followed him. On a sudden impulse, seeing a light under his cousin's door, he stopped and said softly, "Are you still up, Cousin Sylvy?"

For a second or two there was no reply, then Sylvy's low voice answered, "Yes, Christie."

"Would you mind if I came in for a little while?" Christie whispered. "I'd like to talk to you."

He knew it was not the thing to do, go into the bedroom of a female neither his wife nor mother at this hour of the night. He had been raised that way as much as Sylvy and he was surprised when Sylvy said, "All right, Christie. Just for a minute."

He opened the door, stepped into the room, then closed the door softly behind him. This was the only room in the house which he had not been in and he saw at once that it was quite different from all the others. They, in spite of their furnishing, remained what rooms essentially are: boxes. Here boxiness was hidden behind a froth of creamy curtains, of draperies and coverlets and skirted tables. Christie felt himself to be entering not something inanimate, which a box is, but something alive, something like a flower, say, or the hollow shifting chamber behind a waterfall. Sylvy stood against the dark window, wearing her flowered cape and now a flowered, pucker-crowned cap as well.

"What is it, Christie?" she asked.

Christie looked at her without answering. What was it he had come in to say? Was it only the excitement of being still up at the close of a summer night and wanting someone with whom he could mark the occasion? Or was it curiosity? To see Sylvy in her own room where she would be most herself, not housekeeper or daughter or cousin? And in her nightdress?

"What is it, Christie?" Sylvy asked again.

Then Christie, to his own great surprise, for surely he had not stopped in here at three in the morning to talk of a girl neither of them knew, said, "What did you think of Cate Conboy?"

"Think of her?" Sylvy repeated uncertainly. "Why, I was too busy to think, Christie. Though I could see she was pretty."

Christie considered this. "I don't know that I would call her pretty," he said judicially. "No, I think that's going too far. Her face is too short. Don't you agree?"

"She looked pretty to me. Papa said you took her home."

"I did. She came over with Bert Cavanaugh but he got fresh, and she had to box his ears. So he drove off and left her. Plenty of spirit for a girl, don't you think?"

Sylvy nodded.

"That's the thing I admire most of all in a girl, I believe. Spirit."

Sylvy didn't answer. Instead, she placed herself on the windowsill and turned her face from him. A whippoorwill called and she said, "He's up late."

The summer night filled the room. The summer air stirred a yellow dress spread out across the foot of the bed. Christie pressed down one of the moving folds as if he were quieting a fractious animal. Sylvy had asked him something about the dress before the party. What? A sudden puff of air lifted the skirt with the roundness of a knee or thigh and he stroked the curve for as long as it lasted.

"This is a pretty color," he said.

His cousin faced him, at that, took off her cap with a weary gesture.

"Gold of Ophir," she told him. For the second time, he remembered.

The dark hair, without the cap to hold it up, fell about her pink sprigged shoulders. He went across to her, his purpose to lift her hair. He felt the night was too warm for any such closeness and heaviness so near the face. Her hair had a real and surprising weight and density and his hands moved through it with the gestures of a swimmer parting resistant water. Encountering unexpectedly her ears, he was startled by their sudden soft nakedness. Touching them he forgot the task of putting her hair aside. Beyond them was the delicate jut of the bones of her jaw, and beneath them her boneless throat, all alive and pulsing in the circle of his fingers. He took her flowered cape from her shoulders and dropped it from the open window, Sylvy leaning with him to watch it fall. It settled, with great deliberation it seemed, on the beauty-bush below and when it no longer stirred they looked at each other.

She had round full breasts neither high nor drooping; the shape of snowball blossoms, blue-white, with the addition of the slightest defect, a little pink-brown discoloration at the center. These defects he covered with the tips of his fingers leaving nothing but the whiteness to show. Sylvy's expression did not change; she continued to look at him gravely and seriously. Presently she took his hands away and pressed the length of her entire body lightly but closely to him. The flesh at the scooped-in small of her back was very warm; heat flowed out to him through the folds of material he had gathered up and which in a minute or two he tried to push aside.

"There is too much nightgown," he said.

Sylvy said nothing but leaned a little away from him so that a solution suggested itself. He lifted the nightgown over her head and the movement of his arms and the billowing fall of the garment as he tossed it aside set the lamp to fluttering so that the naked body, the room and all of the room's delicate, ladylike furnishings swayed together unsteadily like a picture reflected in water. Before the flame steadied, Sylvy cupped the chimney with her hands and blew. Now we are lost, Christie thought, but it was Sylvy's room and she knew her way about it even in the dark.

VI

CHRISTIE spent four more days at Stony Creek. During this time he avoided his Cousin Sylvy. He got down to breakfast late, spent the forenoons helping Uncle Wes and the afternoons driving or walking about the countryside.

On the afternoon of the last day of his visit he met Cate Conboy again, by chance, wading alone in Stony Creek, her skirts looped up thigh-high. She got her skirts down modestly at once and climbed up on a boulder in midstream; there she picked willow leaves from a tree which slanted toward her and dropped them one by one into the shadowed water. Christie sat on a fallen log and, with the stream separating them, they spent an hour or more talking—mostly of the party.

When it came time to part Christie asked, "Will you write to me, Cate?"

"Yes," Cate said without hesitation, "I will. I like to write letters. Especially on Sunday afternoons."

"Why?" Christie asked, meaning the letters or the Sunday afternoons or any part of it, but she wouldn't attempt to explain. It was something she had read in a book, he decided, a ladylike girl at her white desk on a Sunday afternoon writing "answered" across a growing stack of opened envelopes. But whatever her reasons, she promised to write.

And she had done so—long letters with highfalutin descriptions of sunsets and snowstorms and of birds blown down in blizzards. There were extended descriptions too of the Poor Farm, of the people there, of her father's work. It was difficult for Christie to get any clear idea of these, for the descriptions varied in tone from week to week. Sometimes Cate wrote as if the Poor Farm were her father's personal charity, as if all the Conboys were modern Knights Templars devoting themselves to succoring the worn and the weary. At other times, to judge by her letters, the place was nearer a modern Bedlam, a horror of strangeness and sickness. But most often she wrote as if a Poor Farm were simply a large farm like any other with many workers and she one of them.

The letter in his pocket, the invitation that had put him on the train, said: "Mama read my last letter to you." (Did Mama read all of them, Christie wondered? Was she asked to read them, or did she insist? Or was the reading of "my last letter" a "happen chance"?)

Mama said I wrote like a prisoner in a tower, a princess having to sleep with sixteen peas under the mattress and considering herself too delicate for even one. That was not my intention. I do not consider myself more delicate than my surroundings nor too good for anything.

I expect the only way you will know what this is like is to see it, for it is true that I feel first one way then another about it. Sometimes I am ashamed to be mixed up with it and other times I am thankful that I can be of some use in the world, especially to my father.

Mama says that you would be welcome to visit us at any time. Room is no problem here but vice versa. I would invite you for Christmas except that I expect that you are spending Christmas with your uncle Mr. Cope and your cousin Miss Cope. That would be much nicer I'm sure than spending Christmas in a Poor House for I could see what a wonderful person Miss Cope is. But you might never again have a chance to say, "I spent Christmas in a Poor House." And you could see how it really is here and whether there are sixteen peas or none under the mattresses. And if I make things out in my letters to be nicer than they are, or worse, after this you would know it.

Anyway, I wish you a very merry Christmas and success in the "honorable mention" you are working for in selling insurance. My father thinks you are in a very humane line of business.

Your sincere friend,
Catherine M. Conboy

VII

MR. AMES' hand on his shoulder recalled him to the present. "Here's Odis Korby," he said, "who'll give you a lift out to The Farm."

Mr. Korby, a moon-faced man reaching only to Mr. Ames' shoulder, said, "Be a real pleasure to have your company if you haven't got any scruples against riding with me."

"Scruples?" Christie asked.

"I'm taking a coffin out to The Farm. It's here on the train now. Boy of mine's meeting me with a rig, I trust."

"Oh, no," Christie said, "I haven't got any scruples about riding with a coffin. Have to take a trip like that sooner or later I reckon."

"That's the way to talk," Mr. Korby said. "Meet things half way."

Mr. Korby's boy was waiting at The Junction with a light spring-wagon when the train pulled in. Korby himself climbed up into the seat while Christie and the boy—nothing more than a series of promontories in the dusk, peaked cap, peaked nose, ears set at right angles to his head—got the coffin from the baggage-car. It was easily handled; even in the packing-case which enclosed it, it was a light little thing scarcely more than an oversized shoebox.

"I could drive it out for you, Mr. Korby," the boy volunteered.

"You want to have a little talk with Link Conboy about it, maybe?"

"No," the boy said.

"You better stay home then, Earl. No use monkeying with a buzz-saw till you have to."

The boy backed away from the wagon, and Mr. Korby unwrapped the reins from around the buggy whip and headed his team east. The sky had cleared, and the snow, to Christie's surprise, still held some light, enough to let him have a look or two at Mr. Korby: a benign little man with round empty cheeks and a trim mouth.

After the first quarter of a mile, stands of dark leafless timber began to close in about them. The road went down a steep hill, and Christie listened to the coffin move gratingly forward, then as they crossed a branch and began to climb again, move gratingly back. The road was narrow and the trees dense so that looking up he saw the stars overhead like lights floating on a dark river.

Mr. Korby too lifted his round chin and peered upward. "The stars of Christmas Eve," he said. "Just as they shone on the night the little Lord Jesus came down to earth."

"I suppose so," Christie said. "Just as far away, just as bright."

But the stars were not what interested Mr. Korby. "Came down to earth," he continued, "and no sooner here than Grant's overcoat was too little to serve the boy for a thumb-stall. Pride! That was his big mistake. And it's the one thing people can't stomach, so they killed him for it."

They crossed another stream, then began to climb another hill. Branch water dripped from the wheels, and the coffin once again slid backwards.

"Have big thoughts, son," Mr. Korby advised. "Plan big, but act meechin. Look what happened to our Lord. He got to acting biggity. Took to cussing hogs and blasting fig-trees. I'd be the last to fault him for it, understand. Send me down to earth under like circumstances, doves flapping around my ears and dead fish multiplying when I say the word, and I reckon I'd make an equally poor out-of-it. No, no, the poor boy never had a fair chance. Carried around on a chip from the beginning till he finally had to advertise everything in stud-horse type. Couldn't keep his voice down. Had to give them the word with the bark on it every time he opened his mouth.

"But don't think for a minute I haven't profited by the lesson, son," Mr. Korby said. "What this world wants is a sugar-tit to suck on, and a sugar-tit's what I give it. The last thing I do before I close a coffin lid is to plant a kiss on the forehead of the departed. To impress the relatives? No, sir. Nothing but pure love and humbleness in the face of the great leveler. I don't know you from Adam, boy, but if I was to lay you away tonight I'd kiss you like a son."

"You're an undertaker?" Christie asked.

"Where you from, son?"

"Indianapolis."

"They're men under ground in Indianapolis who got there without the help of Korby," Korby said, "but considerably fewer than you might think."

"I've been in college the last four years," Christie said, trying to excuse his ignorance.

"Never heard of Korby?"

"Not many people die in college."

"They're pretty young for it," Mr. Korby admitted. "But undertaking's not my only line. Furniture, Feed, General Merchandise *and* Undertaking."

"That doesn't leave out much."

"No. Manage to get yourself born and I'll take care of you after that. And getting born's no trick. More of that going on than a lot of people'd like." He gave his head a backward nod in the direction of the coffin.

Christie, who had been reluctant to inquire about the coffin, said, "Somebody dead at the Poor House?"

"That's my conclusion," Korby told him. "Dandie Conboy orders a coffin, baby size, blue satin lining, German-silver handles. He don't say anybody's dead but at once I leap to that conclusion. May get out there and find he plans to use the thing for a collar box. The boy's a high-flyer, and for all I know that may be his latest conceit.

"I used to have a nice little business out at The Farm before Link Conboy got a-hold of the place," he went on. "Plenty of dying out there among the old folks, and the county, with my help, used to put them away nice. Know what Link Conboy does now?" he asked.

"No," Christie said.

"Buries them in homemade boxes. Lays them out for their last sleep in a box I wouldn't use to nest a setting hen in. They're paupers, sure. But is that any reason they should go to Kingdom Come in a makeshift horse-trough? What do you think? You've got a good education."

Christie didn't feel his education had equipped him to answer this. "You don't care much for Mr. Conboy, I guess."

"Conboy ought to have his head bored for the simples," Mr. Korby said, "and I'd be just the man for the job."

The last of day had now left sky and snow alike, and the matched grays stepped along, lighted only by the sharp wintry stars. Mr. Korby ceased speaking, and Christie listened to the blurred klop of the horses' hooves, the soft snurr of the wheels turning in the snow, and the intermittent grating movement of the coffin. The sounds made him drowsy and half asleep, he thought of the change four hours had made. Four hours ago he had been amidst people on the Christmas streets of the city. Here he was, God alone knew where, riding along in a wagon with a coffin. He had the feeling, almost, of being bound for his own funeral accompanied by his executioner.

At the top of the next hill Mr. Korby aroused him by pulling up his horses. "There it is," he said, pointing with his whip. "There stands Link Conboy's castle."

Off to the left, seemingly floating unsupported in mid-air, like a swarm of out-of-season fireflies, was a cluster of yellow lights. As they sat gazing, a bell in the direction of the lights began to peal.

Mr. Korby at this sound slapped the reins across the backs of his grays. "You're late, bub. There's Lib Conboy ringing the supper-bell now."

VIII

CATE CONBOY, believing she would have time to tidy herself in the three or four minutes her mother would spend ringing the supper-bell, ran down the hall to the room she shared with her eleven-year-old sister Emma. She intended to do no more than rub a damp cloth over her face, brush her hair, and yes, put on the gold brooch. She had been of two minds all afternoon about the gold brooch. What did she want her appearance to say to

Christie? Did she want to greet him, broochless, austere, a handmaiden in the house of the poor? Or, bedecked and fashionable, did she want to show him at once that she had nothing in common with the others he would be seeing? Now that there was no longer time for dreaming, these two images of herself, austere Cate, fashionable Cate, vanished. They really had nothing to do with her anyway. *She* was going to wear the gold brooch because it was pretty, and oh! those hands of gold clasping. Were they not a sign?

She paused at the circular window—the Eye, Em called it—to look out. Stars reflected the snow, it seemed, and snow, in turn, the stars. The quietness of the winter evening made her bitter with herself. When am I ever quiet, she thought?

But how could she be quiet? All day she had been trying, not to make the Conboys' living-quarters clean (her mother was a clean housekeeper) but neat. When her mother finished cleaning a room it was far worse, to look at at least, than it had been before she started. Her mother was like a storm at sea: she scoured, cleansed, and wrecked. On the mantel she would leave a filled dustpan; behind a door a forgotten dustcloth; over a chair her discarded jacket. In the middle of the floor, would lie scattered newspapers, vacancies where receipts had been cut out. The center table would hold her half-eaten piece of cornbread. An empty glass with dried buttermilk like frost around the rim would stand on a window-sill. And this a room her mother had cleaned! A room untouched by her mother—her mother's own bedroom for instance! Standing in the doorway of *that* room before beginning its cleaning, Cate often thought that its helter-skelter of articles must look like the flotsam left above a sunken ship.

Yet her mother never asked her to clean her room. Indeed, she would cry impatiently when Cate had done so, "Cate, if you must red up things, at least don't hide them." Anything in a drawer, Cate thought angrily, is hidden in so far as Mama is concerned. But now, looking at the tranquil landscape outside, she was angry only with herself. No one makes you spend a whole day dusting the backs of chairs and putting things into drawers, she told herself. It's a way you choose to be. You could be quiet if you wanted to be, meet Christie out there under a cedar tree, not a sound to be heard unless snow slid down from a limb or a dog barked.

She let her hand curve over the doorknob for a second before opening her door. She had never, even when flying to her room angry with her mother, defiant and, as she supposed at the time, heartbroken, touched that doorknob at once. It was always pause, and remember the miracle that awaited her. The miracle of opening the door and of being alone in her own place. Why was that a miracle? It was a small room: four walls, two windows, two chairs, two beds, a bureau, a wash-stand, a deal table, a wardrobe. There was a blue-and-white striped rag carpet on the floor, white curtains with blue grapes stenciled on them at the windows, and a white crocheted tidy on the rocking-chair. Outside the windows there was a beech tree which in windy weather scraped across the glass. Nothing about her room was either fine or unusual. Was the miracle only that it was hers? Was what anyone had for his own always a miracle?

Now, after the accustomed pause, she opened the door and saw to her surprise that Em was in the room. Em, except for the ten hours she slept and the three minutes it took her to dress each morning, was almost never there. Cate did not consider her sister a co-owner of the room but simply an occupant, on the order of the wash-stand. Not even an occupant in the sense the wash-stand was, for the wash-stand would have looked lost any place else while Em was at home anywhere—haystack, duck-pond, mourner's bench at church confessing her sins (which Cate considered many). Em sat in her shimmy at Cate's table, writing. Her black pigtail, tied with a tan shoe-lace, bisected her stooped white back. The room was unheated, and Cate could see the puckering of goose-pimples across her sister's bare shoulders and arms.

"What are you doing?" Cate asked.

Em answered without looking up from her work. "I was going to change my dress, then I thought a holly wreath would improve this. It ought to be in colors, I reckon, but nobody will give me crayons, so if they look a gift-horse in the mouth, what they will see is their own selfishness."

Em shoved her handiwork, now finished, toward Cate, and Cate without enthusiasm picked up the card and waved it through the air to dry it. The holly wreath, which Em had drawn in ink, was unblotted and still damp.

"I could make holly wreaths until doomsday," Em declared enthusiastically. "My three favorite things to draw are holly wreaths, the moon coming up, and a road going over a hill and getting littler. The moon and the road don't mean anything in particular and holly means Christmas. So holly is my favorite, number one. The road going over a hill is my favorite, number two, because it's kind of sorrowful."

"Why is it sorrowful?" Cate asked.

"Because it makes you think of someone going away forever."

"I suppose it could be someone coming forever," Cate said, reading what Em had written beneath her holly wreath.

"No," Em said, "it couldn't. Not the way I draw roads. Getting littler and littler and going over a big hill. It makes me feel like crying just to think of them."

"This is going to make someone feel like crying, all right," Cate said.

"Who?" Em asked with interest.

"Who do you suppose?" Cate replied, reading aloud, "To Mama and Papa: Christmas advice. Do not argue before your children. It is a bad example. Each night write down what you think is not right on a piece of paper and put it under each other's pillow. In the morning read and improve. Yours for peace on earth, good will to men. Merry Christmas, Lovingly, Emma J."

Em, apparently lost in admiration for her writing, was silent. "Who do you *think's* going to cry?" Cate asked her again.

"Papa?" Em asked dreamily.

"Don't be silly," Cate said.

"Mama? It's really for her I wrote it."

"When did you ever see Mama cry?"

"I can make her cry," Emma boasted, "if I want to."

"You'll be the one who'll cry. Mama'll slap you good and hard for this."

Em got up from the table. "What do I care?" she asked and gave herself a solid buffet first on one ear, then on the other. "It's nothing but flesh," she said, tears in her eyes. "Nothing but my old flesh."

[47]

"All right," Cate said, "put some clothes on your old flesh now and come on out. They'll be here any time now."

"You mean *he* will," Em said. She lifted her arms ready to slide into her dress, and Cate, staring in amazement, held one of her sister's arms aloft. "Em," she cried, "are you mortifying?"

Em's armpits were almost entirely black, with curlicues, like wisps of smoke in a child's drawing of a chimney, extending outward and downward onto her chest and arms.

"Hair," Em said modestly. "Imitation, of course," she admitted. "I did it with burnt matches."

She wriggled out of Cate's grasp and with arms upraised admired herself in the bureau mirror.

"It makes me feel a lot better," she declared.

"Better!" Cate gasped. "Why?"

"A girl my size ought to have hair. Airey's got a full set. Above *and* below."

Airey Creagan was the daughter of Mag Creagan, the hired girl.

"Likewise Earnest," Em went on, backing reluctantly away from the mirror. Earnest was Airey's brother.

"Earnest!" Cate whirled silently. "How do you know?"

"Airey," Em said, pulling her dress down over her head. "It was a disappointment to hear it. So girlish. I thought they'd be different from us. Hoped so anyway. Didn't you? Or did you know they were just the same?"

Cate said nothing and Em finished buttoning her dress, then picked up her Christmas card.

"What are you going to do with that?" Cate asked.

"Put it under their pillow."

At the door Em turned to say, "I've made up a conundrum about us."

"What is it?" Cate asked, not out of interest but simply to hasten the inevitable.

"Why are we the opposite of Christmas?"

"I don't know. Why?"

"Christmas gave the world a live baby and we give the world a dead baby."

"We!" Cate said fiercely. "We don't have anything to do with it."

"This house, I mean," Em explained. "It's interesting to think about, isn't it? Kind of like saying the Lord's Prayer backwards."

"Go on," Cate said. "Get out of here. That's a wicked idea."

After Em left the room Cate dampened the cloth in her washbowl, then standing at the west window moved it across her warm face. Five years ago when she had been thirteen and Em six, her mother had come upon the two of them bathing, as they had since Em was a baby, at the same time and in the same tub. Her mother had suddenly stopped in her hurried passage through the kitchen and had silently stared at her as she stood naked beside the wash-tub in which Em sat.

Abashed, Cate had tried to think if there was anything she had done that was wrong. "What's the matter, Mama?" she had asked.

They were at their own place then, not the Poor Farm. It was a warm May afternoon, and Cate remembered that the shadow of a blossoming apple-tree which grew just outside the kitchen door, which was open, had fallen across her feet. Before her mother came in she had been washing dreamily, playing with the idea that somehow she was actually taking a bath while standing in an apple-tree.

Her mother's staring had stopped all that, and for a minute she had stared back. Because the day was warm her mother had taken off her dressing-sack and was wearing it tied about her waist like a deflated bustle. Her great lolloping knot of hair had been held in place by one of Dandie's ties. As her mother continued to stare, Cate had curved protectively forward trying to make herself smaller and less visible. At last, embarrassed by the silence and staring, she tried to say something funny and off-hand which would make her mother laugh. "What's struck you now?" she asked, managing what she thought was a natural smile.

Instantly her mother's hand had flashed out and Cate was slapped hard: twice across the buttocks and once across the mouth.

"I'll show you who's struck," her mother had cried, "and how and where. Now, will you have the decency not to face your baby sister, naked?"

"Face her?" she had echoed, bewildered. "Naked?"

"Cover yourself with a towel," her mother had ordered.

"I never have," Cate had faltered. "You never said—"

"I say now." Her mother had lifted her hand again. "You've changed. You're a woman. You shouldn't display yourself. You're not nice. You'll shock Emma, give her bad thoughts."

Cate had picked up the towel which lay on a chair beside her and slowly and awkwardly tried to cover herself. It was impossible for her to understand how in two minutes all the happiness she had felt, lazily washing in the apple-tree shadow, had vanished.

Em, squatting silent in the tub of soapy water, had suddenly lifted one corner of Cate's protective towel and peered upward beneath it.

"All the girls are in China, and all the boys have gone to Peekin," she said.

"Oh, see," her mother had cried broken-heartedly at that, "what you have already done to your baby sister! The turn you have given her innocent mind."

Cate had felt warmth flood her, redness, a river of sorrow, and wished she might drown in it.

"March to your room," her mother told her, "and remember what I have said."

At supper that night she had eaten nothing, said nothing. She had wanted only to be restored to her mother's esteem and good will. After the dishes were done her mother had walked out onto the grass of the side yard and there, pacing slowly up and down, she had sung. No one but Cate had paid any attention to her. Link had read; Dandie at a mirror had worked to flatten the curl out of his hair; Em had been sleeping.

Cate had crouched in the shadow of the snowball bush listening to the mournful words of her mother's song:

> "One night when the moon was shining
> And the stars were shining, too,
> A jealous lover crept nearer
> Unto a cottage small."

Her mother's voice was low. Some of the notes she prolonged, others accelerated so that the song was like an improvisation rather than the repetition of a set melody. It had seemed to Cate an expression of personal sorrow and she, she believed, was the cause of that sorrow. Finally, she had dared run out and timidly clasp her mother's hand, and her mother, without looking down, had clasped back and continued to pace and sing, drawing Cate with her. Cate was all tenderness and superiority at that touch. The others reading, primping, sleeping—and they might have been with Mother! Fireflies turned their bronze lights on and off, and the lamps from the house, shining onto the pale undersides of the apple leaves, had lighted them so that when they moved in the night air it was as if a silvery spring rain were falling.

When her mother had finished her song, when the innocent maiden stabbed to the heart had died, Cate had whispered, "Oh, Mama, I'm so sorry. I didn't know it was wrong."

Her mother had let go of her hand then and stood still. "I didn't intend to slap you, Cate. But once when I was a girl we had a hired girl . . . oh, she had tufts of hair . . . wads of hair . . . like a wild animal, a sickening sight. I was thinking of her."

Instantly the last of Cate's resentment had vanished. How could she have thought her mother cruel or unfair when actually she had been suffering.

"Poor Mama," she had said, "poor Mama!" She had lifted her mother's hand to caress it, but her mother drew her hand away, crossed her arms beneath the curve of her breasts, and began once more to saunter and sing.

But she had sung only a line or two when she stopped. She had grasped Cate's shoulder so fiercely that Cate could feel each separate finger. "You mind what I told you, Cate Conboy. You keep yourself covered. Nobody wants to see a big naked girl—not the way you've gotten to be."

Looking out into the snow, the cool wash-cloth grown warm against her skin, Cate thought, perhaps it was seeing me then makes Em—so different—and knowledgeable now. Knowing things already that I don't know.

Then, suddenly, she heard the supper-bell's last dripping notes fall from the clapper, and she hurried to empty her wash water and hang up her wash-cloth. She pulled the comb through her short thick hair. She looked into the mirror at her reflected face: broad brow, short chin, bright cheeks. "Oh, I don't like you," she said. "I do not like you at all." She picked up the brooch which lay before her on the bureau, kissed the clasped hands twice, said,

"Farewell," put it back, then ran down the stairs two steps at a time, singing loudly.

IX

AT THE first notes of the Poor House bell, James Abel had stopped his digging. He leaned on his pick, and his breath, for he was winded and breathing deeply, was a white plume on the evening air.

"Stop now, Mary," he ordered.

His sister Mary, without answering, threw another shovelful of gravel from the trench in which she was working.

"We've done enough for one afternoon," James said, "and we've got no right to put Mrs. Conboy out by being late for supper."

"I hate to stop," Mary said. "I've had a feeling Christmas Eve might be the time we'd find it. I've had a deep feeling, James, all week."

"One day's like another," James told her, "till we come on it. You know that, Mary. Sabbath or Saturday or a holiday. It's all one till then, all gloom." James' voice was placid and cheerful.

"We didn't get much done this afternoon," Mary still objected. "Scarcely made a mark."

"Well, it's hard ground to work in," James defended their efforts. "Gravelly and frozen to boot. We done all right considering the opposition we've had." He reached down a hand and helped his sister to step out of the two-foot-deep trench in which she was working. "Tired?" he asked.

"Middling."

"Out of heart?"

"No," she answered, then asked, "You had a strong lead this was the place, James?"

"I did," James told her. "But you know as well as me that I get false leads. I have and I will. There's nothing for it but to take them and find out if they're false. Turn over two shovelfuls and come on it? What'd there be to that? This is no suck-egg job, Mary. We've known that right along."

"What is it, James?"

"Pain," James said, "hard work, and making ourselves a laughing-stock. And a chance to save the world from perishing to death."

As if satisfied by these words Mary turned away from the trench and began the climb to the road which curved above them. From it, the Poor House, a quarter of a mile away, was visible. Resting at the top of the hill, James gestured in its direction. "There it is," he said, "all lighted and awaiting us."

The Poor House, to James Abel, was as much a wonder as if it had been built at a single clap by a wizard. Nothing had meaning for him which did not foster his mission, and this the Poor House did so well that he sometimes felt that it had not only been raised at a single clap by a wizard, but raised expressly for him.

"We've got a mansion to welcome us, Mary," he said.

Mary Abel shifted her shovel to the other shoulder. Her feet and ankles were snow-soaked, and after three hours of digging her hands felt hot and puffy. The coat she wore was a man's, gray-green with age and so rough that it chafed her neck. When she walked it knocked at her heels like a board. She was forty-seven years old. She had not begun to work with her brother until she was forty-five, and though she believed in his mission, she was unable as yet to see all objects with his eyes. The Poor House did not look welcoming to her.

It was a large building, three stories high, built of brick, and L-shaped. It stood on a hill which overlooked other hills. Winter and summer it took the brunt of the wind. There was a cluster of dark cedars about it, and through these the wind blew with peculiar somberness. At the base of the hill on which it stood there flowed a small stream called Bleeding Creek. Some thought the stream had received its name because of the red clay it carried down from the hills after freshets. Others believed it was so named because of an early-day slaughter of pioneers on its banks. Whatever the reason for its name, Bleeding Creek loomed suddenly into sight from around the flank of one hill, widened into riffly shallows just below the Poor House, then as suddenly disappeared from sight beneath the overhanging limestone ledges of a hill beyond. Sycamores, alders, beeches, willows: all water-loving trees followed its course. During the winter storms their lighter creaking was added to the deep boom of the cedars.

No other buildings were visible from the Poor House. From its windows at night not a single light could be seen, unless on some distant hill a farmer with a lantern hunted a strayed cow or sheep. The day Mary Abel rode in under the dark cedars she had entered a remote and private world. Inside, the inmates. Outside, nothing but the wind and the roiled clouds and the clustering hills. She had lived at the Poor House for two years; still she could not think of it as welcoming.

"James," she said, "tell me how things will be changed when we find the answer."

James had told her many times before but he was a good-hearted man and he said once again, "It'll be happiness, Mary. Pure happiness."

"For everybody."

"Pure joy and happiness for everybody."

"No more sickness?"

Happiness was as far as James would ever go in speaking of the new world, and Mary asked no more questions. But she knew a happening that would mark the day they made their discovery, a happening she did not speak of to James but which often occupied her mind. The Poor House would be at once emptied of all its inmates. Did they die? She didn't bother to answer this question. They cleared out; or were cleared out. After that (when she imagined it) she scrubbed, aired, and scoured. She did away with all the old-man-smell and all the old-woman-litter. She filled the rooms with the objects of a home: stand-tables heavy with red plush albums, paper-weights with frozen fountains at their hearts, beribboned pots of bleeding heart. She set up what-nots, fern-stands, easels. She arranged Turkish corners and filled glass-fronted china-closets with hand-painted dishes. On all the mantels she placed fluted shells, each shell intricately convoluted, as pink in its disappearing tunnels as the inside of a mouth.

Buoyed up by this dream, Mary walked on stiffly toward the lighted building.

Odis Korby caught up with the two of them just before he reached the Poor House driveway. "I'll give you some company," he told Christie.

Christie took both Abels to be men, hunters he supposed.

"Where they bound for?" he asked. Except for the Poor House the countryside was as vacant of buildings as the sky.

"Conboy Castle. Them's two of Lord Jesus Conboy's disciples."

"What're they doing with picks and shovels?" he asked, seeing now that the Abels were not carrying guns.

"Digging," Mr. Korby said. "The two Abels have been out doing a little digging."

"What're they digging for? Anything valuable around here?"

"The truth's buried around here somewheres, according to the Abels. It got lost a thousand years or so back according to them, and they ain't going to give up now till they unearth it."

"Are they crazy?" Christie asked. "Do they keep crazy people at the Poor House?"

"Link Conboy's there, ain't he?"

Christie didn't want to talk about Cate's father. "What do they think it is?" he asked. "Something written down on a piece of paper?"

"Something written down on a piece of greenbacked paper," Korby said, laughing. "What did *you* think?"

He pulled up his horses as he came abreast the Abels. "Want a lift?" he asked. "Can't save you but a step but you'd 'bout as well ride now you've got the chance."

Brother and sister clambered stiffly over the wheel and into the wagon. "Sit down, sit down," Mr. Korby told them, motioning toward the coffin. "No use shying off a seat just because it happens to be a casket. We all got to come to it sooner or later." When the two Abels had seated themselves on the coffin, seemingly without reluctance, he asked, "Any luck today?"

"Nothing very promising," James Abel replied. "But then we didn't get started till toward evening."

"From all I hear Link Conboy keeps you pretty hard at it," he sympathized.

"He's got plans for us, all right."

Mr. Korby slapped the reins over his horses' backs. "The man Link Conboy's got plans for is Link Conboy. Don't let him tell you different."

"Either way," James said, "it don't matter much till the lost's found."

Mr. Korby gave Christie a nudge. Then he turned to James

Abel again. "You'll have to tell this young fellow here all about it."

"He coming to stay at the Poor House?"

"Sure he is," Mr. Korby said. "Can't you tell a fellow-boarder from his looks?"

"I don't go much by looks," James said.

Mr. Korby guided his grays without further conversation in under the cedars of the driveway, past the front of the Poor House and around to a side door. While the Abels climbed out he peered at the lighted windows; then he leaned down to ask James Abel in a low voice, "Dandie here?"

"Far as I know," James Abel answered.

"Link?"

"He was gone when I left."

Mr. Korby rolled out of the seat and over the wheel. Christie, admiring the barrel-shaped little man's agility, followed him. Uncertain as to whether he should go in at once or wait with Mr. Korby, he went to the head of the grays and began to fondle their warm velvety noses. The Abels, also seemingly uncertain, lingered at the tail of the wagon. Mr. Korby tramped back and forth in the snow.

"You waiting to see Dandie?" Christie asked finally.

"Don't yell," Mr. Korby said, though Christie had spoken quietly. "I'm standing right here beside you. I don't give two hoots in a hot place whether I see him or not. All I want to do is deliver my merchandise and collect my money."

Several minutes passed. One of the horses snorted impatiently. The Abels, next time Christie looked around, had noiselessly disappeared. Mr. Korby began to fume. "What's come of that boy? He think I've got nothing better to do than wait here in the snow?"

As Christie was wondering why Mr. Korby didn't announce his arrival by knocking on the door, a large figure was momentarily silhouetted against a window. After a second or two of staring, Korby hastily lifted the coffin from the wagon and set it into Christie's surprised and reluctant arms.

"Deliver that with my compliments," he said, and before Christie could either protest or ask for further instructions, Mr. Korby was back again on the seat of his wagon. "You tell Dandie

Conboy merry Christmas and that he owes me a balance of twenty-five dollars. Tell him I'll expect it by the first of the year."

Mr. Korby turned his grays and went out of the yard fast, his spinning wheels lifting the snow in powdery, wedge-shaped sprays.

Stooping, Christie managed to get his bag in one hand while he balanced the coffin on his shoulder with the other. Walking gingerly through the snow, which masked the walk and steps, he got to the door. There, using his bag as a knocker, he gently thumped on the door a time or two. The door was flung open so suddenly that he almost fell forward. A white faced, black-haired young man said angrily, "Why didn't you let me know it had come?" Then he took the coffin with an excess of force, as if half expecting Christie to cling to it, and strode off down the hallway into which the door opened.

2

Christie stood in the doorway, uncertain as to what to do next. He felt considerably abashed to find himself inside a house he had not been bidden enter, let alone welcomed to. A sudden blast of cold air about his legs reminded him of the open door. He was thinking that he had perhaps better go outside, close the door, knock, and start his visit all over again in a more conventional manner, when a girl entered the hallway at its far end. The hallway was semi-dark, its only light coming from a bracket lamp attached to the wall at the hall's mid-point. Christie was unable to make out the child's features until she reached this lamp. She was, he then saw, ten or twelve years old, thin, long-jawed, big-eyed, and with a black pigtail which bounced over her shoulder as she walked.

She came steadily toward him, not pausing until she was almost directly beneath his nose. From this vantage point she inspected him. Then she said,

> "Outdoors the icy air is king,
> Inside, it's quite another thing.
> If you're too hot, please go outside;
> Many a child of drafts has died."

Christie was amazed; also apologetic. After shutting the door he asked, "Did you make that up?"

"Of course not," the girl answered. "What do you think I am?"

This was exactly what he was wondering. When she said, stiffly, "Will you please step down to the parlor," he decided that she was one of the paupers, trained by Mrs. Conboy to be polite and useful.

"Thank you," he answered, "I will." He followed her bobbing

pigtail down the hall, along a strip of flowered in-grain carpeting, past the bracket lamp and the two gilt-framed pictures which flanked it, and so into a warm, densely furnished, and well-lit room.

"Be seated, please," the girl said and Christie, looking about, chose a red, spring-bottomed chair next the center table.

"Thank you," he said again, expecting the girl to leave the room. Instead, she seated herself on the ornate sofa opposite him and resumed the inspection which the trip down the hall had interrupted. Christie was now convinced that the child was a Conboy. However, after several minutes of silence had passed during which she stared, chewed the end of her dark braid, and meditatively scratched her armpits, he gave up caring who she was.

"Are you troubled with the itch?" he asked finally, irritated by the silence and staring.

"I itch," the girl said, "but I haven't got the itch."

"What's the difference?" Christie asked, but the girl would not quibble over definitions.

"What I've really got," she confided, "is a growth."

Christie, deciding once more that the child was an inmate and an unfortunate one at that, said, "I'm sorry. Perhaps it'll go away."

"I hope not," the girl told him. "I wouldn't be normal without it."

"Say, who are you?" he demanded, deciding that tact would not only be wasted but unrecognized in the present situation.

"Emma J. Conboy. And I know who you are. You're Christian J. Fraser. We have our middle letters in common," she observed. "Jane, and, I presume, John?"

"Are you Cate's sister?" Christie asked, somewhat shocked.

"I don't know."

"What d'you mean you don't know?"

"I think I probably was adopted. I'm not like the other Conboys. But they *call* us sisters," she admitted.

Christie decided to keep clear of the Conboy relationships, imagined or real.

"How'd you know who I was?"

"It wasn't any secret that you were coming. Cate hasn't done anything but clean house all day. And besides, I've enjoyed your letters. Don't tell Cate, though."

Sister as well as mother! Christie wondered if the whole family had enjoyed his letters. "Do you think that's a nice thing—reading your sister's letters?"

"If they're interesting, I do. . . . You couldn't hire me to read the letters of Ferris P. Thompson, though."

"Who's Ferris P. Thompson?"

"An old saucer peach."

"Saucer peach?"

"That's what I say instead of shite-poke. The initials are the same."

"You can say shite-poke for all of me," Christie told her.

"If you don't mind, I won't," Emma excused herself, politely. "Papa don't like it."

Christie didn't enjoy being put in the position of urging a child to use a word to which her father objected and decided to end the conversation. "Does your sister know I'm here?" he asked.

"I haven't the slightest idea."

"Will you tell her," Christie asked, "please? I'm already late. I'd like her to know that I've finally arrived."

"Are you eager to lay eyes on her?" Emma asked, looking at him speculatively.

"Yes," Christie said, "I am."

Emma stood up. "All *she* had to do was look out the window, and she could've told you were here. That's what I did."

"Would you mind telling her?"

Emma went to the door, but lingered there. "Do you want to hear a conundrum?"

"No," Christie said, "I don't. I hate conundrums."

"Maybe you never heard a good one."

"Maybe not. What is it?"

"Why are us Conboys the opposite of Christmas?"

"I give up," said Christie, privately thinking of several reasons.

"Because Christmas celebrates a live baby and we mourn a dead one."

"Whose baby is it?" Christie asked.

"Nory Tate's."

With this, Emma went into the hall; then she turned back.

"Actually," she said, as if determined to be completely honest, "we are kind of like Christmas."

"How?" Christie asked, feeling as if he had been mesmerized into a minstrel-show routine.

"It was a virgin birth."

Christie was not sufficiently mesmerized to have any answer to this. "Go on," he said weakly. "Get Cate."

"Have you got a calling-card?"

"No," Christie said, "I haven't."

Emma, obviously disappointed, left.

At the bottom of the stairs she smacked into Cate.

"Look out where you're going, can't you?" Cate asked.

Em tenderly exploring the caverns beneath her stringy arms, said, "He wanted me to hurry."

"Who?"

"Christian J. Fraser. He says he's eager to lay eyes on you."

Cate could not imagine Christie's saying anything of the kind, but she had no intention of arguing the point with Em. She resettled her skirts, ran her hands through her hair and hurried on.

"The coffin came," Em whispered after her.

Cate whirled about. "What coffin?"

"Don't you know?"

"I wouldn't be asking if I did."

"Dandie's."

"Dandie's!" Cate's heart skipped a beat. Then she said calmly, "What's he want a coffin for? He's not planning on dying, is he?"

"He wants it for Nory's little dead baby."

"Oh, no!" Cate said.

"Mr. Korby brought it and he"—Em inclined her head toward the parlor—"carried it in. And Dandie grabbed it from him as if Christian J. Fraser had been trying to steal it."

Cate felt sick. Her father was opposed to Mr. Korby's coffins; to all ready-made coffins and for everyone, but here especially, where the money such a coffin cost was needed for more important things. Now Dandie had somehow, slyly, behind Father's back, gone to Mr. Korby, who was no friend of Father's, and got one. And for Nory's baby!

Cate did not know for whom she felt most sorry, for her father, or Dandie, or Nory. Or herself. Oh, for herself, of course! She could come to *their* sorrows only at second-hand, but her own sorrow she did not have to imagine. It was real. Her picture of Christie's arrival on Christmas Eve was spoiled—and all of her plans for it. Christie was to have been welcomed, first of all by a house like anyone else's: nobody's change of drawers warming by the stove, nobody's switch, like a dead horse's tail, dangling from the mantel; nobody's boot full of hickorynut shells on the hearth. She herself was to have flung open the door, bade him come in out of the snowy night, then stood against the shining background of the orderly house, austere Cate, fashionable Cate, whatever Cate she chose to be, but a Cate calm and gracious.

Now that picture was ruined. Christie had arrived with a coffin, had had it snatched from him by Dandie and had been greeted by Em—she could not bear to think how. And not only did the shattering of this picture grieve her, it angered her to think that she was more troubled by this, a really trivial thing, than by the true sorrows of her father and Dandie and Nory. She grieved for this other picture shattered: the picture of a Cate of pure motives, a Cate who loved others more than herself. For Cate Conboy steadfastly refused to admit that among the persons she loved well was Cate Conboy.

"Oh, poor Papa!" she said.

Em nodded. "I guess I'll go look at it now while the looking's good."

"Look at what?"

"The coffin. I've never seen a little baby casket. Oh, Papa's boxes! But they're not the same. I bet Dandie bought a pretty one."

"Em," Cate said, "you know Papa doesn't believe in caskets. He won't want you to have anything to do with it."

"It's just the money for them he doesn't believe in," Em said. "Besides," she added, from halfway up the stairs, "how'll he know anything about it? Unless somebody tattles?"

11

CATE walked into the parlor. She had spent so much emotion in imagining Christie's arrival that now she seemed without feeling. Instead of going forward in time, as she walked toward him, she felt herself to be moving backward, to be re-enacting a meeting that had already taken place; there was thus nothing for it but to utter some often-imagined and hence second-hand and hateful greeting.

Then Christie made the meeting new and spontaneous. He did something she had not anticipated.

"Cate," he cried, reaching her before she had crossed half the parlor, "you're beautiful!"

"What?" Cate asked as if she had lost her hearing. She stopped suddenly so that she rocked a little on her toes.

"Well," said Christie, "is it news? Have they kept it from you? Covered up the mirrors?"

Cate was very happy, but she changed the subject at once. A minute's reflection, she was always afraid, might make a speaker regret his praise. He would be embarrassed to hear any reference to a statement he was already trying to forget. The only safe thing to do with praise was to take it and run—clasp it close, while pretending it didn't exist.

"Was your ride up from The Junction all right?" she asked, imitating a hostess.

"Was it!" Christie said enthusiastically. "What a ride! It was wonderful. I came up with an undertaker, Ordis Korby."

"Odis," Cate corrected him, her meeting with Christie becoming newer and newer. What she had supposed Christie would like, what she had wanted to provide for him was the surrey, side curtains up, lap-robe neatly folded and Nigger Bob driving. And what he had really liked was Odis Korby's spring-wagon with a coffin in it. Oh, the situation was far from second-hand.

"Odis," Christie corrected himself. "Anyway, Kissing Korby. You know what he said, Cate? That if he was to bury me tonight he'd give me a fatherly kiss first. What an oddity."

"You wouldn't really like him," Cate said, "if you knew him. He's not a good man."

"Oh, sure," Christie agreed. "I didn't miss that. That was one of the reasons I liked him."

"He's against Papa," Cate said, defining Mr. Korby's lack of goodness.

Christie understood at once. "That's different. He is a rascal, then. Anybody who is against the Conboys is a rascal and I'm against him. I'm pro-Conboy. Especially the lady Conboys. Especially Catey Conboy."

Cate rocked on her toes again, speechless.

"Merry Christmas, Cate," Christie said.

Cate, looking up, saw the shadow of Christie's eyelashes on his olive-colored cheeks.

"Merry Christmas, Cate," he repeated. "Happy New Year, Joyous Easter."

Cate longed to make a sparkling reply, but only commonplace greetings came to her mind.

"Happy forever, Christie," she said, ashamed of her lack of inventiveness.

When Lib Conboy entered the parlor door Christie jumped to his feet. He had been prepared to greet Cate's mother, a middle-aged woman. Middle-aged women were divided, in so far as he was concerned, into two classes: the first, which he preferred, was made up of plump motherly women, gray and bespectacled. They liked to cook, asked him if he was hungry, and told him to clean his feet before coming into the house. With them it was only necessary to pretend that he was still fourteen, that his chief interest was food and his chief sin not washing behind the ears. In the second class were those thin, faded rose-petal women, with dry hair piled high and veined fingers clattering with rings. Sometimes they were old maids, but just as often they were not. But married or unmarried they showed him their scrapbooks filled with columns of newspaper poetry, spoke of the temptations which a young man on the road must encounter and asked him if he drank, and were disappointed, he could see, when he said no. The pretense with *them* was that *they* were sixteen; since it was easier to imagine himself once again fourteen than that any woman over thirty was sixteen, he was more at home with the motherly ones. Mrs. Conboy, he saw at once, could not be easily identified with either of these classes.

"Mama," Cate said, "this is my friend Christie Fraser."

Lib crossed the floor with a quick graceful step, extended a veinless, un-ringed hand, inclined her simple frizz of chestnut curls and said, "I was beginning to think that Christie Fraser was just a young man made up out of whole cloth by Cate."

Christie, a little at a loss, said, "You'll see I'm no one she made up. Otherwise she'd 've made up someone better."

"Are you fishing, Mr. Fraser?" Lib asked, but didn't, he was glad, wait for any answer. "What I'm trying to decide," she went on, "is whether we should wait for Link or sit down now and eat without him. If we wait he'll be sure not to be here before midnight. If we sit down now, he'll get here just as we're half through and everything's cold."

She went across to the tall window, pushed the curtains impatiently aside and leaning with one cheek against the glass said, "The trouble with Link is that he's so good-hearted he'll let people talk a leg off him rather than remind them he's missing a meal because of them."

Christie gazed at Lib in her stylish red bombazine, surprised to find here in the parlor of a Poor Farm in what was agreed to be the lonesomest corner of the most God-forsaken county in the state, a woman as fashionable as any he'd ever seen in Indianapolis. Lifting the white lace curtains, as she did, so that they fell in an arch of froth about her red-clad figure she looked, to him, like a woman in a play, sustaining a pose of graceful, anxious waiting.

"Dressed up," Lib Conboy was undoubtedly the most attractively dressed woman in Rock County; but she no more thought of "dressing up," except for special occasions, than an actress thinks of putting on her Lady Macbeth costume for supper at home. Tonight was a special occasion, Christmas Eve plus the fact of Cate's entertaining a beau and she'd left off the extraordinary hodge-podge of old scarves, petticoats, dressing-sacks, mismated stockings, feather boas, faded wrappers, bedraggled skirts and, if she felt so inclined, hats and shoes of Link's, with which she customarily surprised her many times surprised, but never completely prepared, family.

The sweep of her arm, holding the folds of the white lace curtain in an arch above her somehow grieving head, spoke to Christie in a way which was appealing, but for which he had no word, though he recognized it as being of the theater. The word he could not find was dramatic. The pose was dramatic: which does not mean that it was in any way calculated, but only that Lib unconsciously assumed those attitudes which affect in one way or another the onlooker. Her vanity as an actress was much greater than her vanity as a woman. She had in addition to this sense of drama an ironic humility which pleased her, when the ingredients were at hand, to try for a comic effect. Then she would put on the most incongruous combinations her wardrobe afforded: the discarded hat of Link's, whose battered manliness would appear most laughable, set above the tattered ruchings of a frayed, long-tailed lavender wrapper. Thus arrayed she would sit down at the breakfast table and go about her morning work. Cate, who could see her mother in one rôle only, that of Cate Conboy's mother, suffered accutely when Lib appeared to her to get thus out of character. Link, Em, and Dandie, however, enjoyed the changing rôles and costumes.

Now she let the curtains fall and came back to Cate and Christie. "Here you are in a Poor House for Christmas, Mr. Fraser. How does it seem? Pretty awful?"

"So far I wouldn't know I was in a Poor House."

"That's Cate's work. She's got everyone on the place so bulldozed because of your coming they're afraid to make themselves seen."

"Oh, Mama," Cate implored.

"Don't 'Oh, Mama' me," Lib said. "The inmates of the Rock County Poor Farm think they'll end up in the pen if they do any more than breathe easy while Mr. Fraser's here. And believe me, that's Cate's doings. That's not the way things ordinarily go here."

Lib would work as hard as Cate, though in a very different way, to prepare house and inmates for a visitor. But she could never resist afterwards the comic effect of telling about it. It was a kind of double value, she felt, for the single effort.

Christie had often heard it said that if you wanted to know how a girl was going to look as she grew older you should inspect her mother. Inspecting Lib, he saw what every whittler at The Junction saw when Lib went past: a sight which made whittling suddenly appear a job fit only for old men and boys. No one, except her husband, had ever called Lib beautiful. And this word, as used by Link, and as Lib well knew, had nothing whatever to do with her face, with its large gray-green, somewhat protruding eyes, long nose, and mouth which was too full and, when she laughed, a little one-sided. The word "beautiful" as used by Link was only one of his ways of saying he loved her.

Lib's figure, though Link never spoke of it, *was* beautiful. Of this Lib was aware unconsciously and the whittlers consciously. Lib's figure, the kind of figure it was, spoke to them in a language limited, but which they all knew and had known since the age of ten. It was the absolute expression of what, for all its familiarity, was most not themselves: femaleness. Lib appeared to every street-corner lounger to be expressly designed to extol what they themselves possessed: maleness. Her small ankles, luxuriant breasts, slender waist, and slightly swaying, pear-shaped hips, emphasized the uniqueness of their own slab-sided, uncurving bodies.

And Lib, when she walked down the street, while unconscious of the whittlers' ruminations, was very conscious of the men themselves. She was no more capable of treating a man simply as a human being than she was of treating a cow as a human being. Nothing—neither extremes of age or youth, neither the utter strangeness of a passerby she would never see again, nor the closest of blood ties—dulled for her the disturbing otherness of the other sex. Even the clay in a coffin had not, for Lib, shed its sex. Over male clay she inclined her head with a sorrow from which the old wonder and interest had not completely departed.

This awareness of Lib's, far from resulting in any laxness of conduct, made her unusually stiff-necked and wary in her encounters with males—as if she were a traveler temporarily lodged with a tribe whose habits, while fascinating, might not be entirely dependable. It colored her thoughts of Dandie, of eighty-seven-year-old David Pen, dying possibly at that very minute in a bed not twenty feet from them; it caused her to put her hand on Christie's arm in studiedly casual, even tomboyish manner. But Christie was aware of the restraint, and pleased by the need for it, as all men were.

"Where's Dandie?" she asked, removing her hand from Christie's arm as abruptly as she had placed it there.

"I don't know," Christie answered, his private thought being that a person who could snatch up a coffin with Dandie's fury might now be out digging a grave in the snow for it with his bare hands. "I saw him when I first came in, but not since."

Cate hurried them away from the subject of Christie's reception by Dandie. "I expect he's changing his clothes for supper. Do you know why he is nicknamed Dandie?" she asked Christie and went on, not waiting for an answer. "His name is really James, and at first we called him Jim. Then because he always liked nice things so much and was so natty a dresser we got started calling him a Jim Dandie. Sometimes we still do."

"Not when I can hear you, you don't," said Dandie, who had just entered.

Em, when the talk about Dandie started, had wasted no time speculating where he might be, but had gone to hunt him. "He was in the Commissioner's Room," she said.

Christie saw at once that Dandie had calmed down but still made no attempt to hide his unhappiness or—if that was too strong a word for it—his irritation. Christmas Eve apparently meant nothing to him nor the fact that Christie was a guest in the house. He gave Christie a long hard stare, as if he had been a stranger encountered by chance at a cigar-stand.

"May I make you acquainted with my son, Dandie?" Lib said.

Dandie said, "We've met." Without surliness, flatly, not extending himself in the least to be agreeable or charming.

He had never needed to do so, Christie understood, with his second and third glances. He could walk into a room, that black head arrogantly poised, stance and gait saying, "I have certain powers. I do not overestimate them. But then I don't underestimate them either," and the people in the room would move toward him. He created, and was the center of, a vortex, wherever he went. But Christie, like everyone else, was drawn to him. He has these powers, he decided, is aware of them, but has no desire to use them for cheap or stupid purposes.

He extended his hand to Dandie, smiling. "I am happy to make the acquaintance of any of Cate's family," he said, "and hope this is but the first of many meetings."

Dandie, at that, moved out somewhat from whatever private world he was inhabiting, gave his hand a crisp, warm shake, and said, "Thank you."

"I think we'd better eat now," Lib said, "and not wait any longer for Link."

III

THE FIVE of them went in to supper together, Lib, her three children, and Christie. At the dining-room door Christie thought, this is a far cry from my idea of a Poor House. The room was filled to the brim, its fullness beginning with a red wallpaper thickly covered with brown trellises upon which tan roses bloomed. Over the roses and trellises hung a number of pictures: pansies with cat-like faces; a St. Bernard rescuing a child from the sea; a still life, hauntingly real, of a single fuzzy peach on a cracked plate; on the peach sat a fly, not so much single as singular. No one could be sure it was a fly; perhaps it was a wasp; or even a moth.

Em, who relished meanings in pictures (or elsewhere), often studied this one. Everything in the picture was so arbitrary that she felt sure it must possess layer upon layer of meaning. Her favorite was that courteous people, each refusing to take the best, had helped themselves to inferior peaches until finally this, the best of the lot, was left to a fly. The moral was plain: take the best at once, while the taking was good.

In addition to pictures the dining-room contained two massive claw-footed sideboards, a large base burner, a window-box (made by Link and looking very much like one of his coffins) filled with coleuses, a hump-backed leather-covered sofa, fourteen chairs, four of which matched, and a long extension table. Over the table hung a suspension lamp with a hand-painted china shade. From this lamp Cate had run upward to the corners of the room innumerable strands of red and green crêpe paper. The effect was festive, but strange: as if they were entering an inverted pagoda. The table, also, was decorated. Strips of the same red and green paper which masked the ceiling had been laid across the table, cutting it into pie-shaped sections. At the center of the table, where the strips crossed, Cate had arranged a pyramid of pine-cones and cedar boughs. To this Lib had objected. "Your beau's going to think you've emptied the wood-box on the table."

Cate had said nothing, but she knew better. It would look like Christmas to Christie, like winter and the woods and their being alone together. To Lib, entering the dining-room, the pine-cones still looked like kindling. They, together with the room's other decorations, the company, and her unaccustomed finery, made her nervous. Ordinarily Lib's nervousness expressed itself, in so far as onlookers could tell, as high spirits; but occasionally the disguise slipped and a glass would be upset, a drizzle of gravy would drop on to her dress, an unexpected word would escape with sudden disturbing emphasis into the conversation.

She went to the foot of the table where she usually sat (opposite Link at the head), letting the others sit as they would; by chance Christie was next to her. She was glad of this for she had no confidence in Cate's ability to entertain a male. She was convinced that Cate was the kind of girl who had better snap up the first eligible young man who made eyes at her. She was certain there wouldn't be many. And there was no use hunting through the woods only to come out at the end with a crooked stick. Still, a crooked stick in the beginning was no good either, and her eyes were already exploring Christie for flaws. The mere fact that he was interested in Cate made her wonder if he wasn't a little queer.

When all knees were under the table and the scraping of feet had stopped, Lib bowed her head. Grace was not said at the Conboy table except on special occasions; it was then brought out like the good silver, one of the accouterments of genteel living. This was not because Lib was hypocritical or wouldn't have liked it for everyday use. It was only that in the helter-skelter of everyday living grace was always somehow mislaid.

"Mr. Fraser," she said in her twangy voice, vibrant as a plucked zither string, "will you please return thanks?"

At these words, Cate felt an enormous thumb and forefinger give her heart a pinch. She had tried to anticipate everything—forestall everything—which would be unpleasant or unsuitable. This was her one lapse. Had Christie ever prayed in public? And, if not, could he rise to it?

There was no sound from Christie to reassure her. Should she rush into prayer herself? Pretend to have been overwhelmed by a sudden prompting of the Spirit? Cautiously she opened her eyes. Across from her Dandie gazed stonily at the lamp which swayed a little in the upward draft from the stove. Em's eyes, squeezed shut, were the shape of raisins. Beneath her mother's lowered lids she thought she detected a sidelong, nervous movement in Christie's direction.

Then Christie in an unhurried, untroubled voice spoke. "Let us each silently return thanks for the blessings of this Christmas Eve."

Cate closed her eyes, very thankful indeed, and prayed for a long time—make me honest, generous, kind, long-suffering—the words piled one upon the other without prompting. Presently she looked up to see all heads except Em's lifted. Em's lips moved silently and only Dandie had the heart to bring her back to this world.

"Prayer-meeting's over, Em," he said.

Em, blinking like an owl roused in daylight, lifted her head. "I was counting to a hundred."

"Next time count by tens," Dandie advised.

Before this feud could develop further Lib interrupted it. "See what's keeping Mag, Cate," she said, and Cate, glad of lesser responsibilities, plunged out to the kitchen.

Mag Creagan ordinarily looked after the inmates' table while Cate took care of the Conboys', but tonight Mag was doing both. Mag was actually an inmate herself (but since she didn't look at it that way, no one else did). She had her four children with her at the Poor House: Earnest, Airey, Icey, and Fessler. And while her wages as hired girl paid for her children's keep, there was not enough left over to pay for her own. The children were all Creagans like herself—and she had been born one.

"Earnest's father betrayed me," she had told Cate one day as the two of them scraped parsnips together in the kitchen.

Betrayal was a political crime to Cate. Benedict Arnold had betrayed his country. "Was he punished?" she had asked.

"Ah no," Mag had answered. "Truth to tell, I was ripe for it."

Truth to tell, she continued to be ripe for it. Mag was everlastingly and unhappily in love. She had no relish for a tame and proffered affection. A man advancing toward her was an unwholesome sight. Only a man in flight and wholeheartedly repulsing her made Mag feel ardent. In the pursuit of such she was at least fifty per cent successful. If there were never any wedding rings to symbolize her victories there were, at least, the four Creagans: evidence that, however wholehearted the repulsion, the flight at some point had occasionally broken down.

Mag was at the range dishing up stewed chicken when Cate came into the kitchen. She hauled a fine yellow drumstick from the iron kettle and placed it beside the other plump pieces on Lib's best flowered platter.

"Hon," she said, "I've fobbed them paupers off tonight with nothing but necks and pope's-noses."

"Papa won't like that," Cate said, secretly approving the opulent platter, heaped with breasts and thighs.

"Time Papa knows," Mag said, "Papa can't do nothing about it." She set the chicken on the oven door while she piled mashed potatoes into a dish. "How's things coming in there?" she asked.

"All right, I guess," Cate answered doubtfully, taking the sweet potatoes out of the baking-pan. "Em counted to a hundred instead of returning thanks, though."

Mag made a nest in the mashed potatoes with her big wooden spoon, then deposited an egg of butter there.

"You think that girl's just right in the head?" she asked. Mag's Icey was a little queer and Mag ceaselessly tried to convince herself that Icey's quirks were no greater than those possessed by others.

"Why, Em's smart as a whip," Cate protested.

"Smart don't have anything to do with sane."

"Well, Em's sane," Cate said flatly. "Too sane."

"Like your Papa," Mag said, picking up the platter of chickens. "You bring on the gravy," she told Cate.

Back in the kitchen for their second load of food, Mag looked at Cate thoughtfully. "Sis," she said, "I didn't think you had it in you."

"Had what in me?"

"The gumption to pick up a man like that for yourself."

The way Mag said "man" startled Cate. It had not occurred to her that *that* was what she had picked up. "Did you like him?" she asked. "Do you think he's nice-looking?"

"He's no fire-eater like your brother Dandie. And not so pretty, I reckon, either," Mag said, wiping melted butter from the edge of the dish which held the mashed potatoes. "But in my opinion, well yes, I'd be free to confess he looks to me like—" Mag's voice trailed off while she licked butter from her fingers and stared back into memories Cate could not penetrate.

"Looks like what?" Cate asked, pausing at the door to the

dining-room, stewed corn in one hand, creamed onions in the other.

"Why," Mag said, "just what I was saying. That he'd make a girl a satisfactory fellow."

When all the food was placed on the table there was no crêpe paper and very little tablecloth left in sight.

"You'll be throwing those pine-cones in the stove yet, Cate," her mother said. "To make room."

Cate, humiliated, glanced across the table at Christie.

"Throw some of the food away first, Mrs. Conboy," Christie said. "Those pine-cones are Christmas."

It was all right with Lib if Christmas went into the stove, with the pine-cones. She was too spontaneous for holidays. She never kept anniversaries of any kind. She had a secret scorn for those who did so. She had seen birthdays celebrated in other households with all the claptrap of candles, layer cakes, and beribboned presents. At these times she had been filled with the same superior, wondering amusement which takes hold of savages at the sight of some outlandish, civilized rigamarole. She had been hard put not to snigger outright on these occasions.

Yet, afterwards, she had sometimes felt envious, and wondered if she were missing something. And she had played at keeping a Christmas or two, a birthday or two, in the way a savage plays at being civilized with a stove-pipe hat to emphasize his nakedness. One December she had gone so far as to make red mosquito-net stockings of the kind she had seen at church parties, fill them with candy and put them aside for Christmas; but before Christmas could strike, spontaneity had descended upon her. This, she remembered, was the year Dandie had been seven, and while they still lived on their own place, long before Link had given up his practice.

She leaned across Christie to speak to Cate. "Do you remember the Christmas Dandie burned Gladys Juanita, Cate?"

It had been, Cate remembered, a gray sleety afternoon. Lib had once told her that when it snowed the angels were beating up their feather beds. What had the angels been doing that afternoon to send down such a mixture of ice and water and snow: a mixture that gritted across the window-panes and brought twilight at three o'clock?

"Who was Gladys Juanita?" Christie wanted to know.
"My doll—a rag doll."
"And you burned her?" Christie asked Dandie.
"If they say so," Dandie answered indifferently.
"Little by little he did," Cate declared.

The three of them, Dandie, Lib, and herself, had been in the sitting-room that afternoon. Without saying a word Dandie had picked up Gladys Juanita by one of her bolster-like legs and, whirling with her, had smacked her against the stove often enough to scorch her. Cate hadn't actually loved the doll until that minute, the minute the scorching began; but she was imaginative about suffering, and pity had caused her love for Gladys Juanita to flare up fiercely. She could not have cried louder had her own head been on fire.

"Shut up," Dandie had shouted; he had to shout to be heard above her bellowing. "Your darned old doll can't feel."

"She can, she can," Cate had declared.

"If she can feel," Dandie had argued, "why don't she say something?" To prove his point he once more flattened Gladys Juanita's muslin face against the stove. "Yell if it hurts," he commanded, and waited attentively for some word; and though smoke curled up from Juanita's lips, now rosy as two coals, there was not so much as a whimper.

"Cate forced me to burn the old thing," Dandie unexpectedly told Christie.

"How did I force you?" Cate asked.

"By saying the doll could feel. I had to burn her to prove you were wrong."

"I felt," Cate said. "I suffered. Didn't you care about me?"

"The doll was the only one you ever mentioned."

"So that was your early Christmas?" Christie asked, and Cate, feeling that he thought that she and Dandie were quarreling—

and maybe they were—said quickly, "Oh, no. That was just the cause of the early Christmas."

Suddenly Lib, at the height of their argument, had said to the children, "Hark, what's that I hear?"

There had been something in his mother's voice more interesting to Dandie than cruelty, more interesting to Cate than martyrdom. The word "hark" was unusual too; it announced something out of the ordinary; but more than this was Lib's expression of wonder and amazement. She had gone on tiptoe to the window and Cate and Dandie had followed her, Dandie carrying the still smoking Juanita.

"Get down, get down," Lib had ordered them in an agitated whisper. "Don't let him catch sight of you."

Cate had dropped to her knees at once without a question; Dandie was more curious. "Who'll catch sight of us, Mama?" he asked.

"Santa Claus," Lib told them. "Blown off his course. Swept down here early by the storm. It's now or never for you two. He's got presents for you, but can't deliver them if there are children in sight. Hide, now! Get flat to the floor."

Cate had burrowed into the carpet, snuffing up dust at every breath. Dandie lay flat, though he peeped out through his fingers. Then the sounds began, a hubbub of pawings and nickerings and of voices: one was their mother's, the other must be *his*. Finally after the talk, and farewells, came the sounds once more of animals: reindeer, of course. What other animals could clink their hooves in that tinkling North Pole way?

"Get up, get up, children!" Lib had cried. "Look what Santy's left you!"

They had taken their noses from the floor, Cate's printed with the weave of the rug, and there in either hand Lib held two red mosquito-netting stockings, bulging with nuts and candy and swollen at each toe with an orange. What a wonderful moment! A mother stronger than calendars and a personal friend of Santa's. Who could care about a set Christmas? It would be no more exciting than the arrival of any Monday or Tuesday, a scheduled, dependable event.

"So you had an early Christmas because Dandie scorched Gladys Juanita?" Christie asked. "What was it? A new doll?"

Cate said, "No. Stockings filled with different things."

"What did you do for the real Christmas then? Get more presents?"

"Do?" Cate echoed as if trying to think back.

On the real Christmas, on December the twenty-fifth, there had been nothing, no presents, no extra food. The day after Christmas when the other children had asked her and Dandie what they got for Christmas, Dandie had told the truth. "Nothing," he said. But she had lied. Not for herself, but to protect her mother. A mother who didn't give presents on Christmas was queer.

"I got something," she told them, "but it's a secret."

"Aw, you didn't get anything," the kids had bawled. "You and old Dandie both didn't get anything."

"Dandie didn't, but I did," she persisted. "My mother gave it to me." She had lied for her mother's sake, but the minute she did so she began to hate her for making the lie necessary.

"Where is it?" the kids wanted to know. "If you got anything, show it to us."

"I can't," she told them. "It's a secret between me and my mother."

Even Dandie began finally to believe her. After the kids left he said, "What'd Mama give you, Cate? You can tell me."

But she shook her head. "No, I can't, Dandie. I can't tell you because you're a boy."

Now she heard Dandie, looking across the table at Christie, tell, as usual, the truth. "More presents! Why, those stockings were so darned wonderful you can see for yourself we can't forget them. More! Why, we'd've been crazy as bed-bugs if we'd got anything more."

Cate willed Dandie to shut up. She jumped from her chair, ran to her mother, and gave her an intense, unnatural hug. With her arms about her mother's neck and her chin resting against her mother's mounds of hair she said, "From doll-burning to storytelling! My brother Dandie goes from bad to worse."

Then she went running into the kitchen, like an actress who has heard from off-stage a summons which the audience has missed.

With Cate in the kitchen Lib began to feel unexpectedly free and comfortable. She was Cate's mother and what she felt for her daughter must be love. Certainly she intended to help her in this delicate business of landing a beau. Still, it was good to be free of Cate's missionary eye which aroused in her, in spite of her best intentions, a defiant mulishness, a desire to shock. She was not proud of this feeling; and she was happy when, as tonight, she felt that she was pleasing Cate.

She had been eating quickly, speaking quickly; now she was thirsty and drank quickly. Then, remembering, she slowed down, began to take gentle sips. Once Cate had written in her diary, "My mother drinks like a horse." Cate had been thirteen then.

Lib, who had read the entry, had first boxed Cate's ears soundly with the diary itself, then led her off to Link.

"Look at what your daughter writes of her own mother," she had said.

Link had been saddened by the entry; but reasonable. First of all he had tried to show Cate that she had been wrong in her facts. "A human being cannot possibly drink like a horse," he had said. "Not out of a glass, anyway."

"She sounds like a horse," Cate had stubbornly persisted.

Link had showed her that this too was impossible.

"I don't like the way the cords stand out in her neck when she drinks," Cate had cried, shifting her ground.

"You're not called on to like everything in this world. Nor to speak up about all you don't like."

"Don't you want me to tell the truth?"

"I've shown you there wasn't any truth in what you said."

"I don't like the way she drinks. It's ugly and that's the truth."

"That isn't what you said. But the point is, Cate, that besides hurting people's feelings by saying such things you show your own narrowness. You do yourself harm. You'll grow out of it, but why harm yourself by showing everyone your limitations?"

"Limitations!" Cate had flared. "Is it a limitation not to like to see your own mother"—she had paused, hunting, Lib had seen, a word which would describe what she meant without getting the conversation cut short with another slap—"is it a limitation not to like to see your own mother gulp?"

"Yes," Link had said, "it is a limitation not to understand that to do a thing with your whole heart is a good trait."

"Even drinking a glass of water?"

"Even drinking a glass of water."

These encounters between Link and his older daughter were always marvels to Lib. Nine-tenths of the time, after listening to Link, she was on Cate's side. You could *not* think to order. There was no use in Link's trying to reason Cate into liking something she didn't like. It was reasonable to box her ears, switch her good and hard, tell her she couldn't have a diary if she was going to write such things; but it was not reasonable to tell her she couldn't think whatever it was she did think.

"Oh, shoot, Link," she had said after this encounter, "maybe I do drink like a horse."

Then Cate had broken down and cried. "Mama, you don't, you don't. Don't say such a thing. It's just my badness. I love you, Mama, and I love the way you drink and everything you do."

Cate had nuzzled up to her mother then; but Lib had only given her another sharp rap over the head with her diary, so that she had been forced to draw back, tears and caresses alike unspent. "Erase that out of your book," Lib had ordered, "and never write anything like it again."

Cate had erased the words and replaced them with a sentence about the weather. Lib had looked in Cate's diary to see if she had done this; but in spite of the change the first sentence was the one which stuck in her mind. The trouble, Lib thought, was that when not drinking, she could easily understand that fast drinking might not be a pretty sight to watch; but the minute she began to drink, there were no watchers, only other drinkers. She identified herself with everyone, particularly so, when she was happy or excited. Then the boundaries which separated her from others completely disappeared; to mince and sip then was to begrudge everyone else a full-sized swallow. But now the thought of Cate restored the boundaries which had been slipping, and she drank as self-consciously and as slowly as possible.

Since Cate stayed in the kitchen dishing up the dessert while Mag did the serving, her spirits rose once again: the season and her desire to celebrate were having one of their unusual periods of coincidence. She bit hungrily into her pie and flakes of the tender crust fell thickly on to her red bombazine, and she brushed them aside as if they were part of the season's bounty, as suitable and to be expected as snowflakes. She felt suddenly exultant, convinced that nothing could go wrong; or, if it did, that even a mishap might be useful in the mixture of things which, for those who love God, work together for good. Cate's crêpe-paper canopy was moving slightly—like the ribs of a breathing animal; the lamplight was yellow on the white tablecloth, and the green oak chunks simmered together in the stove behind her; but Lib was not one to linger over such household effects. Her quick eye soon exhausted even a landscape of many miles, let alone a diningroom of a few feet.

"Em," she said, "go tell Mag to tell all the folks to go to their rooms and close their doors."

"Folks" was Link's way of getting around calling the inmates "inmates" or "paupers." It was sometimes confusing. "Where are the folks?" Dandie would ask Em, meaning Lib, Link, or Cate. "What folks?" Em would answer, happily splitting a hair. "You mean the poor folks or our folks?"

"I mean the poor folks who happen to be our folks," Dandie would answer, contemptuous of distinctions, all of them housed here together, closer than bees in a hive.

Now no one misunderstood Lib. She meant the poor folks. Em rose, willing for anything. Lock all the poor folks in and yell fire, for instance. It would be a new spectacle. She would die to rescue any one of them; but in this case the poor folks' sufferings would be only imaginary, while her pleasure would be real.

Cate, back at the table, asked anxiously, "What are you going to do, Mama?"

"I've got a surprise for the folks," Lib said, "a treat."

Lib was usually without color. Now, the sallow skin over the high cheekbones was rosy and her large gray-green eyes sparkled. "Run on, Em," she said, rising. "Tell them to shut their doors. Tell them old Santy's coming. Come, Mr. Fraser, lend me a hand."

Christie got up from the table. He didn't know what his hand was needed for, but he liked the feeling of excitement.

"Excuse me, please," he said to Cate and Dandie, "while I help your mother"; then, hurrying to keep up with Lib, who moved slowly only when sick, he left the dining-room.

Cate and Dandie remained at the table like two oldsters left to crack nuts and reminisce. Cate leaned forward, elbows on the table, suddenly tired. The meal she had thought about for two weeks was over like any other meal; and perhaps was no more important.

"Well, he seems like a nice boy," Dandie said indifferently, answering her unspoken question. Dandie was two years younger than Christie. "Maybe won't set the world on fire."

"Who cares?" Cate said.

Dandie lifted his shoulders, then his eyebrows. "You, I thought."

"What's he going to think about this?"

Dandie looked about the room. "Circus tent, I guess," he said.

"I don't mean *this*," Cate said, gesturing upward toward the crêpe-paper canopy of which she had no doubts, "but what's to come. Mama."

"What *is* to come?" Dandie asked.

"Let's go see," Cate said.

At the dining-room door she put her hand on Dandie's arm. "How's Nory?"

"She went down to eat her supper tonight, anyway."

"Was she the one who wanted the coffin, Dandie? Is that why you got it?"

"She doesn't even know I *have* got it."

"Papa isn't going to like it."

"To hell with Papa," Dandie said. "I paid for the coffin and it's for Nory's baby. Where does Papa figure in that?"

Cate said nothing. She couldn't imagine such freedom.

Lib came ahead, pushing a rocker down the hall with one hand and holding the sack of plug-cut in the other. Behind her was Christie with the galvanized bucket filled with the sacks of hard candy. Behind *him* was Em with the sleigh-bells. At the other end of the hall, Mag came out of the kitchen carrying a dishpan of popcorn balls. She placed this out of the way against the wall and took a horn from her apron pocket. "Fessler's," she explained.

Lib nodded approvingly. "The more the merrier."

Christie gazed down this hall, new to him, longer and more narrow than the one into which he had first stepped, a hall without carpet or pictures or umbrella-stand, with only the bracket lamp on the wall and the six white doorknobs, three on either side, to decorate it.

"The oldest folks are kept down here," Lib told him. "The ones who can't make the stairs so easy and who need some waiting on. We'll give them their treat first. Shake your bells, Em, quiet at first, then louder. Like you're getting closer. You prance, Mag, and blow your horn. You, Mr. Fraser, neigh like a reindeer. I'll be the sled. They'll think it's the end of the world."

This struck Christie as being very near to what they'd really think. "It won't be too much excitement for them?" he asked anxiously.

"Don't go worrying about the folks. They're so starved for a little excitement an earthquake'd pleasure them. Come on," she said briskly and launched down the hall, the rockers of the chair she pushed squeaking against the bare floorboards, Christie had to admit, for all the world like the runners of a sled on ice. Em swept in behind her, her sleighbells whirring; Mag tootled and pranced, and Christie, with no idea what a neighing reindeer sounded like, clattered at the end of the line, bawling, he was afraid, more like a weanling calf than any Christmas deer. It became less of a bawl, with practice, and whatever the folks thought, the reindeer himself began to have a wonderful time, sweating and prancing and neighing.

Christie saw Dandie and Cate come into the hall and knew how they felt: superior to all this hullabaloo as he too had been at first; he reached out an arm and pulled Cate into the line and felt her respond to the excitement of the noise and the movement.

"Now for the presents," Lib said, and Cate went with Christie to his bucket of candy.

"Are you going to put the candy around?" she whispered.

Christie nodded.

"I'll go with you and tell you their names so you can say, 'Merry Christmas, Mrs. Goforth,' and so on," she said.

Em and Mag continued their ringing and blowing while Lib and Christie set the gifts in front of the doors. "Merry Christmas and a Happy New Year to Miss Lily Bias," Christie shouted, prompted by Cate. "Best wishes of the season to Mr. Josiah Stout."

In the midst of this uproar Cate suddenly said, "Papa's come."

Christie straightened and turned. At the end of the hall was a tall man in a dark overcoat. "What's going on here?" he asked quietly.

For a second Christie thought the question was condemning and that there was displeasure in the voice; but as Link Conboy continued to speak Christie saw that he was after information only, not condemning anything or anybody. "Some kind of a celebration?" Still, it was a dry, critical voice, flat and not very strong.

Lib ran down the hall to her husband. "Link," she said, "I thought you'd never get back."

"Well, I made it at last," he said, putting a hand on her shoulder. "What's all this?" he asked again.

"A treat for the folks," Lib said, indicating the bags of candy, the tobacco, and popcorn balls.

"You mean they're waiting for it?" Lib nodded. "Well, let them have it, then. And I've got a treat of my own to add to it. Come on, everybody," he called, and Christie noticed that Link Conboy, unlike the other members of his family, was a slow speaker.

At the sound of Link's voice the hall was filled with the people about whom Christie had been wondering ever since he'd received Cate's invitation. Those who came out of the rooms along the hall were joined by others who came down the stairs and who began at once to help themselves to the candy, the popcorn, and tobacco. The bracket lamp was oversized, but it lighted clearly only those near it. Christie had half expected to see on each inmate's face a stamp of some kind proclaiming, for all the world to read, pauper. Finishing life in the Poor House was, he had always supposed, the worst fate that could befall a man: far worse than finishing life in prison. The prisoner was perhaps no more than unlucky, caught by chance in his illegal act and able to reform, to swear off, after he got out. Swearing off was not going to help the poor man. You couldn't swear off poverty, and reforming wouldn't make you rich. Poverty wasn't an act a man performed, it was an act he couldn't perform: that of feeding himself; an act which, sooner or later, he'd be caught in: then, the Poor House.

This terrible experience, Christie'd always thought, would alter a man's face, give him a hang-dog, beaten look, leave him leveled, flat as a flounder, unmistakably marked; but it didn't. The bracket lamp revealed the same faces he'd left behind him on the streets of Indianapolis; no difference whatever; the same banter and cackling he'd heard there, too. The smell was different and worse: enough old folks with their winter fear of water were packed in the hall to give it the smell of a cupboard in which a side of bacon has been going slowly rancid. He watched the two Abels, the man revolving a popcorn ball slowly in his hands, the woman, poking about in her bag of candy: they had the heavy red faces which might answer his knock at any farmhouse door. A grandmotherly old lady of the kind that keeps her girlish liking for curls and fans was trading candy with another woman, less old, *her* face a web of good-humored lines. A little lanterned-jawed, foxy man dropped his bag of candy back into the bucket. "A present you can't pour ain't of no earthy use to me," he said.

Christie pulled Cate, who was beside him, close enough to whisper, "I'm disappointed."

"Why?"

"They look like anyone else."

"They don't always act that way," Cate told him.

At the other end of the hall Link had begun to speak, and most of the gabble was quieting down. "I told you I had another Christmas present for you," he said, "and I do. Something a lot better than candy and tobacco." He paused, but no one had anything to say to this so he went on in his slow dry uninteresting way. "Some of you probably have a pretty good idea what it is. As you know we've got fair land here as farm land goes in this section, and it's been my belief all along that with a little help from the commissioners to start us off, we could not only pay our expenses but have something left over. Well, I've been meeting with them tonight—not in a regular meeting, but calling on them. I thought Christmas Eve might be a good time for such a visit." Link paused, but again, if there was any response from his listeners Christie couldn't detect it. "I saw all of them," he continued, "except Mr. Korby, who was away from home, and I got the promise of all for enough money to properly fertilize next year and properly seed. That's one of my Christmas presents, that promise. But it's not the only one. I've got something out in the barn that's no promise." Again Link paused and again there was no response. "Mr. Hummel gave us something better than a promise. A two-hundred-pound purebred Poland China gilt."

As Link ceased speaking Christie awaited once again some response from the listeners. He expected no concerted hurrahing, no "Three cheers for our superintendent," but speech of some kind was surely in order. Here was a man who had spent a snowy Christmas Eve going from one house to another, begging, not for himself—though possibly a self-supporting Poor Farm and a herd of purebred hogs would be a feather in his cap as superintendent— but for the people he was speaking to. And he was getting no more thanks for it, unless the two old men and the middle-aged Negro beside him were thanking him, than if he had handed them a snowball. True, he had announced his gifts in the flat dry manner of a schoolmaster giving out prizes, with nothing of the excitement which had accompanied Lib's lesser gifts; still, Christie was embarrassed for him. Someone ought to do something or say something to show that the speech had been heard and the gifts appreciated.

"Shouldn't I go up and say hello to your father?" he asked Cate.

"If you want to," Cate said. "I was waiting for the folks to go to their rooms first, but come on now if you want to."

Christie followed Cate down the hall. "Father," Cate said, "this is my friend, Christian Fraser."

"I'm glad to meet you, Christian," Link said, and Christie's hand was given a short dry grip.

Christie saw at once where the good looks in the Conboy family came from, Dandie's in particular; though father and son were completely unlike. Dandie was a flag snapping in the breeze; Link, the same flag in a dead calm. Dandie couldn't lift his eyes without proclaiming himself a ladies' man. Link, Christie thought, had never been that. If women's eyes had rested on him approvingly, he had not been aware of it. Now he was grizzled, his hair cut close, clean shaven, dark. Each cheek was furrowed by a single deep line, running, not from the nose to the corner of the mouth, but from the top of the cheekbone to the center of the jawbone.

His eyes were long rather than wide, some color between black and gray. The face looked somehow familiar, and Christie accounted for this at first by thinking that he was already accustomed to parts of it in Cate's and Dandie's faces; then it came to him where he had seen Link Conboy's face before: these were the long narrow eyes, seamed cheeks and wide nostrils that had looked out at him for a year from the front page of his *Gallic War*. Though nothing, he thought, could be less commanding than Link Conboy's mild dry manner. He was as tall as Christie, taller than Dandie (who until a few minutes ago had stood behind his father), and he looked Christie over quietly, making no effort to talk. Christie, who had come up to make amends for the inexpressiveness of those about him, stood inexpressive himself.

"I'm very glad to be here," he managed finally to bring out.

Link circled the fingers of one hand about the opposite wrist, then gently rocked the cradled wrist backward and forward. "Since you're here," he said, "that's a good way to feel."

IV

IN THE midst of his father's harangue about sows and fertilizers Dandie had slipped quietly out of the hall and upstairs. There he knocked on Nory Tate's door.

"Nory," he whispered. "Nory."

He had no intention of going in. It was a Poor House rule that there should be no bedroom visiting between the sexes, and if he broke the rule Nory was the one who would be blamed. His mother would say Nory had enticed him in. It was wonderful how designing his mother considered women, and how susceptible men.

"Nory," he said, "it's Jim." He hated his nickname, Dandie, and never used it either in thinking or speaking of himself.

Nory opened her door about twelve inches. She was the softest thing imaginable, with a little white shawl about her shoulders. Dandie could not see her without wanting to squeeze her, hold her close, surprise himself by discovering beneath the softness, solid bones. It never seemed possible. It was like finding a stone in the cream pitcher. Nory's colors were brown, cream, and pink. She had a low forehead, almost covered by soft brown bangs.

In back, her hair was looped into a heavy figure eight and held in place with big bone hairpins. Dandie was constantly toying with these while he talked with her: pushing them in more securely; pulling them partially out so that the whole slippery mass would be on the verge of tumbling about her shoulders. Nory's eyes were round and small. They gave her a look of thoughtfulness, conveyed the impression that they were large eyes momentarily made small by the concentration of thinking. "I've got something to show you, Nory," Dandie said.

Without a word Nory stepped into the hall, closing her door noiselessly behind her. There she paused, listening to the sounds from the hall below.

"They're having a shindig down there," Dandie said, "speech from the superintendent, popcorn balls from Mama and so forth."

"Popcorn balls," Nory said.

"Could you eat one?"

"It would seem more like Christmas," Nory replied.

Dandie was down the stairs and back in a second with one of the big golden-and-white balls. In his effort to understand Nory's grief in losing her child, and not to minimize it, he exaggerated and distorted it. He had supposed she would not care for anything so trivial and festive as a popcorn ball; but she did. She was eating it now. Dandie, unlike Cate, was not tied to his dreams. A happening was as valuable to him as a dream any day.

"Come on down to the Commissioners' Room," he said. "I've got a fire going there. It'll be warm."

The Commissioners' Room was at the end of the hall into which the inmates' rooms on the second floor opened. It was a long, narrow, oppressive chamber and took its name from the fact that once each month the County Commissioners met in it to consider Poor House problems and policies. Link used it also as his official office. (His unofficial office was the kitchen.) In it he talked to doctors, sheriffs, salesmen, ministers. Relatives interested in ridding themselves of an old uncle broached the matter in the Commissioners' Room. Lodge heads arranged for the burial of one of their brothers there, and keepers from the State Asylum spread out there the papers which would make the transformation of a pauper to a lunatic a legal as well as a medical fact. The Commissioners' Room was the institutional heart of the Poor Farm and, even under Link's superintendency, was ordinarily very cold, dark, and bleak.

The room was always locked. Being so handy to the younger inmates, whose bedrooms were upstairs, it would become, if left open, Lib believed, a "sparking-parlor or worse." Dandie unlocked the door and Nory walked in, stretching out her arms as she did so. "You've had the fire going a good long time," she said.

"I aired the place first a good long time, too," Dandie told her, proud to have thought of it.

Ordinarily, the Commissioners' Room smelled of stale tobacco, brass spittoons, damp leather, and some other uncertain odor: a urine-like smell, perhaps the smell left by the grief of old men, for the tears they shed there were rheumy and yellow. There was a political smell in the room too; the smell of country lawyers and their impatient sweat at the tedium and insignificance of Poor Farm happenings which nevertheless required their bored and exasperated presence.

Dandie turned up the lamp, which he had left burning, but turned low. The room was furnished with table, chairs, and sofa. The sofa was covered with black leather and studded with brass tacks. In spite of the twenty years during which Commissioners had snored on it, old ladies wept on it, and inmates made love on it, it remained a grim object, stiff and unyielding. The chairs, cushioned with the same black leather, were huge portentous affairs capable of diminishing a pauper and inflating a Commissioner. The table was frightening, an object on which tortures might be performed: long, heavy, grimed, and darkened by age. No one had ever eaten at it, and across it there had flowed conversations having to do only with poverty, sickness, and death. Dignified topics, though always sad, here they were robbed of their dignity with nothing but sorrow left and fear added.

As the lamp flared, then settled to a steady flame, Nory saw the coffin which Dandy had placed at the center of the table and which he had surrounded with a thick garland of cedar boughs. She made a little exclamation and dropped her arms, which were still lifted in a gesture of embracing the unexpected and delightful warmth of the room. Dandie, mistaking the exclamation for one of pleasure, raised the coffin lid so that she could see the satin lining, the little satin pillow and the lace-edged coverlet.

"Do you like it, Nory?" he asked, eager for praise from her.

Nory picked up the tiny pillow, touched it to her cheek, then replaced it.

"It's pretty," she said. Then she added, "I wouldn't ever use it, though."

She said this quietly, her face remaining tranquil and composed. Dandie was accustomed to his mother and Cate: neither could have made such a refusal without much talk, much ridging and furrowing of their faces, much clasping and unclasping of their hands. Nory's calm and quietness was very mysterious and appealing to him; because he was a talker himself he believed quietness must hold in its unfathomable depths great wisdom.

"Why won't you use it, Nory," he urged, "if you think it's pretty?"

"I believe with your father," Nory said.

"This hasn't anything to do with Father. No Poor House money went for it. It'll save money, even. Father won't even have to knock together one of those boxes of his."

"It's not just the money."

Dandie took Nory's hand. "I wanted this for your baby, Nory."

"It's not my baby," Nory said. "I didn't have anything to do with it." She closed the lid of the casket and began to push the heavy sofa nearer the stove. Dandie watched her without offering to help. She took off her shawl, spread it across the back of the sofa, then sat down and extended her feet toward the fire.

"You would feel better afterwards," Dandie urged, "if the baby was buried right." *He* would, anyway. Bury it beautifully and forget it forever.

"No," Nory said. "If it had lived I would've given it away."

"Your own flesh and blood," Dandie told her.

"It's his," Nory said, denying this.

"Do you hate it, Nory?"

Nory looked surprised. "No. It doesn't have anything to do with me."

Dandie walked over to a window. Outside, in a shaft of yellow light, he could see snow again sifting downward.

"Take the casket back," Nory said. "Get your money back. Your father will make me one of his boxes and that's what I want."

Dandie came over to the sofa, and Nory leaned her head against him. "I can't take it back. I've bought it. Put the little baby in it."

"No," Nory said. "But I don't hate the baby. Don't think that. I'm going to ask your father to read from the Bible when he buries it."

"We could get a real preacher," Dandie said, beginning to play with the hairpins. "Have a graveside service."

"For a baby with no name? What preacher'd do that?"

Dandie sat down beside Nory. The light from the open damper fell across their extended feet. High in the unused room, with snow and wind sweeping past the window and the paupers clacking and gabbling below, he felt beyond time, launched into the eternity which actually, it seemed, he had before him. He took Nory's hand in his. "Once I thought I'd be a preacher," he said.

"You would make a good one."

Dandie spread her fingers wide on his thigh, like an oak leaf, or coon track. Nory leaned back comfortably. It was easy to be loved by Dandie. He was not beggarly, asking for more than he could get, then inching back again, after each no, for another refusal. Dandie was not in love with failure like some people. What he gloried in, was winning, not losing. He was sure enough of himself to leave a small space between them. He was not one to trace veins with a single finger and finally, bending low, to send his mouth munching and kissing along her arm like some old anteater hoping to lick up a supper unnoticed.

"You would make a good preacher," Nory said again. "I can see you kneeling by a chair, your face in your hands."

Dandie quickly closed Nory's fanned-out fingers. How he would look! That reminded him of his mother and the afternoon he had come into the house and said, "Mama, I think I have a call to be a preacher."

Nory felt the muscles of his thigh suddenly contract and hold. Immediately afterward Dandie jumped up and began to wash his hands in the column of heat rising above the stove. It was a good fire he had built, a mixture of dry hickory and damp oak, the one to race forward, the other to hold back.

"How'd you like to be a preacher's wife, Nory?" he asked, in the mocking voice Nory recognized as the one he used when, no matter what the words, "I've been a fool," was his meaning.

"Do me up a puff-bosomed shirt every Saturday night and listen to me shout every Sunday morning, 'Who among us shall dwell with devouring fire, who among us shall dwell with everlasting burning?'"

He lowered his hands, turned his backside to the stove, and faced her; he had no pity for the fourteen-year-old who, six years before, had found that very text so moving.

"Oh, I could put 'em in a weaving way, all right, Nory," he said contemptuously. "I've got a tongue that wags at both ends."

"You've got a silver tongue, Dandie," his mother had told him that Sunday afternoon. "You can be a second Henry Ward Beecher."

Where did such things begin, how disappear? Was it already beginning in that green hollow, that little dip between two hills through which he passed going to and from school at the age of six? What he had felt there was sadness; but it was a sadness he cherished and looked forward to. He would walk down the first hill thinking happily, Now, I will be sad. He would tell whoever was with him to go on, so that he would be able to enjoy his sadness alone. The little hollow was like a saucer, or the palm of a hand. How many times had he seen it before he began to think of it as the palm of God's hand? Sometimes when he had stood there long enough, listening and quiet, he had heard God say, "Be a good boy, Jim."

He had not been good when he baptized Cate; still it was, in a way, a religious act. An irreligious boy would simply have ducked his sister and been done with it. On the afternoon of the baptism Cate had been sitting in the crotch of a beech-tree which grew above the creek on the farm where they were then living, salting and eating young beech leaves. Each spring Cate went forth with a salt-cellar to hunt leaves: beech leaves were best, she said, but she knew the taste of all. When tree leaves had outgrown their first tenderness she would go to the garden and sitting between the rows there would eat (salting them first) onions and radishes. Link said she was more destructive than a whole flock of geese and threatened to set up a salt-lick for her, as if she had been an old, salt-crazy yoe. In the fall, after green things had vanished, she would sit on the wood-house steps cracking hickory-nuts with a flat-iron and dipping the fragments into a saucer of salt before eating them.

That afternoon she would not come down to hear him preach until she had had her fill of salted leaves. Then she had clambered docilely down and had sat on one boulder while he used a larger one as a pulpit. At eight he could already, like any good backwood preacher, intoxicate himself with the rhythm of his own words. And like them he could run a single word into an hour's harangue. All he needed was a starting-place and that afternoon the stone beneath his feet gave him his start.

"Brethern and sistern," he had said, the customary terminology more important to him than fact, "let us plant our feet upon the rock of God."

His voice had followed the singsong rhythms of all the preachers he had ever heard, and he succeeded in mesmerizing himself as well as Cate. At the conclusion of his sermon he was prepared to move mountains or walk on water. First, he unselfishly decided, he had better take care of his unredeemed sister.

"Sister Conboy," he asked, "do you want to be saved?"

"I do," Sister Conboy answered. "Oh, I do."

"Then you must first be washed in the Blood of the Lamb. Are you willing, Sister Conboy?"

Sister Conboy, her will utterly softened by his eloquence, said, "I am."

"Step forward, Sister Conboy," he bade.

Sister Conboy stepped. "Do you crave baptism, Sister?" he cried. "Do you want the old Adam washed clean out of your sinful nature?"

That was what Sister Conboy had wanted, and Dandie had taken Cate's sunbonnet off and sprinkled her hair and broad low forehead, still winter white, with creek water. "In the name of the Father, Son, and Holy Ghost," he said. Then, bethinking himself of still greater opportunities for good, he had asked, "Sister, do you crave *complete* sanctification?"

"Reverend," Cate had said, "I do."

Cate had been almost Dandie's size then; but by taking a firm grip on panty band and pigtail he put her under the redeeming waters, sanctified her right to the bone. Getting her out was another matter and considerably harder than sanctification. He plowed her nose along the sandy bottom of Rush Creek for some distance before he was able to haul her forth, slightly scratched and thoroughly soaked, and set her upright.

Her utter willingness then demanded a still further show of power.

"Sister Conboy," he cried, "do you crave the second birth?"

Sister Conboy, by now quietly crying, said she did.

"Matthew, Mark, Luke, and John, Bless the thing that I pee on," he said and, for politeness' sake, aimed toward the hem of her skirt.

Cate, for all that she was sanctified, born again, and bleeding like a martyr in the bargain from the bumping her nose had taken along the creek bottom, felt this was too much. She had run up the bank crying as loudly as any sinner, unredeemed and unbaptized, "I'm going to tell Papa on you."

"Don't be an old tattle-tale," Dandie called after her. "That's the sin against the Holy Ghost, to tattle on a preacher."

Caught up as easily then as now into any abstraction, Cate paused and said, "You're not really a preacher, are you, Dandie?"

"The power of the Lord hath descended upon me," he assured her, and like a true born preacher was convinced by the sound of his own words; his conviction in turn convinced Cate: a perfect circle and vicious. Seeing that Cate would not tattle, bored by preaching and fatigued with baptizing, he had gone off to hunt doodle-bugs for his doodle-bug herd. Cate, since she was already wet, went back into the sun-warmed shallows to play.

Here Lib found her, and when Cate had protested her whipping by saying that Dandie had both baptized and sanctified her, Lib had answered, "I'll sanctify you, miss. I'll sanctify you with the flat of my hand in a way you won't soon forget."

Dandie, listening from the bank above, had then come down and told as much of the truth as seemed advisable. "Mama," he had said, "it's my fault. I did baptize Cate."

Lib had looked at Dandie as if he were a greater George Washington: to George's truth-telling *her* son added evangelical leanings. "But Cate asked me to," Dandie admitted.

Lib had then given Cate another sharp smack on her tight wet panties, through which her bottom, red from the earlier smacks, glowed.

[92]

"Cate," Lib had asked, "must you always be a temptation to your brother?"

Had that been the beginning of his disenchantment with religion, Dandie wondered? If so, it had been a small disenchantment and hadn't lasted long, for at fourteen he had really decided to become a preacher. He well remembered that Sunday morning; by its smell for one thing, the smell of all mornings when his mother was "dressing up": the smell of her hair burning in the curling-iron; of Florida Water and Pears' Soap, and perhaps the penetrating odor of wool being pressed with an iron (as Lib's were liable to be) scorching hot.

But that particular summer morning the smell he remembered was of the sweet alyssum blooming beneath his mother's opened bedroom window. He had been sitting beside that window helping her get ready for church by running the ribbon through the eyelet embroidery of her corset-cover.

Lib, in petticoat and dressing-sack, was curling her hair—hurriedly and impatiently, for it was late. A thin spiral of smoke rose from the iron about which she had wrapped a strand of chestnut hair; when she removed the iron half the curl came away with it. "The dickens!" she cried loudly but without much feeling for she had so much hair that the loss of a curl or two was nothing.

When the curling was going well Dandie loved to watch, and to smell and hear, too. He liked the rhythmical clink of the iron against the lamp chimney; the hiss of spit on the iron as his mother tested its heat; the deft turn of her wrist as she wound up the spiral of hair; and finally, the released curls vibrating, with Lib's quick movements, like flowers on their stems. He would watch the hair-curling with half-closed eyes sometimes, so that all of the movements ran together, deftness and danger mingling until he felt as he did at the top of a swing on a wild grapevine, wholly excited and half sick.

Though Lib believed that everyone should always go to church, she herself would not go unless she had clothes which she considered suitable, and suitable meant new and fashionable. That morning Dandie remembered she had had a new hat: a large gray straw piled high with lilacs and half-opened roses. She had new shoes, too. He remembered squatting on the floor to button them while his mother pinned on the new hat. Lib was never able to help her children in *their* dressing; the shoe was always on the other foot in that respect. As soon as they were dressed, the children would join Lib in her last-minute skirmishes with her articles of apparel—locating them or getting into them.

"Find me my pocketbook," she would cry or, "Will somebody tie my shoe-string together, it broke," or "I'm out of handkerchiefs. Hunt me up a nice little handkerchief-sized napkin, somebody."

Dandie always enjoyed the nervous excitement of these occasions. Would they make it? Would his mother find the clothes she needed and find them soon enough for them to get to wherever it was they were going on time? Cate often cried before everything was found; but not Dandie. He would not care for a quiet and tame pulling-out of drawers to find shoes, corset-covers, pocketbooks, all in the same old expected places.

Once in a while, as a boy, he would stay overnight with a friend; but the mothers of his friends disappointed him. They seemed always to be completely combed and fully dressed. They evidently got up that way in the morning. Getting "dressed up" was a tame business with them. They would walk into their bedrooms and five minutes later walk out calm as the Sabbath and unchanged, as far as he could see, except for the addition of a hat or sunbonnet, or perhaps a duster. When *his* mother "dressed up" the difference could be plainly seen.

These other mothers dressed so fast that they always had time, before the surrey was by the side door, to get out a wash-rag and give him a rough scrubbing around the ears and under the chin. They would comb his hair with such energetic strokes that he felt as if his head had been creased by chain lightning; an hour later the part they had made in his hair would still be burning like a piece of hot wire laid along his scalp.

At home, Link, while they all waited for Lib to finish her dressing, would sometimes run a wash-rag over somebody's face or twitch Em's or Cate's skirts in order to bring petticoats and panties to about the same level; but mostly they were all left alone. Perhaps this was one of the reasons he had never hated church as much as most boys: he wasn't nearly so tightly trussed up as they were. He wore his Sunday clothes, of course; but there were usually enough splotches on them and buttons off to make him feel as comfortable as on a weekday.

They sat, that Sunday morning, as they always did in church: first Cate and Em, then himself, then next to the aisle his mother and father. His mother and father sat very close together in church—as they did everywhere. But his father didn't, as the other fathers in church did, rest his hand on his wife's thigh or let it hang over her shoulder, fingertips curving just above the starched curve of her shirtwaist bosom. He was glad his father didn't do this; and glad the other fathers did. It was a sight he enjoyed watching but which he did not care to think of as connected with his own parents. The longest sermon was made endurable for him by the sight of those fatherly hands. How boldly they spanned and touched! How mysterious marriage was, which made it as proper for these men to rest their hands on a woman as for him to put his foot on the chair rung in front of him. Sometimes he would spend a whole sermon watching a single hand; and be rewarded, sometimes, for thus limiting himself by seeing that hand undertake some particularly intimate movement.

The mysteries of hands! And the mysteries of preachers who, through the power of God, had made holy what these hands did. And finally the greatest mystery of all: God himself. Ideas about these three mysteries often ran together in his mind, so that he would start thinking of one and slip, without knowing when, into thinking of another.

Oh God, he thought, what a dirty, holy little bugger I was in those days. Suddenly, catching sight of the casket, he wanted to touch it; for anything rich and ornate, whatever its purpose, attracted him. He unlaced his fingers from Nory's, went to the table and lifting the lid of the casket, stroked the cushiony satin of its lining.

"Oh Jesus," he said.

"What's the matter, Dandie?" Nory asked.

But he wouldn't say, for what he had been thinking about was that Sunday morning at church, the going up front and the kneeling down; the praying and laying on of hands; the whole, holy show he had made of himself.

It hadn't even been a revival meeting. He had weathered them and all their temptations. The minute some son of thunder started a holy tug of war he was able to resist; he could stick to a church bench tighter than the bark on a tree, then. But that morning there had been no tug of war to build up his resistance.

The preacher was a visitor, over from Dogtown, a spindly old fellow, thin as a rake-handle and aiming his preaching, it seemed, more out the opened window than at the congregation.

"Friends," he had said, "if I was to speak to you from July to eternity, I couldn't tell you more than the Bible does when it says, 'God is love.'"

He was a little white-haired preacher, more hair than head, as Dandie remembered him; he had put him in mind of a dandelion gone to seed. But he had seemed, in what he had to say, as clear as a deep well after the rainy season's passed. Dandie could remember that while he preached, a butterfly had come in the opened window, tried the roses on his mother's hat for honey, then flown out again. He remembered that while he had listened to the preacher's words he had heard the soft music made by a belled cow as she slowly munched her way across some field of grass.

The old man had said, "A human being without love ain't fit to bait a bear-trap," and outside some jaunty Sabbath breaker had driven his horse past the church in a fast rack. Dandie had let his mind follow horse and driver for a second or two and when he returned to the sermon the preacher was saying, "Sin makes a man as crooked as a pack does a peddler."

He had watched a mud-dauber stitching in and out of the opened windows, hunting a spot to lay down its load of clay.

"Man is the spit and image of God," the preacher had said. Then looking out the window and as if he had just caught sight of God standing in the timothy patch beneath it, he had exclaimed, "He is the rose of Sharon and our bright and morning star."

It was at that minute that Dandie, no one asking him, the preacher preaching out of the window, the congregation in a June day drowse, had pushed past the knees of his father and mother, walked to the front of the church and interrupted the sermon by saying, "I believe that God is love."

What he had meant by that or what he had expected to come of it he didn't know then—or now.

What *had* come of it, of course, was that the worshipers took for granted that he, for the one minute of his life immaculate and complete, wanted saving. They closed in about him, prayed over him, wet him with their tears, laid their hands on him, spoke in tongues, had the shakes and the jumps over him, and at the end of an hour turned him over to his family, saved.

He had ridden home in the back seat of the surrey, saved. It was a new way to ride and he felt uncertain, tender, shamed, and jubilant. Cate reached across Em and laid her hand on his, as if he were sick, and in his new gentleness he couldn't push her hand away. On the front seat his father and mother sat, as always, close together but now strangely silent.

At home no one told him to take off his Sunday clothes, so he left them on. When he sat down to dinner, with Em and Cate barefooted, his mother in a slap-dash wrapper, his father in a work-day shirt, his clothes already set him apart. Already he was a man of the cloth. His mother passed him the fried chicken first and when he, in new humbleness, took the neck she added breast and drumstick to it.

Cate, not understanding the connection between religion and food, had snatched the drumstick from his plate and between bites had said, "It's not fair for Dandie to have the two best pieces."

"Go to your room, miss," Lib had said instantly. "Don't you understand what's happened to your brother?"

"I forgot," Cate had said, but she was not forgiven. She left the table in tears. Lib took the last drumstick from the platter and put it on Dandie's plate. "There you are, son."

He had felt shamed and miserable. God is love and here, as the result of his saying so, were crying and quarreling.

"I'm not hungry, Mama," he said and pushed his plate away. His father, he noticed, wasn't eating, either. Only Em and Lib seemed to have kept their appetites in spite of the morning's happenings.

"There's always been a preacher in the Griffith family," Lib had told them. "Dandie don't look like a Griffith," she admitted, "but these things go by contraries. You *act* like your Grandfather

Griffith, Dandie. He converted one hundred and nineteen people at one protracted meeting. That's a Rock County record. But maybe you can beat it."

His mother had taken for granted that he would be a preacher. But had he? If you got yourself into a battle the only honorable thing to do was to try to lead the charge; and in religion he supposed the honorable thing to do was preach.

"Your Grandfather Griffith," Lib went on, "wasn't one of these easy-going preachers—fold his hands and expect the Lord to provide. He preached and worked. He wasn't beholden to a single human being when he died. And long before he died he owned a section of land, had it cleared and planted, and a big two-story brick house built on it. Maybe you'll do better."

"That's hardly a very good goal to set up for a preacher," Link remarked.

"Why?" Lib flared. "What's wrong with a preacher's having a good house?"

"There's nothing wrong about it, except as a goal."

"Except as a goal," Lib said, "nobody's going to ever get anything. You think two-story brick houses just spring up out of the ground?"

"Greater miracles have happened."

"Who's talking about miracles?" Lib asked.

"We are, if we're talking about the Christian religion."

"What I'm talking about is preaching, here and now. And there's no two-story brick houses in that without planning and planning early."

"The foxes have holes and the birds of the air have nests; but the Son of Man hath not where to lay down His head."

"Well, Link Conboy, do you think that's a good state of affairs? Do you want your son living in a burrow just because he's a preacher?"

"I want him first of all to be a good preacher."

Lib had clashed her coffee-cup down into the saucer. "Are you saying Grandpa Griffith wasn't a good preacher?"

Now Lib began to talk about her own people—the Griffiths and the Goodhues and McFaddens. How steadfast, firm, and successful they were, whether on the farm or in the pulpit. So different from the shiftless, rootless, roving Conboys.

"Just because a man doesn't have any place to lay his head down doesn't mean he's holy—not by a long shot," she said. "I could name a Conboy or two who was as far from the one as the other."

Em got down from her chair and crawled under the table for her Sunday afternoon nap. In the swirling argument only Dandie noticed her leave. He was trying to sink back into himself, to rediscover the feeling he had had when he rose to say, "God is love." Then he had felt united with everything in the church— not only with the people but with the wasps and butterflies, with the artificial lilacs and the real hands. And with passing horses and faraway cows, and whatever the old preacher had caught sight of outside the window. Now he felt separated from everything. He listened to his own father and mother from a great distance. Under the table Em, far from asleep, was running the end of his shoe-lace up and down his bare leg, pretending it was a bug, biting him. All at once he gave a couple of sharp kicks: not so much at Em and her imitation bug as at all he did not understand and which hurt and bewildered him. What he hit, though, was Em. She came out from under the table quietly, but with her nose bleeding. It was much worse than if she had screamed. Before a word could be said the future preacher ran outside, spattered a little about his best pant-legs with his sister's blood.

He had paused at the opened window of Cate's room. There she had stood, red-eyed. The first thing a Christian did, seemingly, was to make his sisters suffer.

"Come on out," he whispered urgently.

"I can't," she told him. "Mama won't let me. I took your chicken."

"I didn't want it."

"Why didn't you say so?"

He walked about the back yard, heavy hearted. It was already the middle of the afternoon. The shadows were so dark and soft they looked like pools deep enough to dive in. The old hens sat under the currant bushes, drowsing. He went into the barn and gave Doll another measure of oats. Doll was a young mare, a beautiful dappled gray with dark velvety smudges above her nostrils. "Poor Doll, poor Doll," he said over and over again and finally he leaned his face against hers and cried, "Poor Dolly, poor, poor old horse."

He went back to Nory, made a motion as if to lay his head in her lap, then sat bolt upright, not touching her. He had never formally recanted. He simply let people judge him by his actions. And judging by his actions, it was believed that Dandie Conboy had surely backslid. No boy who had been in so many fights, whose name by the time he was sixteen had been connected with so many girls, could possibly be considered permanently saved, let alone good preacher timber. As to his ever *being* a preacher, they were right. No sum of money, not wild horses, could have got him into a pulpit now. But neither his mother's admiration of preachers, nor his father's reverence for reason, had convinced him that there wasn't a mystery somewhere worth finding out about. He had stopped trying to give it a name. He thought he got near it sometimes fighting or making love. Sometimes just talking. Then, that moment—the moment he had risen to say, "God is love"—returned to him. But of that moment, he never again intended to speak. He put his head in Nory's lap and, as she traced with her soft fingers his lips and eyebrows, soon forgot it altogether.

v

BY TEN-THIRTY Christmas Eve, though there was still an occasional flurry of snow, the storm of the past two days was dying out. At the Poor House everyone, with the exception of Nory, Dandie, and Link, was in bed. In the sitting-room, Link, roused by the sudden quiet, for the wind had been roaring down the sitting-room chimney all evening, rattling the stovepipe and fluttering the blinds, looked up from his writing. He tipped his head to one side, listening. The coming of quiet was like the break-up of a wall which had imprisoned him. Now he was free to survey in his mind the calm of the snow-covered hills which surrounded the Poor House. He liked the quiet and he liked the promise that Christmas would be a still day. After listening for a time to the silence, he picked up his pen and retraced the last word he had written, which was "prospect," then finished his sentence with, "of a good second year here." He was writing his weekly letter to his brother Fred in Colorado: a letter which he knew quite well didn't mean much to Fred, but which satisfied his own desire to set things down in words without exposing himself to ridicule as the keeper of a diary or journal. Diaries were for young girls and journals for philosophers and invalids. There was just enough kindness in Fred's infrequent replies for him to keep up the pretense that his letters were looked forward to and enjoyed. He had begun a new sentence, "I have no desire to set myself up as a prophet but in my opinion . . ." when there was a knock at the door. A knock meant one of the folks. None of his own family, unless it was Cate in a fit of politeness, ever knocked before entering a room.

"Come in," he called, pausing reluctantly in his writing.

Nory Tate came in hesitantly and stood, one hand still on the doorknob, as if the feel of it gave her assurance.

"Come sit down by the fire, Nory," he said.

No girl, he thought, could possibly look more like a good girl than Nory. Beside her, the innocent Cate was a head-tossing, bosom-arching hussy.

He angled his chair away from the secretary so that he could face her. "Shouldn't you be in bed, Nory?"

"Yes," Nory said, "but I wanted to tell you something."

Nory found it hard to talk to Mr. Conboy. Not because he was Dandie's father. Not because he was the head of the Poor House and she was an inmate. Not because he wasn't kind. It was mostly, she thought, that he said so little. She liked and trusted Mr. Conboy more than Mrs. Conboy, but she was more comfortable with Mrs. Conboy. If she had to spend a whole day with one or the other she would choose Mrs. Conboy. She felt all the time, with Mr. Conboy, that he was asking her some question for which she had no answer. She always left him disappointed with herself. She often left Mrs. Conboy filled with resentment and anger; but it was anger and resentment turned towards Mrs. Conboy, not herself. She, herself, would feel quite superior. Now, Mr. Conboy sat looking at her, saying nothing. If she wanted to tell him something, his silence seemed to say, do so. She said it all at once.

"Dandie's bought a coffin to bury the baby in."

"Dandie bought a coffin!"

She had heard it said that Mr. Conboy had a very bad temper. He had once burned up a clock. First, stamped on it as if it had been a live animal then thrown the pieces, its mainspring unwound and dangling like entrails, into the fire. That was what she had been told. Someone had seen him knock down an inmate. No fight, no words. Just walk up to him and hit him so hard he had toppled over. They said you couldn't tell where you stood with Link Conboy. No more than a hint or two from him that he thought what you were doing was wrong, then suddenly he'd turn on you. He had half risen when she told him about the coffin. What would he do? Go upstairs, get the coffin and burn *it*? She watched him take hold of his wrist as if to keep his hand from some action he'd be sorry for.

"Why did Dandie buy you a coffin?"

"He thought I'd like it—for the baby."

"Why did he think he was the one to do such buying?"

This seemed a strange question to Nory. Didn't he know? Hadn't his wife told him? Lib had berated her a dozen times for seeing so much of Dandie.

"You'd better ask him," Nory said. Then for fear this sounded saucy, she added, "He thought it would ease me to have the baby buried nice. And there was no one else to do it."

"Where did he get the money?"

"I don't know."

"Who'd he get it of—Korby?"

"That's what he said, Mr. Conboy."

Mr. Conboy rocked his wrist back and forth in his hand. "So that's where Korby was."

After a while Nory said, "I don't want it."

"Don't want what?"

"The coffin."

"Why, what's wrong with it?"

"There's nothing wrong with it. It's beautiful." Nory tried to think of some way of describing it so that Mr. Conboy could appreciate it. "It's the nearest thing to a wedding dress I ever saw. The satin and lace, I mean. But I believe with you, Mr. Conboy."

"Believe with me?"

"Not to waste money on the dead."

[102]

Mr. Conboy nodded approvingly. "That's wise of you, Nory."

"Besides," Nory added, "I don't like the dead." She didn't want credit for wisdom she didn't have. "Not this baby. But I don't hate it, either."

"Nory," Mr. Conboy said suddenly, "who is the father of this child? He ought to make restitution."

"Restitution?" Nory asked.

"Repay you. Make up to you for what he did."

"How could he do that?"

"Marry you. Tell me who he is, Nory. I'll see that he marries you."

"Would you want to be married to the person who had done you the most harm of anyone in the world?"

"No, I can't say I would."

Nory pushed her shawl back feeling that, that settled, the worst of her visit was over. "I want the baby to be buried in one of the boxes you make, Mr. Conboy. And I want you to read from the Bible over its grave. Will you?"

Mr. Conboy looked startled. "I will if you want me to, Nory."

"Read, 'Suffer little children,' will you?"

"I thought you didn't like this child, Nory."

"He could have one good thing happen to him, I guess. I don't hate him that much."

Mr. Conboy turned and stared out of the window. Perhaps some day I'll have a child who looks like him, Nory thought, and was glad she admired his face. She waited, expecting him to speak; when he did not she got up and pulled the ends of her shawl together under her chin.

"Thank you, Mr. Conboy."

Mr. Conboy said nothing, so she walked across the room. As she opened the door he said, "Are you going?"

"Yes," she said, "thank you," and closed the door feeling uneasy, as if she had said less or more than she should have.

VI

IT WAS eleven-thirty before Link got to his and Lib's room. He and Lib had a small air-tight heater in their room, and the warmth, though the fire had died down, was comforting after the dead cold of the stale air in the hall. Lib had left the lamp turned low on the dresser, and he picked his way across the littered floor to the window. The sky had cleared; it was alive with stars now, twitching, it appeared, with a distant but brilliant life of its own. He had had a long day, had been tired, and had now gone past the boundaries of tiredness into that state of dry elation which is like being drunk and keeping a clear head. He had accomplished, in talking Hummel out of that gilt, something he had long wanted to do for the folks: put them on the way of being something more than paupers. He thought of them all—poor folks and his folks alike, twenty-seven, if he hadn't miscalculated, twenty-eight counting Nory's poor dead babe—under the same roof tonight. If the Christmas experiences of the entire twenty-seven were heaped together there would be a pyramid of happiness and unhappiness of such a size as would lift the roof which covered them all right off its rafters. Power, he believed, did not interest him. Yet he had to admit there was some sense of power in the feeling of elation he had standing there wide awake, exposed to all that wintry starlight while the rest of his household slept. Forgetting that pig, too? He treated himself to a little scorn for such a feeling, if he had it. He had descended to pretty small potatoes if his pride could feed on such trivial matters. But trivial was all in the way of one's looking. When John Manlief, who had come to the Farm lost in a stupor of staring and forgetfulness, had reached out a hand to touch that shoat's pink ear—was that trivial? He couldn't believe it. That was a semi-dead man taking his first step forward in the direction of the procession of life from which he had somehow become separated. That extended hand and opening fingers had been as moving—oh, a thousand times *more* moving than any opening flower, Link thought, turning away from the window.

He began to pick up Lib's scattered clothes and without thinking what he did held them to his face. He believed he could tell Lib's clothes anywhere by their scent, a scent more fruit- than flower-like, the combination perhaps of Lib and Florida water. But mostly Lib.

While he was sniffing and pondering he heard a light snicker from the bed and turned to see Lib, herself, sitting up, her hair tumbling down about her long-sleeved white flannel nightgown.

"Blow your nose on my drawers, if you have to blow it," she said. "That corset-cover's clean."

"I'm not blowing it," Link began, then understood that Lib was joking. Lib liked to shock him. And he was perpetually pleased with her perpetual interest in doing so. It was a kind of taking pains—as he realized—to be entertaining. Not that it didn't come perfectly natural to Lib.

"What *are* you doing?"

"Hanging up your things." There was no reproval in Link's voice. No assumption of superiority.

"What time is it?"

"Eleven-thirty—a little after."

"Is it still snowing?"

"No, it's faired off. We'll have a clear day tomorrow."

"What kept you up so late?"

"I was writing Fred," Link said, taking off his shirt.

"Oh, Fred!" Lib said, beginning to rebraid her hair. "You could copy him a page of the Almanac. Fred'd never know the difference."

This was too true to contradict.

"You must've wrote him a ream."

"I wasn't writing the whole time. Nory Tate came down to talk with me."

Lib stopped her braiding. "Nory! She's got all day to talk to you. Why does she wait till everyone else is in bed? Isn't one Conboy man a big enough feather in her cap?"

"She was seeing me about burying her child, Lib."

"And thinking already about getting herself another one, no doubt."

Lib threw back the heavy winter comforters with an angry despairing motion and got out of bed. She stood shivering for a second, then snatched up Link's discarded coat and put it on.

"So that's how you were spending your evening!" She stood, coat over nightgown, like someone roused up in the night by a fire. And jealousy *was* a fire in her. In a second it could fill her breast, burn out every other emotion. Afterward, she might be shamed or remorseful, but while it blazed she felt nothing but pain and a savage desire to inflict pain. There was no reasoning with Lib when she had one of these seizures, as Link thought of them. Earlier in his life he had tried to do so. Now he knew better and went on as if he had not heard her.

"Dandie bought one of Korby's coffins for Nory."

"Korby!" Lib exclaimed, the fire veering suddenly in another direction.

Link was naked now, reaching for his night-shirt. Lib laid a warm unexpected hand on him. Goodness, she told herself, was what she most respected in a man, and if goodness took a pot-bellied, bird-shanked form she would try not to mind. But she had got better and she appreciated it. "You've got a fine figure, Link. For a man of your age," she added, some flicker from the first fire still burning.

Link pulled his night-shirt over his head and, inside the shirt, smiled. These sudden calms.

"She wheedled him into it, no doubt."

"What?" Link asked, emerging.

"Nory Tate wheedled Dandie into buying this coffin."

Link gathered the fullness of his night-shirt to his body, hands on hips. "As a matter of fact," Link said, "she won't even use it."

"Ah, then Dandie is a goner. If he bought it of his own free will. Look what you've driven him to, Link—where the best Christmas present he can think to give a girl is a coffin for her woods colt! Why did you ever bring us here, Link Conboy?"

Afterward, in bed, Link asked himself the same question. Or rather heard again the same question asked. Not by Lib who, in the central hollow of the feather bed, lay close to him, sleeping deeply. But by the voice which, in the middle of the night, sometimes asked him, "Who are you, Link Conboy?" Now the same voice was asking, "Why are you here, Link Conboy?"

That was a harder question to answer than "Who are you, Link Conboy?" To that question he needed only to say, "I am the boy who was born on a farm; the son of a man who ran a small second-rate academy. I was educated there, I taught, fell in love, married, read law, and practised law in that same town. And I gave up my practice to become the superintendent of this Poor House. That's *who* I am."

Sometimes the voice asked, "But why? Why did you give up law?"

"It was a talkative, nerve-racking, double-dealing profession, pretending to hand out justice while it supported privilege and fed on the sorrows and evils of the community."

"You weren't very successful as a lawyer, Link Conboy?"

"No."

"Why?"

"I've told you."

"Why did you decide to come to a Poor House?"

"I wanted to be of greater service to my fellow-men."

"Why?"

"I was forty years old. My life was half done. I wanted to leave some better record of the fact that I had lived than a few decisions handed down in favor of clients, possibly guilty."

"Why?"

"I had come to the sudden conclusion. . . ."

"Why? Why had you come to this conclusion? Why suddenly?"

Link, as this question was asked, once again turned quickly to Lib. He curved his body to fit the curve of her body, then drew her still closer. His motion awakened her.

"Where am I?" she asked uncertainly.

"Here," Link said, "with me," and with his face warmed in her loose hair he sank into drowsiness and finally slept.

VII

CHRISTIE had been placed for the night in what was called the Visitor's Room. It was on the second floor at the end of the hall next the Commissioners' Room and, except for its furnishings, was exactly like the rooms occupied by the inmates on that floor. At first glance Christie saw that it was the kind of room his mother used to call "fixy."

Cate had collected articles from all over the house for its embellishment: pictures, cushions, tidies, books, even a rocking-chair, carried up from the sitting-room. The soap, in its dish on the wash-stand, had a paper frill about it, like a fancy cake. The chamber-pot lid was covered with a crocheted silencer. There were more towels on the towel rack than he could use if he took a half dozen sponge baths; and he had no intention of taking even one for there was already a film of ice over the water in the pitcher.

He had wasted no time in assessing the room's niceties but had thrown off his clothes, blown out the lamp, and plunged into what he had expected to be an icy bed. Then he had stretched full length with pleasure. Someone, Cate he supposed, had placed two hot bricks, nicely wrapped, at the foot of his bed. He uncurled his toes and thought, This has been a strange day, and before he could review its strangeness further, was asleep.

He awakened so gradually that he remembered his dream. He did not know what had awakened him, for the wind had died down, and except for the occasional sound of a nail snapping in the bitter cold, the night was quiet. The sky had evidently cleared, for light—starlight or moonlight—lay on the alternating blue and gray stripes of the rag rug that covered the floor. The bricks at his feet were still warm so he knew he could not have been sleeping long.

He had been dreaming that he was back at Stony Creek, asleep in the upstairs bedroom there. It was a summer night, warm and light as day. As he lay there, his Cousin Sylvy had come to his bed, taken his hand in hers and said, "Get up, Christie." In his dream this had seemed a perfectly natural thing for Sylvy to do. He hadn't responded at once, but had lain for a time looking at her. She had been wearing a soft white nightgown, thin enough to show him much more than the outline of her body. In his dream he had been aware of this semi-nakedness but without the surprise or excitement which such a revelation would have brought him, waking. Finally, unconcerned that he himself was sleeping in nothing more than thin summer drawers, he had got out of bed and stood beside her.

"I want to see us in the mirror, Christie," she said.

Without a word he had put his hand in hers. Barefooted, they had gone noiselessly down the heavily carpeted stairs and into the front hall which was filled with the summer night. The outside door had been left open to cool the house and through it they could see mysterious shadows on the lawn and hear the whippoorwill's calling.

They went at once to the mirror and stood there, hand in hand, watching. In the depths of the mirror he had seen (rather than felt) the two of them meet and kiss. It had been a long kiss followed by a long close embrace; and they had stood watching silently until it was finished. Then, without a glance for the sleeping rooms about them or for the shimmering night outside, they had glided back up the steep stairs and at his bedroom door had parted solemnly and courteously.

In God's name, Christie thought, smiling at this memory and permitting himself, now that he had retraced his dream, to become wide awake, why didn't I kiss *her*? What kind of a man am I, dreaming of pictures in mirrors, with the real thing standing by my side?

He shifted about in the delicious warmth and softness of the deep feather bed, opened his eyes, and saw what had no doubt awakened him in the first place: a dark figure in the rocking-chair by the head of his bed. Before he had time for fright or speech this figure said, "I've been waiting for you to wake up. I don't hold with robbing any man of sleep, but if you woke up I thought I'd have a talk with you. Are you awake?"

"I'm awake all right," Christie said. "Who are you and what do you want this time of the night?"

"You know me," the figure replied. "I'm James Abel. You rode up to the farm with me."

Ah, Christie thought, the digger, the crackpot. "Why don't you wait until morning to talk, Mr. Abel?"

"Night's the best time to get at the truth," James Abel said. "Nothing but the dark, you, me, and the truth." He hitched his chair nearer the bed and Christie saw that, as he talked, James Abel pushed his big head back like a chicken with the gapes.

"Maybe I'm not interested in the truth."

"You're fertile ground for it. I noted that the minute I laid eyes on you. There's a boy with the sign on him, I told Mary. There's a recruit for us. It would be better to learn early and easy, than late and hard, Mr. Fraser."

"I'm pretty sleepy," Christie said, "I don't know whether I can stay awake to learn anything tonight."

"I'll undertake to keep you awake. Mr. Fraser, how much happiness do you figure there is under this roof?"

"I don't know," Christie answered. "I don't even know who's under this roof, let alone whether they're happy or not. I'm happy."

"You're not in pain. It's not the same thing."

"Mr. Conboy looked like a passably happy man."

"Mr. Conboy is a man with a load of sin."

"I don't suppose a Poor House is the best place in the world to look for happiness," Christie said. "Are you happy, Mr. Abel?"

"No," Mr. Abel said, huddling forward in his eagerness, "but I've got sense enough to know the cause. Do you think we were born to be unhappy?"

"Maybe," Christie said.

"No. The truth is we were born to be happy."

Sinking toward sleep and anxious to speed Mr. Abel to his conclusion, Christie asked, "Why aren't we then?"

"The word was lost."

"The word? What word?"

"I don't know. The secret word. Someone stole it and buried it."

Mr. Abel's big head, askew on his shoulders, moved back and forth with the misery of this fact.

Christie slept for a second. "Who would do that?" he asked, uncertain as to whether or not he had already been told.

"The devil would," Mr. Abel said calmly. "For one."

Mr. Abel's words were portentous but his voice was a mild monotone. He spoke of the devil as if he were an inmate of the Poor House; happiness, as if it were porridge and could be evenly divided and dished out. You oughtn't to go to sleep, Christie told himself, with a crazy man sitting at your elbow; but Mr. Abel's voice hummed on like a summer fly caught in a crack.

"You got the sign on you," Mr. Abel said. "I marked it the first thing. Come dig with us."

"Do what?" Christie asked, his eyes closed.

"Hunt for the lost word."

"Certainly," Christie said, rousing himself. "Count on me. Any time."

Before James Abel left the room he was asleep and once again dreaming.

VIII

CATE opened her eyes and saw that the room was filled with moonlight reflected off the snow. a clear cold light. Christie is here beneath this roof, she thought.

"Are you awake, Cate?" Em asked.

[110]

Cate didn't answer. Em was a great night-time talker and just now she didn't want to talk, but to stay half asleep dreaming of tomorrow and Christie.

"I know you're awake," Em said. "I can tell by the way you breathe."

Cate tried to mend her breathing but Em wasn't fooled. "Cate," she whispered, "I can't stop thinking about Nory's little dead baby."

"You can stop talking about it," Cate said.

"No I can't," Em said. "I looked at it when I looked at the coffin. It didn't look quite dead, Cate."

Cate gave an impatient sigh.

"What I've been thinking," Em said, "is that maybe God is saying to Himself, If one single person cares enough for this baby to get out of bed on Christmas night and pray for it, I will bring it life."

"God doesn't talk to Himself," Cate said.

"He thinks, don't He?" Em asked.

"Hush up," Cate said, not liking to deny this. "I want to go to sleep."

"God might be waiting for me to pray, and I wouldn't want to keep Him waiting just so you could sleep."

"Pray then," Cate said irritably.

But Em wasn't ready yet. "Nory's little dead baby was born of a virgin just like His own Son," she reminded Cate.

"Don't keep saying virgin all the time."

"Why not?"

"It's not a nice word."

"It's in the Bible."

"That doesn't make any difference. You can't go around saying Bible words out loud."

"Why can't I? If they're good enough for the Bible they're good enough for me."

"The Bible was written a long time ago and people use nicer words now."

"Not me," Em said matter-of-factly.

Cate thought this was true, but was too disgruntled with Em to agree with anything she had to say.

"I keep hearing God say, 'Em, Em,'" Em said, "the way He said, 'Samuel, Samuel.'"

"You ate too much supper. Turn over on your side and go to sleep."

"He says, 'Em, My good and faithful servant, pray for My child.'"

"Well, go on then," Cate said. "Pray. Do it to yourself and don't talk about it and get it over with."

Em lurched out of bed and dropped noisily on to her bony knees.

"Oh, Em," Cate cried, exasperated, "can't you pray in bed? You'll catch your death of cold out there."

"Dear God," Em said, disregarding Cate, "if it be Thy holy will, I pray Thee bring back to life this son of a virgin struck down while still in the bud."

"Pray to yourself, can't you?" Cate asked.

"No," Em said, "I can't. My mind wanders if I don't hear myself talk. He has been dead two days, as Thou well knowest, and now on the third day, if it be Thy holy will, raise him up from the dead as Thou didst Thy own Son. For Jesus' sake, Amen."

Em got back into bed and Cate could hear her rubbing her feet together to warm them.

"Maybe He has answered my prayer by now," she said.

"Oh, Em," Cate groaned.

"Maybe the baby is lying up there now, fully alive and freezing to death because of my lack of faith to go up and get him. Then I would be a murderer."

Once more she got out of bed.

"Em," Cate said, "you are not going up those stairs. You know you're not supposed to go up there."

"Circumstances alter cases," Em said, first putting on a jacket, then pulling on her stockings.

"This is crazy of you, Em," but Em went ahead with her dressing which, when she had put on her garters and shoes, was finished. Cate got out of bed and into her own shoes and wrapper.

"You don't have to go with me," Em said. "I'm not afraid."

Cate knew Em wasn't. Cate did things all the time because she *was* afraid; but not Em. Em only did what she wanted to do or thought needed doing; and for both she had plenty of courage. Half of Cate's reason now for going with Em was that she was frightened to make that trip upstairs, past the rooms of men like Doss Whitt and James Abel and into the cold dark room where the dead baby lay. The other half was that she was imaginative enough to think how she herself would feel compelled, for whatever reason, to make that trip; but not imaginative enough to think how someone else, as different from herself as Em, might feel. Her imagination had depth but not breadth. She was always doing unto others as she would be done by, not as they would be done by. No one need ever tell Cate, "Put yourself in my place." She never did anything else. Em might hear the voice of God; but Cate *was* God, ubiquitous if not omniscient. She had strong feelings and these often rescued her from her wearisome Godlike and wholesale living; then she became herself, concentrated around a core of emotion that was nothing but Cate. Being in love had so rescued her; that was why love was so restful to her: it narrowed and simplified her world. But fright and death had nothing to do with love, and she put herself in Em's place and knew that she must go with her; though she was unable not to resent the need of going.

Em lit the little bed-side lamp and, carrying it, led the way.

"This is crazy of you, Em," Cate objected, "wicked," but she followed, close behind.

They went down their own hall, into the inmates' hall, up the stairs, past Christie's room and into what Em called the "funeral room": an inmate's room, unoccupied now except for the dead child. Cate herself half believed that the baby might be alive. Putting herself now in God's place, such a resurrection seemed to her a fitting way to commemorate the birthday of a dead Son. If she had been God she would have done it.

But God had not done it; He could not, evidently, put himself in her place; at least it had not been His holy will to resurrect Nory Tate's little dead baby; and if He had said, "Em, Em," as Em believed, it was for another purpose than resurrection.

Nory's little baby lay, as Em had last seen it, stretched out on a marble-topped stand-table, dressed as if for a journey in a long white cape and with a white crocheted cap tied under its long, bony, old-man's chin. The baby had been born ailing. For the last week of its life it had swallowed nothing but a few drops of lime water and barley broth. Now it seemed never to have been flesh at all, to have been born a husk; or to have been carved, as Cate had seen faces carved, from peach pits. It was little, shrunken, the color of leather, sad, sad. It had come to the edge of life and had been pushed back. Cate began to cry. Now she was putting herself in the dead baby's place and she saw all of life as cruel and unhappy. All of life marched forward to this: to death. Every one of them beneath this roof would soon be dead: her father, her mother, Dandie and Nory, she and Christie, Em, all the poor folks. Not a soul on earth would be left to know that a one of them had ever lived or to care what their thoughts had been or whether they had been happy or unhappy, good or bad. The very Poor House would fall, brick from brick; the foundations would wear smooth to the ground, and finally even the great cedars would topple and rot away. One nail, one broken cup-handle on the bank of Bleeding Creek would be the only sign left to speak for them to coming generations. Cate, doing as she would be done by, bent and kissed the dead baby.

"Would you like to stay up all night?" Em asked practically. "Have a wake like a Catholic?"

"Oh no," Cate said. She could put some of herself in the dead baby's place; taste, as she kissed the baby, how bitter death was. But she could not achieve death's indifference; she was still Cate: alive, freezing, crying, shaking with cold, worrying about the future, frightened.

"Well then," Em said, having done what she set out to do, "let's go to bed."

3

It was a single day, Christmas, December 25, 1899. It had certain set aspects: the sun shone; there was snow on the ground; the mercury rose from a low of 17 degrees at four A.M. to a high of 45 degrees at two P.M.; the wind (gentle southeasterly) died down early; then the smoke from the four chimneys rose straight up, thin and blue in the still morning air; by noon the cedars had shed all their snow; an hour later the eaves were dripping.

One thousand eight hundred and ninety-nine years ago, Christ had been born. Three years ago McKinley had been inaugurated. Three days ago Nory Tate's baby had died. Two days ago six hogs had been butchered and there would be fresh pork for Christmas dinner. These were the common facts of the day, of everyone's day, the shared Christmas of 1899 at the Rock County Poor Farm.

In addition to this standard, general day there existed the twenty-seven particular days of the twenty-seven individuals who were at The Farm that Christmas. It was a different day for each: a hundred years later the twenty-seven, meeting to report upon it, would hear twenty-seven different accounts. Except for Nory Tate's baby's funeral, the weather, the fresh pork, and some seconds or minutes shared by the lovers, each person had known a private and unsuspected day.

Old David Pen, who at eighty-seven was dying, spent the day as a baby. A happy baby. He was in no pain. "Sleep, baby, sleep," a voice said to him, all day long. Not his mother's voice but his own, as the man he had once been, comforting the baby he had become. Once only did he open his eyes, Christmas day. Then there was a white milky radiance in the room. "Sleep, baby, sleep," a voice comforted him and he closed his eyes again.

Hoxie Fifield, aged twenty-seven, who was also sick, though far from dying, spent the first half of his Christmas day in bed. He believed that faith could cure him. He had begun the day with faith the size of a mustard seed and his faith kept growing. It became cherrystone-sized, new-potato-sized, old-potato-sized, mushmelon-sized. Not a thing had happened as the result of this growth in faith. He continued to burn like a red-hot poker. He discarded faith, got out of his bed, and stripped himself. He thought of going out to roll in the snow.

Doss Whitt came in and looked him over.

"Turpentine's the thing for clap," Doss told him. "Rub it in good and expect a cure within twenty-four hours."

After that Christmas, for Hoxie Fifield, became hell's hinges and chain lightning. No one else who had been at The Farm in '99 would remember anything like it.

Mrs. Goforth's and Lily Bias's days were alike in that neither day contained pork, weather, burial, or birthday. Mrs. Goforth was sixty-three, plump as a chipmunk, and too good for her surroundings. She lived all of Christmas day in the dream that her son Herschel would come for her. In sight of all, he would toss a sealskin cape about her shoulders and say, "Why didn't you let me know where you was, Ma?" Then he would slide her under the buffalo robe in his cutter, speak to his pair of matched blacks, and they would be off, without a backward look for that passel of low-lived paupers.

Lily Bias was seventy-three. What *she* looked like was a worn-out brown shoe-lace with a few knots tied in it. She called Link "Old Mr. Conboy," and deported herself in his presence like a comely, thoughtful daughter. She was by turns start-uppish and full of maidenly languors and hesitancies. Inside, Lily had not changed in sixty years. She was true to the unchanging reality of her thirteen-year-old heart. Other women feigned to be the creatures their mirrors reflected. They had heard, perhaps read, how the middle-aged and old should conduct themselves. They lived from the outside, in, trying to follow these rules. They met each other, play-acting. They pretended they were nothing but porcelain teeth and steel-rimmed specs. But not Lily. Oh not Lily! She was her own, her inward, throbbing girlish heart.

The night before, Christie, in distributing the candy, had given her the largest bag. Planned, prearranged? Of course. He had held her hand, how long? Minutes, long minutes, anyway, and said, "Miss Lily Bias, what a pretty name."

Where had he seen her before? Or was it all chance and split-second recognition? She despised women who loved old men. How could they? It was a sign of some lack of fastidiousness or innocence. Lily felt as innocent and trusting, as perishable and fastidious as any girl. Christmas day was nothing but Christie for her. That pretty boy. He had a long mild sleepy brown face. His thumbs bent backward, she had noticed. She liked that in a man. It was a sign of heedlessness. She had a little present in her room she could maybe rig up for him. She began to work on it at daylight. It was an old whiskbroom-holder, personal but not too personal. She prided herself on not being too forward. The man must take the lead. But let the woman be ready to follow. She sat on her bed, a quilt wrapped around her legs, sewing. The whiskbroom-holder already had her initials on it. She added his, C.F., to the L.B. No curlicues below the line in either. It looked meaningful. She began to sing, "Jesus Savior, pilot me."

Mrs. Goforth, her roommate, turned over in her bed. The singing disturbed *her* dream. "Oh, hush your bellering, can't you?" she implored.

Lily couldn't. She had bent back thumbs herself.

John Manlief, the man with the apathies, leaned sidewise in his bed so that his cheek rested against the icy window-pane: outside, a snowy world lit by a pink and gold sun-up; far, far away was the word "beautiful"; a word he could remember having once used about such a world and such a sun-up. Between that word and the man who had used it, and himself, the man on a shuck mattress in the Rock County Poor House, was a chasm bridged only by the frailest thread of memory. Between himself and the world outside his window there was even less connection. His eyes reported the facts to him: the colors, the growing light, the movement of birds, the birth of shadows. Inside himself there was no response. If his eyes had seen a fire about to engulf the building, his response would have been the same: what did fire mean to him? He was locked inside himself, beyond all harm. Beyond all pleasure, too.

When he had arrived at this place he had heard them say, "Looks like he's planning to do away with himself."

Oh God! From what a distance he had listened to that lively summary of his situation. "Do away with himself." You could not do away with the non-existent. What a belief in life the man had who troubled to "do away with himself." Rigging up a gas-proof room. Fixing himself and the gun so his toe could reach the trigger. Fighting to keep his air-filled body at the bottom of a pond. Slicing and reslicing the rubbery flesh. What a wonderful belief in life such efforts took! He had nothing of that kind. He was already dead—except that he suffered. He could no more kill himself than feed himself. The suicide is like the jealous lover who throws a stone crashing against his sweetheart's window and shouts when she appears, "You'll never see me again." He could not do that. He did not believe in the existence of the sweetheart.

He read the newspaper accounts of a murder with the same emotion with which others read of children saved from drowning or mountain-climbers rescued. What a belief in life! He could imagine committing a murder only as a means of breaking through the walls of ice which housed him. You see the victim walking down a street. You put a knife into him and he topples over, bleeds, twitches, dies. That change proves that earlier the victim lived. It proves that you also are alive, that you are in affective contact with life. How optimistic was murder, how filled with hope the murderer: would he ever again believe in life that much?

He could not believe it. He took his numb cheek from the window, lay back on his cold bed. It was now full daylight outside.

In all weathers the Poor House stood alone. Even in summer when lush vegetation seemed to bind the other farms together, the Poor Farm was isolated. But in winter, with the snow increasing all distances, then it was solitary indeed. Then it rode the white crest of its hill like a ship lost in an empty sea.

Christmas morning this wintry isolation was at its height. Not only were fields blanketed and wood-lots obscured by the snow, but the one road leading into the Poor Farm was, in so far as the eye could see, blotted out entirely. Winter has a thousand aspects, some hateful and forbidding, others miraculously beautiful. One of the most beautiful is that of a still, sunny morning after heavy snow. The sense of cessation, of rest and quiet after the commotion and flurry of a storm is in itself bemusing and pleasant. Add to that the eye's astonishment at finding the night-before's drab earth glittering in unstained white, and the result is almost intoxicating. After so great a change, any change seems possible. Life can start over again. It *has* started over again. The deepest scars have been hidden, the ugliest blemishes lost to sight.

No one at the Poor House, not the oldest nor most ailing, but felt something of this on Christmas morning. The sun came up and filled their rooms with the peculiar blaze of light reflected off snow. Each window had its frost garden, flowers as thin and sharp as if cut from tin. For a minute, as the sun-up frothed with wintry pinks and golds, these metallic flowers were actually flower-colored: lovely as blossoms planted years before in gardens unforgotten. The older inmates lay for a time recalling the past. Life had gone by so quickly! It could just as well be a summer morning now and they at their mother's heels and she bending lovingly over her flags and cinnamon pinks. That it was, instead, winter, old age, and the Poor House, they could scarcely believe.

Then, in the kitchen, they heard Mag Creagan's energetic fire-making; the thump of the grate as she shook down the ashes, the rattle of stove-lids as she shoved in more corncobs. They heard the commanding meow of the Poor Farm cat, a big-headed yellow tom who was given by each of them a different name—that of the last cat he had himself owned: Mike or Nigger or Duchess, as the case might be. They heard the creak of the pump, the squeal of Nigger Bob's boots on the dry snow as he came up from the barn with the milk pails. Then the yellow tom was heard no more. He had gone into the kitchen with Nigger Bob, was already under the stove, eating the first dollar-sized test buckwheat cake.

The smell of oak smoke, fried sausage, and boiling coffee began to fill the building. The fire in the base burner in the women's sitting-room was blazing up briskly; that in the men's sitting-room was doing less well. Too much tobacco juice was sprayed into that stove to permit a really first-rate combustion, Link, who did not use tobacco, always contended.

Link and Lib lingered abed far later than usual because of the day it was. Now they were dressing hurriedly, Lib, slap-dash and helter-skelter, Link, in his usual orderly fashion.

Dandie was still sleeping heavily, one arm across his face.

Nory was in the kitchen helping Mag Creagan, as was Mary Abel.

James Abel was out in the barn throwing down hay for the stock.

Christie had just awakened, curled his toes away from his now cold brick, remembered first, where he was, next what he had dreamed.

Cate opened her eyes to find Em snuggled unexpectedly in beside her.

"How did you get here?" she asked. She didn't, ordinarily, like to sleep with Em, who took the middle of the bed and lay there unyielding, her hind-quarters hard as a cannonball, though less round and hence even less comfortable.

"You asked me," Em said.

Then Cate remembered that, shaking with cold and unable to get warm, she *had* asked Em to get into bed with her.

"Merry Christmas, Em," she said.

"Same to you," Em replied graciously. Then she rolled out of bed and gave a tremendous shudder. "Cold enough to freeze the ears off a brass monkey," she announced between teeth rattlings.

"Don't say that," Cate told her. "It's not ladylike."

Em, stepping into the legs of her union suit but leaving her nightgown on until the last minute, said, "Doss Whitt told me that *was* the ladylike way to say it. He told me always to say ears, not—"

Cate interrupted her. "I'm not interested in what Doss Whitt says."

Em wrapped a leg of her union suit tightly about her ankle, preparatory to pulling her stocking on over it. "It don't make sense any way," she admitted, good-humoredly.

Cate watched Em dress, her own comfort under the covers increased by Em's shiverings. "Is it going to be a nice day?" she asked.

"If you don't mind freezing, I guess it is," Em said, taking a look.

It would be a happy day, too, Cate thought; though the funeral couldn't, of course, be thought of as happy. Yet in a way a funeral would be appropriate, solemn and holy, very like a church service, reminding them that all earthly things passed away. They would stand together in the snow of the Poor House burying-ground while her father read from the Bible. Christie, beside her, would touch her arm and say, "Don't cry," as Nory's little baby went down into the earth. The world was so strange and mysterious, so enticing, and sad, that she gritted her teeth in the sheer pleasure of thinking about it.

Em, at the mirror, her tongue following between her blue lips the movements of the match she held, was renewing the maturity of her armpits.

"Come on over here," Cate said, to her own surprise, "and let me do that."

Em looked at her suspiciously. "You'd just rub it off."

"No, I wouldn't. It's disgusting, but if you're bound to have it done it 'bout as well be neat, not smeared all over."

Em, still suspicious, sat down on the edge of Cate's bed, handed her the match and lifted an arm.

"Are you in love?" she asked.

Cate paused in her work. "Why? What makes you think so?"

"You act lovesick."

"How do I act lovesick?"

"Mealy-mouthed. Letting me sleep with you. Doing this."

Cate broke the match in two, threw the pieces across the room and boosted Em off the bed with her knees. "Now do I act lovesick?"

"Yes," Em said. "Are you?

"It's none of your business. It's not nice to talk about a private thing like love."

"Even if it's pure?" Em asked, pausing in buttoning her dress, so as to be able to catch anything Cate had to say on the subject. Cate said nothing.

"Even—" Em began again, but Cate cut her off.

"You be quiet about love, miss," she said.

"And be quiet about brass monkeys and be quiet about virgins and be quiet about hair and be quiet about love and be quiet about—"

"Just be quiet," Cate said, "about everything."

"Be quiet about Ferris Thompson?"

"You don't know anything about Ferris Thompson to be quiet about."

"I know he's going to eat his Christmas dinner here."

Cate sat up again. "Why? Who asked him? He's got his own home to eat in. Why's he coming here?"

Em hung her gilded wishbone about her neck before replying. "Ferris Thompson's in love with you, so you wouldn't want me to talk about that," she said primly and went out, closing the door behind her with a smart little snap.

11

LINK, as soon as he was dressed, headed for the men's sitting-room. Bare and bleak, it resembled, both in smell and appearance, the waiting-room of a small country depot. Lib, when they first came, had tried to make the room look what she called "less Poor-Farmy and more homey," by hanging curtains at the windows. The curtains had not been a success. The old men had slowly twisted them to pieces. It was their habit to stand in front of these windows at twilight, gazing off in the direction of the farms and country stores they had once known, worked on and in and perhaps even owned. After the curtains were up they had added curtain twisting to their standing and staring; added it, Link supposed, without knowing what they did. The curtains were at first soiled, then frayed, and finally completely worn out, fringes of grimy tatters like battered old eyelashes around still good eyes. Lib reluctantly took them down. Then the old fellows, who had probably not noticed the curtains when they were up, began to miss them. "What's 'come of the curtains?" they complained. Their hands, suddenly without anything to knead and fondle, felt more than ordinarily empty and useless. Link would turn away at evening time from the sight of those old hands fumbling about the empty window frames.

The sitting-room, though once more uncurtained, and always unfurnished except for the necessities of stove, chairs, and table, was not totally undecorated. On its walls hung three objects: a calendar advertising Korby's General Merchandise and Undertaking Establishment; a picture of McKinley; and a fly-specked gilt embossed motto declaring that "Christ Is the Unseen Head of This House." "Korby, Christ, and McKinley" was the way the men in the sitting-room listed the three when referring to them. Korby, they said, should come first because no one could finally miss the undertaker, while many a man got through life—and out of it—with no visible connections with either McKinley or Christ. You couldn't qualify for those two without being either a Christian or a Republican: a state too high for some and too low for others. Korby, on the other hand, wasn't so choosy. All you had to be, to qualify for him, was dead: a goal everyone sooner or later was pretty sure to reach. Some of the folks did argue that the Republicans also took (and voted) dead ones; but by and large Korby was admitted to be in the lead in this respect. These three, together, were referred to as "Father, Son, and Holy Ghost." McKinley, with his plump, big-jowled face was, of course, the Father; and Korby, dealing with the dead as he did, was naturally the Holy Ghost. Christ alone they permitted to remain in his historic rôle.

Visually, McKinley had fared least well of the three. His picture, a relic of the 1896 campaign, had suffered both additions and subtractions. At present it was embellished with both burnsides and imperial and in an aperture made by the removal of a couple of teeth someone had inserted a big-bowled pipe. Going up in smoke from this pipe was a cloudlike substance lettered, THE PEOPLE'S HOPES.

Link himself, when he first came, had tried now and then to do a little improving in the room by setting a crock of sweet-william or prince's feathers in the middle of the big deal table. But this effort at improvement hadn't lasted long. Hoxie Fifield who was, Link supposed, just simple-minded enough to be truthful, had said, "This stuff gets in the way," and had gone to the window and dumped the flowers out.

Link stood outside the closed door for a second, pleased to hear issuing from within on Christmas morning sounds betokening pleasure: an immoderate amount of laughing and talking. When he opened the door they died down, as he knew they would. He closed the door and said, "Don't let me put a damper on anything. I just stopped in to wait breakfast with you."

"Hear that, Neddy," Doss Whitt said. "Mr. Conboy don't want to put a damper on anything."

Neddy Oates, Link then saw, was standing a little apart from the others, off to one side of the stove, arms behind his back.

"Trying to get warm, Neddy?" he asked.

"He don't need to scrooch back there behind the stove to do it. He's got the wherewithal on his person."

"Well, Neddy," Link said, and Neddy, arms still behind him, came one step forward.

Neddy was sixty-some, an old ex-jockey no larger, except for his Adam's apple and nose, which were of full size and manly shape, than a scrawny twelve-year-old. Neddy had not spent all of his life in Rock County. He'd got out into the world, seen it and tasted it and, in his day, had booted more than one winner in first past the checkered flag. He had pictures of himself to prove it: pictures of himself astride horses necklaced with floral horse-shoes. Pictures of himself afoot, with dark-eyed females languishing down at him from under the shade of their big plumed hats and ruffled parasols. These women, he didn't scruple to declare, had been, one and all, soft on him. One and all, he declared, had hounded him for his favors until, the truth of the matter was, he'd been hard put to fend off enough of them to keep himself in shape for riding.

When this irresistibility was scoffed at, Neddy, with no hint of boasting but only the air of a man who imparts a fact well known in his own profession had explained, "Horse smell's the one thing a real lady can't hold out against."

Neddy had lost his horse smell but the ladies still liked him. Men, too. Looking at him, Link thought, except for his weakness Neddy might've got somewhere. As it was he struggled with his weakness, which was a liking for strong liquor, and his struggles were a source of everlasting interest in the men's sitting-room. When all else palled, when nobody had a word more to say about women, politics, the weather, the cussedness of life in general, and superintendents in particular, Link had heard them turn to Neddy. How was Old Neddy getting along in his tussle with likker? Who had the upper hand?

Neddy believed that some day he was going to win this tussle, in spite of the setbacks he continually received. His strategy was to make whisky so repulsive by certain additions that, sooner or later, his stomach would flinch at the mere sound of the word. Link recalled off-hand a dozen diluents: buttermilk, lard, molasses, baking-soda, mustard, castor-oil, axle grease, Lydia Pinkham's. These he knew for a fact and he'd heard reports of others. And worse. None had been just right. Neddy's stomach had been turned, but not permanently. He was keeping up his search. He had a horror of admitting that drink had licked him. The mere fact that so many ingredients had failed him argued that he was nearing, among the few left untried, the proper repulsive diluent. And when he found it he would stick to it. Whisky with *that* or nothing. And since he wouldn't be able to endure *that*, why nothing. It would be simple.

Link considered Neddy a happy man. He was a man with a cause. Two causes, really. First, he had the job of finding himself a drink, a job Link didn't make easy. And that found, he had to decide on the new addition. What would it be this time? How about a little horse liniment? And having downed *that* mixture, there were the boys in the sitting-room waiting his report. Was horse liniment what he'd been looking for? Did he feel as if he'd hit on the cure? Link looked at him, wizened, holding a bulging sock. Like an undersized Santa Claus except for the spirit of merry-making, which was absent now.

"Ask him what he's got," Nigger Bob urged Link. "Ask him what's in his sock."

"Did you hang up your sock, Ned?" Link asked.

"Hung it up last night," Ned admitted, fondling sock and content.

"He come in from the treat last night," Josiah Stout said, "and give his candy and popcorn away. Said that wasn't his notion of Christmas. Tacked up his sock and said he invited Santy to do better. And from the looks of things he's done better. Open her up, Neddy."

"It feels like a bottle," Neddy said, with a sliding look in Link's direction.

It looked like a bottle to Link. Nigger Bob was as impatient to see the contents of the sock as if it had been his own. "Go on and look," he urged. "Santy's brung you something and you'd oughta look at it."

Bob was supposedly one of the Farm's simple ones. Link didn't know. He'd been here since the beginning time: they said a patch of volunteer oats had once sprung up from his thick matted wool after he'd taken a soaking in a spring rain. A sign his head was dirty, Link thought, rather than empty. He had his doubts, seeing how much work the man was able to miss, how simple he was. He was childlike now anyway, in his excitement, running his finger along the curve of the sock. "Peel her off, Neddy, see what you got."

"I ain't got the heart to look, boys," Neddy protested. "Me with the only present. It jars on me to find myself in a fix like this."

Link supposed it did, with the rules, his rules, against drinking, what they were. But Neddy was the only one troubled by the rules apparently. Bob, Doss Whitt, Earnest Creagan, Dexter Bemis, James Abel, Josh Stout, everyone in the room with the exception of himself and John Manlief were crowding around Neddy, urging him on. Finally Bob took the sock from Ned's hand, shucked it aside and handed what it hid (it *was* a bottle) back to Ned. Ned held it aloft, his round blue eyes rolling around like marbles in a basin and read the label, "Old Crow. I'm flabbergasted," he said in Link's direction. "Taken by complete surprise."

Link was, too. Such open rule-breaking was pretty near to mutiny. Ned continued to move the bottle about, put it between him and the light, regarded its amber depths with what was undoubtedly a knowing eye.

"Boys," he said finally, "it ain't believable."

"You don't doubt your own eyes, do you?" Doss Whitt asked. "Wet your whistle."

"You know I don't never drink it straight," Neddy said.

Doss Whitt lifted his heavy eyelids, dark and wrinkled as a bat's wings, to give Neddy an incredulous stare. "On Christmas day?" he asked.

Earnest Creagan who, because Mag was his mother, had the run of the kitchen said, "What you want to go with it, Ned? Ma'll give it to me. Tell me what you want and I'll go get it."

Ned didn't answer but took his eyes from the bottle and looked at Link. Link turned from him, from the whisky and the seven men crowding about them both, and stared out of the curtainless windows at the snow-covered hills. He understood to some extent what the men thought of him. Try as he would he could never get close to them, never be accepted by them. He felt sometimes that he lived in a cage, a cage which opened to admit Lib, occasionally Cate, but no one else; a cage from which he couldn't escape. Once in a while he thought that words were the keys which would unlock his cage. He lived in a family of talkers and saw daily what talk could do. They gave a man another self, a self to run ahead, open doors, and make easy the way. But he had no forerunner. He went single and caged. And when—as he was going to now—he made an effort to escape, people looked at him uncomfortably. They didn't feel easy with him unless they saw the shadow of bars across his face.

"Neddy," he said, "I reckon that's what's called Christmas cheer."

Neddy admitted it. "Yes, sir," he said stiffly.

"You know what the rule is here, no likker. In the first place if you've got money for it, you don't belong here. In the second place, even if it bubbled up out of the open ground, scot-free, there's a multitude of reasons why it shouldn't be used."

"Yes, sir," said Neddy.

"But this is Christmas day," he went on reasonably, "and within the limits of good health and the rules, I'd like you to be happy. That stuff's no doubt a gift, didn't set the county back anything—"

"Didn't set the county back a red cent," Doss interrupted him.

"Under those circumstances," Link said, "I think you might keep it."

Link was taken aback by the popularity of this announcement. Bob Beeson slapped his thighs, the two boys snickered, Doss Whitt laid his arm across Neddy's shoulders and said, "Show Mr. Conboy your appreciation, Neddy, by having a drink right now.

Don't hang back like you didn't have gumption enough to take a present when it's put in your hand."

Everyone, in fact, seemed happy except Ned himself. "No," he said, "likker's my weakness as you well know, Mr. Conboy. I been rassling with it for fifty years, likker winning most of the time. This morning something tells me I got the upper hand at last." He pulled the cork from the bottle, took a sniff, and shook his head. "Nothing on God's green earth could make me take a drink out of this bottle on Christmas morning. I thank you, boys. And you, Mr. Conboy. I appreciate your kind intentions, but I guess common sense has caught up with Neddy Oates at last."

Neddy walked over to the window, shoved it upward and with head turned away from the sight, let the bottle's contents gurgle out into the snow. As the last drops fell from the bottle he said self-reproachfully, "I guess I hadn't ought to have done that, Mr. Conboy."

"I can't say I agree with you, Ned," Link told him. "I was willing for you to keep it, but pouring it out was one of the smartest things you ever did."

Link was surprised at the amount of laughter this caused. Even James Abel and old man Stout chuckled.

"I wasn't talking about pouring it out," Neddy said, "but where I poured it. It looks kind of dirty there. Kind of looks like somebody took a leak out the window and I don't want us getting any reputation like that here, Mr. Conboy." Neddy took another squint out of the window. "Yes, sir, that's just what it looks like. If I didn't know for certain it was whisky I'd say it was pot lye there in the snow. I sure would."

"No, no," Link protested. "Nobody's going to think anything of the kind." He reached out and took Ned's hand. "You did the right thing and I congratulate you."

As soon as Link closed the door he heard their uproarious laughter behind him. He walked slowly down the hall toward breakfast, the cage as solid about him as ever.

III

EM WENT out to the woodshed after breakfast to watch her father make the coffin for Nory's baby. It seemed to her that a man making a coffin should look different from a man making a hen-coop or a hoghouse—but her father looked just the same. He fed the nails out of his mouth into his hand like a mother bird feeding her young. He was very sure-fingered and deft and he gave each nail an extra rap-tap after it had already been pounded in, for the sake of the sound alone. It was strange to Em that making a coffin should cause such jolly, lively noises. She looked at the boards from which the coffin was being put together: the tree that grew that wood had been a coffin-tree. How would the tree have felt if it had known it was going to end up as a coffin? Or had it known it?

"Em," her father said, "I read your Christmas note."

Em had forgotten her Christmas note. And she had never imagined that her father would read it, anyway. It was for her mother.

"I agree with you, Emma. I fully agree with you," her father continued. "We all love each other. There oughtn't to be any bickering. Forgive me."

Em was embarrassed and miserable. It was one thing for her to accuse her parents. It was another for them to accuse themselves.

"What time's the burial?" she asked, trying to change the subject.

Her father went on as if he hadn't heard her. "Once I remember hearing my mother tell my father that she wished she had never laid eyes on him. It hurt me worse than being shot."

"I better go help Mama," Em said.

"Your mother and I," her father continued remorselessly, "have our lives in each other."

"Mama argues," Em said. "She yells. She says the Conboys are no account. She says you look at other women. And it's not true. She oughtn't to do it."

"She oughtn't to do it when you children are around. But the Conboys *were* pretty footloose. And I haven't made as good a living as your mother expected. And—"

"It's all a lie," Em said, and before her father could add any more, she shot out of the woodshed toward the house.

IV

AS SOON as the breakfast dishes were washed, Cate and her mother began to set the table for dinner. There would be enough hurry and scurry at noontime with just the food to dish up, without any table-setting to slow them down. They were using the best they had of everything: the celery vases with the ruby thumb marks; relish dishes shaped like fish; the big centennial bread plate with its cracked liberty bell; the stemmed cut-glass spoon vases, one at each end of the table; and finally the elegance of a small saucer beside each coffee cup to hold the cup, while the larger saucer held the coffee for drinking. In the center of the table stood the twinkling castor; for Cate had at last admitted that her stack of pine-cones took up too much space. Cate would have insisted on the best of everything for this occasion no matter what Lib said; but with Ferris Thompson coming to dinner, Lib was as anxious as Cate that they put their best foot forward.

Lib and Cate were both quick in their movements. They went back and forth, light-footed, between china-closet, safe, pantry, kitchen cabinet, and table. Cate was very happy. She loved the balancing movements of table-setting, the danger of turning a corner at an angle so sharp that the juice in the dish of pickled beets would be almost, but not quite, sloshed over. She was pleased with the symmetry of the set table, with the colors of the plates against the glistening white tablecloth, bright she thought, as a summer flower bed.

She was pleased with her mother, too, this morning, for Lib was again "dressed up": trim, corseted, and curled. She didn't of course look like a mother, that is, gray-haired, pink-cheeked and with a bosom like a bolster for daughter to weep on. She didn't act like a mother, either, in Cate's opinion. Cate, like Dandie, sometimes stayed overnight with friends and in their homes she had seen just how motherly a mother could be if she were so inclined. "Has daughter slept well?" . . . "Has daughter had enough breakfast?" . . . "Has daughter brushed her hair?" . . . "Has daughter's bowels moved?"

Why, Cate thought, remembering this, my bowels could never have moved once since my birth and Mama would be none the wiser. She remembered staying all night once at a house where there were four daughters, girls between fourteen and twenty. Each morning before breakfast their mother had lined the four up for inspection: she would feel each girl's waist in turn to determine whether or not she was too tightly laced. "I can't have my girlies ruining their health," she had said, as Cate, watching in envy, thought how little concern there was at home for her health (which she had to admit was perfect). The inspection, for all its loving, motherly-kindness, had come to naught however: out in the privy after breakfast and inspection were alike past, the four daughters had cinched themselves up so tight that they had trouble in keeping their tongues from hanging out. But the loving care of their mother's interest! It brought tears to Cate's eyes just to think of it. Mama would not know nor care if she wore a suit of armor, let alone a corset. Take the one corset she had ever owned, for instance. At the age of thirteen she, like Em now, had felt the lack of something; of some *one* thing. If she had *it*, she had thought (whatever it was), she would be confident and sure of herself. With the boys, of course. What else mattered? She had decided that what she lacked was a corset. A better decision than Em's, she believed. Certainly more romantic and appealing than *hair!* If she had a corset, snug about her waist, she had been convinced, it would be evident to all that she knew; was initiated, belonged.

"You don't need a corset," her mother had said, "you never will wear it, and it will just be a waste of a dollar and a half." But she had given her the money—then let her do the buying of it alone, without help. The result was that she had bought herself a maternity model and had become the laughing-stock of the town. Those flaps over the busts, which could be buttoned and unbuttoned, had looked to her like ventilators; and ventilators, she had thought, regarding all that length of reinforced muslin and steel would certainly be needed. No one in the store had said the word which would have set her straight in the matter, and Mama's friends and Mama herself had laughed themselves sick over the purchase. And Mama had been right about her wearing it too. Ventilated or unventilated, she couldn't abide the thing. It was still some place around the house, and she was still uncorseted, uninitiated and didn't belong.

Thinking about that unused corset, and her mother's unmotherliness, she stood holding the butter dish with its pound square of butter on it. Her thoughts suddenly veering, she said, "Fly butter," and set the dish on the table.

"Well, Cate," Lib asked, coming in with a dish of corn relish, "what now?"

Cate didn't answer, but not until that moment had the significance of that butterfly, with which all their butter was stamped, been clear to her. Butterfly—fly butter; of course. Was she going to go through life missing half its meanings? "Mama," she said, "why did you ask Ferris Thompson to dinner?"

"A little competition never did a girl any harm," Lib told her.

"Competition!" Cate cried. "Why, Christie's only interested in me as a friend."

Lib made a disdainful sound. "Friend," she repeated. "What that boy wants is a sweetheart, Cate. If he wants anything. And if we want him. Maybe we don't. He's a traveling salesman. That's unstable blood. I've seen enough of that blood in the Conboys to shy away from it."

"I'd be proud to think Christie was like Papa," Cate said.

"I didn't mention your father. I was thinking of the other Conboys. Drifters and renters."

Renters was about the worst word Lib could use in describing anyone, a word too low for respect, too high for pity.

"A salesman has to move about."

Lib ignored this reference to Christie. "Ferris is a good boy. His folks are well fixed and well thought of."

"We don't know him."

"He's asked you to parties time without number."

"Four."

"That oyster supper makes—"

"Oh, I don't care. Ask him. Let him come. Let him eat. Let him sniff."

"Sniff?" asked Lib, bridling.

"Oh, not that way. But when he drinks he wrinkles up his nose like a dog."

"Miss," said Lib, "if you're going to judge a man by the wrinkles in his nose you'd as well resign yourself to be an old maid on the instant."

"I'm resigned," said Cate, lying.

"Don't be a fool," Lib replied, undeceived. She snatched up a pickled beet from the dish and a drop of juice fell onto her dress. "Good thing they're both red," she declared optimistically.

Cate walked over to the window. Outside Christie, Dandie, and the two boys, Earnest and Dexter, were clearing the snow from the path in front of the house. Dandie went at it furiously as if he hated both snow and shoveling; he left an arc of snow-dust as he swung first left, then right. Christie was taking his time, but moving as much snow as Dandie. He looked up suddenly and seeing Cate at the window lifted his face toward her. It was the gesture of a kiss. Cate felt kissed, too weak to move or nod. She leaned back against the window frame as if nailed there. As if the imagined kiss had impaled her.

v

CHRISTMAS dinner was to be served at twelve-thirty. Ferris Thompson arrived at twelve. Lib herself went to the door to welcome him. Lib's feelings about the Thompsons, as about all people who had more money, education, and community standing than she, were mixed. Consciously, she said, "I will never truckle to such people." And she did not. When she met them she was scornful, stand-offish, and short. Unconsciously, she revered them. Her vivid, untiring imagination inflated them to dimensions totally unlifelike. Then, when by chance she came to know them, they were a great disappointment to her. But her many disappointments taught her nothing. Her temperament demanded someone of impossible and arrogant stature for her to defy, and her imagination could manufacture such individuals from the most unlikely material.

Her own father, through hard work and thrift, had become a man of property and "standing" in his own community. Lib had felt, as had her people, that in marrying a Conboy she was lowering herself. Link himself she considered an exception, no true Conboy; and true Conboy or not, at the time of her marriage—as now, for that matter—she would have defied all the McFaddens to be with him. Still she considered it her duty to remind Link constantly of the source whence he had sprung, and to see to it that he did not slip back toward it. Though she had honestly to admit that, except for being somewhat footloose and shiftless, there was not much wrong with the Conboys. Sometimes, Lib wondered if the real reason for her feeling about them was her jealousy. Was she jealous, even of Link's own people? Did she believe that by running them down she could enhance herself in Link's eyes? Make him think how fortunate he was that this daughter of a well-to-do, upstanding, Christian farmer loved him, the son of the shiftless, irreligious, renting Conboys?

Actually, she knew that the matter did not work out in that way. Her railings against the Conboys did not endear her to Link. But the hot irresistible desire to attack the Conboys would sweep over her, and in words too bitter for a mortal enemy she would describe her in-laws. Why did she do it? Did it have some connection with her father? For it was always with an admiring reference to her father that she ended her tirades against the Conboys: "Papa always said. . . ." "Papa would never have tolerated. . . ." "I remember that Papa. . . ."

Link usually listened quietly to her outbursts, replying with no more than a calm, "There's very little truth in what you're saying, Lib." Sometimes he could not help laughing, for Lib was full of irresistibly droll exaggerations, and he would steal Lib's thunder then by saying, "Yes, that's Uncle Mort to a T." Nor did he seem to resent her admiration of her own father. He admired his father-in-law himself. No one had a greater regard than Link for veracity and rectitude. Lib knew that Link believed that, in addition to these virtues, her father possessed an unnecessary amount of narrow-minded, suspicious caution, and an exaggerated concern (which she had inherited) for what the neighbors would think. But Link kept these opinions to himself: partly through a natural delicacy, partly through the conviction that nothing could be accomplished by contention and wrangling. Occasionally, however, he would break out, not in words but in action—action which was the more startling because it was so unusual.

Once, in the days before he had given up his law practice, he had accompanied a lady client to The Junction where she was to catch her train back to Seymour. The lady client had had no bags to carry; she had been young, able-bodied and, in so far as Lib could see, perfectly capable of walking the quarter of a mile to The Junction unattended. When Link returned to the house Lib had begun to speak of the irresponsibility of the Conboys and of the rocklike steadfastness of the McFaddens, particularly of the rocklike steadfastness of her father, a man who had never demeaned his wife by an unnecessary midday walk with a grass-widow. Dramatically, Lib pointed to the clock which had been her father's wedding present to them, an elaborate contraption with simulated marble pillars on each side of its face and simulated bronze lions with rings in their mouths on each side of the pillars.

"When he gave me that clock," Lib cried, "Papa said, 'Libby, may that clock never strike anything but happy hours for you and Link!'"

The clock at that minute had struck three.

"If Papa only knew what kind of an hour it was striking for me now! My husband waltzing off in the middle of the afternoon with a divorced woman! Right through the town in the full sight of everybody. What can they think? Not a reason in the world for it except you're tired of me and hankering after a change. Lawyering is full of temptations, Papa always said, particularly if a man is weak. And the Conboy blood is full of weakness."

She had swept to the mantel and turned the clock about so that at five after three it faced the wall. "I can't bear for it to be a witness of what's going on here," she had said, "after all of Papa's high hopes for us."

Link had then said quietly, "It might happen again. Let's not take a chance on its twice witnessing anything so improper."

With that he had placed the clock, lions, pillars and all, face down amidst the burning logs in the fireplace. There, jarred by its reversal, though Link had handled it temperately—and this had made his action seem the more deliberately cruel to Lib—the clock had begun to strike. It had pealed forth from the midst of the flames—like a martyr crying for mercy. The memory could still make Lib shudder. Dandie, who had been in the room at the time and who loved the clock because of its ornateness, had tried to rescue it. Link had thrust Dandie aside with no thought for his son's badly burned hands and had silenced the clock with the poker, beaten it down to fragments. But the clock had died hard. Its mainspring had coiled and uncoiled among the coals like the intestines of an animal, broken open, but still alive and suffering.

Such action, however, was unusual in Link; and it had no effect, either in putting a stop to Lib's jealousy or in curbing her belittling of the Conboys. When she married Link, he had been a young teacher saving money to buy a farm. He had bought his farm and had then been for a while a young farmer studying to pass his bar examinations. He had passed his examinations and during the twelve years that followed had become a moderately successful lawyer. She had been very proud of him during this time. Then, overnight, Link had decided to put his career as a lawyer behind him and become the superintendent of the Poor Farm. It was a good job, as respectable as being the head of a flour mill or the manager of a dry-goods store. And she understood too that the superintendency was a political job, a job no one could get unless he belonged to the party in power and had done the party a good turn or two. And because it provided the man who held it with opportunities for "honest graft" it was considered a political plum, a reward for services rendered. That all such opportunities would be lost on Link, Lib well knew, and, until the day they moved to The Farm, she had urged him to reconsider, to go back to farming even, if he had to give up the law, rather than move them all to the Poor House.

It still galled her to tell anyone that she lived at the Poor House, though she was always quick to explain in what capacity. She had known the people over in this corner of the county only by hearsay; and no one here seemed to have ever heard of the McFaddens. She might as well have been born a Conboy herself for all the good her McFadden connections did her. And in her own community the McFaddens had had as much standing as the Thompsons had here.

Ferris' mother, Mrs. Orville Thompson, was a small, bow-legged woman who looked, Lib thought, a good deal like an anxious hen searching for a spot to drop an overdue egg. If Hannah Thompson had been an anonymous female Lib would not have given two cents for her. As the wife of Rock County's richest farmer, and in her own right an authority in church and Ladies' Aid circles, Lib inflated, magnified, snubbed, and despised her. If Mrs. Thompson had been old, feeble, or impoverished Lib would certainly have gone out of her way to do her a kindness for it was only with those who were plainly her inferiors that she was ever truly at ease. This was the real reason for her happiness at the

Poor House, for she *was* happy. Since she was touchy, haughty, and independent as a hog on ice, anyone thoughtfully hunting a matron for a Poor House would have rejected her at once. Yet once she was set up on a pinnacle and called Matron, she leaned down from that height until she reached the level of the most sorrowful and unfortunate. Link, who was full of natural humility, did not succeed with the inmates half as well as she.

Except that both Ferris' mother and sister were sick, Lib could never have brought herself to ask him for dinner. It would have smacked of truckling. But with Ferris' sister down with the measles and his mother down with not only the measles but pneumonia as well, Lib considered her invitation a neighborly kindness, not a social overture. And in addition she completely believed what she had told Cate: a little competition never hurt any girl.

Ferris Thompson could never have guessed from Lib's welcome that she looked on him as competition; as anything less, in fact, than the one thing necessary to make her Christmas complete. She was full of hyperbole and exaggeration and invariably welcomed her guests so heartily that they outstayed their welcome. Then, closing the door upon them after their reluctant departures, she would wring her hands and demand that Link tell her what she had ever done to deserve so long-winded a visitor. Link *would* tell her, told her time and again, but she could never learn that guests, when urged to do so, frequently linger; or that others did not discount, as she did, all the soft soap and palaver of visiting, including her own.

"Ferris!" she exclaimed admiringly. "You got here through all the snow! First rig out on the road this morning, I bet."

"Well, I didn't see any other tracks," Ferris answered modestly.

"With a horse like yours, though, I guess I could drive it myself. But Merry Christmas and come in. I'm so busy welcoming you I keep you standing out here in cold until you'll be down sick with the rest of your family. How's your mother this morning?"

When the door had been closed behind him Ferris said, "Mother's resting pretty easy this morning, thank you."

"And Wanda? How's Wanda?"

"Wanda's beginning to pick up a little."

"That's a relief, that's a great relief. I'm happy to hear it."

Lib looked Ferris over. Let this traveling insurance agent of Cate's see what their own community could produce in the way of beaus, she thought.

Lib considered Ferris' chief beauty to be his hair, which rose above his high white forehead in a springy pompadour of golden brown waves. Middle-aged mothers, demonstrating how well they still understood the romantic impulses of the young, would ask their daughters, "Wouldn't you just love to get your hands into all that curliness of Ferris'?"

Beneath his pompadour, Ferris had a small-boned, plump, fresh-colored face. His eyes were blue, fringed by long lashes, and his ears which were small and set close to his head were covered with a multitude of soft white hairs. Except for his mouth, which she thought too round and small for a boy, Lib considered Ferris far better looking than Christie. Not than Dandie, of course. Though Ferris dressed better than Dandie, who, even for her taste, was a little too fond of Madras stripes and rhinestone stick pins. Beside Dandie, Ferris looked restrained and genteel; beside Christie, who was not very sprucy in her opinion, he looked trig and fashionable.

"Come on into the sitting-room," Lib urged him. "They've been looking forward to seeing you. They're talking pigs. Link's got a sudden craze for them, and to hear him you'd think this farm was the pig center of the state; pig center of the United States, according to Link." She paused at the sitting-room door as Ferris stepped into the room. "Ferris," she said, "may I make you acquainted with an Indianapolis friend of Cate's? Mr. Christian Fraser, Mr. Ferris Thompson."

When the two had acknowledged the introduction Lib went back to her dinner preparations. Dandie, who knew Ferris and didn't like him, nodded. Link said, "How'd you leave the sick folks at your place this morning, Ferris?"

Ferris went over to the stove before answering. "They're on the mend, thank you." Then trying to put everyone at ease he said, "Hogs, I hear, have got the center of the stage here this morning."

"Not with me," Dandie answered.

Dandie sat, one leg cocked over the arm of his chair, waiting;

[138]

waiting for the morning to pass, the dinner to be eaten, the funeral to be over. Waiting for the time when he and Nory could begin their life together. He had only half heard all the pig talk: Christie's endless and evidently interested questions: What breeds were best? How much cold could a hog stand? Would a brood sow attack a human being? Was a hog as dirty as it was said to be? Did it have any intelligence at all? Was there more money in corn turned into pork than in corn sold outright? And his father's endless, and not to him interesting, answers.

Christie had listened, though. As Link talked he had hitched his chair closer and closer. Link was full of information about hogs; it seemed impossible to Christie that he should be so ignorant of this amazing animal which was to become the backbone of Indiana husbandry. The gilt Link had received the night before, he intended to make the beginning of a herd second to none in the state. "In building up that herd," he told Christie, "I hope to help the folks here get something they can be proud of."

"You sound like a reformer, Mr. Conboy."

"No, I reckon not," Link said. "I'm doing this for my own sake mostly."

Like everyone else, Christie had been hunting all of his life for someone he could look up to, someone he could admire. He had a bump of veneration and no use for it. People in general were fine, but he felt a crying need for someone a thousand rungs or so above him on the ladder. A person of whom he could truly say, "There's no one else in the world like him." A friend, but something more than a friend; someone he had to reach up toward. Perhaps that, as much as anything else, had been what he was looking for when he took up insurance peddling. And it would be a fine how-de-do if he should have come over to Rock County to court a girl and found himself falling in love with her father. Oh, love, he thought, that bedraggled word! But beside "like" and "respect" which were not right either, what words were there for the feeling he was beginning to have for Cate's father?

"A sow don't seem a very likely thing to start a reform on," Ferris said.

Christie, as if he were Link's appointed advocate, explained, "This isn't any ordinary gilt. She's a blue-ribbon Poland China."

"Hardly blue-ribbon," Link objected. "Yet, anyway."

"Yours?" Ferris asked, "or the county's?"

"The county's," Link answered, "and the folks' here at The Farm."

"They're a pretty motley crew," Ferris said, "from all I hear. Aren't you afraid somebody'll get hungry for fresh tenderloin some night and cut her throat?"

"Nobody here'd do that."

"We hear you got some pretty leaky vessels on The Farm right now," Ferris insisted.

"No more than usual, I reckon."

"Half the county, they say, was out about a month back watching those two diggers of yours at work."

"I'd put a stop to all that if I had my way," Link said.

"Can't you just say, 'No more digging'?" Ferris asked.

"I meant the staring, not the digging," Link said.

"Well, I wasn't there," Ferris reminded him. Then as if to make amends he said, "One real doll-baby here now, I understand."

Dandie swung his foot down from the arm of his chair.

"Old man Wade's niece, I mean. Never did understand how she was entitled to free board and room."

"She's got no folks," Link told him.

"Don't an uncle have to look out for a niece?"

"She ran off from Wade's."

Ferris pursed out his underlip knowledgeably. "So that's the way of it." Then he added, "There was one time with somebody when I guess she didn't start running quite soon enough."

Dandie was out of his chair in an instant. He was half a head shorter than Ferris, but it was plain that he could break Ferris into little pieces and stuff the pieces into the heater, if he was of a mind. Christie grinned: it's me, he thought, who ought to be fighting Cate's old beau, not her brother.

Ferris looked surprised. He was a nice-talking boy and would never have thought of saying "knocked up" or "got caught," like the rest of the Rock County men. "I heard she was in a family way. Likely no truth in it."

"It was the truth all right," Dandie told him. "The baby was born and died. We're going to bury it this afternoon. You're invited to the funeral."

"Funeral for a woods colt? That's kind of—" Ferris began but Dandie didn't let him finish.

"Shut up," he said.

Ferris flushed and looked unhappy. "I wish you would tell me some safe subject, Dandie. I didn't know it was any crime to talk about Miss Nory Tate."

"It is if you haven't got something better to say than anything you've said so far," Dandie answered. "I'm going to marry Miss Nory Tate." He turned and looked at his father. "At the soonest possible chance."

Christmas dinner, in spite of this announcement, went off in fine style. The crêpe-paper canopy was holding up beyond all belief. The light off the snow shimmered across the laden table. The stove was red hot, its sides glowing like July berries. The meal struck a hard balance: it was both dignified and festive. Even Cate was satisfied with it. Earlier she had wanted Lib to roast a whole weanling pig for the dinner.

Lib had said no to this nonsense. "Your father's gone crazy about pigs all of a sudden but I declare I'm not going to have them trotting across my Christmas table."

"We could have just a head," Cate had urged. "Roast it with an apple in its mouth."

Lib had said no to this, too. "What do you say when you pass a hog's head?" she had asked. "Help yourself to an ear? Please take an eyeball?"

Cate had giggled in spite of herself. "We could at least eat the apple," she had said.

"If I want an apple," Lib had replied, "I'll take it first hand, not wait until it's been wowsled around in a hog's mouth." When Lib was feeling good she made up words so fast she seemed to be speaking in a foreign language.

The hog's head had been only a dream anyway. Cate had let it fade without sorrow in favor of tenderloin, sweet and Irish potatoes, creamed onions, stewed dried corn, two kinds of pie: sour cream raisin and pumpkin; and two kinds of cake: spice and ribbon.

Because she was self-conscious with Christie, Cate talked more with Ferris than with him; but her talk with Ferris was all for

Christie to observe. She would look up at Ferris and use her mother's trick of blarney, which in her mother she hated. "Oh, Ferris, how exciting!" she'd exclaim.

Ferris, who had got over being miffed by Dandie's rudeness, let himself expand beneath Cate's showers of exclamations. Before the meal was over he had told her the story of his life. There wasn't much to it and what there was bored Cate. While she listened she kept her eyes on Christie who sat across from her and was still talking hogs with Link.

Dandie was in fine fettle for two reasons: he had told Ferris Thompson what he thought of him and had announced his intentions concerning Nory. His face, usually white, burned with color. He darted in and out of the conversations on each side of him, supplying a fact here and contradicting an opinion there. He dominated the dinner table.

He knew that he possessed a certain power to direct and control the actions of others. If he used it infrequently it was because he was, for the most part, filled with indifference for the life which went on around him. He scorned to exert himself in situations which did not fire his imagination. There must be something better to do in the world than play hired hand at a Poor House; something a little more lasting in life than fighting or even lovemaking.

All of his power lay with people; he knew that. "That Dandie Conboy! He sure is one prince of a fellow." They said that about him without troubling to lower their voices. But who said it? The loungers in a saloon who called any tin-horn sport who set up the drinks "a prince of a fellow." It was possible to be a prince in a mighty small and nasty kingdom. He did not intend to settle down to princing it at the Poor Farm, nor The Junction, nor even Rock County. If his early desire to preach had been impossible because he couldn't reconcile his twin desires for holiness and power, now that the one desire was shelved, he ought to be able to forge ahead in the other.

After dinner they were free to go their separate ways until the funeral which was set for three. Link expected them all to attend that. Leaving the table he said, "It would be a mark of kindness for all of you to be there. Death, even if it's not among your own kin, is nothing to overlook."

Ferris, dodging a strand of sagging crêpe-paper said, "That's mighty true, Mr. Conboy. Death won't overlook us."

This sententiousness from Ferris, smoothing down his pompadour while he philosophized about death, tickled Dandie. "Ferris," he said, "it sure won't. And you better stay away from Korby. He would just love to bury you, you would look so pretty laid out."

Ferris was uncertain how to take this, containing as it did, references both to his good looks and his death. Dandie was a show-off, he supposed, and perhaps should be ignored; but he answered good-naturedly, "Korby wouldn't want me. I wouldn't try his mettle enough. What he likes is somebody kicked in the head by a horse or chopped up by a mowing-machine."

Ferris was careful to see that all the women had left the dining-room before he said this. He considered it one of the marks of a gentleman to protect women from whatever was coarse or rough. Sometimes at home when sex or filth or sickness was mentioned by a hired hand at the table he would get queasy and excuse himself.

VI

OUT IN the hall Dandie asked for volunteers to help him dig the grave for Nory's baby. Both Ferris and Christie offered to help, but Lib protested. Let some of the folks help Dandie. She had more fitting ideas for entertaining Cate's beaus than sending them out on Christmas afternoon for a little grave-digging. Paupers' graves at that! What a report for Ferris to take home. "Come on into the parlor," she urged. "I've got some new stereopticon views of the Pyramids. It'd just ruin my day if I had to think of you two out there digging in this weather."

In spite of her protests, Lib had expected the boys to go dig. She had done her duty as a hostess by protesting against the digging; let them do their duty as guests by ignoring her protests. Ferris, who was inclined to be literal, went off with Cate to look at the Pyramids, leaving Christie to help Dandie.

Christie, who had no more suitable digging clothes than the ones he was wearing, went out to get his tools while Dandie changed. He met James and Mary Abel as he stepped from the barn door.

"Ready to go!" James said with approval, nodding toward the pick and shovel which Christie carried.

Christie, in the rush of the day's events, had forgotten the visitation of the night before and believed he was being offered some help with the grave-digging.

James set him right at once concerning this. "Mary and me's got something more important to do than dig graves," he said. "And last night I got your word to go with us."

Christie was feeling exuberant, excited by the snow, by love, by his own life in the face of death; even by being so much in demand, wanted for all kinds of enterprises.

"Got other plans now," he said jauntily.

"You gave me your promise last night," James answered.

"A man's not responsible for what he promises in his sleep," Christie objected. He felt irresistible, so full of obvious good will he could charm the circles off a racoon's tail.

"Last night you said, 'Count on me.' "

Christie laughed. He was already imagining how he would report this encounter at his boarding-house in Indianapolis; and in doing so he felt enhanced, multiplied by two, or even three, stretching time like a rubber band. Here he was involved in this affair, observing it, and at the same time imagining its outcome and describing it to his friends. Looking at James and Mary, he simultaneously explained them to his Indianapolis friends. "Crackpots. Red as lobsters. Bugged-out eyes. Diggers. Can't say what for. Something lost in the world. They considered me a fellow-digger. Said I had a sign on me. I tell you it's like the Dark Ages down there in Rock County. They still believe in witches, that's what they call those two: witch diggers. You don't know a thing, I tell you, buried up here in the city, about what goes on out in the 'world.' "

Darkness seemed to flow in under the redness of James Abel's face when he heard Christie's laugh. "It ain't in my power," he said, "to let you off after you promised."

Christie stopped laughing. "I've got this grave to dig," he said. "I've got no choice."

"We all choose," James said, "every minute."

Mary Abel spoke for the first time. "Let the dead bury the dead."

"What you're willing for the dead to do and what they're capable of doing's two separate things," Christie told her and started on toward the burying-ground.

"That's your final answer?" James Abel called after him.

Christie nodded without turning around. What was the use of trying to reason with folks who had lost their reason?

"You elect the dead instead of the living?" The voice was Mary Abel's and something in its tone made the back of his neck prickle; but he continued without answering. When he had mounted the first little rise in the direction of the burying-ground he took a quick glance over his shoulder. They were still there, immovable in the snow, watching him.

VII

DANDIE was coming down the hall, pudding-footed in his arctics on his way to join Christie in the grave-digging when Lib, opening the door of her and Link's room, reached out and drew him in. There was anger and unbelief on her face as she shut the door and stared up at him. Over by the window Link, with his back to the room, appeared to be studying the landscape.

"Dandie," Lib cried, "I can't credit my ears!"

Dandie was unperturbed. Things were coming to a head. "About what, Mama?"

"About you and Norah Tate." So she was rejecting the familiarity of "Nory."

"What about us, Mama?"

"Marriage," Lib said, as if the word would choke her.

"What's wrong with marriage, Mama?"

"Nothing," Lib said, "except that that girl is getting her dose of it about ten months late."

"Not for me," Dandie asserted.

"What's your grandfather going to think?"

"Grandpa Conboy?" Dandie asked.

For a minute he thought his mother would box his ears. He leaned down laughing to make the job easier for her and Lib, throwing her arms about his neck, pulled his cheek down with a thump against the fleur-de-lis pin which held her watch to her shoulder. She rocked him back and forth momentarily then pushed him away.

"It's all Link's fault," she said and marched across the room to confront Link once more with the fact.

Dandie watched his mother. It did not trouble him that Lib was not one of these sweet little mothers, gentle as starlight and content to glimmer dimly in corners. Nor did he care that she wasn't reasonable and manly, with a sense of proportion and a feeling for justice. About all anyone could bank on, in an argument with Lib, was that he wouldn't get kicked or scratched. Anyway, with *her* little tongue, what need was there of such defenses? Dandie admired his mother. He was not like Cate, perpetually suffering because she thought Lib made Link suffer. His father had a tongue of his own, hadn't he? If Lib handed him a sockdologer let him hand her one back. A man, he had already decided, got from a woman just about what he wanted.

"Link Conboy,'" Lib cried, all the zither notes in her voice vibrating, "look what you have brought down upon your own son by dragging us all here to the Poor House!"

Dandie had heard his mother before they ever came to the Poor House tell Link a thousand times that such a move would not only be a come-down in the world for them, but that it would expose the children to all the rag-tag and bob-tail of the county. If Lib lacked motherliness in the matter of Christmas and birthdays, she made up for it in her concern about her children's playmates. Unconsciously, the wicked of the world seemed much more appealing to Lib than the virtuous; and she worked overtime trying to protect her children from those charms which she herself felt so strongly. She dinned the shortcomings of the neighbors' offspring constantly into their ears: "Stay away from those no-account Rices. The Burfords are a trifling lot. Don't let me catch you playing with the Murphys."

Cate, innocent of evil, protested against these warnings and thought them only one more indication of her mother's unfairness. Not Dandie. He knew there was a good deal of sense in them. He knew about the things that happened in fence corners and the goings-on in musty spare rooms, couplings not to be whispered about; yes, but often impossible to hide, too. Each year someone in the county was killed in a shooting fray, and cutting fracases accounted for another fatality or two. There was no use pretending: it was a dark county. Look at the names: Bleeding Creek, Deadman's Crossing, Bears Tits, Dogtown. Plenty of the people in the county had been standing behind the door when the brains were passed out—yes, and the decency and respectability, too. Dandie understood this and didn't blame Lib for trying to build up dikes to protect her own home; though what she used for dikes might not be the best material in the world: Brussels carpets and lace curtains and crocheted tidies and Boston ferns and picture postcards in wire racks and peacock feathers in stone jars painted a purple-brown. That these would stop the flood, he doubted. The ferns would certainly die of neglect. Lib's motto was live and let live. She had never asked any favors of ferns and didn't expect in turn to be asked for favors by them. And the postcards, unless Cate kept at them, would soon all be upside down, and the peacock feathers broken under the weight of one of Lib's hats. Nevertheless the point was, whether Cate knew it or not, the world wasn't a place to walk out into saying, love, love, love. There were people in it who didn't understand that word and there had to be dikes and walls. But not between him and Nory, and Lib was building in vain if that was her purpose.

"I'm going to marry Nory," he said. "If Father's coming here caused that, why, he never made a better move in his life."

Lib joined Link at the window. In some ways this was worse news than if Dandie had announced his intention of taking up bank-robbing. To marry a pauper was bad enough—but one who'd been in trouble! It was a denial of manliness. A real man didn't take another's leavings. And when a son chooses a wife he chooses a substitute for his mother. How have I failed Dandie, she thought, so that this loose-living girl is the one he chooses?

"Dandie," she said, turning back to him, "if only I'd been a better mother to you none of this would've happened. If I'd been a better example you'd picked out some nice girl."

Link said quietly, "In spite of what's happened, Nory seems as nice a girl as you'd care to meet."

"Seems." Dandie's anger flared, unreasonably, against his father. "You can drop that word. She *is* nice."

"I don't feel I know her well enough to say more than that. For a girl who's been in trouble she seems—"

Dandie swung his father away from the window, a hand on his arm. "Shut up that kind of talk."

Link wrenched himself loose. "I will not take orders from a son as to when and what I can speak."

Lib went between them. "Hush up, both of you. This is no time for words. What we've all got to do is figure how we can get Dandie out of the fix he's in."

Now Dandie took hold of his mother's shoulder. "You try to get me out of this fix," he promised, "and you'll wake up to look back on all this as a summer picnic."

By the time Dandie reached the burying-ground, Christie had almost finished the grave.

"Isn't that pretty small?" he asked, looking down into the gravelly pit. "I made it the size your father told me."

As Dandie stood there he began to understand that the child, who had bulked so large in its mother, was a very small mouthful for the earth to swallow. When the grave was finished he asked Christie to go with him to cut cedar boughs to line it. He had an idea that Nory, for all her protests that she would've given the child away, if it had lived, would be comforted to have the raw wet earth covered from her sight. They were still busy with this job—and it was not easy to attach branches to the sides of the grave—when the inmates began to assemble for the services.

The funeral was a great occasion to them, an event to which they had been invited, like a party; to which they could say yes or no. It provided them with an alternative, a luxury they had very little of any more. They were reminded by it of the past, of the times when there had been decisions to make and they had opportunities to come or go, to accept or refuse. They marveled at Mrs. Goforth who had used this power of election to choose to stay in her own room. "In this country," she said, "the bottom rail's come to be the rider. But no Goforth's ever gone to the funeral of a woods colt and I'm not going to be the one to start it."

In addition to an alternative the funeral provided the inmates with another luxury, that of pity. Part of their poverty was that they had no one to pity. Nory was at the minute in a sorrier fix than any of them: not only was she a pauper, but she was a pauper betrayed and bereaved as well. They came out to the funeral, all their own hurts and wounds salved over by their pity for her.

When the coffin arrived every inmate, with the exception of Fifield and Pen, who were sick, the two Abels, who were digging, and Mrs. Goforth, regretting her high-mindedness, but too stiff-necked to recant, was at the graveside. Even John Manlief was there, his apathies evidently having let up enough for him to appreciate the fact that there was some difference between life and death. Whether or not he considered that difference important couldn't be told from his expressionless face.

Link's pine coffin, which *was* small, and which, against the endless-seeming stretch of snowy hills, seemed smaller still, no larger than a shoebox, was carried to the grave by Earnest Creagan and Dexter Bemis. It was the custom in Rock County for the coffin of a child to be carried to its resting-place by other children; partly on the theory that innocence merited innocence in its final handling, and partly because it was thought that the experience might, in reminding the young pall-bearers how slight was their hold on life, teach them to mend their ways while there was yet time.

Em had begged to be a pall-bearer. When Link had said no to this she had suggested, as an alternative plan, that she be permitted to precede the coffin holding aloft a cross. She had the cross already made and waiting: an old broom handle sawed in two then lashed together with cord string and covered with cedar boughs. She longed with her whole soul to carry it. After all her praying of the night before she felt that she was bound to the baby almost as closely as Nory. Lib, who liked people to have a good time, would have let Em carry her cross; but Link, feeling that Em should not use the occasion of Nory's sorrow for her own personal dramatics, still said no and Em had to walk out to the burying-ground with Cate, Christie, and Ferris, a completely undistinguished mourner.

Cate, as she had imagined herself doing, stood close beside Christie. The baby who was being buried represented not death to her, but love. And not love either, but the unknown, mysterious act of passionate love. It lay there before her, the visible symbol of that unknown, strange, and often imagined union. She felt herself wicked to be entertaining such thoughts at such a time: in the presence of death and sorrow and on the anniversary of Christ's birth. But she could not rid herself of them, and finally she indulged them. It seemed to her that the fact that she and Christie were together in the presence of this symbol of passion—and sin—was a sign of some kind. If by chance his thoughts were the same as hers, they had already experienced some kind of binding together. And since at that very minute Christie took her hand in his and held it close against his side where the crook of his elbow hid it, she believed that he had been with her in thought.

Dandie, who until this time had kept his meetings with Nory secret, escorted her out to the funeral as boldly as if he were already her husband, and at the same time, as happily as if bound for his wedding. In a sense this was the case since he and Nory both felt that the burial of the child would be the burial of the past which separated them. The child to them was not a symbol of the act, but a symbol of the man who was its father; when the baby went underground that man would go also and so cease to trouble them.

Link and Lib, delayed by talk of Dandie, came last of all; Lib hurrying, Link pacing more slowly, they advanced across the already trampled snow toward the group which awaited them. It was a bright afternoon but very cold; the sky a pale taut blue, like skin stretched across bloodless lips. Link left Lib with the mourners and went to the opposite side of the grave. There he faced in silence his family, his two guests, and his charges.

Dandie regarded his father belligerently. Let him suggest, ever so slightly, any condemnation of Nory and he would—what would he do? He knew very well that he could no more think of touching his father in anger than he would of touching a tree in anger. Actually, what he felt, rather than apprehension, was curiosity. He did not consider his father a religious man. At the time of his conversion his father had looked at him, he thought, as if he had caught him taking a bath in a public horse-trough. The Bible said, "Go ye and spread the good tidings," and whatever his father thought about the tidings, the spreaders, Dandie was convinced, didn't rank high with him. His guess was that for this occasion Link had found some ready-made burial service and would read it dryly and slowly, his emphasis on the sense of the words.

Link took a small Bible from his overcoat pocket but did not open it. Without bowing his head, shutting his eyes, or making any other of the gestures common to preachers, he said, "But the fruit of the spirit is love, joy, peace, long suffering, gentleness, goodness, faith: against these there is no law."

This, Dandie thought, was a strange beginning for a funeral, but before he had a chance to see what Link intended next, the services were disrupted by Hoxie Fifield who burst screaming from the back door of the house. Between the burying-ground, which lay at the top of a gentle rise, and the Poor House below were a number of objects, clothesline, wood-pile, chopping-block, sawhorses, hog-houses, and the like. Hoxie, screaming with pain or craziness, Dandie couldn't be sure which, aimed straight for the wood-pile. Just before reaching it he gathered himself and by some miracle flew up and over it. His coming down was not as successful as his going up, however, and he landed face down in the snow. Since he was dressed only in a long union suit and since the back flap of this garment dangled unbuttoned he presented to the eyes of the astounded mourners a plump behind, curving upward out of the snow like a pumpkin missed at harvest time.

The on-lookers were at first too amazed to make a sound or move a muscle. They watched and listened in dumbfounded silence as Hoxie, again roaring, reared himself up out of the snow and raced toward the sawhorses. These he soared over, obviously without extending himself, and charged on toward the hog-houses. The first, he cleared by several feet. In fact he went so high that he appeared to have discovered some law negating gravity. Then, turning, he had a go at them from the opposite direction and his red behind blazed upon the eyes of his beholders like an Indian summer sun past its meridian but by no means quenched of light. The hog-houses appeared to have bewitched Hoxie. There were six of them in that group and he went up and over them so fast that he seemed to be hovering in midair like a swarm of evening midges. There seemed to be not one Hoxie but a multitude.

The first wild, strangled snicker came from Earnest Creagan. Everyone turned to look at him; a pall-bearer at a funeral laughing!

How unsuitable, how sacrilegious, even. They stared poor Earnest down with stern looks of reproof, then turned back to Hoxie. Hoxie, now leap-frogging the final hog-house, was near enough the grave so that it was possible for those about it to understand his screams. "For Christ's sake, somebody stop me," Hoxie was crying in a hoarse despairing voice every time he reached the zenith of a leap.

"For Christ's sake, somebody stop me," Doss Whitt whispered to himself, like a man testing out on his own piano a tune heard elsewhere and about which he has not yet made up his own mind. "For Christ's sake, somebody stop me."

It was this whispering, like an echo, which set off their uncontrollable laughter. They gave themselves to it, then leaned against each other, weakened and weeping and hysterical. For laughter, too, was one of their luxuries at the Poor House and they laughed like people who don't know where their next laugh is coming from, uncontrollably.

Tiring, finally of hog-houses, Hoxie came spurting up the hill toward the open grave. "For Christ's sake, somebody stop me," he implored, as he came abreast the mourners; then, without pausing, he started down the farther side of the hill heading toward the barbed wire fence which the snow half hid at the bottom.

"Stop him," Link cried, "before he hurts himself," and at once Christie, Ferris, and the two pall-bearers, as if released from a spell, sprang after Hoxie. Christie was first to reach him, and in a split second Hoxie changed from a runner and jumper into a jumper and fighter.

"For Christ's sake, somebody stop me," he continued to plead, as he pranced and flailed.

Christie, still laughing, did no more than try to protect his face. He couldn't bring himself to hit a man so obviously beside himself.

"Stop me, for Christ's sake, stop me," Hoxie implored, battering away at Christie's upraised arms.

Dandie, who had been reluctant to leave Nory, arrived in time to take one of Hoxie's windmill blows full in the face. "Stop me, Dandie boy," Hoxie begged, "for Christ's sake, stop me."

Dandie did so at once. He hit Hoxie twice, once as he went up on a prance, and once as he came down in a float. Hoxie fell on his face in the snow, at peace at last. Earnest Creagan, experienced in buttoning younger brothers and sisters, leaned over and buttoned Hoxie's drawers for him. Then Hoxie lay there, a long lank figure, decently covered and apparently gone to sleep in his underwear.

They were standing over him, uncertain as to what to do next, when Doss arrived and explained matters. "It's the turpentine," he explained. "He wanted a cure for the clap and I told him, turpentine. Who'd of thought he'd be simple enough to use it? I reckon it's burned him clear to the bone."

"Well, he can't feel it now, I guess," Dandie said.

"You're hallooing before you're out of the woods, boy," Doss assured him. "He'll wake up any minute now, and it'll be all to do over again."

"Since you're the one who set him off," Dandie said, "what's your advice on how to cure him?"

"Lard," Doss said. "Lard's the only thing to counteract turpentine. Lard him from stem to stern."

Doss and Christie took Hoxie back to the house for the larding, while Dandie and the two boys returned to the interrupted funeral. All the mourners were now too spent with laughter to have much emotion left for Nory's poor baby.

Link gazed across the grave pit to the quietening group, uncertain as to how he should continue. The day was ending. The western sky had become a clear, glassy green. A few birds—chickadees, a couple of jays, a crow or two—swung in toward the Poor House, hunting a bite to eat before nightfall. Deep shadows, the bluest, Link thought, he had ever seen them, lay on the snow. The last of the sunlight was staining those at the graveside a peculiar purple; they looked, one and all, as if they'd been steeped in pokeberry juice. Dandie, reddened by his exertions and empurpled now by the strange light, appeared dark and forbidding. Cate, standing alone, was lost in some dream. Only Em remained constant to the occasion, a faithful mourner. Link thought, as he gazed at his children, of the saying, "a face that only a mother could love." He felt that he loved the three faces of his children not because of his fatherhood but in spite of it: that his fatherhood caused him, out of over-familiarity and modesty to underestimate them. Had he come upon the three of them on any city street his heart would have said: how beautiful; he thought their beauty was more than any special arrangements of flesh and bone. It was the uplifted, waiting alertness of all young people who have not yet had enough of their gifts refused by life to have begun to doubt and fear.

He yearned to speak to *them*. There was no need to speak to or of the dead baby. It was gone, it had escaped. But surely in forty-five years of living he should have discovered some truths which he could hand over to his children. Truths which in times of crisis and despair they could use for their guidance; and remember, after he too was gone, from whom they had had them. But what were those truths? The wise fatherly words? In the face of Lib's accusations he particularly longed just now to find them. Was it true, as she said, that coming to the Poor House—which had seemed a way of salvation to him—was a stumbling block for them?

While he stood silently pondering, Mag Creagan started a hymn. "There'll be no parting there," Mag sang in her hearty carrying tenor. This was a terrible thought to Nory, for whom it was intended as consolation; but it was relished by the others and they sang verse after verse, their throats, rasped by earlier hysterical laughter, relaxed now in the gentle rhythms of the hymn.

When they had finished the song, Link said, "And now abideth faith, hope, love, these three; but the greatest of these is love." Then he put his Bible back in his pocket.

They waited some seconds after this, expecting a prayer; at the very least, a line of benediction. But that was the end. The funeral services were over. Earnest and Dexter lowered the little box to the bottom of the grave, then dropped the cedar boughs which Dandie and Christie had piled about the grave's edge, into the pit. Link turned and, with Lib beside him, led the way back to the house. Some of the mourners could not resist stopping en route for a look at the trampled snow in those places where Hoxie had performed his marvels of leaping.

VIII

CATE had tried all day to live inside the pattern of what she had imagined "the perfect Christmas day" or the "most suitable mode of entertaining a young man" to be. Since the pattern she had imagined was narrow and inflexible she had been cramped. Now the pattern was broken and she was free. There was no use pretending that the "perfect Christmas day" could possibly contain any such jumping and screeching as Hoxie's, or that "the most suitable way to entertain a young man" could by any stretch of the imagination include a wrestling match between the young man and a simpleton crazed by turpentine which he had used in the hope of curing a bad disease.

And though she would never have imagined it, she was glad to be free. Before, she had been trying so hard to squeeze the day into her pattern that she'd had no chance to enjoy the happenings which didn't fit. Now that the pattern itself was completely smashed, she could take each thing as it happened and like it or dislike it for itself.

She and Christie had waited all day for a private time and place in which to exchange presents. She had two presents for Christie: a leather collar-box, and Elizabeth Barrett Browning's *Sonnets from the Portuguese*, leather bound: a practical and an impractical gift; one for the body, one for the soul, a perfect balance. Now, having been given by Hoxie a small taste of the pleasures of being unbalanced, she began to wish that instead of dividing her money and trying sensibly to provide for every want, she had spent it all on some one single breath-taking present. It was after four o'clock, already twilight before she and Christie found the place and the time for their exchange.

"I haven't seen your father's sow yet," Christie told her in the parlor after the funeral. "Would you care to go have a look at it with me?"

The time had been, and recently, when she would have been repelled by such a suggestion; but she was becoming less choosy by the minute and saw this as the opportunity they were both looking for.

On the way out to the barn Christie paused for a minute to examine the whorls left in the snow by Hoxie's union suit. "I'd've sworn no living man could jump so high," he said and Cate saw that Hoxie's jumps, like Korby's ride, had given Christie more pleasure than all her careful plans put together.

The barn, when they reached it, felt warm; it wasn't, of course, but the wind, at least, was shut out and the stored hay and the animals gave it a scent warmer than that of the raw wet snow outside. Link had not risked putting his prize with the common hogs, but had made her a private pen by boarding up one end of an unused stall. Cate and Christie both knew that their purpose in the barn was gifts, not animals; still they spared, Christie out of real interest and Cate out of regard for what she considered seemly, a few minutes for Link's pride.

"She looks real independent," Cate said doubtfully. "Though I don't suppose that's why Papa prizes her."

"Your Papa prizes her," Christie said, "because of three points. Point number one is her length of body. Room to store the fat. Point number two is her bones. Strength to hold up the fat. Point number three is her height from the ground, none. You can't put fat on a long-legged hog. That is the whole art of judging hogs, and now you know as much about hogs as I do."

Cate looked at him with surprise and admiration. "Why, Christie! I didn't know you knew anything about hogs."

"I didn't until today. Your father's a good teacher."

"Do you like Papa?"

"Yes, I do."

"I do, too," Cate said.

Neither wanted to be the first to say, "I have a present for you," so they began to walk about the barn, Christie pretending a greater ignorance of farm machinery and animals than he had.

"What's that?"

"A mowing-machine."

"What big lawns you have down here, Miss Conboy. And what's that animal, may I ask? A swan?"

"It's a gander," Cate answered, too filled with feeling for Christie to do much pretending. "He's mine. He was born with a club foot so they gave him to me to raise."

"Looks like a swan to me," Christie insisted. "And what may I ask is this?" He laid his hand on the two-seated sleigh.

"It's a cutter," Cate said, "to drive in the snow."

"Well, this is just the day for it, Miss Conboy. Hop in and I'll take you for a spin." He helped Cate into the front seat, got in beside her, unfolded the buffalo robe and put it over their knees.

"What are you going to use for horses?"

"Horses? Do you think we are earthbound, Miss Conboy? Look at that! We don't need horses." The gander had followed them to the sleigh and stood now, tail to the dashboard, like a steed awaiting the slap of reins. "We're going to travel in style. Go flying and sailing like Venus with a swan to pull us."

"Like Venus?"

"The Goddess of Love. And her swan, Eros."

"His name's Samson."

"Not any more. I've renamed him. He's Eros. He's love. We'll follow Eros wherever he goes. And you must never kill Eros and you must feed him the best food and pet him and coddle him. And give him a kiss for me when I'm gone. Will you?"

"Yes."

"Promise me?"

"I promise." Eros limped off at that minute but neither of them noticed.

"Cate," he said, "I've got a little Christmas present for you."

He took a small package from his pocket and began to untie its ribbons himself. "I don't know whether you'll like it or not. But it looked pretty *to* me and I thought it would look pretty *on* you."

When he had the paper off, he handed the box to Cate, a blue box with the name of an Indianapolis jeweler printed on it in gilt letters. Inside, on purple jeweler's plush, lay a gold heart attached to a fine gold chain. The heart itself was cut diagonally by a line of blue enamel; above this line was a blue enamel forget-me-not with a drop of dew, made of a single rhinestone, glistening at its center. The gift seemed so beautiful, and so personal, that Cate could say nothing at all. She hated even the thought of the practical collar box and impractical book of poetry and wished that they were actually sleighing so that she could drop both into a convenient snow bank.

"Don't you like it?" Christie asked.

"Oh, yes."

"Why don't you put it on then?"

Since she made no answer Christie took the locket from the box and began to fasten it about her neck himself. He lifted her curls which were a little long at the back so that he could see to fasten the catch.

Cate waited to feel his fingers touch her neck. She thought, I can't bear it if they don't, if he puts the locket around my neck like some terribly careful-fingered old bachelor jeweler. Touch me, touch me, all of her flesh cried, and she did not try to silence it, but let it speak as loudly and plainly as possible. At last she felt Christie's fingers, warm, steady, and assured. Did this mean no more to him than the proper arrangement of a chain, the nice settling of an ornament? Then, when the clasp was fastened she felt his hands on her shoulders and was turned toward him so that he could see whether or not his gift became her.

"Yes," he said, "it looks fine. I was right to get it. That's your heart all right."

He let his hands remain on her shoulders and Cate thought, Why is he so terribly slow? Surely he intends to kiss me? Then she began to hate him for his slowness, thinking of all the ways she would later shame and humiliate him for the delay. If I were a man, how bold and quick and commanding I would be! I would kiss and kiss, be fiery and savage, not dilly and dally. She began to want with all her might to hit him; she could feel along the whole length of her arms the pleasure she would have in beating his bare flesh with her fists. Then just at that moment she saw that he *was* going to kiss her and, she thought bitterly, it is too late, he has ruined everything. But it was not too late at all. When his mouth touched hers all her aching fury vanished. The kiss was exactly right and had come at the one most needful moment.

IX

THE HOUR for supper at the Poor House was five, Christmas or not. At four-thirty Mag had the lamps lit in the kitchen and had recruited the fire (never allowed to die out completely) with some of the shavings left over from Link's coffin making. Supper was always a pick-up meal and tonight, with all the left-overs she had from dinner, it would be a shorter horse than usual and sooner curried. She slapped her kettles onto the stove, then seeing the yellow tom outside in the snow, opened the door and let him in.

"Well, Mister," she said, "what's your fancy for Christmas supper?"

She was still holding the cat when Lily Bias scuttled into the kitchen for her evening chore of table-setting, took up the knife-and-fork box, and scuttled out. Mag, who had a talent for such things, saw that Lily was once more in love. "The poor old fool," she said to Mister and set him down with a slab of cold pork for his supper.

Mrs. Goforth paced in with a reluctant stateliness: like an old maid forced to go to the backhouse but trying to act as if it was a matter of free will, not necessity, Mag thought. "Well, Lodema," she asked, "what's biting you?"

Mrs. Jesse Mercer, the oldest woman at the Poor House, tottered in, and Mag pushed a chair toward the stove. "Sit down and toast yourself, grandma," she said.

Leathy Wade, a soft shapeless old woman of sixty-nine, always giggling, came in giggling now.

"What's tickling you, Leathy?" Mag asked.

"Hoxie," Mrs. Wade said. "That Hoxie. Say, how was that for high?" she asked.

"He went up and up," Grandma Mercer said, gazing at the ceiling, as if Hoxie might still be poised somewhere in midair. "I never in my life seen the like."

"Then he come down," Leathy added, "and lay there in the snow like a great big lightning bug, his tail a-blaze like a lantern."

"Mighty big lantern for such a little bug," Mag said, making potato cakes out of the left-over mashed potatoes.

Mrs. Goforth stopped her bread slicing to say, "I thank my lucky stars I was spared that sight."

Mag agreed with her. "Would just of het up your blood to no purpose, Lodema. Hoxie's got a girl in town."

Mrs. Goforth said nothing, but cut bread so fast the slices flew away from her knife like leaves.

Leathy Wade, who heard all the gossip, was reminded by this of her news. "Dandie is going to marry Nory Tate," she said. This stopped all work in the kitchen. Mag, first to recover, flipped the potato cakes into the hot grease. "Wait until his Pa and Ma have had their say before you count on that." She nodded toward the window through which Cate and Christie could be seen coming up the path from the barn. "There's the marrying couple."

Lily, back in the kitchen, shot to the window for a nearer view. She could not deny that the two were walking mighty close together, but she knew the reason. "He's polite," she said. "But marriage! Why, a girl like Cate, halfway between grass and hay, don't hold any interest for a man like Mr. Fraser."

"Hay might interest him," Mag agreed, "but not a bunch of old straw, long since gone to seed and been winnowed God only knows how many times already."

Lily took no offense at this. She no more expected the common run of people to understand love than a saint expects the man in the street to understand God. And she was glad that Mag knew her secret. Love was better that way, when there was someone to share the glory with.

"Such goldy eyes he's got," she said, "and such soft furry hair!"

Mag swooped down, picked up the cat and thrust him into Lily's scrawny arms. "Hold Mister," she said, "while you wait the real thing. He's furry and goldy-eyed enough if that's what you're hankering for."

Lily pressed her face close to the cat but continued to gaze out the window at Christie and Cate who had paused to talk. "I just spend the livelong day hoping for a little glimpse," she confided softly.

Mag paused in her frying. "Sweet Jesus," she ejaculated. "I pray God give me a little relief by the time I've reached your age."

x

AFTER supper was over Ferris suggested that they play charades. No Conboy, not even Cate, would ever have thought of charades; charades took planning; they seemed pretentious and formal, like using a bookmark or deciding ahead of time what to cook for a meal. But charades suited them all that evening. They were all filled with strong emotions which they could not express directly. Indirectly, through the play-acting of the charades, they could let themselves go; they could kiss, or embrace, strike or defy, and give no secrets away. Ferris, since the idea was his, was naturally the captain of one side; Christie, as a guest in the house, was the other captain. Ferris, who got first choice, took Lib: not because he wanted her but because he knew it was the polite thing to do. Christie, paying no attention to politeness, chose Cate. Ferris' motto, "Ladies first," made him chose another player he wanted even less than Lib. Em. Christie then took Link, and poor Ferris was left with Dandie, too rambunctious tonight to fit into any organized game, let alone one so formal as charades.

Cate, Christie, and Link retired to the dining-room to decide on their first word. Link watched his daughter, transformed almost beyond his knowing. By what? he asked himself; then looking at Christie he had his answer. By love transformed; purged of all her painful alternations of shyness and show-off; her spirit, rid of all its dreads, lighting face and body so that every expression and gesture came blooming outward with a lily's natural curve and radiance. The dining-room was unlighted except for the small bedroom lamp they had brought in with them and in the half-dark Cate was bright as a firefly; she had the same bronze sheen.

She was full of suggestions, bubbling with words they could act out. *Masticate, Washington, illuminate*—they flew off like sparks. But she could listen tonight, too.

"What's your idea, Papa? What do you think, Christie?"

My daughter, Link thought, what have we done to you to keep this ease and happiness hidden?

"How do you act out masticate?" Christie asked.

She teased him. She was sure enough and happy enough for that The little gold heart was swinging against her breast. "Christie, what did you *do* in college? Just waltz? Just play baseball? Didn't they teach you anything about words?"

"Since I got to Rocky County words don't seem so important."

Link recalled them. "How do you act out masticate?"

She could tease him, too. "Lawyers and college men," she hooted. "Do you know what the word means, Papa?"

"I know what it means, all right, Cate. You tell us how to act it out."

"It's easy. It's next to nothing. It's *mass* and *tea* and *Cate*. For *mass* don't either of you remember some Latin you can reel off fast? And for *tea* we'll drink pretend tea out of real tea-cups. And the last syllable will be me alone—Cate. They'll never guess it."

They never did, though Lib, who was quick as a wink at charades, was near to guessing when the time was up. Christie, as winner, chose Em for his side; but as loser on the next word he lost Cate, so the score was even.

Cate was rescued by Lib who tired quickly of any one game and who broke the charades by sitting down at the organ and beginning to play: not any Christmas songs, as Link well knew, but her old favorite and his, *Tenting Tonight*. He wouldn't go so far as to say that Lib had a contrary streak, but Christmas songs on Christmas day made her feel, as he'd heard her say, "like a round peg in a round hole"; which was too much of a muchness for Lib and gave her no sense of being separated from her surroundings. And Lib wanted to be Lib; not mingle and mix and lose her identity. "That's buttering bread with bread," was a saying of hers when something blended a little too thoroughly for her taste. Lib was a woman for contrasts; thunderstorms pleased her, while a spell of pokey weather gave her a nervous headache. She would choose the piece of music which suited *her*, not the occasion; and what always suited Lib was *Tenting Tonight*. Why? Link didn't know. She was at the organ now, lifting the song, it almost appeared, in great shafts of sound from the keys.

"Many are the hearts that are weary tonight,
Tenting on the old camp ground."

Did she choose this particular song because it increased the comfort and happiness of their own four walls? To help them imagine, not only the sorrow and pain and hardship of that past weariness, but the sorrow and pain everywhere, at the very minute? Link couldn't say. Perhaps it was the tune alone she enjoyed and she would've played it, no matter what the words. All were singing now:

"Many are the hearts that are weary tonight,
Waiting for the war to cease."

Link backed away from the others and leaned against the hall doorway. That song always brought tears; he was ashamed of them and was glad when Mag, opening the door, whispered, "You're wanted in the kitchen."

XI

IN THE darkness of the dimly lighted hall Link quickly dried his eyes. "What's the trouble?" he asked.

"Old Mr. Dilk's come," Mag said.

Link groaned. Settling a new inmate was a hard business at best. Evening was always a bad time for the change to be made, and Christmas evening was certainly the worst time of the whole year.

"What's he mean coming this time of the night?" he asked, following Mag down the hall toward the kitchen.

It was not really late, only a little after seven, but it was late for this kind of business. Old Mr. Dilk's nephew, Cady Gutherie, had been over earlier in the week and made all the arrangements for placing his uncle at The Farm. The old man was really his wife's great-uncle, no actual blood relation of Cady's.

"Cady says they're starting butchering tomorrow, and this was his best chance to bring him in," Mag explained.

Link followed Mag into the kitchen, a room which served Mag and her children in the evenings as a sitting-room. Mag's three eldest and Dexter Bemis sat on the floor by the stove playing jackstraws. Cady Gutherie, a raw-boned young farmer with his red face screwed up tight, was warming his hands by nervously clasping and unclasping them about the stove-pipe. The uncle, head bowed clear to his chest, sat at the kitchen table. Before Link had time to utter a word, Cady began to speak.

"The old man's nursing a fit of the sulks, and I'm free to admit I don't envy you the job of handling him. He agreed to come down here. He knows as well as I do that I've got six mouths of my own to feed and that I'm hard put to do that. We've had him two years and for a while he could make a little return in the way of work, but he's too stiffened up now to be any account. And I'm dogged if I'm going to deny my own blood just to salve his feelings."

Cady Gutherie spoke in a gust of words, angrily and complainingly. Link could tell that he was unhappy to be leaving the old man and mad that the old fellow was making it harder for him.

"He's ruined our Christmas. Hasn't swallowed a bite all day and made us herd him out to the sleigh like a balky steer."

Now it was plain to be seen his one desire was to be shut of him as quickly as possible.

"I've got to be going," he said. "My kids are out in the sleigh. They've been hounding me for a sleigh ride all day so I said all right, we'll kill two birds with one stone—give you your ride and deliver your uncle."

He walked over to the table, put his hand under his uncle's chin—as if the old man had been a pouting child—and tried to pry it up. Failing, he said, "Suit yourself," and turned to Link. "Don't carry him around on a chip just because he's surly. It goes against my grain always seeing the squeaking wheel get the grease."

Then he said good night, banged the door behind him, and left Link face to face with a job he hated: a job of sorrow and a job he had to work his way through with talk. The children, who had stopped their game while Cady Gutherie spoke, had gone back to it. Mag stood, back to the stove, hands on her hips looking at the old man. He hadn't moved a muscle, even when his nephew left. Link went toward him reluctantly. This, he reminded himsef, is what you asked for; this is what you thought would be no more than your just deserts.

"Maybe he'd like a cup of hot tea to warm him up," Mag suggested.

Link sat down at the table, across from the old man. "Could you use a cup of tea?" he asked. There was no answer. The old man had a clean, white, well-shaped beard and above it a thin, blue-veined nose. Since his upper face was shadowed by the visor of his cap and since his chin was deeply entrenched in the frayed bosom of his coat, beard and nose were all Link could see of the new inmate.

"How about some tea for yourself?" Mag asked, when there was no reply from Mr. Dilk. "Wouldn't you relish a cup?"

"Yes, come to think of it," Link said, "I would."

The kettle was already on and steaming and Mag had the tea ready in a second. After she had poured Link his cup she poured another for Dilk and put it by his elbow.

"Some people don't know what they want unless it's right under their nose," she said. But though Mr. Dilk's cup steamed under his nose, he didn't move a finger toward it.

Mag poured a cup for herself and stood stirring and sipping. "Have a seat," Link said, but Mag shook her head. She wouldn't think of sitting down with Link; not because she had any feeling of inferiority as hired girl, but because for Link's sake she didn't want to stir up any trouble with Lib. And no use the name and not the game, she thought: though with Link she hadn't much hankering for the game. He was the best-looking man she knew, and the most desirable, but she wouldn't trade what she had with him, this talking and drinking together, for what was so easy to come by, with any man, out behind the corn crib.

Link sipped his tea, listened to the singing in the parlor, watched the children's delicate unpiling of the stack of jackstraws. Mag's Icey seemed to have brains in her fingers, even if she was a little lacking above. He finished his cup and said, "Mr. Dilk, your bed's all made up for you. I'll show you to it."

There was no movement from the old man to indicate that he knew that he'd been spoken to. Link put a hand on his arm and felt resistance hardening there.

Mag set her cup down and came over to the table.

"Want me to give him a little boost?" she asked.

"No, no. But you might bring me the Fraser boy."

He had thought of Dandie, but Dandie was too impatient: he would get the old man down to his room in a twinkle, but feet foremost, like as not. He didn't know what Ferris would do; argue, he guessed. Lib was the one who could've wheedled the old fellow out of his mulishness; but he didn't care to give Lib any more cause today for finding fault with his having come here in the first place.

Mag brought Christie in, sent the children off to bed, then left the room herself.

"Pour yourself a cup of tea," Link told Christie, pointing to the enamel pot, "and sit down."

Christie did so.

"This is Mr. Dilk, a newcomer here," Link said.

Christie, who had been gazing uneasily at the old man over the rim of his tea-cup, said, "I'm pleased to meet you."

For all the response he made, Mr. Dilk might've been dead.

"Mr. Dilk's sorry to find himself here," Link said in a matter-of-fact way.

"I've taken a liking to the place myself."

"That's because you're free to go. That makes a great difference. Set you down here with no other place to turn to and you'd have a different story to tell."

"I can't see that there's much lacking here."

"You get word tonight that there's a new law saying you're to stay here for the rest of your life and you'd tear the place down to get away."

"Yes," Christie agreed. "I guess I'm a born traveler."

"Born stay-at-home, and it would be the same. A man with no choice ain't happy. Mr. Dilk," he said, "if you want to spend the night here in the kitchen you can. It'll be a botheration to everybody and you won't rest comfortable. But it's up to you. Suit yourself."

The old man collapsed on to the table then, as if broken, his head lying on his arms and his shoulders shaken with his crying.

"Would you like to get out of here?" Link asked him.

The old man rose. He kept his eyes tight shut, as if trying not to see where he was; Link took his arm and guided him out of the room. After they left Christie looked at the smear on the table. It took him a minute to realize that what had made it was tears. Blood, he thought, would somehow have looked less terrible.

XII

CATE, sitting across the kitchen table from Christie, felt shy of him. A kitchen, she thought, is the most intimate room—after the bedroom, of course—in a house. It is the room where husband and wife face each other after the night is past. It is the room where the wife cooks for the husband, sets the table for him, learns things about him which only a wife can know. He has a hollow tooth; sugar makes it ache. He likes parsnips, but parsnips don't like him. Thick gravy is the one thing he can't stomach.

"What about another stick of wood in the stove?" she said. Like a wife, she thought.

Christie put it in. Like a husband. "No use sitting in a glare, is there?" he said, indicating the lamp, burning brightly.

"No, it's hard on the eyes."

They were beginning to talk of small things as if they were important. The way married people do.

"Shall I turn it down?"

"Silly to waste oil, I reckon."

Christie pointed to the table. "That's the spot where he shed his tears."

Cate nodded. They were beginning to have a past in common. Soon they would be able to say to each other, "Do you remember?"

Christie reached across the table and touched the heart he had given her. "Do you still like it?"

"Yes."

"Will you wear my picture in it?"

"Oh, yes."

She felt herself climbing over so many barriers to reach him; she being herself and reaching the real person he was. Not reaching some person she imagined him to be: not Donovan or St. Elmo or Steerforth. She was at home with *them*; had been kissed by them and swooned in their arms a thousand times. But to stretch her hand across the oil-cloth to Christian J. Fraser —could she do that?

So much separated them: being teased about boys. "Is Tommy Briscoe your little sweetheart, Catey?"

Knowing since she was ten that she must find a husband, but must never appear to be hunting one.

Hearing Lib say, a hundred times over, "I'd far, far rather see a girl of mine in her grave than have that happen."

And all the little barriers: of cheapening herself; of going too far; of not appearing to hold back; of letting a boy know you liked him; of not having enough self-respect.

The stove, with the fresh stick in it, was humming steadily. Beneath it, the yellow tom was sleeping, folded into sphinx-like lines. Outside were the snow and the wind and the hills: what was called the world. Here at the very center of it was Christie. Christian J. Fraser. Cate tried to detach herself from her feeling about Christie long enough to see who he actually was: the insurance salesman, she thought; the man who goes from town to town; from house to house; who is listened to by strangers; the man other men pay attention to when he tells them how much money their wives will need to live on after they are dead; girls in the houses he visits flirt with him; play *Star of the East* on the organ for him; make big platters of panocha for him after supper. Oh, but he remembered me, came back to me, gave me a gold heart, asked me to wear his picture in it! Without thought her hand slid across the oil-cloth into his. When she stopped thinking, it was not so hard for her, the real Cate, to reach him, the real Christie.

"Catey," he said, "with a C."

"Spelled that way to match your name."

"Catherine-Christian. They were meant to go together, I guess."

Cate thought, I'll always remember today because it was our first Christmas together. Then she thought, We always know the first, but the last time can come and we don't know it.

"What's the matter, Catey?"

"Nothing." Then trying to be truthful, "Oh, yes, a solemn thought."

He kissed her then and it disappeared.

When Christie went up to his bedroom he found on the floor outside his door Lily's whiskbroom-holder. Since Cate had not yet given him any present, he supposed it to be her gift.

A whiskbroom-holder! He turned it over and over. The darndest present a man ever got. Last thing in the world I wanted. Made by her own dear hands. The sweet girl. It was velvet covered, and he held it against his cheek. Then he kissed it.

Down the hall, watching, Lily observed the caress and the kiss. After all these years. After all the false leads. And the long golden brown face. She floated down the stairs to her room. She thanked her God she had waited for this one.

"He loves me," she told Mrs. Goforth.

Asleep, dreaming of her son, Mrs. Goforth said, "Yes, dear."

Lily crawled into her bed, dazed with happiness.

XIII

IT WAS almost midnight when Link got back to the kitchen. Cate and Christie had left the cat in, the lamp burning, and had forgotten to stoke the stove. He stirred up the fire, put in more wood, and turned up the lamp. Then he took the big ledger out of the drawer in the kitchen cabinet in which he kept all the Poor Farm papers. He sat down at the table with it and opened it to the page entitled "Inmates—1899." This page had two columns on it, one headed male, the other female. Link let his eye run over the familiar listings.

Male

1. David Pen—87—bedfast
2. Robert Beeson—36?—simple
3. Hoxie Fifield—27—simple
4. John Scripture—73—ran away
5. Valentine Worst?—died cholera morbus
6. Sam Pheasant—colored?—died
7. James Abel—57—digger
8. Neddy Oates—62—drunkard
9. John Manlief—apathies
10. Doss Whitt—48—peeper
11. Fessler Creagan—9 mos.—born poor house
12. Earnest Creagan—14
13. Dexter Bemis—15—orphan
14. Hiram Webster—30—picked up by Jennings Co. Sheriff
15. Josiah Stout—72

Female

1. Mrs. Jesse Mercer—78
2. Nettie Trask—20—died consumption
3. Leathy Wade—Mrs?—69
4. Lily Bias—72—man crazy
5. Baby Trask—3 wks.—died
6. Mary Abel—45—digger
7. Nory Tate—18—orphan
8. Baby Tate—born poor house
9. Icey Creagan—12—simple
10. Airey Creagan—12
11. Mag Creagan—32—hired girl 1.50 per week
12. Mary Hesse—age?—bedfast

Under Stout's name Link wrote: "16. Marvin Dilk—74." After "Baby Tate" he wrote "Died stomach complaint." Then he put the ledger back in the drawer, picked up the tom and carried him to the door. On a sudden impulse he walked outside, the cat still in his arms. He went up the pathway toward the burying-ground, then turned about so that he could see the house. Except for the light in the kitchen the windows were all dark, the building black and heavy against the snow. Overhead the stars blazed bright and sharp as swords; the snow-covered hills rolled away toward an infinitely distant horizon; there were no sounds, even the cedars were silent for a change, the air dead still and freezing. He buried his chin in the cat's warm dense fur. He thought, I could be standing outside a monastery in Tibet, or a farmhouse in Sweden or a palace in Russia; be a priest, or a Swedish farmer or a driver waiting on a feasting duke and no more surprised than finding myself here outside this Poor House —its Superintendent.

He went back toward the house, the cat still in his arms. At the door he put him down, then seeing the cat sitting gingerly on three feet, one foot pitifully lifted above the snow he picked him up again. He dropped him down by the stove. "This being Christmas night," he said, "we'll chance it."

Then he blew out the lamp and felt his way in the darkness toward his and Lib's room.

XIV

THEY kept Christmas well at Stony Creek. They had a Christmas tree garlanded with ropes of popcorn and cranberries, a Christmas table laden with every kind of holiday food, and two dozen friends and relatives to eat the food and admire the tree. In the midst of all this celebrating Uncle Wes forgot, for a couple of days, that he was a widower; and though Sylvy never forgot that she was unmarried, and that not from choice, she was too busy during the Christmas season to think much about it. Both she and Uncle Wes had expected Christie for the holidays and both were disappointed that he had chosen to go to Rock County; but they refrained from speaking of their disappointment. Uncle Wes even pretended indifference and relief.

"We can be thankful that that traveling salesman cousin of yours has got an itchy foot," he had said, "and will be out on the road Christmas week persuading some poor ignorant farmer to gamble his life's savings away on insurance. We'll have a full house without him and his fool ideas."

Sylvy was not deceived by her father's manner nor about his purpose. He knew very well that she was in love with Christie and tried whenever he could to spare her feelings. She herself, out of pride, and for her father's sake, struggled to keep her feelings about Christie hidden. Not that she was ashamed of them, but she knew the general feeling of pity for a woman in love with a man who doesn't love her—particularly when that woman is five years older than the man and his cousin. After Christie had left she had kept herself perpetually busy; pickling, preserving, drying fruit, canning fruit. She had taken up all the carpets, cleaned them and put them down again over fresh straw. She had gone to church every Sunday and before church had taught a Sunday School class. In the evenings, Sundays or weekdays, she had played hymns for her father. And in her spare time she had made herself a number of unneeded dresses of the kind Christie had liked and praised; clear soft colors embellished with petal-shaped flounces and flowerlike overdrapes. She knew very well what she was doing when she wore these dresses—reliving the hours of Christie's admiration and love. For though the time of his loving had been so short, she had never doubted that it had been real.

She would stand in front of the hall mirror, wearing a dress the green of a dead-ripe Summer Sweeting, a green shot through with yellowness and transparency, not seeing herself, how warm her colors were against those fruity shades; not even seeing what, before Christie's time, had been her first concern in any mirror, her damaged lip; not seeing Christie, either. In those minutes before the mirror she was given over to sensations at once more general and more specific than those of sight. Unseeing, before the mirror, she lived in the eternal moment—not of Christie's loving, but of his love.

She did not berate herself for that love or that loving, as she would have expected herself, before the fact, to do. They seemed to her now, those hours with Christie, an unexpected bounty. She was grateful for them in a religious way. She thanked God that she had been permitted so complete an expression of her deepest feelings. Deepest and best, she was sure; so that since that summer night six months ago she had experienced a union with the world and its inhabitants beyond anything she had known before. And though Christie's falling in love with the Conboy girl—there was no doubt that he had—and his continued absence and infrequent letters made her unhappy, they did not make her wish that she did not love him. For love expended, one did not have to receive a return; as if love were a mortgage clapped onto the loved one and paying interest at an approved rate. Love expended, whether there were any returns or not, increased, within the loving heart, the store of love available; and while she had often, before loving Christie, felt empty and bereft, separated from other women, now because her life was centered in Christie, because she desired his happiness and well-being more than her own, she was attached to every other loving being in Stony Creek.

On the evening of December thirtieth Sylvy and her father were in front of the sitting-room fire. Both had had their fill of holiday food and holiday frills. They were filled with a revulsion for tinsel, ribbons, wrapping-paper, useless gifts, and sentimental palaver about how good it was to see Cousin Bessie, when they were both going to spend the rest of the year trying to avoid Cousin Bessie. Their teeth were on edge with peanut brittle and black walnut panocha, and Uncle Wes had taken the last half dozen popcorn balls out to the hogs. They had kept the two or three oranges that were left, but they had no real stomach either for their tropical look or exotic smell. Sylvy had dismantled the Christmas tree with zest and Uncle Wes had carried it out to the wood-pile with pleasure. There was a little piney fragrance left in the room; but that blended with the smell of the pine chunks they were burning and spoke to them of winter rather than Christmas. There was still turkey in the house but those marble slices had begun to taste like pasteboard to them both. "Just as lief eat a slab of boiled shirt," Uncle Wes had said, "as another slice of turkey."

Sylvy felt the same way. They had had sausage cakes and fried potatoes (peppered to a fare-ye-well) for supper. No dessert of any kind. Uncle Wes, who ordinarily could eat a crockful of cookies and top it off with half a jellyroll, bespoke his pleasure at this arrangement.

"In my opinion the world has been steadily going downhill since the discovery of sugar," he said. "If you want to make a sensible New Year's resolve, Sylvy, I advise you to resolve to cut down on the use of sugar in your cooking."

Sylvy had smiled tolerantly. By day after tomorrow, at the latest, her father would come sniffing into the kitchen at mid-morning, open the oven door and say, "Seemed I caught a whiff of something baking from out at the barn. Kind of smelled like a fruit pie of some kind—from out there." And knowing her father, it would be a fruit pie.

But now they had both had their fill of fleshpots and easy living.

Uncle Wes was busily rubbing tallow into a pair of boots. Sylvy was cutting designs along the edges of newspapers preparatory to using them for shelf paper. Tomorrow she would clean the pantry and reline the shelves. Outside it was snowing. As if the world, too, had had its fill of complexities and luxury and was trying to clean and scour and simplify. The calendar itself appeared to be moving away from redundancies; first month for twelfth, first day for thirty-first and a tidy 1900 for the crowded 1899.

Into this atmosphere of spareness (Uncle Wes, Sylvy, weather and calendar, like-minded about fol-de-rols) Christie, powdered with snow and happy with the completeness of his surprise, stepped exuberantly.

Sylvy stood up, scissors and paper sliding to the floor. "Christie," she whispered, "oh, Christie."

Uncle Wes spoke at once. "How'd you get here, boy?"

"By hook and by crook. By hoss and train. By main force and determination. You didn't think I'd let Christmas go by without seeing you and Cousin Sylvy, did you?"

It was unforced, it was hearty—it was impersonal. Sylvy stepped behind Christie to help him get out of his overcoat. When she came back from hanging it on the halltree her face was composed; she had accepted the fact that Christie's return, whatever its purpose, had no connection with her or last summer. She looked at him, lovingly but calmly. He was heavier than when she had last seen him; his hair was cut in a new way; he had let the beginnings of sideburns grow. But there was the same long-eyed and sidewise looking; the same rather slow smile, as if his mouth followed exactly the development in his mind of the humor of a situation. And there was the same olive smoothness of cheek and hands. And oh, olive smoothness elsewhere. She turned away for a second to attend the fire. Here is the only one I could ever call husband, she thought, and now all that is settled. I know it, and I know it isn't to be, so I needn't think about it and suffer about it any longer.

When she faced the room again, Christie said, "Cousin Sylvy, how have you been?"

She answered quietly, "I've been well, Christie."

The matter-of-factness of her reply, without any banter, appeared to give Christie pause. He seemed not to know how to go on from there and picked up a boot from the floor beside Uncle Wes and offered to help with the greasing.

"You're a little late, Christie. I finished that before you arrived. Both done now," he said and put the two boots beside the hearth. "Pull up a chair and warm yourself. How's it out? Pretty cold?"

Christie sat in his old favorite, a low rocker, with his legs extended toward the fire. "No, it's mild. Snow's just barely sticking."

"How's business?" Uncle Wes continued. "You been swindling as many people as you figured on?"

Christie laughed, head back and smooth jut of Adam's apple rising and falling. Sylvy, still standing, leaning against the fireplace, smiled down on him, happy in his happiness.

"It's good to be home," Christie said, "no more pretense, recognized for what I am."

After a few minutes of insurance talk Uncle Wes picked up his boots and rose. "Insurance is like train robbery. A little of it goes a long ways. I'll wish you both good night and we'll hear the rest of the story in the morning."

Sylvy understood completely the purpose of her father's departure and feared that Christie did, too. She was very near Christie, within touching distance, but the inches that separated them made no difference one way or another. She could no more touch him than if he were as far away as the North Pole; and in another sense she had no need to touch him at all, because she still lived and would forever live within the eternity of that moment of their complete touching. It was a very contradictory matter, one she was far from understanding; and she dismissed the complexity of her thoughts about touching to fully enjoy the pleasures possible to her at that minute—in seeing Christie and listening to his voice: here in the very room where, since last August, she had a thousand times imagined his being.

"Did you have a nice Christmas, Christie?"

He looked up and something like embarrassment flickered across his face. "I was down in Rock County for Christmas, you know."

"At Cate's?"

That word, from her, appeared to release some spontaneity in him. He had spoken of "being at home" with her and Uncle Wes, but it was apparent to Sylvy that only in speaking of Cate did he truly come home. He reached a hand toward the fire, opened and closed it, and it was Cate, not warmth, Sylvy saw him reaching for and fondling.

"Well, I was at Cate's father's. And not even at his place, in a way, since his home is the county Poor Farm."

"But you went down to see Cate?"

"Yes." He laughed. "But not to see the Poor Farm, certainly. My God, Sylvy, you can't imagine a place like that. Except for a man like Link Conboy it could be a hell on earth."

"You liked Mr. Conboy?"

"Yes. You know, Sylvy, sometimes I had the funny feeling that I'd gone down there for the purpose of seeing him, not Cate." When Sylvy didn't reply, he went on. "People get the wrong idea about Cate, people who don't know her very well."

"How?" Sylvy asked.

"She seems contradictory, stand-offish, blow hot, blow cold. Well, she *is*. But it can all go, it all does go when she's with somebody she—trusts, I guess, is the right word. You don't know how sweet she is, then. How funny she can be. She lifts that bright head of hers like a little banty and says the most comical things. All those old women out at The Farm love her to death, and she'll work herself to the bone for them. I never heard her say a hard word about anyone, but she's hard on herself. Too hard. That's her main trouble, poor darling."

He stopped suddenly, a naked look in his eye. He had said more than he intended—for her sake, Sylvy understood.

She said, "You love Cate?"

"Yes. Yes, I do, if I know what love is." He begged her forgiveness with that. And she was happy seeing that his feeling for Cate was complete only in speaking to her of it.

"Yes," he repeated, "I love Catey."

Those words—no new knowledge in them, and repeating only what she had asked for—rested suddenly like weights on her eyes and shoulders and mouth. She felt it impossible to remain any longer talking. "I must go to bed," she said.

"Not yet," Christie exclaimed. "You can't go to bed until I've given you your present. Sit down while I get it."

He pushed her down into the rocking-chair he had vacated,

went out to the hall and returned with a large package wrapped uncertainly in holly paper and tied with red ribbon already slipping out of its haphazard bows and rosettes. He stood watching her as she untied it. "I tried to find you something useful."

It *was* useful, she supposed, though it was an object *she* never used: a scarf or shawl, soft, delicately woven, with an intricately knotted fringe. Brown, too, a color she never wore. But she put it around her shoulders and said, "Thank you, Christie. This is warm and lovely."

"Do you really like it? I wasn't sure. I wanted to find something you'd use, no trinket."

A sudden impulse made her ask, "What did you get Cate?" She was sorry for the question the minute it was out. It was nothing she had any right to ask and the answer was sure to hurt her.

"A locket."

Without being told she knew the shape of it: a heart. She rocked listlessly for a few seconds, then got up.

"Can I light your lamp for you, Sylvy?" Christie moved ahead of her toward the table at the foot of the stairs and its array of bedroom lamps. But before he reached the table Sylvy saw him glance at the big mirror which had so often in the summer held the two of them, glance, and turn back. "I expect you'd rather do it yourself," he said.

It was a very small thing, a negative thing, but it comforted her. As she went up the stairs, carrying her lighted lamp, she told herself, He remembers, oh, he remembers.

4

Toward the close of the last day of the year Link began a restless walking about the house. He opened doors and peered into rooms without entering them; took down books and flipped pages without reading a word; wandered out to the kitchen and pieced on shreds of this and that without being hungry or having any idea what he had eaten ten minutes later. Finally he settled himself somewhat by mending a skillet of Mag's, which had long suffered from a wobbly handle. That done, he took up his stance at the sitting-room window which looked out toward The Junction.

Lib, who knew exactly what ailed him, and had let him pace, fidget, nibble, and mend, now let him stare without saying a word. At last he came to her where she sat sewing carpet rags by the stove. "I never had any notion it would be like this."

"What'd be like what?" Lib asked. If she, as Cate was always telling her, began her stories too far back, Link started his too late. His stories were nothing but the endings. "They lived happily ever after." Who? Where? Why? When? All this had to be pried out of Link, word at a time.

"The last day of the nineteenth century."

"How'd you think it would be?" she asked.

"I don't know," he admitted and Lib sighed. Then suggested, "Sad?" A conversation with Link was occasionally no more than Link's repetition of words suggested by her. It had the sound of a conversation, she supposed, to an outsider; but she herself wasn't fooled.

But he was not content to repeat this afternoon. "Not sad," he said, contradicting flatly.

"Well, what then?"

"Empty," he said.

"That's Dandie's being gone—more than the New Year."

She watched Link chafe a wrist, then, stopping that, smooth down an eyebrow: was it already developing, that eyebrow, some old-man bushiness?

"I had a notion I might drive by The Junction. Just see how they're making out."

Drive by, she thought, smiling into her sewing. As if that fooled her for a minute, that acting as if the visit to Dandie would be no more than a side issue tacked onto some larger more important trip elsewhere. "You haven't forgotten Dandie's note have you, Link?" she asked.

She hadn't, certainly. It was the first thing she had seen when she woke the morning after Christmas—stuck under the door, a white blur in the early gray light. (The morning before Em's note had been under her pillow. Were their children giving up speech for writing? And when would Cate's note arrive?) Link had climbed reluctantly out of bed and had begun, standing there goose-pimpled in the cold, to read it to her. "This is to let you know"—no bothering with Dear Folks—"that Nory and I have gone to Carrolton to get married. There is no use whatever in your—" But she hadn't been able to endure Link's slow reading, word by word, as if the note were on the same level of importance as a seed catalogue, and had thrown back the warm covers and gone to read by his side. She had reached the final sentence, "All we ask now is the great kindness of being left alone," before Link was half finished with the page.

" 'The great kindness of being left alone,' " she had repeated angrily, flinging herself about the icy room. "All we ask is to be left alone! It will be a pleasure, him and that trashy girl. We take that girl in, nurse her, wait on her hand and foot, bury her baby. And what are her thanks? She runs off with our son. The fourth or fifth, for all we know, she's run off with. Oh, we'll leave them alone all right. That's a gift they can have free for the asking."

Now she put down her carpet rags. "Link, haven't you got any pride? Go running where you're not wanted?"

Link said, "I can't bear to think of them living there in that little room back of Korby's, short on rations for all we know. Unless Korby's paying them a lot more than I think he is, they're more than likely short on everything."

Lib didn't try to hold back her shrug of scorn, or the sound of scorn that contracted her throat. "Short on rations! You misjudge your boy, Link. Dandie's not one to not look out for number one. You'll go there and have the door shut in your face for your pains. Or meet Korby and have another run-in with him."

She saw Link's purpose harden and fix with those words. "What Dandie does when he sees me is *his* responsibility not mine," he said. "It's mine to go see the boy. And as to Korby, why, I owe the man my thanks, don't I? He's given the boy a job and a roof over his head when I couldn't. Not one to suit him anyway. I hope I do see Korby. I'd like to thank him."

Lib got up, letting the ball of carpet rags roll unheeded from her lap. "Link, you old fool. You old softie!"

Link paid no attention to that. "Come on with me," he urged. "For the sake of the ride, if nothing else. I'll do the talking and visiting, if you don't want to see them."

But she was not to be budged. "You go on if you want to, but not me. I'll wait till I'm asked. And I'm not sure I'll go then."

The evening and the road were perfect for the trip. I love winter, Link told himself. But he knew winter was only one name for what he loved. What he really loved was weather, any kind, all four of the seasons and the whole face of the earth, wild or cultivated. His brother Fred had answered one of his letters saying, "Dear Link: Your weather report rec'd. We'd be glad to have some news of you and the family too if you can get around to it."

Link had to admit that Fred was right: the news of rain and drought, clouds and crops came first; then, time and paper holding out, the human news. He sometimes wondered if there was a law whereby those who loved nature were to be denied any close relationship with their fellow men. If God had decreed, "Let there be a fair division: love of earth, or love of human beings; but not both."

If a man loved snow, did some of its coldness enter his nature? If he responded to the sound of rain, did human voices come to mean less to him? Lib, for instance, was no nature-lover. Views and panoramas and sunsets made her impatient. She let her potted plants die. She threw away the curious stones and bright leaves he brought her, as soon as his back was turned. And as a result, if it was a result, she was close to people: close in love or hate, but close. She did not stand apart, as he did, and she could've talked to Dandie as he would never be able to.

Link thought that The Junction in winter, particularly after a fresh snowfall, was a pretty little town; and that it was pretty again at the height of summer, embowered in its maples and elms and sweetened with its flowering stock and honeysuckle. But at other seasons, awash with mud, desolate with flying dust and leaves, it was hard to understand how man, in his thousands of years on earth, hadn't been able to figure out something better in the way of a habitation than these ugly, ramshackle collections of little wooden buildings called towns. The fifteen hundred people of The Junction lived in about two hundred houses: forlorn little one-story wooden boxes, for the most part, though there were a few forlorn big two-story boxes and a few built of brick. Korby's house was both. Link passed it, noticing with unusual interest its gaunt maples, its walks swept clean of snow and its overly-fancy, overly-high wrought-iron fence. The place was lit up tonight; spokes of yellow light rayed out across the snow from almost all the downstairs windows.

He had always taken for granted that when the time came, he would help Dandie "establish a home" and find his "life work." Then in a flash, while he was involved with his own affairs and still thinking of Dandie as a boy, Dandie had married, had established a home without his help and found himself work: that is, if the back room at Korby's store could be called a "home," and if being clerk or handy man for Korby could be called "work." Dandie had begun to live without any help from him: Korby was the man who had given him help and Link could not escape feeling some resentment. Not, he thought, because Korby had usurped his own place with Dandie; but simply because Korby was the person he was.

The Junction was a two-street town with the two main streets meeting to form what the residents called The Flat-Iron. Korby's store, located at the point of this triangle, was The Flat-Iron Building; the store had two departments, the one facing on Main Street being given over to "General Merchandise," while the section facing on Indianapolis Street bore the sign "Furniture and Undertaking." Link tied his horse to the rack in front of the

Furniture and Undertaking section and walked around to the back of the store. A light shone there from behind the sagging red calico which curtained the glass in the door and he knocked twice, hesitantly. A week ago he would have walked without knocking into Dandie's room and said, Go here, go there, do this, do that. How had the fact of Dandie's marriage altered all this?

Dandie's voice, cordial and strong, called, "Come in," and before Link could turn the knob Dandie himself swung the door open. He was dressed in his best, his hair damp from recent combing, and his face lit up in the way which at home had announced: "Dandie's going on a tear." You could not ask, Link thought, for a better picture of a happy and triumphant bridegroom. He stood, not saying anything, waiting for Dandie to speak, Lib's words and the words of Dandie's note in his mind, in spite of his loving intention.

"Why, Father," Dandie exclaimed, not attempting to hide his surprise at seeing him there. Then as Link continued to stand on the doorstep, he took his arm. "Come in, come in. We can't heat the whole outdoors, you know."

Link stamped the snow from his feet and stepped into the warm, dirty, half-furnished room. He felt ashamed of the room for his son's sake and tried not to look at it. But Dandie didn't permit him to ignore it.

"This," he said, "is the nastiest, dirtiest little hole in Rock County, I reckon." He gave the sagging bed which occupied a good quarter of the room's space a slap. "Up hill and down dale. After a night in that you feel like the floor'd be a treat. Take your choice of chairs. One's got half its bottom out and the other's minus half a rocker. Nothing wrong with the table that a wad of paper in the right spot won't remedy though." He put a hand on the battered, begrimed center table and rocked it back and forth to show what it needed. "But the stove," he licked his finger and ran it, hissing along the pipe, "draws like hell's fire. Damnedest hottest little cubby-hole in Rock County, wouldn't you say?" he asked, smiling with pride.

Link opened his mouth to reply but before he could say a word Dandie, treading about the faded rag carpet like Jay Gould in his mansion, pointed to the floor. "Look at that," he said.

Link looked. The rag carpet was every now and then lifted off the floor—as if beneath it some hard breathing animal had taken up residence.

"Wind," Dandie said, "and no weather stripping. Some stove," he boasted, "to counteract that." He threw another oak chunk in the already red-hot heater.

"You'll burn the place up," Link warned.

"Not much of a loss, eh?" Dandie asked. "But wait. We've been here four days, only. Wait till we dress the place up. Look at this." He brought out from under the bed in one quick movement a paper-wrapped parcel. "Got it on tick from Korby." He unwrapped a bolt of soft red silk. "That'll tone things up, don't you think?"

"What's it for?" Link asked.

"Curtains," Dandie said. "Coverlid. Can't *sleep* on the damn bed. 'Bout as well make it *look* good." He fondled the material. "Good goods!" he pronounced. "Best Korby had in stock."

"You working for Korby, Dandie?"

Dandie nodded.

"Clerking?"

"To begin with."

"Which side?"

"General Merchandise. But Furniture and Undertaking's where I'm headed."

"Mr. Korby," Link began, "isn't—"

Dandie rose up from sliding his package back under the bed and finished the sentence. "Korby ain't worth a damn by lots of cussing."

"I wouldn't go so far as to say that."

Dandie sat down on the center table and by shifting his weight rocked back and forth on the uneven legs.

"Pop," he said, "you wouldn't recognize the devil if he put his hoof in your hand."

"Korby's no devil, but he's shifty. I had a run-in or two with him before I went out to The Farm. And he's the last man I'd pick for any of my children to get mixed up with."

"Don't worry about me. I know beans when the bag's open. Don't you want to see Nory?"

"Is she here?"

"Is she here?" Dandie exclaimed. "Do you think I'm spending

[182]

my honeymoon alone? She's out in the kitchen washing and dressing for the party."

"Party?" Link asked. "You two bound for a party?"

"Korby's," Dandie said. "New Year's supper. Champagne at midnight."

"Champagne," Link repeated, both disbelieving and disapproving.

"Maybe not champagne. But I reckon there'll be stagger juice of some kind. Korby said he was going whole hog on this."

Link was surprised that Dandie had been invited to Korby's party. After all, whatever you thought of Korby, he was not only the richest man in the county, but a political power as well, a member of the board of commissioners, and would sooner or later, everyone said, be a candidate for the state legislature. He was an oddity, he was "Kissing Korby," but his queerness seemed to please people, to reconcile them to his power and money. And he could invite anyone he wanted to his parties, and Link didn't know anyone who would refuse.

Dandie jumped off the table. "Wait till you see Nory! I bought her a new dress in Madison. She's prettier than a May-apple in it." At the kitchen door he turned about. "Explain to me," he said, "men who pick ugly wives. Are they mad at themselves?"

Link changed from the chair with half a bottom to the chair with half a rocker while Dandie was gone; and got out of that when he and Nory entered. Nory was carrying a little coal black kitten.

Dandie took it from her. "Stop nursing that cat," he said, "and let Papa see your dress."

Link was taken aback by this abruptness; but perhaps it was a good thing. It swung their attention away from the fact that this was the first time he'd seen Nory since she'd run away from the Poor House with his son; the first time he'd seen her, actually, since he stood across the grave from her, her dead baby between them.

Dandie brushed some cat hairs from the sleeve of Nory's dress. Nory looked up hesitantly and asked, "Do you like it, Father Conboy?"

Link swallowed. Father Conboy! But what did he expect? He wasn't Superintendent Conboy speaking to one of the folks now.

"Well," Dandie said, "have you got an eye for beauty or haven't you?"

"I have," Link said, "I have. Trouble with me is, I've got a one-track mind. I can't look and speak at the same time."

The dress was of wool, creamy and flecked with minute splashes of gold and green. Nory was made on a less spectacular plan than Lib or Cate: rounder, softer, plumper. She had never been half-boy, he reckoned, at ten and eleven, as Cate had been. Nory had been born a little woman, round brown eyes and sweet pink mouth, from the first. There was in Lib and Cate some defiance, some resistance, so that they maybe appealed to men who needed a woman as a test, as a proof of strength. In loving Nory, you wouldn't be proving anything to yourself; there'd be no self-love in turning to her, not needing to be won.

Dandie began pushing the hairpins more firmly into the shining loops of his wife's hair. "In Carrolton," he said, "I had some serious second thoughts. Shall I marry this woman, I asked myself? Ain't she too pretty, I asked myself, for a serious man to get tied to? Won't I want to be hanging around the house all the time instead of out making my million?"

Link looked at Nory. Lib couldn't stand public love-talk of this kind, but Dandie had always been a talker and now, being a lover, he was naturally combining the two and Nory didn't seem to take either amiss.

Dandie put both arms about her. "I'm her red-hot Armstrong heater," he said.

Well, Link thought, this has gone about far enough. "That dress," he said, "looks pretty light for winter."

Dandie lifted a fold of it. "Goods don't have to be dark to be warm. Feel it. Thick as a horse blanket."

Proud as a dog with two tails, Link saw, taking the proffered fold between thumb and forefinger. He was holding it thus, testing the weave and the weight, when Korby walked in, not troubling to knock. Surprised, Link held onto the cloth for a second. I suppose he thinks it's his own place, he decided, but if I was Dandie I'd insist on a little privacy.

If Dandie minded, he didn't show it. "Come in, Odis," he said, as if Korby weren't already half across the room. Odis: Link

[184]

couldn't remember ever hearing Korby called that, even by Mrs. Korby.

Korby progressed toward the stove in a series of bounces, shedding snow as he came. "Howdy, all," he said. "Nory, you're pretty enough to eat. I'd relish you in a saucer with a little cream. Wouldn't need any sugar. Well, Link, you over to see how I'm treating the young folks? Come to see if they're living in the style they've been accustomed to? Little run down here, I admit. Kind of gaumed up at the present. But Dandie and Nory ain't fine-haired, I tell myself. They ain't biggity. After Poor House fare this'll be maybe a cut above what they're used to, but they're smart, they'll rise to it, I tell myself, eh, Dandie, boy?"

Link felt anger and shame. Such plans as he'd had for Dandie when he was born—everything better than he'd ever known, and then in a twinkle the boy'd gone, set up for himself in this rat hole, and even that due to the help of another. And Korby there saying to himself, "Old-Wind-and-No-Weather Conboy." Got plans for everybody: going to set up the paupers as pig-fanciers, will save the county money on coffins, and eat the same grub as the simple. Lord Jesus Conboy! Oh, yes, he'd heard that. Lord Jesus Conboy of Conboy Castle; but when your son marries, he marries trash, and when he sets up housekeeping it's Korby he turns to.

"I hear you wheedled a sow out of old man Hummel on Christmas Eve, Link," Korby went on. "Nice evening to—"

Link interrupted him. "There wasn't any wheedling."

"No need cutting me off shorter than pie crust, Link. I was aiming to congratulate you. Hummel's tighter than the bark on a tree. Didn't know you could pry him loose from a nickel, let alone a two-hundred-pound sow. Ask me over the day you butcher."

"We won't be butchering that hog."

"Brag's a good hog," Korby started, but before he could finish Link took hold of his shoulder.

"You got the wrong sow by the ear this time, Korby. I've had enough of this. Get out and let us alone. I came here to talk to my son, not to argue with you."

"Get out?" Korby tried to shrug loose. "Whose place do you think you're in?"

"My son's," Link said, shoving Korby along toward the door.

Korby, resisting, was pulling the flimsy rag rug into heavy folds about his feet. "Conboy, you got poor house manners. You ain't dealing with paupers now."

Dandie wrenched Link's arm from Korby's shoulder. "Odis," he said, "let's go." He had snatched up his and Nory's coats from their pegs at the foot of the bed.

Korby looked at Link. "There's nothing to keep us, I guess."

"Not a thing," Dandie agreed.

At the door he turned back to Link. "Can I trust you to turn out the lights and bank the fire?" he asked.

11

"DID YOU make a vow never to take off Christie's locket?" Em asked.

Em, in bed, was watching Cate get ready for the New Year's party at the Thompsons'. It was going to be a fashionable party, late. Ferris wasn't even coming for Cate until ten. Cate, in her shimmy, was washing her neck and lifting the locket out of the way with one hand while she scrubbed with the other.

"No," Cate answered, "of course not. That would be silly."

"Why?"

"I might *have* to take it off sometime."

"Why would you *have* to?"

"I might get quinsy and my neck swell so that if I didn't take it off I'd die."

"Well, you could die for love then."

"No sense to that." Cate was drying her face and neck.

"Is that what you want to be?"

"Is what what I want to be?" Cate asked, taking a corset-cover and petticoat from her underwear drawer.

"Sensible?"

Cate put her arms into the embroidered ribbon-laced corset-cover, very sweet smelling because of the bar of Pears' Soap she kept in the drawer with her underwear.

"Yes," she said, "it is. Reason and sense are what separate us from the animals."

"Doss Whitt says animals are better than humans in lots of ways."

Cate tied the blue ribbon that ran through the insertion of her corset-cover in a firm bow knot. "You would be a lot better off, let me tell you, Emma J. Conboy, if you didn't talk so much to that Doss Whitt. He's the next thing to a criminal and you know it. He's here on good behavior only."

"Why is it criminal to want to look at people? Doss says God wouldn't have given him eyes if He didn't expect him to use them."

Cate stepped into her petticoat and pulled it up neatly over the shorter shimmy. "God doesn't expect us to use our eyes looking at people who haven't got any clothes on. And who don't want to be looked at. That's the same as robbing."

"What does Doss rob them of?" Em asked.

Cate buttoned her petticoat and put on the combing jacket Indiana Rose Cavanaugh had sent her for Christmas, before answering. Then she said, "He robs them of their modesty."

"Their modesty," Em said doubtfully. "Doss never said anything about that. What would he want that for?"

Cate didn't stop brushing her hair. "Don't ask me. I'm no robber."

"You make *him* a robber though."

Cate turned away from the mirror to face Em. "I never said two words to Doss Whitt in my life. I don't make him a robber."

"Yes, you do. You pull down the blinds all the time so Doss can't look in and Doss says that drives him crazy."

"You're the one who's crazy, Em Conboy. Look, do you think no one ought to have any money just because it makes some people want to steal? Do you?"

This was too much for Em. Silently she watched Cate settle the rhinestone comb in her hair. Then she said, "I miss Dandie and Nory." Cate without answering took off the combing jacket and put on her dress. "Cate," Em asked, "why do people sleep together after they're married?"

Cate was busily buttoning. "Because they're usually poor and don't have enough money to buy two beds," she answered shortly.

"Oh."

Cate pulled Christie's locket out from under her blouse so that it could be seen. "After they get enough money," Em objected, "and aren't poor they still go on doing it."

"By that time they're in the habit."

"Do they look at each other when they're undressing?"

Cate whirled away from the mirror and stamped over to Em's bed. "Nice girls don't think about such things."

Em felt humble. "What do they think about?" she asked.

"They think about helping other people. And good books. And how to be good housekeepers. And the beauties of nature. And religion."

Em gazed up at Cate who looked, she thought, very grown-up and fashionable in her new dress. "Do they?" she asked, though she was already full of belief.

"Oh, Em," Cate cried distractedly, "they try to. Or at least they ought to try to."

Cate went out to the sitting-room to wait for Ferris, in an uplifted mood. The change from one year to the next always impressed her, and this, being a change not only from one year to another year, but from one century to another, made her feel unusually solemn. She was filled with resolves to be thoughtful and loving, particularly toward her mother. Now, seeing that her mother had waited up to tell her good-by, a very unusual thing, she paused in the doorway and emotion making her voice husky cried, "Oh, Mama."

"Cate, are you catching cold?" Lib asked unaware of the emotion.

Waiting up for her, asking about her health! It was all she had ever dreamed. "No, Mama, I haven't the least cold."

Lib stood with her back to the fire, skirts well hoisted.

"Aren't you too warm, Mama?"

Lib lifted her skirts another inch. "It's peculiar how things repeat themselves. My mother was always throwing open windows in zero weather and saying, 'How balmy,' while I froze to death. I had a little spell of comfort before you got big enough to open windows, but now it's the old story all over again. 'Aren't you too warm, Mama?'"

"Am I like Grandma?" Cate asked, always entranced with remembering.

"I think so. I hope and pray so, for there's no use denying there's bad blood elsewhere in the family."

Cate's heart began to harden. The Conboy blood! She was filled with mulish disbelief. But it was not the Conboy blood at all.

"My mother's two sisters, her only sisters, were wild." Lib sank into a chair and rocked for a minute as if debating how much to tell. "They had to be married," she finished starkly.

"Aunt Soph?" Cate asked. "Aunt Myrtle?" She could not think of these old women as girls, let alone—bad girls. Aunt Soph, the massive white-haired mother and grandmother. Aunt Myrt, the frail, religious widow of a preacher.

"They were loose," Lib said. "It had as well be admitted. Aunt Soph fell in love with this scamp from nobody knows where. Aunt Soph's folks told her she couldn't marry him. When she heard that, she said, 'The time will come when you'll beg Leonard Arbuckle to marry me.' That time came all right and very soon."

"Uncle Len?" Cate asked. "Was this Uncle Len?"

Uncle Len was the good-natured, portly owner of a livery-stable, a pillar of church and community.

"Uncle Len's turned out all right. But he didn't start right. Aunt Soph's baby was born four months after she was married. Aunt Myrt's was born three months before she got married."

Cate felt stunned. "But Aunt Myrt was married to a preacher. Uncle Sloan."

"Uncle Sloan got his religion later," Lib said grimly. "But there wasn't any excuse in the world for Aunt Myrtle's behavior. She was just weak and loose and dirty."

Cate folded herself up on to the footstool in front of the fire.

Lib leaned forward. "My mother told *me*. She said, 'Lib, there's weak, bad blood in the family. It's in us too, but we don't have to give in to it.' And I didn't. And you don't have to either, Cate. But it's there and we've got to be on our guard."

Lib reached down and put a hand on Cate's shoulder. It was an unusual gesture. With her other hand she smoothed Cate's curls away from her face; "roaching your hair back," Lib called it. Her touch was wonderfully nervous and vital, no dead weight of motherly duty and maternal unction and Cate trembled beneath it.

"Dandie's wild," her mother continued. "Em's a good girl but she's got a queer turn. It's you we're looking to, Cate. We're banking on you. Our first-born daughter."

Cate began to cry, from happiness, not sorrow. It was so wonderful to be loved and trusted, to be depended upon. To start the New Year in this way. She lifted her shoulder so that she could touch her mother's hand with her cheek. "Mama, Mama," she said. She wanted to say how much she loved her mother, but that seemed so bald-faced. "Mama, Mama," she cried, "I've always been good, and I promise you I'll never disappoint you. I promise. You can depend on me." She picked up her mother's hand and kissed it, then sat holding it against her cheek and Lib, for a wonder, permitted her to do so. And though she was so happy, feeling indeed as if this were an enchanted moment the tears continued to slide down her cheeks. By the time Ferris came she had stopped crying, though she was still red-eyed and red-nosed when she left for the party.

Lib thought the two had gone for good and had already taken off her corset when Cate came tiptoeing back into the sitting-room. "Mama, I forgot to thank you for waiting up to see me off. It was so wonderful of you."

For a minute Lib thought her daughter was going to kiss her again. But she didn't. She said only, "Happy, Happy New Year, Mama, I love you," and ran out of the room.

III

SINCE she had been waiting up for Link, with no thought whatever of Cate, Lib was surprised by Cate's words. They're self-centered at that age, she thought, believe that everything hinges on them. But even if the talk with Cate had been no part of her plan for that particular evening she was glad for it. You can tell a girl, "Stay out of the woods. . . . Make him keep his hands off you. . . . Have some respect for yourself," and then something wells up in the girl which makes her want to run counter to everything she's been told: if going to the woods and sweet-hearting is dangerous, then that's what she'll give her young man; whatever is riskiest and most forbidden she'll want him to have, as proof of her love. Only it won't be a proof of love to him, but proof of something else, a lot easier come by. I've been too mealy-mouthed with Cate, she thought, and it's high time she was put on her guard, high time she knew about her aunts.

She took the pins from her hair and let it slide across her shoulders. She rubbed her scalp, and seesawed her uncorseted body comfortably backward and forward, and finally unbuttoning and unhooking the fashionable red bombazine, took it off and hung it with some care across the back of the rocker. Lib had long since decided she wasn't pretty but she didn't despise herself for this; what she despised was a woman without any style. She saw women at church and on the streets of The Junction in outfits she wouldn't wear to a dogfight. Your naked looks, your beauty or lack of it is the Lord's affair, she thought. He'd done a good job or He hadn't. You aren't responsible for that. But stylishness is all up to you, and that is how the world judges you. Not the family, of course. They're a part of you, they stand with you, looking outward: rats, curling irons, feather boas, corsets, chatelaine watches, Semper Goo-ve-nay; your family knows you've got all those tools of stylishness and can use them if the occasion calls for it; but to use them at home, why, that'd be like a hunter keeping his gun cocked and over his shoulder while he sat in the kitchen talking to his wife. She switched her heavy hair about, kicked off her shoes, pulled a rocker to the very edge of the fire, and began to worry about Link. What was keeping him?

It was after eleven when he came in. "Link?" she called when she heard him open the kitchen door. She could tell by his voice, before she had seen him, that he was tired and discouraged. She was no husband-coddler. When Link was in health and spirits she expected him not only to look after himself but to defend himself against her onslaughts. He was that big a man, she thought. Protect him? Spare him her belief that he was eternally wrong about some things? Bolster up his pride and ego? Why, Link was the man in this family. He was also, she thought, about half the time wrong-headed, soft-hearted, and as a result, put upon. And she would tell him so. And tell him about his family: shiftless and no account. Except for her he'd be put upon by them, too. But Link himself! He was her idea of what man should be: better than she was (but less practical), smarter (but less shrewd), calmer (but capable of violence). She pitied from the bottom of her heart women with bacon-colored, tame-tabby, big-bellied husbands. A woman who'd got herself a man who wasn't dark and lean had got herself half-a-husband. They were men, she thought contemptuously, if a human being with the label "man" on it was all you wanted. But she wanted more.

She had more, too. And was jealous of him. Women set their caps for Link. Minced and palavered around him. Arched their busts and fluttered their big buttermilk eyelids. And Link claimed not to notice it. "Common courtesy," he said. "Neighborliness." Neighborliness! The neighboring those women had in mind would increase the population mighty fast. If only once Link would admit that he noticed their actions. But he wouldn't. "Just being friendly." Friendliness like that was headed straight for a roll in the nearest hay-mow.

He must not have the look of a completely contented husband —though his looks belied him, then. They were a pair, and she knew it. Their life together made her feel biggity. She could act meechin enough, put on a false Irish humility, but underneath the layers of soft soap was nothing but scorn for those she was fooling. Did they think for a second she would step out of her shoes into theirs? She hated people who were forward at neighborhood sociables, the women who wanted the flashy jobs, the waiting on tables and making announcements. She took the dirty kitchen work and listened with ironic pleasure when she heard the waitresses, in their fancy big-bowed aprons, saying, "Poor Lib! Back there pot-walloping."

Poor Lib! Well, she might be Cinderella for the minute, but at midnight onto whose foot did they think Prince Charming was going to slip the glass slipper?

"Link?" she called again.

He came in, a cup of milk in his hand, and Lib got up and pulled him down into her chair. She put more wood on the fire, drew up one stool for Link's feet and then another for herself.

"What do they mean keeping you out to all hours?" she asked, scanning his tired face. "And didn't they give you anything to eat?"

She could forgive Dandie the wrongs he did anyone else, but when he wronged Link he'd have his mother to deal with.

"They didn't keep me," Link said.

"What then?" Lib asked suspiciously.

Link had finished his milk, and Lib took the glass and put it on the mantel. "They're staying at Korby's?"

"Yes."

"What kind of a place is it?"

"Not good."

"Not good," Lib said impatiently. "I can't see not good. What do you mean by that?"

"Well, dirty," Link said. "drafty, broken-down furniture."

"Is Dandie working for Korby?"

"Yes."

"Yes, yes. What kind of talk is this, Link Conboy? For heaven's sake, don't make me drag everything out of you piecemeal. Were they home? Did you see them? How'd Dandie look? Did he ask about me? What'd that Nory have to say?"

"They were home," Link said. "They looked fine. They were fixing to go to a party."

"A party? Who invited them to a party?"

"Korby."

"Korby!" Lib was astonished. Not that he'd asked Dandie—Dandie was asked everywhere and went everywhere—but Nory: out of the Poor House and over to Korby's in one week. That was quite a jump. "How in the world did Korby come to ask them?"

"I don't know. He didn't say."

"*Say.* Did you see Korby, too?"

"He came to take them over to his place."

"Did you go? Is that what kept you?"

"Korby's more particular who he invites than that."

Lib, from her stool, looked up into Link's face. He looked past her into the fire. "Link," she said, "did you have words with Korby?"

Link moved his eyes slowly from the fire and finally gave her a straight look. "Well," he said, smiling a little, "there was a scarcity of words if anything."

"Oh, Link! Well, go on," she said. "Let's have it."

"I'd of set him outside in the snow if I'd had my way."

"What stopped you?" Lib asked dryly. "Not that little puss-gut himself, surely."

[193]

"No—Dandie."

Lib stood, turned her back to Link and faced the fire. "Link, you harm nobody but yourself this way. Korby's on top here. Face it. He has the say-so. He's a Commissioner. You can't run this place and not be on good terms with him."

"I won't truckle to a man like Korby," Link said.

Lib whirled about. "Truckle! Who's asking you to truckle? Why, I could manage a man like Korby with one hand tied behind my back and never truckle an inch."

"I don't misdoubt, you and Dandie both. But saying one thing and thinking another don't come so easy to me."

"Thinking and saying! What's the connection? Even God don't try to say all He thinks. Are you better than God, Link Conboy?"

"Less sensible anyway," Link said, smiling, "I reckon."

"This is no laughing matter, Link. You weren't content till you got us all here. Determined to break our lives in two to come, no matter what I wanted. I never understood that and I never will. If it was so important to you to come I'd think it would be important to you to stay."

"It is."

"Don't go having fist fights with Korby then."

"I tried to make some amends to Nory and Dandie after they left for the ruckus I stirred up."

Lib felt very skeptical. "What was your idea of amends, Link?"

"I heated a boiler of water, got out the soap and the lye and scoured that place of theirs from roof to ceiling. Working by lamplight, I don't suppose I did a very good job but I thought it'd be a sign to them when they got home that I saw I'd been in the wrong."

"In God's name, Link." She put a hand on his shoulder. "Be a sign to them you thought their place was dirty. Be a sign to Nory her in-laws are going to mix in her affairs. Be a sign to Dandie you got a poor opinion of the best he can provide."

"Find fault, but don't help?" Link asked.

"That's about the size of it."

"I left him ten dollars—all I had."

"It'll be back in the first mail."

Link rubbed his forehead, then let his hand rest over his eyes and Lib saw that with his eyes, which were the livest part of

[194]

Link, shut from sight, how tired his face was, how lined and sorrowful. "Link," she cried, "what's our aim here? Where are we heading?"

Without taking his hand from his eyes Link said, "The Poor Farm, you mean?"

"The whole kit and caboodle. Poor Farm, us two, and the children."

"I came here, Lib, because my life seemed to've taken a wrong turn. It was time I figured to try to make a little amends." He took his hand down from his face. "A man has his own conscience to deal with."

"Amends, amends," Lib said. "That word makes one uneasy coming from you. Your amends so far turns out to be Dandie's marrying a girl like Nory. What'll be for Cate and Em?"

"Something half as good, I hope."

There was no use talking, Lib thought, if that seemed good to Link. "I expect you're famished to death, Link, after all that scrubbing and beating. Could you eat a bite?"

"Yes," Link said, "come to think of it, I could. I'm hollow from hunger as much as anything, I reckon."

"What strikes your fancy?" She went into the hallway and got a discarded jacket of Dandie's, came back and held it before the fire a minute before putting it on.

"Whatever's handy," Link answered.

"Oh, handy," Lib said. "Let's have something good."

When she left the room Link got up, replenished the fire, and cleared a spot on the center table. If he knew Lib, she'd bring them in more than a smidgin. There on the floor was her corset and her scattered hairpins. Across a chair, her dress, What of it? If he didn't like them he could put them away in two seconds. He'd seen too many neat housewives, the whole of their living centered in clean windows, scrubbed floors, and polished furniture. They seemed to live in and for their eyes and their eyes took in nothing but household arrangements. Lib, thank God, didn't center her life in any one organ. She was considerably more than an eye for dust. She was back in what seemed like a minute or two with big slices of fried pink ham, fried eggs, quince honey, hot soda biscuits and coffee.

"The fire was still up in the range," she said. "It wasn't any

[195]

trick." She took off Dandie's coat and sat in her short-sleeved, ruffle-necked shimmy, back to the fire. "I hope none of the folks chance in and find me here half naked."

She was far from half naked; her flounced petticoat came to the floor, her shimmy was hollowed only a little at the throat. But whatever was absent was all to the good. Was there another woman past thirty, he wondered, who, the less she had on, the better she looked?

"I got a pinch or two too much soda in the biscuits," she said, a little self-consciously, as if she might be imagining his thoughts. But she was not refusing biscuits either because of soda or thoughts. Lib was not a woman who takes the pleasure out of eating by saying, "I can't swallow a bite after standing over that hot stove." Lib swallowed many a hearty bite.

"I don't recollect ever eating better biscuits," Link said.

"You're too easy satisfied. You don't put me on my mettle."

Maybe he didn't. Maybe that was one of the things human beings should do for each other, ask each other for his best. Maybe a man sinned through his own good nature, held his family down by asking too little of them. Asked the boys no more than, "Pay your debts." Asked the girls only, "Stay out of trouble."

"Listen, Link."

The clock on the mantelpiece, the one that had replaced the wedding gift, was striking midnight. The new year, the new century. He didn't wish Lib happiness. He was too close to her for that, would've felt as foolish as if he'd whispered to his image in a mirror, "Happy New Year."

"The year's brought some changes," he said when the striking had finished.

"We can look forward to being grandparents now, I reckon," Lib replied in a curious wondering voice.

"Grandparents!" he said. It seemed impossible, too hurried. He and Lib. Those two young folks. They hadn't learned yet to be parents.

"I had a talk with Cate tonight."

"Cate, too?" he asked.

"She'll be married before the year's out."

"Em, thank goodness, don't think of the boys yet."

[196]

He got up, stacked the dishes, brushed the crumbs from the table into his hand and threw them into the fire, then banked the fire. "You about ready for bed?"

Lib leaned forward and blew out the light. The room, even without it, was not dark: the fire still cast its blossom of rosiness upon the floor, and a three-quarter moon, enhanced a thousandfold by the snow, lit the room with a milky radiance. They went together to the window and gazed out into the intricate tracery of the night-time tree shadows which lay across the white drifts. Link shifted Lib's corset, which he had picked up, to his other hand, so that he could draw her close to him. In the new year— the new century—he'd be reasonable as never before. Think twice —and thrice, if need be. The world was not so muddled—nor man—that you couldn't, by exercise of sense and reason all along the line, bring about some kind of ordered goodness. His desire for it was so great, for himself and his children, that without knowing it he had folded Lib to him and was painfully and unreasonably clasping her to him, as if she were as boneless as a leaf —or a cloud.

5

"Well, Link," Lib said, gazing out into the sleet one morning two weeks after New Year's, "I hope you're getting your fill of weather these days."

As near a fill as he'd ever get, he reckoned. If there were five hundred different ways for snow to fall he believed he'd seen in the last ten days at least four hundred and ninety-nine of those ways demonstrated. He loved them all: a lodging snow that had pressed down the trees until you walked under a roof of marble; a wet snow that had clung to the window-panes and shut out half the light; a snow with wind, so that snow-sprays had risen fifteen feet in the air; snow dropping like salt, dry and coarse; a sugaring of snow, fine, delicate granules light on the face as the touch of a hair; a spitting snow, all angry squalls and flurries; a heavy, straight-falling, continuous snow, so that he had come into the house with coat pockets half filled.

Then there had been finally a lull in the storm and the mercury had gone so low that the clocks had stopped and the roofs had sparkled like diamonds, and the western sky at sunset had been hard and gray as a piece of graniteware.

Rain followed this cold snap; then freezing weather had returned so that the fields were mirrors and the trees glass. One day would be prolonged by a twilight that lingered in the snow until midnight, it seemed, while the next day would end abruptly at four, the evening star already visible through a rift in the steel-colored clouds.

After the snow and the hard freezes were over the weather became dependably changeable: blustery and sleeting at one minute and at the next a thaw with the promise of spring in it, harder on everyone than an unrelieved cold snap.

At the end of a day that had set the eaves to dripping old David Pen had died. The next afternoon they buried him in the teeth of a bitter storm of snow and sleet.

Lily Bias, out roaming and dreaming in the thawing weather, came down with the grippe. In bed, she read and re-read a letter from Christie in which he thanked her for the whiskbroom-holder. He was sorry he had not had a chance to thank her before he left, but he would thank her in person on his next trip to The Farm, a visit to which he was already looking forward. The gift was both pretty and useful, he said, a distinct adjunct to his room and more than one person had remarked on it. He hoped she was in good health, as he was himself, and he signed himself, "Faithfully yours, Christian J. Fraser."
That "faithfully yours" put her back on her feet. "Faithful unto death," was the way she read it. She would reward his faith by being up and out of this room, which Lodema Goforth's presence sullied, when he arrived.

Lodema Goforth, bedeviled by the bad weather, by her son's failure to come for her at Christmas, and by Mag's and Leathy Wade's taunts, took to deliberate lying about him. Up to this time she had confined herself to stretching the truth. Now she branched out, left the truth far behind her. Herschel, she told the women in the kitchen, was in California; he had struck gold. He had written saying, Should he come for her?
"I wrote him by all means, stay. Develop your gold mine first, I advised him. Gold won't wait, I said, and I will."
Mag, for a change, had nothing whatever to say to this.

Hoxie Fifield—recovered from his triple affliction of clap, turpentine, and exposure—was set to work by Link at the carpet loom: work he could do well and which kept him indoors while he was still a little feverish.

James Abel didn't let many kinds of weather keep him from digging, but during January he was often housebound. He tried to put the time to good use by making a convert of Nigger Bob. In past times, he had had several converts, but now, through death or instability of purpose, or simple laziness, he had lost them all. He did not consider the present inmates a very promising lot for his purposes: those with sufficient understanding to appreciate what he was attempting to do hadn't the strength for digging; those capable of digging had closed minds. The colored man was his one real hope.

He came into the men's sitting-room early one dark morning looking for Bob. The beams from the lamp struck steely sparks from the icicles outside the windows, and the firelight washed pleasantly across the splintered floorboards. Morning was the time for new enterprises, the hour when he hoped for converts.

Before supper was the glum time at the Poor House, the time of remembering and despairing. But after supper the glumness disappeared, day was finished then, what was, was. Then they played checkers, cut each other's hair, talked politics, quarreled, cussed Link, went to bed, and didn't care whether they ever woke up. But they did wake up, and morning would bring all its old infection of hopefulness. This stay at the Poor House? Why, it was just a bad spell, just a piece of hard luck. They'd get their health back, get a little piece of land; why, God knows, maybe even marry again. This wasn't the end, nothing but a little spell of rest, a time they'd look back on saying, "I went busted along toward the end of the nineties. Didn't begin to really get on my feet again 'til about 1900."

Nigger Bob was late coming in from his morning's work and James waited impatiently, sorry to see the other men arriving; they'll interfere, he thought; the truth don't mean a thing to them—Neddy Oates, an out and out drunkard; Dilk, too old to dig; John Manlief not all there; Josiah Stout, too old and too lazy, both; Hoxie Fifield, simple minded; Doss Whitt, cracked on the subject of peeping. There were some who thought Nigger Bob simple; but to Abel's mind, getting out of slopping hogs and shelling corn wasn't a necessary sign of simpleness: it might be the beginning of putting first things first. There was altogether too much hog-slopping going on, anyway, to his notion.

As soon as Nigger Bob came in James called him over into a corner. "Bob," he asked, "you been thinking about what I told you?"

"I thought about it oncet or twice."

"You think everybody's happy?"

"No ways to tell, I know of."

"You think everybody ought to be happy?"

"No, sir. I don't. There's a fellow—"

"You'd like good people to be happy, wouldn't you?"

"Nope, not unless they're a mind to and I figure it's their business."

"Well, they're a mind to, I can tell you that without pause or preamble."

Bob said nothing.

"If you could vote for happiness, you'd do it, wouldn't you, Bob?"

"I reckon so."

"You can, Bob. That's just what I want to tell you. That's the chance I'm offering you. All you got to do is stretch out your hand and take it."

Nigger Bob laughed. "Stretch out my hand and catch hold of a shovel. No siree, that ain't the ticket I'm voting."

In spite of James' care, everyone in the room had heard the conversation and everyone laughed.

Doss Whitt came over and laid a fleshy hand on James' shoulder. "Whyn't you let people alone?" he asked. "Everybody don't have to do what you do. Diggin' ain't everybody's line."

He's got a face like scum water, Abel thought, and he lifted Doss Whitt's soft hand off his shoulder as if it had been a toad squatting there. "Peeping ain't everyone's line either," he said.

"I ain't recruiting peepers," Doss reminded him.

11

"I FEEL like a man without a country," Em declared at breakfast the last Monday in January. School, because of the continued bad weather and a fresh outbreak of the measles, was closed for the week.

"Don't feel too downcast," Lib advised her. "I've got a new country in mind for you soon's breakfast's over."

"What country?" Em asked suspiciously.

"Country of dried apples to be picked over for worms."

"Worms," Em said with disgust. But it was not the work she

minded, she told herself, it was the lack of a plan—at home you could never depend upon anything—work or not work.

At school there was system and order: a thing called a schedule. You knew what to expect at school. 9 to 9:10, Singing; 9:10 to 9:20, Bible Reading; 9:20 to 9:30, Memory Gems. . . .

Em was the star of the Memory Gems program. Each morning she was prepared to recite more and longer Gems than any other pupil at the Bleeding Creek school. She scorned such short and easy lines as "Truth lies at the bottom of the well," or even, "If we were without faults we should not take so much pleasure in remarking them in others." Her Gems were of the length and on the order of the Gettysburg Address. Once Em was on her feet the Memory Gems program paused indefinitely. This suited the Bleeding Creek pupils very well; but the teacher there had other ideas: any selection, she ruled, taking more than one minute to recite was not a Gem. Although this new rule restricted Em, it flattered her, too: the ordinary rules of the Bleeding Creek District School could not contain Emma J. Conboy.

Home contained her all right, but too loosely for comfort; and besides feeling adrift in its planlessness, she missed at home those daily draughts of envy, admiration, and hate with which she was customarily refreshed at school. At school she was somebody, a person to be reckoned with. Only modesty had caused her to say that she was, at home, a man without a country: in actuality she was a queen without a country. At school when she said "Jump," they jumped. And the difference was not that at home she was dealing with grown-ups. Miss Longnecker, the teacher, couldn't possibly have been more grown-up, and she jumped with the others. Here, Em thought discontentedly, I could yell murder and no one would move.

"Murder," she yelled to prove it, and no one moved.

"Em," said Lib, "since you're feeling so bloodthirsty, you get right on out to the kitchen and begin taking care of those worms."

Taking care of the worms did not involve murder: all you did was shake them off the circles of dried apples into a pie-pan. They were mild pale creatures and after the first few shakes she lost her distaste for them and began to imagine what the change from a dried apple to a pie-pan might mean to a worm. What were they saying as they landed? "Terrible earthquake we just had," or

"Have you seen my wife and children?" or "I think my back's broken," or "Interesting prairie country hereabouts." Through these imaginings about worms she noted Dexter Bemis' approach with cynical detachment. There was no need to wonder what he'd say because he always said the same thing: "Where's Cate? How's Cate?"

Now he held out, of all things, a butter paddle. "I whittled this for Cate for a Christmas present, but I didn't get it finished in time. D'you think she'll like it?"

Em took the paddle without enthusiasm. "No," she said frankly, "it's the last thing in the world Cate'll want."

Dexter looked downcast, "Well," Em said sensibly, "Cate don't ever churn, not if she can get out of it. What's she want with a butter paddle?" Even for a butter-maker, Em considered a butter paddle a sorry Christmas present.

Dexter was not down-hearted long. "She can gild it and hang it on the wall for an ornament. Or she can paint a picture on the paddle part and just gild the handle. That's what my Aunt Edna did. She painted two of them, then crossed them and tied them together with a ribbon and hung them in the parlor."

Em stirred up the worms and apples with the prospective ornament. She didn't believe in Dexter's Aunt Edna and her gilded butter paddles for a minute. Everybody at The Farm had some important relative to talk about. Mrs. Goforth had her rich son and his gold mine. Lily Bias had a man who was in love with her. Now Dexter had this painting aunt. She handed Dexter back his butter paddle.

"Cate can't draw a straight line," she told him coldly, "let alone a picture on a butter paddle. I'm the one who draws."

"Roads and hills," Dexter said. "And fences! How'd they look on a butter paddle?" He walked off belaboring a forearm with the intended gift.

"And the sun coming up," Em called after him, "or going down. That's in the picture, too."

To her mind this made all the difference. Just the road, the fence, the hill: that was nothing, she agreed. It was the sun that changed it all. And she had discovered a new way of drawing the sun, a way that seemed to her to fill the whole picture with rays of quivering light. She began to work faster: as soon as she had finished the apples she would show the picture with the sun drawn in the new way to her friend Doss Whitt. Doss could draw, too.

She climbed the stairs, looking at her picture as she went, and knocked at Doss Whitt's door. "Don't waste your strength pounding," Doss called, and she went in.

Doss' room was cold and dirty. Through its one window she could see the snow in the back yard, grimy and streaked. There were four pieces of furniture in the room: a washstand, two beds, and a chair. The chair stood between the two beds and was covered with a litter of odds and ends: a whetstone, two or three pencils, matches, a pipe, old letters, a collar-button, a broken shoestring, a stack of newspaper or magazine pages. Doss was stretched out on one bed so Em sat down across from him on the other.

"This is your center table, I guess," she said, thinking it would be polite to have general conversation for a minute or two before showing him her picture.

Doss made this politeness unnecessary by saying, "What's that you got there?"

She handed him her picture diffidently, but with pride too; it was not wonderful, probably, but it was the most wonderful she had been able to make, yet.

"Same old thing, I see."

"Oh, no. This one's lots different."

Doss stretched out his arm and tilted his head. "Can't say's I see any change."

"The sun's rays are different, can't you tell?"

"No, not 'til you mentioned it," Doss admitted, "I didn't."

"I guess it's not a very good sun. It's pretty lopsided."

"Why don't you draw round a quarter or the end of a spool for your sun? That way you'd get you a nice neat circle."

"Oh, no," Em said. That was tracing, work for Fessler. She was beyond all that. What fun would tracing be? She was embarrassed for Doss, that he would suggest such a thing, and to hide the mistake he had made, she picked up the top two sheets from his stack of papers, unfolded the first sheet and felt, as she looked at it, a sudden growing warmth and weight in cheeks and fingertips. Nakedness! She ought, she knew, to refold the paper and put it down, but she kept on staring. Lifting her eyes, she saw Doss watching her as she stared. It was nakedness, and nakedness not like a statue's, but like a person's living nakedness and what she could not understand was how such unclothed women came to be in a paper at all. For this was a newspaper or magazine picture with printing above it to explain its meaning. "Baptists Lay Cornerstone" were the words over the picture, and that was actually what the two women and the two men (clothed) were doing, and doing, to make the nakedness stranger still, in snowy weather. She unfolded the next picture, not because she wanted to see it but because she couldn't look at the one she had any longer and didn't know what to say. And there, in it, was more nakedness. The words this time said, "Riding Club Prepares for Canter," and this picture showed a man holding a horse for a woman, who, unclothed, without so much as shoes on, had one foot already in the stirrup.

Em's throat felt dry as sawdust and her hand shook as she replaced the pictures. Over the top of her pictured sun, which he still held, Doss was quietly smiling at her, as if to say, And you thought you could draw!

"I never saw any pictures like these before," she whispered.

"No, I don't suppose you did," Doss said.

"Papers don't print pictures like that."

"No," Doss said, "they don't."

"You did it?" she asked.

Doss nodded.

"How?"

Doss picked up a cube of rubber, one thing she hadn't seen on the chair between them, and tossed it over into her lap.

"You erase their clothes?"

"I set 'em free," Doss said.

"Don't the paper tear?"

"Sometimes."

"And you draw." She kept seeing the big flowery navels, like cabbage roses, Doss had given the ladies. "Beside you I'm no drawer at all."

"I've had considerable more experience."

She looked out of the window where dark gray clouds were hurrying across a lighter gray sky. "You don't take the clothes off men?"

"So that's what you'd like to see?"

This is a dirty, gritty room, Em thought, postponing the truth. "They would be more interesting to me." Now, she thought, he can make me ashamed.

"Why?" he asked.

"I know how ladies look."

"Know," Doss Whitt said. "That's like never wanting to eat again because you had a square meal once," and Em thought suddenly, this is a part of his peeping. He wants to peep even at people in pictures.

"You steal from people when you stare at them," she said.

Doss got off his bed. "Who says so? Who's got the right to say what's to be seen and what's forbidden? Who made this world? Them that say so or God? Where's their license to wrap up and hide? God made 'em and He made 'em without any clothes on. Who's going against God's will, me or them? God didn't cover up a single part, and then after He had invented nakedness He invented eyes. I tell you the man who uses his eyes is carrying out the will of God. I tell you I'm God's eye sent down to earth in the form of man, and what there's here to be seen I'm going to see."

Doss had been standing over Em. Now he turned and hurried to the window as if there might be some nakedness out there in the tramped and dirty snow he was missing. "Who said it was stealing?" he asked without turning around.

"Cate," Em said. "Cate said that."

"Cate!" Doss said. "That sister of yours could be the most sinful of God's creatures, she's so shamefaced. She's so backward about the shape in which she's been cast, maybe she's Satan's image, not God's? What she got to be so shamed of? Or so proud of? The blinds pulled down ain't enough for Sister Cate. She ain't safe with just the blinds down. Get *them* up and Sister Cate's over behind the wash-stand. Get on the far side of the wash-stand and she's cowering behind a towel. What's she hiding? What'd God give Sister Cate that's too good or too bad for the rest of the world to see?"

Em's neck ached from staring upward at Doss but she couldn't turn away.

"I ask you what she's got?"

"Nothing," Em whispered, "nothing that I know of."

"I walk the whole livelong night and, oh, let my eye be refreshed and give me a little ease, I pray."

He stopped as if remembering those nights. "All hands are turned against me," he went on. "Most men don't believe in God, but I ain't one of them. There must be a God to make a man like me for I sure never made myself and time and agin my Mammy and Pappy'd say to me, 'Doss Whitt, you're no son of ours.' So I'm God's handiwork. And *you* are," he said.

"Yes," Em whispered. Doss hung over her like a wave, topheavy and about to break. Slowly she was crumpling her picture, with the sun drawn in the new way, between her hands.

"Believe me, I pity the human race from the bottom of my heart," Doss said. Then he dropped onto his knees, and laid his face against the bed Em sat on, and Em got up and tiptoed around him to the door. When he heard the squeak of the opening door he said, "I'm a lost soul. Go on and leave me."

Em paused, filled with pity and embarrassment. "We all are," she said, wanting to share his misery and wondering, as she said the words, at the unexpected ring of truth they had. She made herself walk down the stairs slowly, quietly, one step at a time.

III

1 lb. condition powder	.20¢	Use of bull	$1.00
Indenture papers	$1.00	Repairing bull halter	.25¢
Castrate pigs	.90¢	30 lb. Lion Coffee	$3.75
Ironing wagon tongue	.25¢	Rec'd for 34 lb. lard	$4.25
Pulling tooth	.50¢	Marshal's fee for Arrest	$1.50
2 bbl. salt	$2.20	Threshing 406 bu. wheat	$18.27
Chain for windmill	.05¢	10 bu. lime	$1.50
600 cabbage plants	.25¢	½ doz. lamp flues	.30¢
2 hame strings	.20¢	14½ gal. molasses	$7.25

LINK sat at the kitchen table that evening checking back over the year's accounts. The room seemed to him to be filled with a kind of living silence, to hum with sounds he couldn't identify but which pleased him. At his elbow the big glass lamp, burning with its steady, saw-toothed flame, gave out heat as well as light, for he could feel a warm spot on the cheek next it.

January was the hard month at The Farm, the steep frozen hump of the year that had to be climbed. Once over that, they could coast down the far side into spring; snow and ice all the way, like as not, but easy sledding after that ugly uphill climb. He didn't mind the month so much for himself, but it was a long tedious pull for the folks: the old ones were racked with aches and pains, pinched blue with cold; the younger ones were cranky and restless, out of sorts at being shut in and because of having too little to do. And they all suffered, he thought, from the name they had: pauper; and from the name of the place they lived: Poor Farm.

He was of two minds about these names and their meanings. Should they be considered a part of a man's punishment for being poor, be made as shameful as possible, burned into the inmates at every chance, until finally they had them for life like the old-time brands for thieving and whoring? He didn't know. He was of two minds about these words because he was of two minds about poverty itself. Was poverty a crime and this a house of correction and punishment? Or was poverty a misfortune only? Or even the result of a kindheartedness that had refused to grind its neighbor down for the sake of an extra dime?

There was proof, he thought, for every kind of belief you'd care to hold on the subject, right there under this very roof. Old Josiah Stout was probably most people's idea of a pauper: an improvident, lazy ne'er-do-well, a man who'd lived easy in his young days, lapped up the cream while his neighbors made do with skim milk and now, come to old age, was still living easy at his neighbors' expense. As far as the neighbors were concerned, Josh Stout's story was the story of the Prodigal Son all over again with them playing the rôle of the Prodigal's father: a rôle they didn't feel cut out for in the first place, and which in the second place, they didn't ever intend to play with Old Josh Stout as son. Nor did they intend for Link to serve up the fatted calf, or anything that smacked of fatted calf, in their stead at the Poor House—for Josh—or anyone else. They didn't hold with letting paupers starve to death in Rock County; but they'd be damned (the men) and switched (the women) if they could see any justice in carrying a man like Josh Stout around on a chip. They'd gone hungry in their day and never asked any man for a red cent: now old Stout, who'd never done an honest lick of work in his whole enduring life, was lapping up more grits and gravy than they themselves sat down to. So they heard anyway, and so they said.

If everybody here was like Old Josh, Link thought, he could see eye to eye with his neighbors. But the ones like Dilk? And the women who, except for the unluckiness or laziness—whatever it was—of their husbands would be in their own kitchens or parlors tonight, bossing hired girls and playing with their grandchildren? And the simple ones, like Hoxie and Mag's Icey? And the ones with a screw loose like the Abels? Or gone off half-cocked on a single subject like Doss? Or only half living like John Manlief? What did you do for them? God knows, he thought, I bit off a lot bigger bite, coming here, than I had any notion of.

He wondered about more carpet-weaving as a job for the folks who needed inside work. And how would it be for the ones who needed something they could do over and over again, something not full of new problems? Carpet-weaving in Rock County was nothing but getting old rags together in a shape lasting enough to cover the floorboards for a few years. Was there any reason these carpets couldn't be pretty—couldn't be bright and cheerful? And if they were pretty, wouldn't they sell? And who would object to a little extra cash coming into The Farm?

The hogs, of course, ought to prove the chief money-makers—that is, if he could get shut of that bunch of first cousins to the mast-fed razorbacks of forty years ago which he'd inherited with The Farm; get started with something a little modern in the way of porkers. Raciness was fine in a horse but it wasn't what you asked of a hog. That herd he had out there now, he reckoned, could outrun most horses in a road race—but who wanted to meet Dan Patch on a meat platter, all bone, muscle and County Fair ribbons?

Carpet-weaving, more and better hogs: they would mean extra work, to which the county wouldn't object. And hogs and weaving'd mean in the long run less taxes, which year in and year out was what the county yelled loudest about. But they'd mean too, if they succeeded, that The Farm would be less of a Poor Farm and the poor folks, because they earned some of their keep, something more than paupers. How would the county stomach that? They'd call it biggity and fine-haired, if he didn't miss his guess. But that, sure as shooting, whatever the county thought or the Commissioners did, was the way he was heading.

He dipped his pen into the ink well and began his posting of the January bills.

Whip lasp	.15¢	Shoeing mule	.50¢
Caustic	.10¢	Repairing wash-house stove	$1.50
14 lb. tobacco	$1.75	Lamp black	.15¢
Turpentine and castor oil	.50¢	Livery bill	.25¢

Because it was her bounden duty, Cate came out to tell her father. He was at the kitchen table writing and didn't turn or speak until she sat down opposite him.

"Well, Cate?" he asked, without stopping.

"Papa," she said.

Papa, the close name, and this person writing, this man, so far away. Lib had seen to it that she remembered that Papa was a man. "I've seen some girls," her mother had told her, "riding around on the front seat of the surrey with their fathers, while poor old Ma bounced along in the back seat, a back number in more ways than one. But not me. If Link gets girls on the mind, like some men, he'll at least have to go outside the family to find them." And Lib would spring up into the front seat with a flourish, leaving her and Em—neither of whom had any wish to be any place else—to the back seat. And Lib had sent her, aged twelve, scurrying from the room shamefaced, a little of her flesh showing at the top of her shimmy by saying, "Cate, you're too big a girl to be displaying yourself in that fashion before your father." She'd seen her Normal School friends throw their arms around their fathers' necks and kiss them! Didn't they know that fathers were men? She'd as soon hit her father as kiss him. And because what she had to tell him had to do with—nakedness—she was embarrassed as well as troubled now.

"Papa," she said, "Em's been up in Doss Whitt's room again."

Link finished writing a word. "How many times," he asked, "must I tell you children you're to stay out of the folks' rooms? They're entitled to a little privacy. Just because you're the superintendent's children you needn't think you can go running in and out their rooms whenever the fancy for a little visiting strikes you."

"*I* don't, Papa," Cate reminded him.

Link put the cork in his bottle of ink and cleaned his pen on the corner of his handkerchief.

"You would, I reckon, if you wanted to."

"No. . . ." Cate shook her head. "Papa, Doss showed Em pictures."

"Pictures? What kind of pictures?"

"Women." Her father stopped polishing his pen. He could see, she supposed, that she hadn't told everything. "Women without clothes on." She finished in a very low voice.

Her father's hand went slowly down to the table, and his fingers slowly put down the pen. "You go and get Em," he said.

"She'll be mad," Cate said. "I told her I was going to tell you, but she'll be mad. I had to tell you, didn't I, Papa?"

"You have, anyway," Link answered.

Em brought the little potholder she'd been sewing on since she was seven or eight into the kitchen when she came and stood working on it industriously, waiting for her father to speak.

"Stop that sewing for a few minutes," Link said, "and listen to me. Were you up in Doss Whitt's room?"

"Yes, sir."

"You know you're not supposed to go into the folks' rooms?"

"Yes, sir."

"Stop sirring me," Link ordered. "What did you go up there for?"

"To show Doss Whitt a picture."

"What kind of a picture?"

She put her holder down on the table beside her father, took a sheet of paper from her pocket, unfolded it, then pressed it flat beside the potholder. It was one of the kind she always drew, Cate saw, road, fence, hills, sun—going down or coming up.

"Why did you want Doss to see this?"

"The sun's drawn in a new way."

"Look's like the same sun I've been seeing you draw for the past five years. But that's beside the point. My understanding is that Doss showed you some pictures. Did he?"

Em refolded her piece of paper and with eyes intent on getting the creases just right, answered, "No."

"Cate said . . ." Link began.

"Did Cate swallow all of that?" Em interrupted. "I told her the pictures were naked women, too. I reckon she swallowed that. Did you, Cate? Poor old Cate'll swallow anything she's—"

Link didn't let her finish. "Besides lying, which is wrong, didn't you think of getting Doss into trouble with a story like that?"

"Papa," Cate urged, "she was telling the truth. I know she was."

"Were you, Emma?"

"I was lying," Em stonily repeated.

"You girls wait here while I go see Doss," Link said.

At that Em ran to the door leading into the hallway and placed her back against it. "Don't," she cried, "don't go. He didn't show them to me, I just saw them. They're not bad. They're just people put back the way God made them. That's all Doss wants. He wouldn't have to be a peeper if people didn't hide themselves. He worships God's handiwork with his eyes. He said—"

"Hush, Em."

Cate couldn't remember when she'd ever seen Em cry before. Em had been braiding and unbraiding her hair as she talked and now she took the braids' stubby ends and wiped her face with them.

"You go to your room, Cate," Link said. "What I've got to say is for Em's ears alone."

While she waited for Em, Cate turned back the covers on her sister's bed, plumped up her pillow and put her drawing papers back in the baby casket. Link had let Em keep the casket, despite all Cate's protests, as a chest in which to store her valuables, after Dandie had refused to return it to Korby.

"It's nothing but a box," Link had reasoned sensibly with Cate, "made out of wood like any other box. If Em can get some use out of it, let her. What've you got against her keeping her belongings in it? It's a good deal more reasonable to use it the way Em wants to than to put it under ground."

It was a coffin to Em, though, not a chest for valuables. "A coffin," she crowed to Cate, "in our room! How exciting! We'll be almost like monks who sleep in their coffins every night to remind them how they're going to end up."

Cate believed Em would actually have slept in this coffin, too, if she could've figured out a way to crowd herself into it. Why would anyone want to do such a thing? Why did people want to remember how they were going to end up, dead and under ground, or need coffins to remind them? She remembered—without this coffin or box—whichever it was now—standing under her eyes day and night to remind her.

She had been writing Christie when Em had come in with her news about Doss' pictures. She put her hand on the letter now but she couldn't go back to it; it was a different world from this of Em and Doss and naked women. "I had to tell, Papa, didn't I?" It was Christie to whom she addressed her question and asked for justification. While she had been writing Christie she had felt herself to be the most loving, kind, and gentle person in the world. Here thirty minutes later she didn't know what to think of herself. She had got Em into trouble, even though her intention had been to help her. Oh, what was the right way to love and why didn't Em come? Was she being razor-stropped? When Link whipped, it wasn't like Lib, one sharp slap and the matter done with, but a hard, serious session.

After a long time, it seemed, Em did come in, red-eyed, but quiet and began without a word to undress. When Em's drawers went off Cate cried out, "Oh, Em."

Em touched the welts contemptuously. "Nothing but my old flesh," she said. But once she was in bed, lying face down to protect herself, she began to cry, without much sound but so heavily that her thin shoulders were jerked up and down under the covers. Cate watched in silence for a while, then she went over to Em and began hesitantly to smooth her black hair. "Em, Em," she said. She knew she was responsible for Em's crying and knew how hateful, "I'm sorry," is to the person who has seen you, a minute before, cause his pain: as if you were determined to have *all* pleasures, being forgiven as well as pain-giving. But she was sorry and said so.

Em turned over slowly onto her welts, groaned, and with her face hard under her tears, said, "What've you got to be sorry about?"

"Sorry I told, sorry you were whipped, oh, sorry I'm alive," Cate said and dropped onto her knees and pressed her face against Em's outflung hand.

"Cheer up," Em said. "You taught me an extra good lesson tonight."

"Lesson?"

"To keep my mouth shut and especially to you."

Cate looked up and the tears were still rolling down Em's stony face. "Em," she said and reached again towards Em's hair but Em moved away from her. "Let me alone," she said coldly, "I'm going to sleep now."

Cate went to the kitchen and found her father still there, one hand—the one that had licked Em?—stretched out toward the cold stove.

"Papa," she faltered. She had come out to be comforted, but standing in the doorway she changed from that to wanting to comfort: "Papa, you had to do it."

"Had to do it?" Link said. "Nobody has to do anything."

"If she said she lied, you had to—"

"Go on, get out," Link said. "Get to bed. I've heard enough out of you for one evening."

Cate went outdoors, not to bed, and walked up and down in the slush, shivering and crying, miserable and suffering; and fully aware of her misery and suffering. From some distance overhead, suspended in the starless stormy sky she saw herself, a girl of eighteen out in the winter night, without a soul to turn to. And above this Cate, who observed her suffering, was still another Cate, observing the observer. So she got no pleasure out of her unhappiness finally, but added self-hate to it.

Her father came out and she thought, Now I'm keeping him up, and she tried to stop crying and said, "I cause everyone trouble."

"You'll catch cold out here," Link said, "and that will cause everyone trouble. Now, get on to bed."

Cate wished she could act like her school-girl friends, put her head on her father's shoulder and cry. But she could not. They stood facing each other in the winter darkness, unmoving as poles or trees, neither able to give or take comfort.

[214]

"Now go on in, Cate," her father urged, "and try to be sensible. Try to use a little reason occasionally. Stop and think once in a while before you act."

Without stopping for a minute to think Cate promised eagerly, "Oh, Papa, I will. I promise you I will."

6

*F*or a day or two in the middle of February they had spring weather at The Farm, no snow anywhere, a blue unclouded sky and sudden warm breezes touching their lips and throats like the flick of unexpected tongues. They knew it wouldn't last, knew winter'd be twice as hard to bear afterwards; still they couldn't forbear giving themselves up to it, treating it like a lasting possession. For those two days even Bleeding Creek had a summer sound and slipped by with the murmuring smoothness of sunny weather. The cedars were quiet for a change: quiet and fragrant, and everyone took deep breaths of their bitter-sweetness, deeper and deeper, like drunkards for whom each drink is tied to another.

Hoxie Fifield, James Abel, and Bob Beeson, supervised by Marvin Dilk, were grubbing and burning on a tract above the burying-ground which had never been properly cleared. When Link had asked Marvin Dilk to oversee the job he had complained about his crew. "That man Abel," he said, "will be mighty hard to keep moving. Once he gets a pick in his hands he'll freeze in one spot. He'll dig plum down to Chiny unless somebody calls a halt."

The trouble with Hoxie and Bob was just the reverse. If they had to dig to it, China would never be discovered. "They use a mattock like it's a toothpick," Mr. Dilk said. "They delve round an old stump as tender as if it was a live tooth."

Link himself, with Doss Whitt as a helper, was spreading manure. Doss drove and Link stood in the back of the wagon forking out the dressing. It wasn't a sweet job but it was a satisfying one; he could already see the August stand of corn they would have in that field, man tall, blades arching up as strong as shoulders and tassels thick as hair.

Lib had been working all day at the sewing-machine, running up new house-dresses for the womenfolk. When Lib launched into a long seam, she pushed the treadle so fast the whole machine rocked like a boat. The needle ate up the goods like a prairie fire eating up grass. Lib hated sewing and she didn't propose to spend any more of her life than need be turning out house-dresses for the female inmates of the Rock County Poor Farm. When she hit a long seam the poor old Singer hummed and whined. The seams Lib sewed were saw-toothed, but they were in to stay. She sewed a firm stitch and she put the stitches far from the edge. The ladies of the Rock County Poor Farm would have to do something pretty energetic before Lib's sewing gave way. When she held up one of her uneven seams for inspection, she consoled herself by saying, "It'll never be seen on a galloping horse." Leathy Wade, Lily Bias, Mrs. Goforth, and Grandma Mercer were the four women in Rock County least likely to mount any horses let alone a galloping one, but off a horse, or on, each was going to have a new dress, the calico fresh and crackling, the colors so strong even boiling wouldn't faze them.

Lib had set Neddy Oates to swabbing out the men's sitting-room, a job long past due. He had the windows wide open, the chairs stacked on the table, and was sluicing and scrubbing as happy as if he had been in a horse-stall.
Mag stuck her head in the door. "Everything so quiet in here I thought you's off somewhere playing hookey, Neddy."
Neddy winked at her. "Mag, don't you know you can't catch a weasel asleep?" he asked.

Mag went back to her kitchen and pursued an unseasonable house-fly with a rolled newspaper—then repented her attempt to kill it. Poor thing, she thought, to live through all this cold snap, then be laid low by an Indianapolis paper. She shooed the fly outside, and stood for a few minutes on the back porch, tasting the fresh, sun-filled air. Over by the barns the manure pile was steaming. Back of the burying-ground strands of pale lavender-gray smoke moved upward. Down in the south forty she watched the breeze pick up straw from one of Link's tossed forkfuls and carry it, glinting, toward the house. Em and Dexter, who were cleaning nests in the hen-house, went by, and she called to them, "I'll trade you jobs. You two cook supper and let me get outdoors for a change." Em, who seemed these days to be getting a little less talkative, didn't answer but Dexter called back, "Supper'll be nothing but potatoes boiled with their jackets on, then."

Dexter had the dirty part of the cleaning to do: he took the old straw out of the nests and Em put in the clean. Em made good deep nests; she ignored the size of hens, and patted and deepened simply for the pleasure of the work. Dexter ran his hand around the latest of these edifices. "Hens'll be so worn out getting in and out of these nests they won't have enough strength left to lay," he said.

Em went on to the next nest and made it just as big and just as deep.

"A hen's going to think she's got in the stew-pot when she falls in that," Dexter said.

"How do you know so much what a hen thinks?" Em asked.

"I'm part animal," Dexter told her.

Em sniffed. "Why don't you talk to hens then instead of me?" she asked. But Dexter wasn't bothered by that. He would have preferred hens to Em any day if they could've told him anything about Cate. "Is Cate in love with that fellow who was down here at Christmas?" he asked.

"Yes," Em answered shortly.

"She say so?"

"No."

"How d'you know then?"

"Cate goes by contraries. If she don't say so, she does." Em picked up a china nest egg and watched a big louse labor around its slipperiness. The Columbus of lice and no West Indies to get in his way.

"Is she in love with Ferris Thompson?"

"No."

"What's she keep going with him for, then?"

"To show Christie she can have her pick."

"Can she?"

"Yes," Em said. "Now you answer a question."

"What question?" Dexter asked.

Em stopped work. "Did you ever see a naked woman?"

Dexter's face got red and his voice thickened. "That's none of your business."

"I guess anybody who wants to see one is out of his mind?" she suggested.

Dexter scooped out old straw furiously. "Don't talk dirty," he ordered.

Em went over to the nest Dexter was working on. "Why is it dirty if you take your clothes off?" she asked.

Dexter flung his armload of straw down into the wheelbarrow and turned to trundle it out. "You finish up here," he said. "I got to go split wood for supper."

Em didn't miss him with his everlasting Cate, Cate, Cate. Cut-cut-cut. He really did sound like a hen. She finished the nests, put the wheelbarrow away and walked aimlessly about the side yard stooping now and then to examine a pebble or a piece of broken glass. I will have a secret life, she thought, do everything and not tell a soul. She squatted down by a short brown feather, touched it, then picked it up. This is a sweet little feather fallen off a live bird and nobody knows I have it, not even the bird. It is a secret between I, me, and myself. "What is your secret?" . . . "The bird is minus what I am plus." She stayed, squatting, imagining that conversation. They had asked her ("they" were her enemies) the question, and she had answered them thus. They couldn't make head nor tail of it, naturally, "Tell us," they threatened, "your secret. What is it you are keeping from us?" But all she would say was, "The bird is minus what I am plus." They were baffled, they threatened torture, but threats could not unseal her lips. They stripped her naked (she could see herself standing before them, long and white, like a lily), they beat her, they broke her on the rack. She died without uttering a word, the little feather hidden, where? Some secret place. It was with her in death.

She got up, dizzy from death and torture. She opened her eyes and the winter-killed grass and bare trees looked fresh and sweet after where she'd been and what she'd done. She put the feather in her apron pocket and continued her stroll. If I had a prayer-book, she thought, I could read it as I walked like a nun. She felt brimming with tenderness and solicitude. I would like to do someone a very great kindness, she thought. She paced up and down, ruffling gently the feather's edges and tried to think who: there was Cate, at the front door, but Cate wasn't the one. It was someone else, entirely, to whom a kindness was due; Cate's opposite, if anything.

Cate leaned against the doorway waiting for Christie who was arriving for a visit at The Farm that evening.

"Be on the lookout for me a little before sundown," he had written. He had a new horse, a blood bay, Ajax, and a new rubber-tired buggy. "Be prepared for something kind of classy," he had advised. "No more arriving to see you in the undertaker's wagon with the coffins. I'm moving up in the world. Sold $7,000 worth of policies in the month of Jan. Outsold everybody in this end of the state. If it suits you, let's go to Madison and celebrate. The Orpheus Club is having a concert and I've got tickets."

It suited her, everything suited her this afternoon. She was tired, scrubbed clean, scented with Lib's Florida water and had on her second-best dress. (It was only sensible to save the best until tomorrow.) The silky air was moving just enough to lift the hair about her forehead. All around her the farm work was going on. Down the road she saw her father and Doss spreading fertilizer. Back of the house somebody was chopping wood. She could smell the smoke from the stumps burning in the clearing and nearer at hand, the smoke from the supper fire Mag had already started in the kitchen. Her mother's sewing-machine was still racing; when Lib started a job she finished it. Em went by, gave her a sidelong look then glanced quickly away. For a minute Cate's happiness wavered, but she heard the creek's full-voiced sound and the cedars' deep murmur, and her happiness returned.

Behind her were the shining rooms that she herself had cleaned; though cleanliness was only the half of it. She had made them, the way an artist makes a picture: placed the slat-backed chair in the one spot where the light from the western windows would be reflected from its dark polished wood; picked cedar boughs and put them in a big yellow pitcher, then set the pitcher on the sitting-room mantel where the boughs drooped downward in a curve which was an echo of the curving picture-frame above the mantel.

The day was coming to a mild and colorless end. The sun was going to slide out of sight with no more commotion than a smooth stone makes when dropped edgewise into quiet water. Just sink, just finish, that would be the way of it. The air stirred her blue surrah skirt: and there was the same interaction, she thought, between herself and the plum-colored hills, the big cedars (bitter or sweet she could never decide which), the bare silvery-purple raspberry canes—even between her and the weathered slats of the picket fence; though nothing in them or her moved visibly (as her skirt was moving in the wind) to show the connection, the interaction.

In the minute when she had not been watching, Christie had come in sight, driving at a nice natural clip, something halfway between the show-off of too-fast and the show-off of too-slow. He lifted his arm—to her she thought—but it was a greeting instead to Doss and her father, for he pulled off to one side of the road and, as she watched, wrapped the reins around the buggy whip and started across the field to where they were working.

11

AT EIGHT-THIRTY that night Marvin Dilk, who had gone to bed at eight, got to worrying about Link's sow and reluctantly hauled his old legs from under the quilts. "I'd ought to go have a look at her," he told himself.

He talked to himself because, as he got older, there seemed to be two Dilks: the Dilk who knew what needed doing and was willing to do it, and this other, newer Dilk who, unless he was eternally jawed at, would sink back and take his ease. The real Dilk was the talker and doer; this other, the old fellow shivering on the edge of the bed, was a stranger. "Get your pants on," he told this old shirker (somehow he seemed to be huddled over with him), "and get into your coat. It ain't really cold. It's just the first shock." He talked the old codger into his clothes, then talked and walked him out to the kitchen. Once he'd got him on to his feet and moving, the differences between the two Dilks weren't so noticeable.

The kitchen made him blink, it was so full of commotion. Here, in the middle of the night, kids were playing, dishes being washed, food eaten. Mr. Conboy and the oldest girl's beau were at the kitchen table with a pie and a coffee-pot between them. Seeing them, he began to question his right to visit the sow. "What right've you got to put in your oar here?" he asked himself. But he couldn't feel that anybody who'd started out as Mr. Conboy had, as teacher and lawyer, could understand animals. Men like that weren't ordinary flesh and blood or they would never've picked such jobs in the first place. And Mr. Conboy's intentions, while good, wouldn't tell him what to do for a farrowing sow.

He said no to the offer of pie and coffee. He didn't want them to think he'd come poking out in hope of food. He told the old fellow, the Dilk who would've set down at the first hint of an invitation and polished off all that was left of the pie, "You're here on charity and you've had your three square meals already today."

"I was wakeful," he told them, "and thought I'd walk out to the barn." He was trying to make the trip sound like the result of a weakness of his own, not of any suspicion that Mr. Conboy didn't know how to look after a hog. "Being a farmer so many years, the stock's still on my mind, even at night. Does me good, seems like, if I'm wakeful, just to see them snoozing." He looked anxiously at Link.

Link drank the last swallow of his coffee, pushed back his chair, and said, "Christie, you've never seen our famous sow. Want to come out for a look?"

"I had one look," Christie told him, "at Christmas."

"No rule against two," Link said. Without asking Dilk any more about it, he poured him a cup of coffee, sugared and creamed it heavily, and thrust a slab of pie into his hand. "Don't waste good food," he admonished, and since waste was involved, Dilk ate and drank.

Outside they found that the wind was up again. The sky was scoured clean of everything but stars, and they had been polished to a fine point and glittered overhead like Fourth of July sparklers. The cedars were booming, and the wind, once they were away from the protection of the house, hit them with cannonball bursts of iciness.

"Goes right through me," Dilk said, both Dilks, talker and listener, sharing this opinion. He was speaking to himself but Link, leading the way with the lantern, answered him. "It'll be warm soon's we're in the barn."

It was warmer, anyway, the wind no more than a thin whine through the cracks. The gilt still had her private pen, and when Link held the lantern over her she opened one eye then shut it again like a wife disturbed by a husband home late from a lodge meeting. "She looks hoity-toity, don't she?" Link asked, pride in his voice.

Dilk wasn't content with looks. He went into the stall and laid a hand on her. "She knows me," he told them. "I do Abel's feeding for him a good part of the time."

"Is Abel scamping his work?" Link asked.

"I'm no tale-bearer," Dilk said and began to scratch one of the leafy ears. The gilt herself lay quietly, but the litter inside her continuously rippled her sides with their movements.

"She look all right to you?" Link asked.

"She's fine, going to have a banner litter or I miss my guess."

He came out of the stall and stood with the two men, waiting for them to make the first move to leave and when they did so, followed them into the cutting wind. He walked behind them listening to their talk. They were speaking of the stars, calling them by name and pointing them out. He'd never before heard a star called by name, like a door-yard animal. He'd spent his life beneath them, but had had no more mind to name them than to name the gravel under his feet. In all his life there'd never been a person who'd mentioned such things, or if asked, "What's that star's name?" wouldn't have thought him out of his mind. He looked up at them, a pretty sight, like seeds on fire. I've lived a hard grubbing life, seen nothing, done nothing, and come to nothing, he thought; don't know the name of even one star. He scraped his feet carefully at the door and followed Link and Christie into the warm lighted kitchen.

III

CATE awakened early next morning. She loved firsts and the day would hold a lot of them: first train trip to Madison; first whole day alone with Christie; first concert. She lay still, counting firsts, wondering if she had missed any, and added, first day for my new dress, first ride with Ajax—they were going to drive into The Junction, leave Ajax at the livery-stable, and take the train from there. And first time in Kentucky. Christie had said, if the weather stayed fine, they'd take the ferry across the Ohio, just for the trip, just to be able to say they'd been there. She ran to the window to inspect the weather and it was perfect, made for a day in Kentucky, sky unclouded, air mild and warm as new milk.

She went to the mirror with less faith, not expecting to find perfection or even any firsts; but something was reflected there; if not a first, at least the first time she'd ever seen it. It was in her eyes, mostly, but her mouth was changed, too. What was it? Love? Being loved?

Em was still asleep, bow shaped, her face out of sight against the wall. Cate dressed on tiptoe not to awaken her. She put on her new dress with trembling fingers. This would be the test. Before, when trying it on, she had been able to reassure herself by thinking, "It will look better when the real time comes." This was the real time, it was now or never for her new dress, the costume she had tried to devise as practical enough for a train trip and elegant enough for a concert. Had she fallen between two stools? She had badgered Lib into making it for her and it was so complicated (a zouave jacket of hunter's green velvet, trimmed with gold passementerie, and worn over a brown bengaline dress) that Lib had had one nervous headache after another, simply trying to figure it out. *Had* she figured it out? Cate wondered, inspecting herself and the dress in the mirror. The armholes cut into her flesh. The zouave jacket, which was made to hang open displaying the tight basque and its buttons (shaped like little gold beehives), displayed also, she saw to her dismay, a great deal of bust. She tugged unsuccessfully at the basque to loosen it and unsuccessfully at the jacket to close it, but neither would budge, and her only reassurance, as she gazed at the too-visible curves was that, if she acted very matter of fact and sensible, perhaps no one would notice them.

She put on her hat, also hunter's green velvet and also homemade, a capote, the *Ladies' Home Journal* had called it. Lib, in making it, had wavered in her conviction as to which was the back and which the front and this uncertainty showed up now in the finished article so that Cate stood switching it end for end, undecided as to which way it looked best. Or least worse. It looks like an old moldy pancake, she told herself, whichever way I wear it.

She went out to the sitting-room, uncertain of herself, and saw there the picture she had worked so hard to make the day before, broken and ruined. The cedar boughs were in the woodbox and the pitcher which had held them was on the floor, empty, its water gone, no doubt, into the foot tub which stood unemptied in front of some foot-soaker's chair—Lib's, it appeared, for her discarded underwear was on the chair back. Bottles, left by the folks for fresh supplies of turpentine and castor-oil, were lined up on the mantel and ashes had been scattered about the hearth by some careless fire-banker; and a careless reader had strewn a newspaper, all its eight sheets separated, from one corner of the room to the other.

Christie came in as she was bending shamefaced (underclothes under her arm) to pick up the foot tub.

"Let me take this," he said.

But she ignored his offer, tried to ignore the tub, and swept, water slightly splashing, to the kitchen. The confusion in the sitting-room was nothing to that she found in the kitchen. Mag was banging away at the range; Nigger Bob was noisily stacking wood, not in the woodbox (Mag had Fessler bedded down there) but against the wall at the oven-end of the stove. Fessler was wrapped to the ears and sucking noisily on an empty bottle. With another bottle of Fessler's, this one filled, Icey and Airey were feeding an orphaned lamb. Old Grandma Mercer, huddled up, was half in the oven, half out, sipping tea-kettle tea with smacks that equalled for loudness Fessler's or the lamb's. Leathy Wade and Mrs. Goforth trailed back and forth between kitchen and inmates' dining-room, setting the table and discussing Mrs. Goforth's female complaints—loudly and intimately. Under the stove the big gold tom, Mag's Mister, had imagined a bacon rind into a mouse and was killing it slowly with nasty growls and slobberings.

Cate saw all this, going through the kitchen with the tub, and no sooner was she back from emptying it than the outside door once again opened. In backed Dexter Bemis, beaming with pride and dropping corn; behind him, progressing from grain to grain like a well-oiled machine, was Cate's gander. The minute the gander was inside, Dexter banged the door behind him and dropped a whole handful of corn for his reward. "Look who's come up from the barn to surprise you, Cate!"

Cate was usually too self-conscious, when Christie was about, to show anything so natural as temper, but a gander in the kitchen, with everything else that was there, was the last straw. "You get that bird out of here," she ordered, stamping her foot, and when Dexter, surprised at this, was slow to move, she flew at the gander herself. The poor bird, frightened, first soiled the floor, then, dragging its misformed foot, half-slid, half-flew toward Fessler and the woodbox. Fessler, as frightened as the gander, and more helpless for he was pinned down by his tightly wrapped quilts, could only scream and throw his bottle. Grandma Mercer dropped her tea-kettle tea and got farther into the oven. Airey, Icey, and the lamb clattered up and down the kitchen, the girls screeching and laughing and the lamb adding further disgrace to the floor already thoroughly disgraced by Samson. When finally gander, lamb, and even poor old dainty Mister—so great was Cate's zeal to have all livestock out of the kitchen—were removed, everyone except Cate and Mary Abel was weak with laughter.

Mag mopped things up; then, tears of mirth still on her cheeks, hooked a comradely arm across Christie's shoulder. "Guarantee me a show like this every day," she said, "and I won't ask for wages."

Cate and Christie were halfway to Madison before Cate was able to break through the shell of humiliation which these happenings had forged about her and which had kept her silent. Then, for some reason, she began to speak of the Thompsons.

"Ferris' mother is a very unusual person," she said. She looked away from the window to Christie, who was reshaping the dents in the crown of his gray felt hat.

"How's that?" he asked politely.

"For one thing Ferris' mother has a little miniature bellows she uses to blow the dust out of corners with." She had watched Mrs. Thompson do this, one afternoon when she had been visiting Wanda, and had been astonished at such cleanliness. She was so accustomed to thinking of herself as a model housekeeper that the discovery that there were those to whom she might appear slovenly stirred her imagination.

"Where does it go?"

"Where does what go?" Cate asked, thinking, he isn't listening to what I say, and I don't blame him.

"The dust."

"Oh. Well, it just disappears."

"It can't just disappear. It has to go somewhere."

"There wasn't ever enough to notice in the first place. But it looks so nice to see Mrs. Thompson going around with this little miniature bellows."

"Why?" Christie asked.

"I guess because it's so orderly. Friday is her day for doing it and every Friday, no matter what, she goes around with this little miniature bellows, blowing."

Christie put his re-dented hat on his head and leaned toward her so that she could see his reflection in the window; but he didn't touch her. There was a good six inches between them, as there had been since they had got on to the train. Not so much as a thread of her zouave jacket had touched a thread of his blue serge. "It's like clockwork," she said, further explaining Mrs. Thompson and the bellows.

"It must be," Christie said.

Stop, stop, Cate told herself. This is your perfect day and you are deliberately ruining it. Stop me, she bade Christie. He could rescue her—why didn't he? He had only to put his hand, or one finger even, on the green velveteen of her sleeve. He knew she was, in a way, committing suicide; committing a murder, killing their day. Why didn't he stop her? Rescue me, she pleaded, save me.

"Wanda Thompson is also very unusual," she said.

"She got a little miniature bellows too?"

For a second, that sounded so ridiculous, Cate thought she *was* rescued; but it wasn't enough. She was stronger in her intent to harm than that.

"Oh, no. But she went to the Cincinnati Conservatory of Music for one term. She improvises."

Why was she talking and talking about these Thompsons anyway? Was it because she wanted to say, Look, I'm a good friend of these people—people who don't have ganders in their kitchen and bathtubs in their sitting-room? A way of saying, only not in so many words, I'm ashamed of Mama and ashamed of the Poor House?

"Mama can play a lot better than Wanda Thompson can, though," she made amends.

"I believe it," Christie said. "So why don't we talk about the Conboys instead of the Thompsons?"

"Oh, I don't know," Cate said, fearful that a word too much would close the Thompson prison doors behind her again.

"The Conboys are the ones I'm interested in," Christie said, and touched one of the beehive-shaped buttons. "And the Frasers." He moved nearer and she felt his shoulder and thigh press close to her. "Let's talk about them," he said.

For the rest of the day that was what they did, even when they seemed to be talking about something else. And they both knew it. When they got off the train exclaiming, "What wonderful weather," they meant, "How wonderful it is to be together." When they walked down Main Street in the midst of the Saturday crowds and said, "How many strangers there are in the world," what they meant was, "But we're not strangers, we're together." When Cate exclaimed about a passing woman, "Isn't she beautiful?" she asked too, "Can you love me when there are others so much prettier?" And Christie answering, "She's nothing so much," answered yes, to her unasked question and added in unmistakable tones, "You are more beautiful than anyone to me."

They stopped before store windows and bought, in their minds, the merchandise they saw there. Christie bought rings: pearls, garnets, and a single huge bloodstone, and slipped the rings, one at a time, on to Cate's square-tipped fingers. He bought, in his mind, a chatelaine watch and fastened it with the anchor-shaped pin which went with it, just above one of the curves which Cate, for all of her sensible, matter-of-factness, had not been able to hide from him. Cate, when they passed grocery stores, imagined buying, for their pantry, supplies of Epp's Comforting Cocoa and Carl's Imperial Granum—even lowly things like potatoes and onions. They stopped for a long time in front of a hardware store, admiring a Majestic A-1 Wood and Coal Range, imagining it in their own kitchen and a meal which they would share, cooking and eating, on it. They shared everything they saw until they came to a furniture store displaying a brass bed, bulbous and glittering as an Eastern temple. Cate, feeling it unladylike to stand staring at such an object in the company of a young man, hurried, after one sidewise glance at its opulence, on down the street.

At a drug-store the imaginative buying stopped; there Christie paid real money for real perfume, a new scent, just on the market. "Blue Lilies of the Nile" it was called and the sign in the window declared it to be "Delicate as a cobweb, lasting as the hills." Cate, who had never owned a bottle of perfume before, was wonderfully pleased and too excited and impatient to wait until she got home to try it. In the middle of the sidewalk with the Saturday shoppers flowing by on either side, she opened the bottle. "It's so sweet," she told Christie, breathing deeply. "Blue Lilies of the Nile! To think, that it came all the way from Egypt." Christie, who doubted it had come quite that far, said nothing and the farmers and their wives walked around her, smiling as she dabbed the scent on to her throat and ears.

At lunch the waitress sniffed appreciatively, "That's a sweet toilet water you're using, miss," she told Cate. "Thank you," Cate said, "but it's not a toilet water. It's real perfume."

After lunch they took the ferry, as Christie had planned, and crossed the Ohio. "So this is Kentucky," Cate exclaimed as they walked ashore. She had half expected that the houses and trees on the Kentucky side of the river would have some exotic foreignness which would set them apart from the common run of Indiana houses and trees. But they were just the same, the same white or unpainted farm houses; the same bare or evergreen branches. Even the road, up which they began to walk was exactly the same as the roads which wound across the Indiana hills, narrow, rutted, and ungraveled.

"This looks like one of Em's pictures," Cate said. Below them was Em's snake fence and above them her hills, and the very road they stood on was Em's, turning and twisting as it climbed the rise, and waiting for some traveler, leaving forever, to walk down it. Em's setting or rising sun, however, was absent. In its place was an early afternoon sun, so warm that Cate, careless of the resulting exposure, took off her zouave jacket and carried it over her arm. After a mile or so they came upon the ruins of a burned-out farm house, its stone chimney standing in the midst of the charred trees like a neglected monument. They sat down for a minute on the hearth to rest and watched, from there, the river below them, brimming with light in the afternoon sun.

"It's strange, isn't it," Cate asked, "to be sitting here uninvited in the very center of someone else's house?"

"It's not a house any longer."

"Last times and first times! Aren't they sad? The night this house burned down everybody sat by this fire and talked and no one had any idea it was a last time. But it was. And somebody said one word, and nobody knew it was the last word that would ever be said in this house. How terribly sad."

Christie said, "If they'd known it was the last word it would've been sadder yet."

Cate protested. "Oh, no. Not knowing makes it ten times worse. If this was our last time together, wouldn't you want to know it?"

"Something tells me it won't be."

"It could be. The ferry could sink, going back to Madison, with all on board." The Ohio, below them, looked big enough and ruthless enough to swallow ferries like gnats. "What would you do if you knew it was going to sink?" she asked, and waited for an answer out of one of her novels: "I would thank God for the time He has already given us," or "To die in your arms would be sweet."

Christie said, "I'd cross on the bridge."

Cate was unprepared for this matter-of-factness. Was she so far ahead of him in her feeling? When they had talked of the color of the Ohio and if blue lilies really grew on the Nile, had he really cared about those things? She hadn't. She was making conversation, passing the time until they came to what really mattered: themselves, touching and loving. She was nothing to him and she knew it. A companion on a walk and the walk more important than the companion. Oh, why had she been so gullible, so taken in and believing, so unable to see or hear anything but Christie, while he had ears and eyes for everything and was calm as a meeting-house in the face of her drowning? He had betrayed her confidence and she gave him one straight, knowing look, then walked to where the front door had been and threw Blue Lilies as far as she could, as far as the river, she hoped.

"What's the idea of that?" Christie asked.

"I'm tired of it."

"What're you going to do about the way you smell? Tired of it or not, you can't throw that away."

"It will evaporate."

"Lasting as the hills," Christie reminded her.

"The hills aren't lasting. They're washing away. Look." She made a commanding gesture toward the Ohio. Deny it, she implored him, contradict me. If you don't love me, fight with me. That is the next most personal thing. But he said not a word.

She gave him one more chance. "This isn't even the same river that went up here yesterday."

"So they say."

Indifferent, indifferent. She ran away from him at that, jumped over the stone foundation and raced down a pathway lined with shells till she came to the winter skeleton of a summerhouse, gray boards scaly as snakes, bare and desolate, and the bareness and desolation pleased her. She sat on the bench which extended the length of the back wall and thought, This is the end of things. On the river below, the sun glinted across the steel-colored riffles and winked off the brasswork of a passing steamer. She heard passengers shouting to riverside loiterers, and saw one loiterer toss a shining object upward, which was followed, as it dropped toward the water by some river bird. On the flats beyond the river two men were burning brush, and the smoke from this fire rose in a great transparent blue column. She noted all this. She told herself, This is a beautiful day and for no reason at all you are ruining it; but, though she could hear reason's voice she was powerless to heed it. Reason told her, call Christie and tell him you're a wicked fool. Save your beautiful first day in Kentucky. But she was determined to suffer; and to inflict pain.

She heard Christie's steps and, in spite of herself, turned and watched him go, slowly searching, down the hillside below the burned-out house. After a while he stooped, then rose, and holding her bottle of Blue Lilies so she could not miss seeing, threw it in a sweeping loop some hundreds of feet nearer the river.

Cate jumped to her feet. "Why did you do that?" she shouted. "It was mine, you gave it to me and now you throw it away." He came to the summerhouse without answering and Cate told him, "If there's one thing I've always scorned to be it's an Indian giver. If I make a present, it's for good."

Christie listened, his hands in his pockets. "Make up your mind, Cate Conboy," he said finally, "which it is you want. Your cake or the pleasure of throwing it away. There's no known way of having both."

He was giving her a choice and that was what she least wanted; given a choice she would have to choose whatever was most painful, wouldn't she? But he took his hands from his pockets and shook her lightly. "What's the matter with you, Cate?"

The prison doors opened at his touch and her head drooped forward on to his shoulder. He led her back to the summerhouse, seated her, took the fancy, big-knobbed side combs from her hair and began to smooth her curls comfortably away from her face. "What got into you, Catey?"

"I don't know," she whispered. Whatever it was, sickness, craziness—while it lasted she couldn't speak. He sat beside her and she leaned against him, and watched, no longer separated from them, the beauties of the still winter hillside and the quiet river. "Help me, Christie."

"With what?"

"Being that way. Hurting us."

"I'll try."

"It isn't that I don't love you. You know that."

"Yes," he said. "I know that, Catey."

"I'll always love you."

"I'll always love you." With his hand following, but not touching the curve of her breasts, he said, "You are so beautiful; here, Cate."

Trembling, she pulled his head down until it rested on the fullness of her breasts and holding him so, she pressed her face against his soft heavy hair. "Do the buttons hurt you?" she asked.

"A little," he said.

She undid them quickly and passionately. "I don't want ever to hurt you, not in any way. Tell me if I ever hurt you, Christie."

He settled his head against the softness of her white chemise and, above its scooped-out neck, the first swelling of her beauti-

[232]

fully full and rounded bosom. "You could never hurt me, Cate," he said, "never."

For the rest of the evening they hurt no one, least of all themselves; arm in arm, unable to stop looking at each other long enough to make sure where they were going, they bumped into townspeople and were forgiven because of their happiness. If they had been old, ugly, and in pain, their lurchings would never have been overlooked; but they were young, comely, and in love, and passers-by were moved at the sight of them as by the sight of the first snowfall or the reappearance of Venus after long absence in the evening sky. Moved beyond that. For the passers-by had never been snow or evening star; and they had been young and in love, and seeing Cate and Christie, it was easy for them to believe that they had been beautiful as well.

The Orpheus Club Singers were presenting their program in the Opera House, the grandest building Cate had ever been in. She took color always from her surroundings; amidst dirt and poverty she was poor and dirty; on the sweeping stairway of the Opera House, amidst the velvet wraps and feather boas, with plumes tossing about her face and taffeta petticoats whispering along the stairs at her ankles, she too was gay and feathered and rich. The capote and jacket, which at The Farm had seemed too ornate and dressy, here, if anything, seemed too plain. And her bosom, which had there appeared frightfully noticeable, was here, she saw at once, a curve quite natural to ladies and nothing to hide or complain about. Blue Lilies of the Nile, extraordinary on the winter hillside, here, mingling with rose and violet and carnation, was only another sweet scent. She was rescued from singularity, at home among concert-goers. She went up the stairs, her hand on Christie's arm, joined completely with the hour, herself and love.

The red velvet curtains opened with a movement like the parting of waters, and the Orpheus Singers swept onto the stage and were framed like a picture by the arch of the proscenium with its gilded mingling of fruits and flowers and faces. The ladies wore what Cate thought of as "ball-dresses": bare ivory arms and naked shoulders, delicate, it appeared, for the opulent burdens they supported, breasts swelling up out of their swathings of tulle and chiffon, solid and creamy as mushrooms in the midst of lacey grasses. Their dresses were of all colors, but shades of red predominated, and the ladies flamed along the edge of the stage like a live fire, full of the same eddying and swaying. Behind them were the men in tails, slender cavaliers, rugged desperados, not a single lawyer or hardware merchant hidden under the menace of the black claw-hammers.

Then they opened their mouths; they sang like birds, but richer; like organs, but more trillingly; like the night wind, but with greater assurance: *Oft in the Stilly Night, Come Where My Love Lies Dreaming, Who Is Sylvia?, Canadian Boat Song, The Bullfrog on the Bank, Italian Street Song.*

Cate whispered to Christie, "It is so beautiful."

They were hand in hand and Christie, smoothing and turning her fingers, said, "Are you glad we came?"

"Glad!" She was scornful. "Oh, Christie."

Glad? These sounds so clear and passionate. Lifted beyond living into meaning. (She who had never heard music heard them so.) The boat borne so smoothly along the dark river; the lover, faithful, by his sleeping love; the street singers, daring to say that life is pleasure! Oh, glad! She was enraptured and transported. In the darkness she lifted Christie's hand to her cheek. Here, on this pinnacle, she would live. In the intensity and pleasure of these flying sounds; in the beauty of those shimmering dresses; in the frankness of those arms and breasts. She remembered a phrase of Link's: "days loaded and fragrant." Such days were possible, and they would be hers and Christie's.

There was time, after the concert was over, for them to have ice-cream at the Madison House; and, there amidst the other concert-goers, Cate moved and spoke as Christie had never seen her before, delicately poised, aware of giving pleasure.

"That is a very sweet perfume you're wearing, miss," the waitress said. "May I ask its name?"

"Blue Lilies of the Nile," Cate said, "and thank you for liking it."

When they left the dining-room they found winter outside in the streets. They had seen the first warnings, as they recrossed the Ohio, in the green and glassy sunset. Now in the icy winds that swept down from the hills about the city, winter no longer warned, but struck. Coming home from The Junction, Ajax's hooves rang against the already freezing ground with a bell-like clangor. After a day of livery-stable rest he was eager for travel, and Christie, reluctant for the day to end, kept reining him in. The result was vertical movement, the light buggy responding to Ajax's curveting in a series of birdlike swoops. Cate and Christie rocked and swayed together, held close not only by Christie's arm, but by the lap-robe, chin high and tight as a drumskin about them.

Cate listened and looked, put out her tongue to taste the icy air and quickly put it in again. At the beginning of the day, she thought, she had missed her happiness because of the way things had been at home; then she thought her own bad heart had ruined happiness for both of them. But she had one good trait: If, before the event, she imagined disaster, and she often did, afterwards, if there had been any happiness in it at all, it was the happiness she remembered.

Looking back she recalled the day as pure happiness: the Orpheus Club, singing like angels, but better dressed—in evening clothes! Raw oysters for supper, a great marvel to taste and to look at, open and staring as eyes in their socket-like shells. The mighty Ohio, and they afloat on it. The wonder of Kentucky, its wonder being chiefly that it was so un-wonderful, a picture of Indiana by Em, and nothing she herself couldn't have imagined, sitting at home. But there were matters she could never have imagined, sitting at home, that one had to go out and seek; and she marveled at the humdrum lives people led, content never to have heard an Orpheus singer or eaten an oyster on the half-shell. And never to have seen that burned-out house above the river, nor rested in the skeleton of that summerhouse, nor have been kissed and held by Christie. At first, the memory of those buttons, so quickly undone, had troubled her, but now the act appeared to her as she had intended it—though intended was the wrong word, with its sound of planning, for there had been no plan, only the act itself which was a way of saying love. And it was love which caused her now to say to Christie, "Let's go back sometime and build a fire in that fireplace and cook our supper there."

"All right," Christie said, "when'll we go?"

"When's the best time?"

"Go when the grapes over that summerhouse are ripe. I like grapes."

"So do I. That'll be this fall. And we can hunt my bottle of Blue Lilies."

"No, we'll leave it there. It was meant to be there, as an offering, a libation."

That was a new word to Cate. "Libation?" she asked.

"A thank-you to the gods for today. We should've poured some in the Ohio, too. Tribute from the Nile to the Ohio."

"From Antony and Cleopatra to Christie and Cate," Cate said, feeling shy at this far-fetched comparison but wanting to show that she caught on.

Christie hugged her closer, a feat that hadn't seemed possible. "My serpent of the Nile."

They rocked on together, laughing, their warmth exhaled into the bitter night in wreathing clouds.

"I am so happy, happy," Cate said. "And I'm so glad I put some Blue Lilies on me before we made the offering. Can you still smell it?"

Christie inclined his head. "I'll always smell it," he said, pulling the determined Ajax once more down to a walk.

Cate thought, probably this is the beginning of my life, my real life. It didn't seem likely that she could ever again be selfish or cross or unreasonable. Ajax's hooves struck light from a stone, and Christie said, "Steady, boy," and they went on at a walk past the unfamiliar dark shapes of trees and fenceposts and past a patch of corn left ragged and desolate in a little field. She drowsed on Christie's shoulder and kept track of where they were by the turns and the tilt of the buggy going up hill or down.

Christie roused her by saying, "Looks like a party at The Farm. All the lights burning."

She didn't bother to open her eyes to look at them but wondered if by some wonderful chance, Lib had waited up for them, had hot chocolate ready in the dainty chocolate pot, and cups and spoons laid out on a table before the fire.

Because Christie told her not to, she didn't wait for him to unhitch but ran ahead of him through the cold to the house, imagining hot chocolate in the lighted sitting-room. She opened the door with a flourish, imitating an Orpheus singer graciously coming back on stage in answer to prolonged applause. She closed the door slowly. This is my punishment, she thought, for expecting too much. Though what was wrong? Four quiet people, two sitting, two standing: Papa dressed as usual, leaning against the mantel; Mama in a wrapper, leaning against a chair. Em, barefooted, with a coat on, upright, on a straight-backed chair; Doss in a rocker, pants pulled on over his undershirt. Where was the wrongness in that? The desolation?

Beneath their folded and puckered lids, Doss' eyes were round as a turtle's. Without a collar his neck was turtle-long too, naked and exposed—stretched, it came to Cate, from all his years of peeping. Em was stone, the way she could be; her lips were blue and she had one foot on top of the other and they were blue too. Her father seemed to be short of breath. Lib's mouth was on one side, her eyebrows pulled down so that the ridges, which they usually covered, were exposed, sharp and bare as knives.

Her father's voice was low and quiet, no relief as a shout would've been. He said, "Please tell Christie to go on up to bed, Cate. This is a family affair. Then you come back."

When she came back, Lib let go her chair and was standing in front of Em, speaking. What she was saying came to Cate like speech heard from a distance, or heard when the wind was blowing and the cedars booming: some words were very clear, loud even, exploding inside her head, and others were blurred, and without meaning. Finally, Lib put a hand on the lapel of Em's coat and spoke with scorn and contempt. "Show us too, miss, what it is you're so proud of, what you've been parading around in the middle of the night to display, what you've roused up a whole household to see. Get up here and now," she said and tugged at Em's coat while Em, her stoniness all vanished, sank away from her. "Don't begrudge your own flesh and blood, your own family the sight of what you were so proud to force on others. If a sideshow's where you're heading, get up here and now and start your practising, give us a taste of the wares you think so much of." And she hauled Em, by main force, upright.

Cate, even if her mother's hands had been hot white pinchers, would surely have loosened them from Em's coat at that minute without thought of pain to herself. She saw Lib's hand, the one she had succeeded in loosening, flash out and heard the sound and knew she had been slapped, but felt nothing whatever. She understood clearly how easy it is, sometimes, to die; how impossible, really, not to.

"Let Em alone," she cried and then her father's hand too betrayed her.

"Go to your room," he said, turning her after his punishment in that direction.

"Em, Em," Cate cried, but she was already moving. "Mama," she entreated finally.

"Your mother was exaggerating," her father said, and she betrayed Em with that funny word in her ears.

In her room she undressed, letting each piece of clothing lie where it dropped, capote, zouave jacket, bengaline dress in one pile; in another, a little nearer the bed, her underwear, and finally at the bed's edge, her shoes and stockings. She got into her freezing bed, naked, too tired or too indifferent to care about her nightgown, and lay there, shaking.

7

That night the winter everyone had said would return, did return, sharp and bitter, to surprise them all. For in spite of all their talk about "this can't last" each one had wondered in his heart of hearts if it might not; if this might not be the year that "spring began in February." Why not? They weren't so unlucky, were they, as to prohibit all pleasant surprises? The weather, before this, had taken unusual tacks, hadn't it? There had been the year, hadn't there, when butterflies drifted by in droves, when a minute's walk would plaster you over with wings? The year of the great blizzard? The year when the smoke from prairie fires mixing with river fog had rested along the course of the Ohio as thick as paving blocks? Why not the "year of the early spring" then? And why not this the year for it? The mere fact of their being alive didn't put all wonders out of the question, did it?

Maybe not; but 1900 wasn't, in Rock County anyway, the year of the early spring. 1900 was the year of the usual wintry story, there. Owls hoorer-a-hooing in the cold dusks and jays screaming in voices sharp enough to splinter ice. True winter sunsets, first, mother-of-pearl tints then a clear green, followed by woolly flocks in a gray sky. Hard coarse rain flung in the face like a handful of wet gravel as you went out to feed the stock. Black water flowing past the snowy banks of Bleeding Creek. Everybody's clothes, so tight did they all stick to the stoves, smelling of woodsmoke. Everybody snatching up the cat, when he came in from a nap in the hay-mow, to get a sniff of his summery cut-hay smell. And the cat, crying to get outside, but at the first whiff of arctic air, deciding to postpone his trip. Sheets frozen stiff. Outside doorknobs so cold they stuck to the hand when clasped. And where had the crows gone? And who could remember as far back as leaves? Pork in the barrel, flour in the sack, wood in the woodboxes—what else mattered now? Stamp on the earth—it was frozen so hard they could hear you clear to Louisville like as not. A cold tedious frozen time: nothing to do but wait and hope for spring.

John Manlief sat on his bed gazing at the lights which he could see shining out through the cracks in the barn. He felt snagged by them, as if they were so many fish-hooks deep in his flesh and pulling him toward the barn where Link and old man Dilk attended the farrowing sow. He had no desire to help there, to speak to Link or Dilk, or even to be seen. He wanted only to look, to observe, but this he was painfully prompted to do. Painfully, because he was unable to move. He hung upon the windowsill like a drop of water which, lengthening, tries to join the general stream but has not finally the force to escape the confines of its own circumference. What a godsend a call from the barn at that minute would have been; any invitation, however lukewarm, would have been enough to start him moving. But go of his own will? It was impossible. How had this imprisonment started? By a hanging upon the edges of occasions, imagining failure? Now he hung upon the edge of an occasion imagining success: imagining himself there in the lit barn with the other two men, accepted by them and busy in whatever work a farrowing required. He was city-bred and had never seen so much as a cat bring forth a kitten. But it was not the event of birth, mystery as this was to him, which drew him so strongly toward the barn: it was the compassionate care, for so he imagined it, Link and old Dilk were giving the sow. He saw them in his mind's eye bend over her, feed her, encourage her—whatever was done on these occasions—completely unmindful of the cold, the hour, or the fact that neither of them would be a cent richer after their night's work. They were free men, they had escaped from themselves, and it was this freedom which he longed to see, as a man in jail cannot resist putting his eye to the window when anything outside moves. In him nothing moved.

He had looked at everyone at the Poor House in this way, watched them, speculated about them, but was no more able than a tree to communicate with them. He had thought most often of Link: close-mouthed; determined to hand them all equality and self-respect even if he had to work them to death in the bargain: "Work till you can see your hoe strike light," he told them and set them all an example; taking his sole ease, as far as he could make out, in measuring snowdrifts, writing letters. Had the man a friend? Had he ever had one? Except Lib.

Lib: you are someone else, he thought, a live woman. By you I might have been saved: not to goodness—he was not thinking of saved in that way—but saved for living.

Cate: poor wretched girl, half of her harkening to Papa's reason; half, attached to Mama's un-reason.

Em: God knows, I will not try to follow you, miss.

Dandie: loving, hence free. I will smoke one of your cigars some day, Senator, if you can manage to stay out of jail that long. After Lib, my eye's greatest pleasure. Self-consciousness is the devil, and Dandie has none. There is no shadow on him when he moves.

All these people lived in his mind—where he himself lived. Often in the middle of the night he was compelled to get up, light a match and peer into the cracked mirror which had belonged to Doss, his former roommate, to see if he had any existence, outside his mind. In those minutes, he was a peeper like Doss; hunting a greater mystery than Doss had ever looked for beneath doffed drawers or under lifted petticoats; hunting himself, trying to externalize himself. He would look in the mirror to see if he actually existed, to see if there was any more to him than his own thoughts about himself. He never left the house without his little pocket looking-glass. He would take it out, fingers trembling, blood thundering in his ears, and have a quick peep: how beautiful to see reflected there his broad, pale face, as real as any hardware merchant's. Once, when he had first arrived, and in the sight of all the inmates, he had kissed that reassuring reflection.

He had never done so again; not because he had willed himself to stop—he couldn't do that—but because he was beginning to take that reflection for granted. He could light a match, as he was doing now, move over to the mirror which Doss in his hurried leavetaking had left behind, and hold the light in an untrembling hand. Light match after match and trust every time to see a face, the very same face, in the glass.

He heard Link and old Mr. Dilk come in from the barn, he lit a final match, then tiptoed down the stairs to the kitchen carrying his shoes in his hand. There, he put on his shoes, got himself a lantern, and shielding its light under his coat, went silently down the pathway to the barn.

11

IT WAS three weeks after their trip to Madison before Cate attempted to write Christie. It was nine o'clock at night, raining, not very cold. She sat up in bed, a shawl pinned around her shoulders with an old safety-pin, her curls skinned back into an unsteady knot and held there by one of her mother's big backcombs. A lamp burned on the chair beside her bed and beyond it, in her bed, Em lay, either sleeping or pretending to sleep. The March rain, which pelted against the window, was covering it with a continuous wash of dark water. Cate dipped her pen into the ink-bottle on the chair and wrote swiftly.

Dear Christie,
    I am returning to you the beautiful gold heart locket you so kindly gave me last Christmas. I am sure you feel as I do that our friendship should end. Papa says he did not explain to you why he asked you to leave that Sunday morning, since the matter was so personal. He says he did tell you it was a matter of family trouble and that he trusted you would understand it was not a suitable time for your visit to continue, enjoyable as it had been to us all. For the same reasons I think it is not suitable for us to continue going together. I do not expect we shall ever meet again but I want to assure you that no one will have your welfare more at heart or be more eager to hear that you are progressing in your chosen profession.
                                    Your sincere well-wisher,
                                        Catherine Conboy.

The minute this letter was finished she tore it into a thousand pieces, put the torn pieces inside her pillow case, and began another.

My darling,
    I love you so much and I am so weak. What can you think of me? I think we must part. All night long after we came back from Madison, in spite of what had happened, I thought of you. Of us, I suppose.

How many times do you think we kissed? I don't know. You would think we would keep track, wouldn't you? A man always knows how much money he has and I wouldn't trade money for kisses, would you? I could touch every place you kissed me, even if I couldn't count them. I have never been drunk but if that is the way whisky makes men feel I don't blame drunkards.

What can you think of me? That is a silly question because I know the answer. You can't respect a girl who does not respect herself. I can't put into words what I did. You know—so cheap—and immodest. I had as well face it. I love you too much to want to saddle you with the kind of girl I am turning out to be. I would be a millstone around your neck—a walking invitation to men to make improper advances. Doing what I did—you know—seemed at the time, kind, even courteous. But courteous I guess is the last thing a really good person would call it, and kindness seems to be one of the surest ways in the world to get into trouble.

May I keep the gold locket? It will be my dearest possession, always. We must not meet again. I would just drag us both down. You are stronger than I am but perhaps not strong enough to offset my bad tendencies—which are not just chance with me but run in our family. I will love you until I die. Please remember me kindly, always,

Cate.

This letter she wadded into a hard ball and threw with all her force across the room. Em, either awakened or never really asleep said, "What are you doing, Cate?"

"Writing," Cate said. Em, propped on her folded arms, was looking at the ceiling.

"Was that some writing you threw away?"

"Yes," Cate said.

"Why?"

"It didn't suit me."

"Was it to Christie?"

"Yes," Cate said, and dipped her pen into the ink well and began her third letter.

Dear Christie [she began],

I am going to tell you everything, just as it was, and let you judge.

It is now ten o'clock at night and raining hard, but not very cold. I am in my room and Em is here too, but not asleep. She just asked me if I was writing you. This is my third letter. At first I couldn't write you at all, then I wrote to say we shouldn't see each other any more. I tore those letters up because I knew I couldn't bear that. My aim now is not to say what we should do, or not do, but just to tell you what happened.

When I got up that next morning Papa said you had gone—because, he said, he had asked you to. He said that with the Sheriff coming for Doss Whitt, etc., it was not a suitable time for Sunday visiting. I didn't think so then, but he was right. This is why the Sheriff was coming, which Papa didn't tell you.

Cate held her pen in midair thinking how to go on from there and Em said, "Are you going to tell Christie about me?"

"I'm going to try to," Cate said.

"It will make an interesting letter, I guess."

Cate looked at Em who was still staring at the ceiling. She could see that Em had not intended a sarcasm and that she might have said in the same way, "The rain will soak the ground." She was forgiven by Em, she knew that; but she was also excluded. "Nothing but my old flesh," Em used to say. Em was no longer so cavalier. What was hers was hers and she would in no public way disdain it.

"What are you going to tell him?"

"Just what you did."

"I suppose he's got to know?"

"Somebody'll tell him if I don't."

Em said nothing, and Cate wondered suddenly, If that's so, why should I?

"Tell him," Em said, "I did it to cure Doss."

"To cure him?" Cate asked, her mind so busy planning the letter to Christie she had forgotten what the letter was about.

"To cure him from peeping." Em had turned on her side so that she faced Cate, but her looking went past her. "Doss wanted to see a naked woman, and they were always hiding from him so he had to spend his life peeping and getting into trouble. He was a good man and believed in God and only wanted a chance to see God's handiwork. So I took pity on him. How could nakedness hurt me?"

"How could it cure Doss?"

"I thought it was like the gold fever. When you find gold, you don't have to hunt any more."

"Is that true?" Cate asked.

"Maybe not," Em admitted. "How do I know? But it was what I thought: I thought if he saw me he'd be cured."

Cate had never permitted herself to *see* what Em had done; she could say the words, Take off her clothes, put on that coat, climb those stairs, knock on Doss' door, take off the coat, stand there naked while Doss' wrinkled old turtle eyes—but she could not *see*. She would not let herself see.

"Perhaps you did cure him."

Em smiled, years older and wiser by that trip up the stairs. "Oh, no. He didn't even want to see me, he cussed me and made that uproar. That's what brought Papa."

"But there you were," Cate said, puzzling it out, "exactly what he wanted and without any trouble."

"The trouble," Em speculated, "was what he enjoyed most, and I was no trouble. Looking at me was like looking at a tree or a house for Doss. Except he had to go to jail for looking at me."

"Well, that was trouble, if trouble is what he wanted."

"That was trouble afterwards. What he wanted was trouble before."

Something clouded Em for Cate; not sending Doss to jail, which she had certainly done, nor the sin she had committed in stripping herself before a man. It was two things: it was the film Doss' eyes—because for all his uproar he had certainly looked—had drawn across Em, those hard eyes, lodged amidst their folds and puckerings like a spider's swelled and shiny body in its nest of legs and webs; and it was Em's will—Em, the person who was capable of that act, who could walk up those stairs, open that door, take off that coat. And could then walk down again and survive that meeting in the parlor. She felt awe for her; even fear. What could Em not do?

But we *are* alike, Cate told herself. Em had been found out, was all. She was unlucky and I was lucky. I undid those beehive buttons, I was willing to be naked. Oh, we are sisters all right, and we have the same aunts, and what I did, I didn't do to cure anyone, but out of a real love of undressing before a man's eyes.

"I had an only sister," she said suddenly, aloud, and Em looked at her but did not appear to be surprised. She had said it for the same reason she had written Christie, "It is ten o'clock, it is raining." To understand the fact, to separate herself from it and

[245]

perhaps possess it. She had an idea people might travel through the whole of their lives and for lack of ever saying the word "sister" never have a sister at all, though surrounded by half a dozen. But she had said the word and she had a sister, a girl with a high-necked nightgown buttoned under her long chin, pale lips folded in remote thoughtfulness, and stiff black braids lying like gnarled sticks outside the bedcovers: Emma Jane Conboy, twelve years old.

On the wall beside her bed was a rusty stain and Cate traced its outline with a finger. On the night she had come home from Madison and had heard Lib say to Em, "Take off that coat and show us all what you're so proud of," she had made a vow, "I will never forgive Mama for what she did tonight." And to record that vow and remind her of it (for she had no firmness of purpose about hate), she had scraped her knuckles back and forth across the rough plastering next to her bed until there was enough blood left there to be a sign to her in future times. This was a future time, but that stain was now a sign to her, not of unforgiveness, but of greater understanding. She understood now that her mother had had to speak to Em in that way for Em's own good, to save Em from perhaps worse happenings later. And she had flown at Mama at the very moment when she had been most upset, most in need of support from her elder daughter. Since then she had tried to make it up to her mother—for that rebellion and that flare of hatred; and had succeeded a little, she thought. She covered the bloodstains with her spread fingers. If she could now forgive herself she would perhaps be able to go ahead and find in life that stateliness and honor for which she had always so much longed.

She began a fourth letter to Christie:

Dear Christie,

I'm sorry I haven't written you for such a long time. It is late now and I can't write a real letter tonight. The wind is blowing and it is raining and I am thinking of you. I hope you are well and that I'll see you soon. Always, your true friend,

Cate.

This letter she handed to Em. Em read it through, then asked, "Why don't you say lovingly, Cate. You do love him, don't you?"

Oh, yes, she thought, I do love him, Em; I undid the buttons without being asked. We are blood-sisters, Em, and I wrote the calm words to offset the un-calm act. But she could not confess. Silently, she held out her hand for the letter.

Em did not return it, but said, running a finger across its words, "And you didn't tell him about me."

"No. You can, if you want him to know."

"No. I'm never going to tell anybody anything any more. If there's something I've got to say I'll write it on a piece of paper and put the paper in the casket. That will keep me from busting and won't put anybody in jail or get me whipped."

Cate said, "I got you whipped."

"Yes," Em said, "you did."

"Maybe I'll take your papers out of the casket and read them too."

"No. You thought it was honorable to tell on me, but you wouldn't think it was honorable to read my papers."

The word honor, spoken by Em so soon after she had thought it, moved her strangely. "I wouldn't," she declared. "You're right, Em." She stood up and watched the lamp, leading its own steady life of burning, and the storm, blowing up again, sluicing black water down the lighted pane. "I would like to lead a stately, honorable life," she said.

Em said, "Don't read what I write and don't tell on me."

Cate lifted the window two inches, and all the watery tongues of the night spoke inside the room; then she stood by Em's bed for a few minutes hunting a way to say, I love you, Em; but except for those very words, which were certainly too bare-faced, she could find no words which would do. She tucked Em's two braids under the covers, touched her shoulder, then without even saying good night, blew out the lamp and got back into her own bed.

8

WATER and music, Cate thought, break out at the same time in the spring. She and Em were going cross-country to spend the day with Dandie and Nory. It was a bright clean morning, a soft wind blew them along, rippled the ponds and curved the clumps of sallow grass which had survived the winter's snows, and lofted the blackbirds, who alternated flying with singing. Em paused and stroked the arch of a yellowed tuft of grass as softly as if it had had fur like Mag's Mister. Cate watched her without a word. She had not much wanted her company for the trip but Lib had said, "You can go if you take Em with you. And see," she had added for Em's hearing, "that your sister keeps her clothes on while there."

This was an old story to both of them; though what surprised Cate was that her mother did not blame her father more for what had happened to Em, blame him for bringing them all to the Poor House in the first place where they'd be exposed to peepers like Doss. But the person Lib blamed was Em, saying that a person with an itch to take off her clothes would always find an excuse to do so, while anyone with even an ounce or two of real modesty and determination could balk a thousand peepers.

Thinking back, Cate knew that this was no new thing in her mother; that Lib had never found in others any excuse for her own or any of her family's mistakes. If any of her children had trouble at school, it was never the teacher's fault, but theirs; if Dandie came home with his clothes wrestled half off him she didn't blame the other boy but Dandie: either let him stay away from boys like that or learn to wrestle better. If Link bought cheap Hamburg edging from a pack peddler at six times the price they charged in The Junction, it wasn't the pack peddler's double-dealing she railed at, but Link's lack of gumption. A teacher's business was to make life hard for his pupils and a pack peddler's to get the best of his customers; and Lib didn't blame them for practising their business. Whom she blamed was a Conboy for coming off second best in these encounters; for coming off second best in anything. It was the same thing with Doss and Em: a peeper's business was peeping and a Conboy's business was to keep from being peeped at. Em was the one to be blamed, there; no reason in the world, except her own weakness, for her coming out the little end of the horn in that affair.

Away from home, Cate felt an insolent strength observing her friends babied and petted and excused. Lib had made her strong enough to admit failure and not to hide behind excuses. But at home she longed for a little babying and petting. If Lib had ever wiped her tears away and said, pillowing her head on her shoulder, "There, there, Cate, it wasn't your fault," she wasn't sure she could've borne the bliss. Thinking of these matters, she idled along, touching the moss on a fence rail and setting an old last year's sycamore leaf, still dangling, free. Em was a quarter of a mile away, choosing her own routes and her own distractions, but when they reached The Junction they entered it together, the Conboy girls, Em in brown, Cate in blue, the picture of sisterly companionship, though they hadn't spoken a word to each other since they started.

Cate had visited Dandie and Nory a number of times since their marriage, partly for the unending surprise of observing the story-book way in which two people, in spite of obstacles, in spite of inexperience, could make up their minds to live together and do so. Three months ago, Dandie was a harum-scarum bachelor who couldn't locate a pair of cuff-links without help and thought an evening at home a hardship to be endured by the old and crippled. Nory was in even worse case: a Poor House girl without a shimmy to call her own. Now here they were in the midst of their footstools and dustpans and bread-boxes and comb-cases, a solid married couple, unhappy to be separated a minute and at home every evening, laying carpets and lining cupboards. And it had all come so fast. It was almost as startling as if one of her and Dandie's old playhouses, outlined in pebbles and furnished with half-opened milkweed pods and knives without handles, had sprouted overnight a roof and a real cookstove.

Dandie and Nory took all these things for granted, or seemed to. They sharpened butcher knives and hung curtains as if they had been married in their cradles. This matter-of-factness is all the result of marriage, I suppose, Cate would conclude, observing closely. Marriage was a state she was interested in and hoped to learn more about; and with Dandie and Nory marriage was, she believed, still new enough for the outlines to have been unobscured by time; with them she would be able to distinguish between what was "marriage" and what was "ordinary living."

She would watch them at the table, wondering about these matters. "Pass the salt," and "Help yourself to the butter"—that was ordinary living, as two old-maid sisters together might live it. But Dandie's hand, hidden, he thought, by the tablecloth, on Nory's knee, and Nory's care in seeing that Dandie had the largest piece of pie? That, she supposed, was marriage. And Dandie's sudden, "Why so glum, now?" to Nory; or his, "Stop babying that cat." What were these—marriage or ordinary living? It was like taking a course at Normal without her examination papers ever being marked right or wrong.

Nory answered their knock in a pink house-dress, skipping a season, a summer rose in early spring. Cate, when she was not thinking of Nory as "a wife" in the study she was making of marriage, thought of her as truly a sister: Meg, to her Jo, in an Indiana story of *Little Women*.

"Heigh-ho," she greeted Nory in Jo's cheerful, fresh-air way.

Nory was surprised by this, but kissed her, then Em. "How are you, Em?" she asked.

Em accustomed, since her trip up those stairs to Doss, to this solicitude, said, "I'm better, thanks," and walked past Nory into the house, not waiting to be bidden. Cate and Nory followed her and Nory said, "I believe you girls have already been made acquainted with Mr. Korby?" And there, on the edge of the bed, the new feather tick curling up about him like a lily leaf round a frog, did sit Mr. Korby. Em, standing above him, inspected his scalp, freckled as birch bark through the long scant frayings of his twine-colored hair, and said, "I've had the pleasure"; but she laid her hand formally in his, a little frog owned by the big frog: damp and jumpy, like all that tribe.

Cate stood coldly aside from all this hand clasping. It was

improper for Mr. Korby to be visiting Nory alone on a Saturday morning, and she didn't scruple to let him know it.

"Are you waiting for Dandie?" she asked.

Mr. Korby laughed, shaking his lily pad. "You're your Papa's own daughter, aren't you?"

"Whose else?" Cate asked and Mr. Korby laughed a good deal more. "A cross-grained chip from an old hardwood log. Pretty, though." Cate turned her back on him.

"Dandie'll be here any minute," Nory explained. "Mr. Korby gave us a stewing hen for dinner so I asked him to share it with us."

"I hope you'll be asking me to share something beside stewed hen. Pitifulest sight in the world to me is an old hen laid out on a platter naked, not even a dumpling to hide her shame."

Oh, no, thought Em, hearing that word "naked" and after it, the word "shame." If you want to talk about me you'll have to stop beating about the bush. "I made a mistake," she said, "but I did it to cure him."

"I want to know," Mr. Korby said, his eyes round with mystification as he looked toward Nory and Cate for help.

"Talk about hens and mean me," Em explained, before either girl could put in an explanatory word.

"You got me helpless as a sheep on its back," Mr. Korby said politely. "Fact of the business, all you Conboys speak in tongues, far's I'm concerned. Except brother Dandie. Dandie and me speak the same language. Yes, sir, we span together pretty near perfect. Speak of the devil," he said and waved a hand toward the kitchen door.

The kitchen connected directly with the store and Dandie came through the kitchen and into the sitting-room, still wearing his black alpaca jacket like a merchant born and bred; and though his actions didn't speak of merchandise—kiss all the girls and pump Mr. Korby's hand—his words had the true mercantile ring.

"Sold it at last, Odis."

"Sold what?" Korby asked.

"That second-hand organ."

"Gone and unmanned me," Mr. Korby said, with a cock of his head for the girls, but it was all home-furnishings talk, as far as they were concerned.

"You shouldn't've done it, Dandie," Cate said (Nory was in the kitchen leaving her the one responsible for Dandie), "if Mr. Korby didn't want it sold."

Dandie shed his jacket, pooh-poohing at this. "Odis'd sell anything for money. That's his business."

"Dinner," Nory called from the kitchen and Mr. Korby sprang away from the lily-pad, saying, "Selling's my business, but eating's my pleasure."

Nory always managed her cooking easily: the old hen, neatly dismembered, rested in a nest of noodles and ranged around her were dishes of gravy, potatoes, and cole-slaw. Outside, the soft wind pushed the summer-like clouds across the blue sky, and the white tablecloth was dappled by their passing shadows. Through the window Cate could see the Saturday shoppers who already filled The Junction: ladies on foot with market baskets, their leg-of-mutton sleeves vibrating with the energy of their steps; whole families in buckboards or light spring-wagons, come into town from the farms for a Saturday afternoon of buying and visiting.

Beyond the kitchen, where they were eating, Cate was aware of the sitting-room, newly rich with its bright curtains and shining furniture; not neat as she reckoned neatness, the big book always under the little one, but tidy enough in a haphazard way. Mr. Korby and Dandie, in their store clothes on a weekday, made the meal seem festive too; and above all, Cate suddenly understood, the absence of the poor folks made the meal a party. At home she was always prepared for one of them to run in, crying or laughing, crazy or sick; at home she was surrounded by lives that had failed and were ending. Here everything was new and headed toward success. Dandie and Mr. Korby talked business and the gossip of the countryside, and in spite of herself, for she thought it her duty to let Mr. Korby know she didn't approve of him, she joined in the conversation.

"I see you and your brother's both been tarred with the same stick," Mr. Korby said.

"I don't understand you," Cate said.

"Both got a gift of gab."

Instinctively turning away from talk about herself, which she liked, Cate asked, "Has Dandie got that?"

"Has he! Why old Dandie can sell a lady a copper-lined wash-

[252]

boiler and make her think she's getting Cleopatra's marble carved bathtub. Old Dandie here's a past master at fiddling the tune the lady loves to dance to."

"Fiddle the tune that opens her pocketbook," Dandie said, "to name the tune right."

"Should hear him with the bereaved!" Mr. Korby exclaimed. "Mourn with them that mourneth, says the Good Book and brother Dandie does such a good job at this, the ladies forget all about their own troubles, they're so busy trying to comfort him."

"Is Dandie an undertaker now?" Em asked.

"Assistant undertaker," Mr. Korby said. "Going out this very afternoon to visit a family for me. The Fitzgeralds. Lost their twins by drowning. You heard about it yet?" he asked, willing to share the pleasures of his trade with them. "First the girl, then the boy, trying to pull her out. Offer them rates for the two caskets, Dandie."

Mr. Korby licked up the last of the chicken and noodles, ate two dishes of apple tapioca, then rose and stretched.

"There's a box of your wife's belongings," he said to Dandie, giving the box a sharp rap with his toe. "Picked it up yesterday out at her uncle's. Cousin of hers out there called my attention to it. Keepsakes, I reckon."

Dandie thanked Mr. Korby, but after he left he turned irritably on Nory. "Keepsakes? I didn't know you had any. If you wanted them, why didn't you tell me? I'd've borrowed a rig and gone after them."

"I didn't want them," Nory answered in a low voice. "I'd about forgotten I had them, even."

Dandie went over to the box and, like Korby, gave it a rap with his toe. "Looks like they could've found something a little better to put your stuff in."

The box, spotted and cobwebbed, appeared to have spent some time in a barn or carriage house, holding axle grease, horse liniment and the like, before being put to its present use. It still had a smell of manure and arnica. "What's in it, anyway?" Dandie asked, pushing aside the newspapers that covered it.

"I don't remember, myself," Nory said. "Mr. Korby brought it in just before dinner and I haven't had a chance to look."

Dandie lifted the first object. "What's this?" he asked sharply;

though, as it fell out of its folds, it was plainly a baby dress. "I thought you said you didn't make any baby clothes?"

"I didn't," Nory replied. "That's a baby dress of mine. Mama saved it."

Dandie dropped the garment quickly. "Oh, she did," he said. "Well, you girls look at the stuff while I get ready to go to the Fitzgeralds'." He went back to the kitchen where the washing and combing was done, and Em took his place at the box. "I'll unpack it for you if you want me to, Nory," she said.

Nory said nothing and Em began to take out the contents of the box: more baby clothes, a plush-covered photograph album, some loose pictures, a child's play tea-set, a framed wedding certificate and finally a big doll, her body gone flabby from loss of sawdust but her china face still hard and pink and wonderfully knowledgeable—like Nory's little dead baby's had been. Em smoothed the flowered skirts over the limp, rust-stained legs, then handed the doll up to Nory.

"What's her name?" she asked.

"Rose," said Nory, as if just at the minute remembering. She began to rock the doll back and forth in her cradled arms. "I got her on my ninth birthday."

Brushed and washed, Dandie came back into the room for his coat, and Cate watched him watch Nory, at first silently; then he said, "Stop that," in a loud voice, went to her, snatched the doll from her arms, appeared to be considering throwing it to the floor, but ended by tossing it harmlessly on to the bed.

"Stop that," he said again still more loudly, and took hold of Nory's shoulders as if to prevent her rocking the doll she no longer held. "Stop it, I tell you. Stop it."

Since Nory was perfectly still and perfectly quiet it was hard to understand what Dandie wanted by all this shouting and commanding. His actions were beyond Cate. This must be one of the things I don't understand about marriage, she thought, one of its mysteries.

"Stop what?" Nory herself asked, and the mystery deepened.

"Making a show of yourself—and me. If you can't get your mind off that baby, at least have the decency to put off your carrying on until no one's around."

[254]

"Carrying on," Nory murmured as if unable to convince herself that she wasn't imagining the whole conversation.

"Making a show of yourself," Dandie repeated. "Kittens. Pups. Every passing baby. Now, dolls. I'm ashamed to step out of the house with you. It's bad enough to have you carrying on when we're alone. But before people's too much. It's time to call a halt when you begin advertising to every Tom, Dick, and Harry where your heart is. I don't mind being a laughing-stock, but being felt sorry for is more than I can stomach."

"Dandie," Cate said, "nobody feels sorry for you."

Dandie took his hands off Nory's shoulders and came over to Cate with one hand raised as if he might slap her. "Shut up," he said. "You don't know what you're talking about."

He put on his coat and hat and went to the door. Then he came back, picked up the doll and curved Nory's arms about it.

"I won't be back until late," he said. "Have a nice afternoon remembering and grieving. And remember who gave it to you."

11

DANDIE kept his promise and came home late to Nory. After finishing his business with the Fitzgeralds he stopped in at the Poor Farm. Though he had seen all of his family a number of times in town, he had not been home since his marriage. As he turned in under the cedars he had an ache in his chest: Folks I used to know live here, he told himself.

Lib to his surprise, for it was nearly dark, came running down the driveway to meet him, and he gave her a hand up into the buggy. She did not kiss him, in fact he couldn't remember ever having seen her kiss anyone but his father; but she put a hand up to his cheek and said, "Well, Dandie, you old prodigal you, you old marrier."

For the first time in his life Dandie felt sufficiently separated from his mother to see her as a human being. She was, he saw, a woman who would make a man a good companion. Drive on now to Madison with her and she would find pleasure in everything, from the lights on the river to the sand in the oysters served at the Madison House. There was steel in Lib for your steel: toss a word at her and something rang out; Lib reacted.

Cate and Em had evidently told her of his falling out with Nory, for otherwise she would've had some disparaging words to say about his wife. If he was learning his lesson however, without her help, she would keep quiet. On occasions he had heard Lib say, "I'll be spit on, but I'll be darned if I'll have it rubbed in." She was practising what she preached. She had warned him about Nory, but she wouldn't rub it in, rub in the fact that her warnings were being borne out by facts.

At the side door, she jumped down, ran into the house, and came out with Dexter Bemis. "Take care of Dandie's horse," she told him. As Dexter led the horse away she said, "Be just as well if Link didn't see me do that."

"Papa still babying the poor folks, still trying to make them happy?" Dandie asked.

"Oh, I don't know what Link's trying to do and neither do the folks. With the one hand he works them to death and with the other hand coddles them. They don't know whether they're afoot or horseback. Sometimes I think your father acts like he's punishing himself, as much as looking after them."

Supper was over but Lib, declaring that the pickings had been scanty, said she'd run up a fresh batch of fried apple turnovers for everyone; and by the time Dandie was finished with his warmed-over leavings, the first fried pie, glazed and brown and steaming with scents of mingled cinnamon, nutmeg, and apples, was under his nose. "If you ever ate anything better," Lib said, "say so. Speak the truth and shame the devil. If that ain't a turnover fit for a king then I've never fed kings."

"Have you?" Em asked.

"Kings and princes," Lib said—but mentioned no princesses, Em noted.

The dining-room was as long and dark as Dandie remembered it; the coleuses just as flesh-stemmed and the stems just as hairy; and that fly, if it was a fly, astride the peach, just as enigmatic as ever. He was at one end of the table; Link and Lib (when she wasn't in the kitchen) at his right elbow, the two girls at his left.

"Last time I was here this place was as bedizened as a circus tent." There was still a short dangle of green paper hanging from the corner to recall the Christmas mosque.

"A good deal's happened since then," Link said.

Em's forkful of fried pie resisted swallowing: "Sow's farrowed and we've got that back twenty ready for corn." Em's shadow of an Adam's apple made way for pie at these words. "I want you to see the litter we got from that animal before you leave, Dandie."

Lib, with the second round of turnovers, said, "Now, Link, let Dandie do the talking. He's the visitor here tonight. He's the one with tales to tell."

The tales Dandie had to tell were not for family hearing and he began, he didn't know why, to speak of the Fitzgeralds.

"These Fitzgeralds, whose twins drowned, live in a big, half-empty house, off the road, miles from nowhere. Mrs. Fitzgerald's a sandy-colored woman, eyes, hair, all the same color. She took me into the bedroom. She had the twins in bed there, nightgowns on and quilts pulled up to their chins. We tiptoed in and whispered, as if they were asleep."

"Did they look asleep?" Em asked.

"The girl did—the boy'd been hurt in the rescue."

"A grappling hook?" Em suggested.

"Em," Cate said.

"So you're an undertaker now," Link spoke, uneasiness in his voice.

"Undertaker's assistant," Em said.

"If the dead was all you had to deal with I wouldn't have any misgivings. It's the living worries me. Having to pull a long face for them. Making money out of sorrow. Pretty soon you won't feel it, and you'll have to keep on acting it. I hate to think of your getting to be one of those oily two-faced fellows like Korby, Dandie."

Dandie tried to leave Korby out of it. "One face and no oil to notice, so far. You think I had to pull a long face there with the twins?"

"This is the beginning. In time you'll have to bring out the oil to grease the hinges."

"Before that time comes I plan to be finished with undertaking."

"Finished?" Link asked, surprise in his voice. "What then?"

Dandie knew, but he wouldn't say. He hadn't been brought up in the backwoods for nothing: where a man, if his announced plans peter out, is not sympathized with, but made the butt of jokes. "I've got my plans," was all he'd admit. "Clerking and undertaking suit me now, and while I'm working at them I'm getting to know the people in the county."

The look Lib and Link gave him told him how queer his "getting to know people" sounded to them. He supposed the truth of the matter was that they both scorned power, except as it came in personal and spontaneous ways. And he didn't. They both had a kind of pitying disdain for a man who would make a public bid for power, run for an office or make a speech; a congressman to them was as unhinged as the Abels, and unhinged in a good deal the same way. How could one man legislate for the happiness and welfare of any other man? How had they come to this conviction? In the pioneering days, when the Conboys and McFaddens and Griffiths and Goodhues were moving west, were the speech-makers the lazy ones? The politicians, the trouble-makers? The planners, the hypocrites?

While he was eating his second pie and thinking about this, Nigger Bob came in, without knocking, holding aloft an empty, yellow-shining bottle. "How're you, Bob?" Dandie asked.

"I'm poorly," Bob answered. "Bowels clogged up on me and my castor-oil's gone."

"You go see Mag," Link told him, "about that oil." And Lib added, "There's an extra fried pie out on the range, Bob, if you think your bowels could stand it."

Cate, the minute Bob left, sprang up, began to speak, then without finishing more than, "I think that—" ran from the room.

"Excuse her while she pukes," Em said and perhaps it was the truth, for Cate came back pale and was, for a time, quiet.

They stayed on in the dining-room after the last pie had been eaten, talking. Nory was not mentioned but she was in Dandie's mind and he compared her with the women of his family, how quiet she was beside them, like a flower in the midst of a flock of darting, whirring humming-birds. How fast Lib and his sisters talked! How they exalted and suffered in every phrase, leaned forward, gesticulated, made their bodies echo every word their tongues had already said. They were good-looking women, he would admit that; and they were not copies, even of themselves and the minute that had just passed; but they were too intense. After an hour with them he began to want to back off, protect himself; too much was flowing out from them. He could see the pulse beating in Lib's temple and wrist; he turned to Cate, and there was the same blue vein throbbing. The sight of it made him tired. Nory's veins, thank God, were hidden. He didn't have to sit watching her every heartbeat. While the women talked and he watched them, the wind let go with one of its mournful gusts so that the cedars set up their desolate and long-drawn crying.

"I like that," he said. "I'd almost forgotten how much I do like it. At home—" He stopped, startled to see how soon those two rooms behind Korby's store had become "home."

Lib, with her inclination to swallow any truth whole, particularly if it was bitter, took this at a gulp. "Go on," she said. "How's it at home?"

"Quiet. The store's a windbreak. Can't hear a sound of wind, even in a gale."

"When I was a girl at home," Lib said, "I used to go out to the barn just for the joy of hearing the wind whistle through the cracks. It's a taste you come by honest."

They sat together under the swinging lamp, the light falling on their like, yet dissimilar, faces and took pleasure in remembering by what ties, by what common tastes and experiences, they were bound together, and even as they remembered, busied themselves weaving new ties which in the future should hold them still closer: the tie of Dandie's first visit home after his marriage, "the night we all ate so many apple turnovers."

Dandie felt their eyes on his face, searching it for signs of any change which Nory and marriage might've put there. He held it up for their scrutiny, exposed it to Cate, who was looking for something, probably, this world didn't contain; to Link who wanted, his guess would be, goodness; and Lib who would not mind seeing a little unhappiness there, considering who would be its author. He lifted his face confidently: whatever Nory had put there he was willing for them to see.

It was ten before he knew it and strange, in some ways, to be starting out on the drive to The Junction instead of going up to his old room; but it was another person who had slept in that room and in another time. He could never again be anything but a visitor here, someone who comes back to talk and remember but does his living in another place.

Link went out with him, to help hitch, he said, but what he wanted, it was plain, was to talk. "I'm going to turn all the hogs out into the corn this fall," he said. "Going to feed them right in the field. I figure about four to the acre. It's nothing but a waste of effort bringing the corn in to them."

"Won't they founder?" Dandie asked for politeness' sake, no more interested in hogs now than he had ever been.

Link snorted. "A hog's no cow, nor horse either. A hog's got more real sense than any animal I know—not excepting a dog. Set almost any other animal loose and it'll die—either overeat or starve—but not a hog. A hog knows his limits, knows what he can and can't do. You know any other animal that'll stand by its friends in time of danger? No sir, Dandie, the fact of the business is I don't know another animal that's as clean, loyal and friendly as a hog."

Dandie, his hitching finished, heard his father out on the subject of hogs, sitting down taking his ease in the buggy. Night mists had gathered along Bleeding Creek, and the sky which that afternoon had been so blue was beginning to cloud over. The hogs, in their houses back of the barn, were grunting and snuffling restlessly.

"Listen to that," Link said. "Sign the weather's going to change when the hogs get to talking like that."

Link said no more but he was evidently not yet ready for him to leave, for he kept one hand on the seat of the buggy. Finally he said in his dry, judicial way, "You know Korby can't be truthfully called an honest man."

Dandie laughed at this mild statement. "Who can?" he asked. Then he changed his tune. "Well, yes. I think I know one man."

His father's voice couldn't have been more filled with pain if he'd hit him. "Now let's not have any talk like that. Let's have no nonsense."

"Nonsense?" Dandie asked, and his father didn't answer though he still held him by that extended hand, a pale blur against the dark leather of the buggy seat. The hogs grumbled and the crick went lipping by, under cover of the growing mist. Finally Dandie said, "I reckon I'd better be cutting for home." And still his father's hand rested there beside him, saying, Wait.

"Dandie," Link said.

"Yes, Father."

"It was always my plan—I always had it in mind—to do better by you." And before Dandie could make any answer at all, even say good night, Link was gone, far up the path toward the house and walking rapidly. Dandie sat for a while, watched the last light go out in the big dark building, then began his slow drive home to Nory.

She was still up when he came in, seated by the center table in the new oak rocker, feet on footstool, gently rocking. The lamp, she was looking downward, burnished her brown hair and made her plump little hands, nesting together in her lap, rosy. He went to her at once, and taking her feet from the footstool, sat down and leaned toward her, with his hands on her soft firm thighs—so much warmer, through the thin pink dress, than his hands, for he had driven without mittens and the night had turned chilly. He said quietly, "Tell me who he was, Nory. Tell me his name, what he looked like, where you met him, and how it happened. That is all I want to know. Tell me that and I'll never speak of it to you again."

Nory's eyes never faltered. "Why?" she asked. "What would you do?"

"Do?" He was startled. "I wouldn't do anything."

"Why do you want to know then?" Nory began to touch his hair, then his ears and the bones that cupped his eyes. While her hands moved, he said nothing. When she stopped, he said, "I want to know, because if I knew I could stop imagining."

"You told me the baby didn't matter."

"I know I did. But I didn't know what I was talking about. Every man who comes into the store, I think, Is he the one? Everyone. Ferris Thompson. Korby, even. For God's sake, tell me so I can be shut of all that."

He got up and began to walk about the room, touched the other rocking-chair and set it to moving, stopped it as he repassed it; opened the plush album which lay on the center table beside Nory, looked at the pictures, closed it, came back, and touched it again.

"What's this?" he asked.

"A photograph album."

"I don't remember seeing it before."

"It was in the box."

He had forgotten the box. He opened the album again. The first picture was of a girl in a white dress leaning against an ornate chair, a girl who had remembered to put the hand with the ring on it where the ring would show. Behind her, on the photographer's scenic backdrop, was a milky waterfall sending clouds of mist swirling through umbrella-like trees. The girl was obviously Nory's mother.

"How old was she here?" Dandie asked.

"Seventeen."

Nory was eighteen. This picture was taken—perhaps twenty-five years ago—1875. A summer morning. The Civil War a memory. She had gotten up early, this girl, dressed carefully, ridden into town with her father and mother, remembered about the hand with the ring, held absolutely still, and looked with her dark eyes straight into 1900. Straight at him, her daughter's husband, smiling in that perfectly trustful way.

"What was her name?"

"Vickers."

"Her first name, I mean?"

"Jane. She was called Jennie."

He closed the album and Nory looked up at him questioningly. "Let's go to bed," he said.

In the night they were awakened by the teasing rumble of a spring thunder-storm, so different from the thunder-storms of summer which come on quickly and mean business. They listened as it moved nearer, watched the flickerings of its distant blue-white tongue. As they heard the first slow drops on their low roof, Dandie slid his arm under Nory. We are a family now, he thought, remembering the album: pictures of ancestors here in the room with us.

"I forgot to tell you," he said, "we're invited to the folks' two weeks from Sunday. Cate's Indianapolis beau will be there. Do you want to go?"

"Of course," Nory said.

They went to sleep as the rain slacked off.

At daylight Dandie was already up staring out of the window. When Nory stirred he turned toward her. "Tell me his name," he said. "Tell me now and get it over with."

9

THE POOR HOUSE, on the Sunday morning of Dandie's and Christie's visit, was astir early. Their visit alone would have set the day apart; but in addition it was the Sunday of the month when the church ladies of The Junction, uniting under the leadership of one of the seven Protestant ministers of the town, came out to the Poor House to hold religious services. The inmates enjoyed these meetings which were held in their own dining-room, and all not bedfast attended.

Though the spring morning was mild and warm with that particular quietness which seems to mark Sundays, Jake Devlin, a new inmate, had come down to the men's sitting-room at daybreak and built up a roaring fire in the stove. Later, the men coming into the room to wait breakfast found the room too warm; but because Jake had them all buffaloed, they said nothing. All but James Abel; when he came in, he pushed up a couple of windows. "The outside air," he announced, "is fresh and pure."

Jake Devlin banged the windows down again. "Fresh and pure," he scoffed. "Fresh, pure, and freezing! And you poor fools don't know no better than to call this spring."

Jake was a large, stoop-shouldered, one-legged man who had gone west in the 50's, and now considered himself a Californian, temporarily and unfortunately detained in Indiana. All of the inmates occasionally cussed Link, the Poor House, the County Commissioners; but Jake was geographically far more encompassing. He cussed the whole eastern half of the United States and particularly Indiana where, according to him, the second-rateness which first begins to be visible east of the Rockies reaches its climax.

"You call it spring here," he said, "if there ain't snow on the ground. Why, out in California this time of the year, the roses are already as big as cow pats." He spat on the base burner to show his contempt for it and the kind of spring that made it necessary.

The climate of California, since Jake's arrival, was an old story in the men's sitting-room and a dull one. The only way to escape it was not to argue. No one argued now and he said, "I got some news for you."

"News about who?" Josh Stout asked.

"John Manlief."

"No news in him."

"You say he don't talk."

"Unless he talks in his sleep, he don't talk."

"He don't talk in his sleep."

"He don't talk then!"

"You with him at all times?" Jake asked.

"I don't wash his face," Josh said. "I don't go to the privy with him."

They were all eager for any news Jake might have, but they weren't eager enough to make themselves beholden to him; except Neddy Oates, who felt himself Jake's equal. Devlin had California, but he had horses. And for choice he'd take horses any day. What was California, anyway? Nothing but a state, was it?

"You ever hear him talk, Jake?" he asked.

"Yep," Jake said, "every day."

"What's he talk about?"

"Pigs."

"Pigs? Who's he talk pigs to? You?"

"Nope."

"Talk to himself?"

"Nope."

"I ain't going to pry it out of you. I ain't that interested in you or Manlief. Either one."

"Who he talks to," Devlin said, "is a pig."

There was a minute's silence. Then Neddy said, "The pig talks back, I reckon. That's the next part of the story."

Marvin Dilk said reasonably, "Manlief don't ever get in gunshot of the barn or the hog-houses. I never yet seen him slop a hog, let alone talk to one."

"I didn't mention the barn or slopping hogs. What I said was, Manlief talks to a pig."

"What's he say?" Earnest Creagan asked, as if Manlief's silence with humans might be accounted for by the fact that the only language he knew was one understood by hogs.

"He says," Jake said, " 'Eat, eat and grow strong.' "

There was a long silence following this, then a roomful of snickers and Jake added, "He says, 'Eat, eat, little one, and grow up to be a fine hog!' "

"Where'd this pig come from," Dilk asked, "he talks to?"

"Don't ask me. It ain't the pig who does the talking, but Manlief. And he don't talk to me."

"Where's he do this talking?" Neddy asked.

"In our room."

"You mean to say," Josh asked, "there's a pig there?"

"It ain't no ghost pig. I might be able to see a ghost pig, but I ain't so good I can smell a ghost pig. What Manlief talks to and I can smell, I figure is real. I take a sniff. Manlief says, 'Piggy, piggy.' Then I take a look, and what I see looks like pig, and I reckon, hit it on the head and put it in the skillet and it would taste like pig."

"How long's this been going on?" Dilk asked.

"There's times when I can't seem to remember not living with a pig. Was I born in a sty, I ask myself? Other times it seems to me piggy came to us about the time Link's pet farrowed."

Neddy started for the kitchen but at the door Mag stopped him. "What's the matter with you boys this morning?" she asked. "You all lost your appetites?"

Neddy put an arm around Mag's waist. "Mag," he said, "as far as you're concerned, we ain't lost a thing."

11

AT TEN, Cate and Em decided to walk down the road a piece to meet Christie, who was coming to The Junction by train but would ride out from there with Nory and Dandie. After they had left the little swale which lay like a moat at the bottom of the Poor House hill, the full sweetness of the day struck them. At a fence corner, where they stopped to pick Johnny-jump-ups, Cate listened to the silky rustle of the half-formed elm leaves overhead. It is spring, breathing, she thought; and the blackbird's song, loud and rich from the tree's center, is spring's heart beating.

They walked on and Cate expected, each time they came to the top of a hill, to see Dandie's buggy on the crest opposite them. She wondered if Christie thought of her as they moved toward each other, as lovingly as she thought of him, and was as impatient to see her. She had made a resolve about herself and Christie which she thought she should tell Em; partly because the telling would help her to keep her resolve; partly because her conscience hurt her in the matter of those beehive buttons. She had never admitted to Em how closely she was related to the girl who had undressed for Doss.

"Em," she said, "I have made a resolve about Christie."

"You are always making resolves."

Was this true, Cate wondered? This, at least, was a resolve she had never made before. "I have made up my mind not to kiss Christie any more."

"Have you already kissed him?"

"Yes. Yes, I have."

"Didn't you like it?"

"I liked it too much. That's the reason I made my resolve. I must stop before it gets a hold on me."

"What would happen," Em asked, beheading Johnny-jump-ups by hooking one flower over another, "if it did get a hold on you? Finally?"

Finally, Cate wasn't sure herself. But she answered, confident of what she did know. "I would want to be kissed more and more. One or two kisses wouldn't satisfy me. I'd lose my taste for reading and working."

"How can you tell?"

"I don't know how I can tell, but I can."

"Do you like it better than reading?"

"Yes," Cate said, impatience mounting, but determined to be honest.

"I wouldn't think it would be that enjoyable."

"You don't know anything about it."

"I've been kissed."

"By the family. That's not the same. They don't count."

"I've been kissed outside the family."

Cate stopped in her tracks. "Em! Who?"

"Earnest Creagan. But you don't have to worry about me, Cate. Kissing's the last thing in the world that's going to get a hold on me."

Cate, confession a part of her plan, said contritely, "I guess I like it."

Em, seemingly unimpressed, said, "If you're planning on getting married I guess that's a good thing."

III

THE DAY had started with fires in the stoves but by noon the windows were up and the plump ones, like Leathy and Lodema, were hunting last year's palm-leaf fans. In the parlor they were waiting dinner on Cate and Christie. Christie had chosen to walk home with Cate, letting Em ride with Nory and Dandie and now they were an hour overdue and still no sight of them. Em sat apart from the others, watching the rise and fall of the white lace curtains—as if the room occasionally sighed—and watching the room's occupants, Link and Lib, Nory and Dandie. They were unusually observable she thought, solid as statues; though not immovable. But when they moved, it was like marble moving, big heavy gestures as if their arms were weighty and their mouths hard to bend.

Link and Dandie were talking, with long pauses between their sentences. Both were on the sofa, Link as erect as a sitter could be, Dandie as slouched, far down on his spine with the ankle of one leg cocked across the knee of the other; a pose so dashing Em couldn't resist copying it. Nory was in a chair by the window with the *World Atlas* on her lap, very slowly turning its pages. Lib was at the organ playing through the hymns for the afternoon's church services.

Lib swung around on the organ stool. "I'll be switched if I'll wait for those two any longer. I wanted to get dinner over with early on account of the services."

"Let's be in no hurry," Link advised. "They'll descend on us when least we expect them."

"As far as I'm concerned, that's now," Lib said and looked toward the door, but her lack of expectation didn't bring them, and she turned back to the organ. "*Many are the hearts that are weary tonight*," she chorded, and Link picked up the tune, singing the words just loud enough for Em to hear. "*Many are the hearts that are weary tonight, Waiting for the war to cease.*"

Nory looked up from her *Atlas*. "I never do think of the Mississippi's being so long, do you, Em?"

"Yes," Em said, "that's how I always do think of it. If you didn't think of the Mississippi's being long, how would you think of it?"

"You could think of it as the Father of Waters."

"Do you?"

"I never think about it at all—except when I look at a map," Nory admitted. "Then it looks long." She turned a few more pages. "The China Sea. That's a pretty name."

"My favorite is the Horse Latitudes," Em said.

Lib, without stopping playing, said, "Em, you're so interested in geography, you go out and hunt us up Cate and Christie. Tell them we're not going to wait dinner a minute longer."

Em went through the kitchen and there Lily Bias, with her hands out of the dishpan feeling like sea weed, drew her into the folks' dining-room and closed the door behind them. Then she leaned forward, so that her dress fell away from her scooped-out chest, and pulled up an envelope decorated with clasped hands strewn with forget-me-nots.

"This is for him," Lily said in a solemn whisper and put the envelope in Em's hand.

"Him?" Em asked; and Lily pointed to the address: *Mr. Christian J. Fraser. Kindness of bearer.* "I would've said, 'Kindness of Em,' instead of bearer, but I couldn't be certain of catching you."

Em stared at Lily and knew, without being told, what ailed her: Lily was in love. Her face was like Dexter's when he spoke of Cate; and like Cate's when she talked about Christie; it had a look of being not very close to its bones. She would not say that they didn't look better, all three of them, with their faces softened and hidden that way; but it was a look that made her uneasy; it excluded her. She turned Lily's letter about half-heartedly. "Why are you writing to him when he's right here and you can talk to him?" she asked.

"Oh, petty," Lily said, "I hope to do both. In time to come you'll know how it is. My great worry at present is your poor sister. Does she have her cap set for him?"

Em, remembering Cate's morning vow about kissing, said, "I'm afraid so."

Lily was quite downcast. Then she brightened up. "She's young. She's nothing but a girl. There'll be plenty more for her. At my age I can't afford to waste too much pity on her."

Lily's age didn't bother Em—she was too young yet to think love only for the young. What bothered her, for Lily's sake, was Lily's telling what she felt. Telling anything—to anybody—was the one sure way to trouble. "Lily," she advised, "don't go around telling everybody."

Lily was indignant. She fluttered her old eyelids like battered petals. "Petty," she said, "telling is my glory."

Em could see it was; still she didn't think that changed matters. "It's a mistake to tell," she persisted, moving toward the kitchen.

"You promise to give it to him?"

Em dropped the note inside her Garibaldi blouse. "I promise," she said, and Lily disentangled her fingers from her arm.

Outside, the morning's freshness had vanished. Big clouds lumbered slowly across the sky, and their shadows stained the new grass. Cobwebs, strung about the quince bushes during the night and fresh and taunt at sun-up, were already tattered. Old hens, winter bedraggled, tried to stir up some comforting dust in the earth packed hard by snow and rain.

"Cate," Em called, "oh, Cate. Hoo-hoo, Cate." She walked toward the barn, calling as she went, and Dexter Bemis, playing duck-on-rock there with Earnest, came down to meet her.

"You want Cate?" he asked.

"No," she said. "I'm singing a new song. Cate, Cate, Cate."

"That's not funny," Dexter said.

"I know it," she said, though she hadn't until Dexter told her.

"Do you want Cate?" he asked, giving her another chance.

"Mama does."

"There's no use yelling. She can't hear you."

"Do you know where she is?"

[269]

"She's down the creek aways. Down by the falls with that fellow. Do you want me to go get her?"

"You can go if you want to," Em said, unwilling for Dexter to pretend that what he was doing for his own pleasure was done as a favor for her. "Tell her Mama's waiting dinner for her and Christie and for them to come right away."

Dexter threw away the stone he was carrying and went running and leaping toward Cate.

On the way back to the house Em put her head in the woodshed door. The noise she had heard in there was James Abel, pounding away on the edge of his spade to straighten it. Without seeming to look up at all, he said, "Come on in, Emma."

She went in and Mary Abel, who was sitting on a nail keg watching her brother work, pushed another keg toward Em. "Make yourself comfortable, Emma," she said.

Em sat down. The Abels' faces, after Lily's and Dexter's, were calm and restful and close to the bone. Settled faces. "It's good digging weather now, I guess," she said politely.

James finished his pounding and put the hammer back in Link's tool chest. "All weather," he said seriously, "is good digging weather. Bar none. Digging is easier some weathers than others but there's no bad weather for digging."

Just to keep the conversation going, Em said, "Where are you digging now?" She knew, as did everyone else in the county. People kept closer track of the Abels' diggings than they did of Sundays.

"Over at the gravel pit," James said. "There's been enough work done there already to give us a head start."

"Don't you get discouraged?"

"We do. We get tired and downhearted. But at the end of the day we've got something to show for our tiredness. In there," he nodded toward the house, "night comes and what've they got to show for their tiredness and discouragement? Corn planted, knives scoured. Perishable work." He spread his opened, empty hands before him. "It's a shame on earth the way they live and lay waste."

"Me too?" Em asked.

"Emma," James said, "let me put a question to you. Are you happy?"

The question pleased Em, and she considered it for some time without answering. No one before had ever inquired, or cared, as far as she knew, about her happiness or lack of it; and she herself had never thought of the way she felt in such terms or asked herself, Am I happy? Am I unhappy? There was, she knew, deep inside herself, a sore spot; a spot which, when she took her pencils and drawing paper from the casket, began to ache and throb so that she could not draw so much as a single line. Was the name for that spot unhappiness? When she first woke up in the morning this spot ached so she always hoped she might hear at once a piece of bad news: a terrible wreck on the B. & O. or a cyclone that had wiped out a town: then she would have an excuse for crying. Any excuse would do, would be like the needle that lets the water out of a throbbing blister. But without an excuse, how could she wake up and under Cate's wondering look begin to cry? "What's the matter?" Cate would ask. "What're you crying about?" And could she answer, "I am crying because it makes my sore spot feel better"?

"What's the answer, Emma?" James asked.

"I don't know for sure which I am—happy or unhappy."

"I'll give you a test. Which can you do the easiest, laugh or cry?"

"Laugh," Em said.

"You ain't happy then. The unhappy are afraid to cry for fear they can't stop. Laugh, laugh, laugh. That's their whole testament and creed. Stop laughing and the pit opens up beneath their feet."

Em said nothing. Was that why she didn't cry in the mornings? For fear she couldn't stop? For fear a pit would open up?

"Don't you wish you wasn't afraid to cry?" James asked, as if he were peering inside her, investigating the chambers of her heart. "Wouldn't it come as a relief to you?"

"Yes," Em said, and just admitting it seemed to take some of the ache from the sore spot.

"Poor child," said Mary Abel, "poor lost baby," and she made a motion as if to pull Em's head down on to her bosom. But Em didn't know how to put her head on anyone's bosom, and she was still too unhappy to cry.

"Why don't you come with us, Emma?" James asked.

"And dig?"

"She's too young for the work," Mary objected to her brother.

"I could throw out the dirt you dig," Em suggested.

"You willing to be a laughing-stock, Emma?"

"Yes," said Em, feeling that that was exactly what she craved to be; she could see herself, as she had seen the Abels, working deep in some pit, while above her a ring of onlookers laughed and asked questions.

"You could have a full share in the glory of finding it if you shared the shame."

"What will we find?" Em asked, not noticing the we.

"No man knows, till we come on it. Something lost that they had before us. Even you ain't so young you can't feel that something's been lost, are you?"

"No," she answered, for there seemed to be a time in her own life, far back but still faintly remembered, when she had been perfectly happy, without any sore spot. What was it she had lost since then?

"When'll you start?" James asked. "This afternoon?"

Before Em could answer the back door slammed and Lib called, "Em, Em." Then to someone else she explained, "First Cate disappears and I send Em after her, then Cate gets back and Em's lost. Em, Em," she called, raising her voice. "Hoo-hoo, Em."

Em, before answering her mother, said to the Abels, "I'll come help you as soon as dinner's over."

On the way to the house she passed Dexter, sitting on the chopping block, crying. He was silent and motionless, but tears ran out of his wide-open eyes and he paid no attention to her passing. Was this a sign Dexter was happy, because he wasn't afraid to cry?

And did all the laughing in the parlor mean that something sorrowful was going on there? Something unusual was going on she could tell, the minute she opened the door. Everyone was clustered around Cate and Christie, and she stood outside the circle, uncertain, until Christie called to her.

"Em, I've got everyone's permission but yours."

"Permission?"

"To marry Cate."

"What would you do if I said no?"

"Marry her anyway," Christie said, and bent to kiss her. And watching Cate return the kiss, Em thought, Cate was right. Kissing has got a real hold on her now just as she was afraid it would.

IV

ENGAGEMENT or no engagement, Lib sent them all slashing through dinner, pork to pie, in record time. The engagement was a pleasing matter, but it was settled; while the afternoon's services for the folks still lay ahead and were unsettled in the extreme. Lib was worried about them for a number of reasons. Without losing sight of the fact that they were church services, she knew the visitors from town would be judging Link's work as superintendent while they were there, as much as they would be worshiping. Their interest in the state of the folks' souls wasn't going to blind them to the state of the folks' bodies: were they washed and combed, neatly turned out, but unmistakably paupers? Were they in moderate good spirits, but meek and humble and able to recognize a benefactor when they saw one? Link was either blind to such things or refused to see them; but she wasn't, and her plans were all made. The old ladies were not going to wear their new calicoes, but their old ones, mended and freshly ironed; the men could wear their best—nothing they owned would convince the church ladies that county money was being spent for fripperies.

She intended to be well turned out herself. Some of the church ladies were old acquaintances and she didn't propose that there be any looking down of noses at the Poor Farm matron. She had made herself a new dress, a purple silkwarp Henrietta with a polonaise falling aside to display a pastron decorated with alternating rows of gilt and steel nail-heads—or what looked like nail-heads; and if that was not enough to convey the fact that Lib Conboy was beholden to no one, her manner would do the rest.

The minute the last pie-plate was off the table, she pushed back her chair. "There's just an hour and a half before the services start. You men carry these chairs into the folks' dining-room.

After you've finished that, the greatest kindness you can do us all is just to stay out from under foot until the meeting starts."

Christie, after the last chair had been carried to the folks' dining-room, accepted Link's invitation to walk with him up to the newly cleared piece of corn land. They went up the rise at the back of the house, past the burying-ground and into the pasture lot. Bleeding Creek was on their right and to their left the apple orchard, still some weeks short of blossoming, lifted its lavender and blue-gray wood. On the high ground across the Creek a service-berry bush bloomed misty and white. The two men, ordinarily so easy with each other, were not yet accustomed to their new rôles or their new emotions. It was two o'clock when they reached the clearing, the day's dead-quiet center, the least human hour of the day, the hour least adapted to the heart's needs. The sky was cloudless, the sun apparently stationary. They had been brought together by their common love of Cate, and they wanted to speak of her and of the future—but found no words. Link stooped, gathered up a handful of dirt and let it trickle slowly through his fingers.

"Fine open soil," he said.

Christie, for whom one handful of dirt was exactly like another, gathered a similar sample, examined it in the same way, and agreed.

"A very forward growing season," Link said.

Christie nodded. "Whippoorwills were out early this year."

"I noticed that."

They had begun to walk back slowly toward the house when three buzzards, drifting overhead, made a change in the scene which enabled Christie to say, "I think I stand a good chance of selling enough insurance in my district this year to win a trip to New York."

"New York?" Link asked. "A free trip? That'd be quite a prize."

"I thought Cate and I might be able to make the trip our honeymoon."

"Will they send the two of you?"

"Oh, no. But I'm not completely dependent on the Provident Mutual. I've got a little money of my own."

"A trip to New York," Link repeated, struggling to break through the barrier of the hour and his own nature, to say: Cate, the apple of my eye and you, a person I might some day talk to, going together on this trip, seeing at the beginning of life and in love, all of the wonders of which I've only dreamed. And I'd rather have this happiness for you than any amount of ease and pleasure for myself. He felt he should perhaps say: Cate's no unmixed blessing, you know. She's like a snake trying to shed an old skin and she can't be too concerned whether or not in her threshings about she doesn't damage someone near her. But don't try to protect her too much. Women like a sense of danger. He wanted to say, Your children will be my grandchildren. The paths of our lives from here on will cross and re-cross and I'm glad of it. This has been a happy day for me. I feel it's the beginning of happy days. But all he managed was, "Christie, I'm truly glad for you and Cate."

Christie said, wanting to hide nothing, "My Uncle Wes tells me he feels sorry for the girl I marry."

"Uncle Wes?" Link asked.

"My mother's brother. He's about the only family I have. I stay at his place when I'm not on the road. There was a while when I thought I was in love with his daughter."

"She's a first cousin, isn't she?"

"Yes, and five years older than I am. But we didn't see each other much as kids so she doesn't seem like a relation."

"Were you engaged?"

"No. There was some lovemaking, though."

"There's few of us don't get that far—with somebody."

"Uncle Wes considers me a drifter."

"What does he mean—drifter?"

"No real job, for one thing, in his estimation. I don't think I'm lazy though, and I expect to make a fair living. But I admit I'd rather be here talking to you now than out selling a $10,000 policy. I don't want any of Korby's kisses until I've seen a few things and learned a few things, money or no money."

"What, for instance?"

"I don't know. I reckon hunting for what I want to know, along with everything else."

Link held out his hand. "Go on," he said, "go on and find it.

[275]

Cate with you." They stood there for a minute, in the middle of the newly plowed field, solemnly shaking hands; then, a little self-consciously they parted and headed once again for the house.

V

AFTER Lib had all the folks ready and had extracted promises from them to stay in their rooms until they heard the bell ring for the services, she went to her own room to dress. She had finished and was lighting the lamp to heat the curling iron when Christie knocked. "Could you come out to have your picture taken?" he called. "There's just time before the meeting if we hurry."

"Who's going to take a picture?"

"I am. I've got a new Kodak."

Lib was both fascinated and repelled by pictures of herself. Her features were too strong for a camera; her long nose cast a shadow, and the bony ridges above her eyes made her eyesockets appear cavernous. Still she could not, however much she hated these images of herself, stay away from them once they were made. That is Lib Conboy, that is what people see when they look at me, she would think, gazing.

"You go on," she answered, "and don't wait for me. I'm no-wheres near ready." But she was winding up curls on a half-hot iron, and straightening her eyebrows with spit and rummaging through the drawer for a handkerchief, even as she talked.

"You go on," she called again, and she heard Christie's retreating footsteps. But she was out in the south yard, the yard with the summerhouse in its center, by the time Christie had his subjects lined up and their camera smiles in place.

"Come on," Christie called to her, "we're waiting."

"Hurry up, Lib," Link urged. "There's no time to lose."

"Em's going to take this one," Christie told her.

Lib seated herself in the summerhouse. "I'll watch. I'm not suitable Kodak timber."

Dandie alone didn't argue. He came to her and took her arm in a grip too tight for comfort. "We'd prefer the Venus de Milo," he said, "but since you're our mother you'll have to do, Kodak timber or not." She hung back. "If there's anything I hate to see," she said, "it's family pictures all gaumed up with some old toothless woman in the center. What did she have to get in it for?"

"You've got your own teeth," Dandie reminded her, but she broke away from him, running back through the arabesque of blue shadows laid on the ground by the summerhouse.

The two girls, Cate breaking twigs, Nory pleating her handkerchief, watched this performance without a word, their camera smiles fading. Em, more doubtful every minute of her ability to take a picture at all, wiped first one damp hand then the other on her skirt-tail. Link, who permitted Lib every unreason, said, "Lib, I think I hear a rig up the road. We'd better hurry."

Dandie simply took her arm in a vise, lifted her off the summerhouse bench and said, "What do you think this is, a game of wood tag?" and led her without further words to the snowball bush which had been chosen by Christie as a background for the picture.

"Where do you want me?" she asked, genuinely abashed. She made herself, as well as her children, live without the sustaining assurance of being important to anyone. The stark premeditation of posing was silly, preposterous, lined up with their faces poked camera-wards, for whose possible pleasure hereafter? But she went where she was put and smiled when Christie said, "Smile," and held still when he said, "All right now, Em, we're ready."

But this unnerved Em. The responsibility seemed too great. Her sore spot began to ache. She was sure she would touch the wrong button. "I can't do it," she cried. "I'll make a mistake." She put the camera on the ground and backed away from it, waiting for someone to give an order. Christie gave it. "Get in my place and I'll take the picture."

But there was to be no picture taking that day. Before Christie could line them up once again, the Thompson surrey had turned in the driveway and Lib and Link had left to greet them. Ferris had driven his mother and Wanda over to the afternoon services, and he let them out while he went on to hitch his horse.

Mrs. Thompson was a small and neat woman, about to Lib's shoulder. She had a flat triangular little body, broadening as it went downwards and ending in flat triangular little feet pointing in almost opposite directions. Lib introduced her to Christie and Nory, and Mrs. Thompson, in turn, introduced Wanda to them.

"Wanda," she said, "is an accomplished musician, and I have prevailed upon her to offer her services as organist for the singing this afternoon."

"My own music," Lib said, "is already laid out for playing. Reverend Foxe asked me to play. I wonder if Wanda would like to leaf through it."

The irony was lost on Mrs. Thompson. "Wanda is a sight reader," she said. "But—what do you think, Wanda?"

Wanda wore glasses and had the bright piercing look of a musician who can distinguish a sixteenth note from a thirty-second in the gloomy light of the murkiest parlor. She was high colored and flat chested, and her long eyelashes were turned backwards by her spectacles. She spoke in odd rushes, a spatter of words, then a gasping breath; and when she gasped, chest and eyelashes fluttered in unison (the one so thin, the other so full) like a well-balanced passage for treble and bass.

"I have—my own—music," she gasped, and held forth a music roll. "Thank you—just the same—Mrs. Conboy."

Lib was breathing deeply herself. "Don't mention it," she said. "I'm afraid it's time for me to go ring the bell for the services now. If you'll excuse me, please, Mr. Conboy will look to your needs."

When all who were expected had arrived (twelve women, three men—not counting the minister), Link led them into the folks' dining-room. The arrangements were churchly—but the smells were still of winter's foods, boiled cabbage, fried pork, fried potatoes. Since it was expected of him, Link sat up front with the Reverend Charlie Foxe, facing the congregation: the Reverend Foxe on one side of the parlor stand-table, moved in for the occasion, he on the other. Behind them at the organ, likewise moved for the occasion, Wanda played, as a prelude for the services, "Sweet hour of prayer that leads us from a world of care."

The Reverend Charlie Foxe, dark, plump, and deeply dimpled, had been contemplating his fingers set together to form a suitable steeple. Now he unlaced them, stood and announced the first hymn. "Friends," he said, "let us all stand and sing *Old Hundred* together." With outstretched arms and opened hands he lifted his congregation to its feet, and led them in his creamy voice, dimples flashing, "*Praise God from whom all blessings flow, Praise Him all creatures here below.*"

Link, no singer except in the mornings grinding coffee, looked over the top of his song-book (loaned by the United Brethren) at his family, neighbors and charges. Lib was singing (as she did everything) with her whole heart, her contralto warm and lively as her hand. Nory was worshiping God with her eyes on Dandie. The visitors were praising God for His mercies with unusual heartiness, surrounded as they were with so much evidence of what, except for that mercy (and their own industry), might've been their lot. The folks, in voices as broken as their lives, rejoiced in the one kingdom to which their title was as good as their neighbors'. And above all the voices, rose Dandie's big sweet tenor, a public voice, Link had almost called it a pulpit voice—but from that memory and word he shied away; a smooth, gold-flecked voice, a voice at once commanding and wheedling. Link heard the Reverend Foxe let out his own vocalities a notch or two in competition—but it was wasted breath. Dandie could outsoar him all along the line.

The sunlit April air carried with it through the opened windows scents of new foliage and warm earth. It bathed them (in the winter-smelling dining-room) with spring's freshness. Link's eyes smarted with tears at the sound of this chorus of praise rising from those who had so little cause for thanksgiving: creatures ignorant (like himself) of the history of their race on earth and with no assurance of any life—better or worse—to follow.

> "The Lord ye know is God indeed.
> Without our aid He did us make:
> We are His flock, He doth us feed,
> And for His sheep He doth us take."

It was pitiful and strange. He could not say whether his tears were for the courage or the foolhardiness.

> "Praise God and bless His name always,
> For it is seemly to do so,"

they sang, and seemly was the word, in addition to pitiful and strange. It was seemly for them to stand together in this mingling of spring and winter smells, praising the unknowable—and he loved them for it.

The Reverend Foxe had chosen as a theme for his sermon the parable of the Prodigal Son. "Friends," he said, "God loves you. Though you may have laid waste your substance and misused your heritage, the Heavenly Father is still eager to welcome you home. Afar off He waits and watches for you; from a great distance He will see you coming and prepare the feast. Though you have consorted with swine and fed on husks, you are still His children and dear to Him."

Link didn't miss Neddy's wink and jab at the word swine nor Devlin's answering whisper, and he hoped the rest of the folks would be as quick as those two to see that the Reverend Foxe's sermon was funny—for the Reverend Foxe himself, confounding sin and poverty, was going to miss it. In his own mind Link argued with the Reverend Charlie, letting the sermon swell and mount unattended. There's nothing wrong with the folks here, except they're short on money, he told him.

But it was Lib who, in his own mind, answered him. There's more than a lack of money wrong with a lot of the folks here and you know it, Link Conboy. Just because you're soft-hearted, don't shut your eyes. Don't coast along until a contrary sign explodes in your face.

Contrary signs hurt him, he had to admit; as he was hurt now to see the folks so willing to accept the Reverend Charlie's label of sinner. Accept that label, he supposed, and the world looked reasonable to them, a Poor House ending being a just punishment for their fallings from grace. The Reverend Foxe was pacing back and forth now smacking his songbook from hand to hand. Link's mind was lulled by the rhythm, and his attention wandered.

The dining-room windows were too high to give him any view outside, and he fell to examining Mag's well-polished kitchen through the open door at the rear of the room. He had inspected stove, dish-safe, and that third of the kitchen cabinet which was visible and had returned once more to the Reverend Foxe and the Prodigal Son when Manlief appeared in the doorway. The idea of Manlief as a worshiper surprised him; but in spite of his conspicuous location, he motioned him in. The Reverend Foxe would soon be finished, surely, with the husks and the swine and moving on to the feasting and the fatted calf; and there was no one he would rather see at that feast than Manlief.

But Manlief stood where he was, stockstill in the doorway, though Link saw, to his amazement, that Manlief's lips were moving. Link wanted to hush the Reverend Foxe, to say, "Be still, be still. You can talk day in and day out—but here's a man who hasn't spoken a word for a year." He saw Lib and Dandie turning about in their seats to see what was causing the disturbance and in the midst of this activity Manlief's lips continued to move; but as yet Link could distinguish no words. He made a quieting gesture at Foxe, who either couldn't or wouldn't interrupt at this point, his sermon's mounting fervor. Manlief himself interrupted it. In a voice sepulchral from lack of use he cried, "They have stolen my pig."

Link had no idea what Manlief was talking about. The wonder was, he was talking. He felt that the sermon had now a solemn and appropriate illustration. That which had been lost was now found and they should all rejoice. Anxious that Manlief should not, for even a second, be made uncertain of his new power, he called out to him heartily, "Come on in and tell us all about it, Manlief."

The Reverend Foxe tried to out-preach this interruption. Biblical swine were one thing and Poor House pigs another. "Oh beloved," he cried, "oh friends in Christ, I tell you here and now on this precious Sabbath afternoon, standing as we are in the face of eternity and under the light of God's unfailing truth, that the joy of the earthly father when he saw from afar this son, begrimed with dirt, and soiled with sin, is nothing to the joy of the Heavenly Father when He catches sight of one poor wayward human soul groping its way back to redemption and everlasting peace."

The Reverend Foxe had to stop for breath, and in that interval Manlief declared again, his voice rising like a stone tower amidst the still echoing sounds of the sermon, "They have stolen my pig."

The Reverend Foxe now took cognizance of Manlief. "Remove that man," he ordered Link.

Link explained matters in a whisper. "The man's been dumb. Be careful or you may drive him back to it."

Dumbness was what the Reverend Foxe wanted of Manlief.

"He is interrupting divine service. If he can't be silent, he belongs outside."

Manlief, while this discussion was going on, had come into the room and was advancing up the aisle between the dining-room chairs. "Mr. Conboy," he said, "they have taken my pig away from me."

"Are you going to kick that fellow out, or must I?" the Reverend Foxe asked.

"Be quiet," Link cautioned.

The Reverend Foxe said not a word, but leaving table and Holy Writ behind, strode forward to meet Manlief. As he did so, a fact to which Link had been shutting his eyes exploded in his face: the Reverend Foxe was choosing himself rather than his brother, his own voice rather than Manlief's, his church service rather than Manlief's life.

A kind of high courtesy occasionally led Link to the necessity of knocking down one of his fellow-men. Faced with the need of putting into words a conviction of the sort which had just come to him, a blow often seemed the kindest way of doing the job. At the time of the blow no such analysis ever filled his mind; only afterward did the dilemma outline itself in such plain terms. Before, there was only the tide of mounting anger, the stepping back, the loosening of the held wrist, and the picking of the likely spot. The likely spot seemed now the area on the jaw line just below the Reverend Foxe's dimple and he hastened to overtake him before he reached Manlief. But it was Dandie he encountered first; Dandie who, with arm lovingly thrown about the Reverend Foxe's shoulders, had turned him around and was returning him to Bible and pulpit. In passing, Dandie's right hand reached across to Link's cocked fist, lowered it and, in the ear which this gesture inclined toward him, whispered, "For God's sake, don't be a fool."

Link was then left face to face with Manlief who, like Dandie, laid a hand on his arm. "Mr. Conboy," he said, "help me." Behind him, Link heard Dandie's public voice, strong, humorous and wheedling, a voice that could sway women and votes: "The Reverend Foxe wants us to join him in singing 'Come thou fount of every blessing, Tune my heart to sing Thy Grace'."

"Mr. Conboy," John Manlief began again in his unused, inflexible voice, but Link quieted him. "Come on outside," he whispered, "where we can talk."

Dandie's tenor, as they left the room, rose sweet and high, unfolding like a trumpet lily above the worshipers.

> "Here I'll raise my Ebenezer,
> Hither by Thy help I'll come
> And I hope by Thy good pleasure
> Safely to arrive at home."

Link closed the door behind them. "Now tell me," he said, "what seems to be the trouble."

Manlief's trouble hadn't changed. "They've stolen my pig," he said.

VI

THAT evening after supper Link was as nearly talkative as he ever got. "That pig certainly turned the trick," he told them.

They were all in the parlor again, the three Thompsons, all the Conboys, both by birth and marriage, and Christie, who soon would be officially entering the Conboy circle. Lib had asked everyone who had attended the services to stay for supper, and all, with the exception of the Thompsons, had had the good sense to refuse. Mrs. Thompson herself never issued an invitation which she did not hope would be accepted, and she was completely unaware that Lib, bolt upright on the edge of her rocking-chair, was energetically willing her to take her two children and depart. Turning to Link, her well-polished spectacles flashing signals of alert and intelligent interest, Mrs. Thompson asked, "How is it, Mr. Conboy, that this man could have a pig in his possession that you didn't know existed?"

Lib, perfectly willing to skin Link alive herself when she thought he needed it, never permitted anyone else to so much as question him. "That's the whole point of the story, Mrs. Thompson, if you'll just have the patience to let Mr. Conboy get to it."

Only the Thompsons missed Lib's anger. Cate saw anger shimmer about her mother as visibly as heat waves about a red-hot stove. And she saw how untidy Lib was beside Mrs. Thompson, her hair half-uncoiled and her shirt-waist splotched with eating or

[283]

cooking spots. But she didn't care; Christie had rescued her from her concentration on Lib. He was gazing at her now so openly, so lovingly, that her heart beat against her eardrums with the sound of waves locked in a seashell. They had spent the whole afternoon by the falls, new grass and the dance of spring light on running water all about them; but it had as well been winter or summer; they were beyond seasons. She ventured a direct glance at Christie, but it was too much. She was drowning or suffocating or both, and she reached out as a drowning man does for the sight of any object which would save her: the peacock feathers or the wrinkles in Em's stockings. But nothing in the room was strong enough. She returned to Christie. Christie, you are so beautiful and you love me. It was amazing and mysterious. If Christie were to say now, Take off all your clothes and walk across this room to me, could she refuse? She looked across at Em, who was watching her. Oh, Em, I'm your sister all right, she wanted to say. Wanda smiled at her. Ferris smiled. Oh, I love the whole world, she thought, and smiled Wanda and Ferris their share of that love. Mrs. Thompson gave her a nod. "You're looking very chipper tonight, Cate." Why, I'm all right, Cate assured herself, astonished after all the years of worry to find it so. It has all been for nothing. People like me.

Link, bending upon Mrs. Thompson that kind and courteous attention which so riled Lib, said, "You asked how John Manlief could have a pig I didn't know anything about. Ordinarily, he couldn't. But as chance would have it after Dilk and I left the barn the night that sow littered, another pig was born." He paused, wondering how to relate to a mixed company and on Sunday evening the fact that the sow'd had more pigs than teats. He couldn't see his way clear to any explanation of this matter and went on quickly, "Manlief saw that this little runt didn't stand a chance of getting any food with all its bigger brothers and sisters there first, so he hid it under his coat and took it up to his room. He's had it there ever since, taking care of it."

Em listened to her father. Before that night with Doss, her father had stood for whatever was right in the world—all honor, goodness, understanding. Then he had been wrong with Doss, wrong with her; wrong in listening to Cate and Lib; wrong in being willing to listen to everyone but to her and Doss, the only ones who knew. He was her father, and she loved him but she would never again depend upon him or confide in him. She would rely on her own judgment, decide things for herself. She would not tell him, for instance, that she had been out digging with the Abels this afternoon; or that on the way home she had watched Cate and Christie on the bank by the creek making love. She would not tell him; but she was not like Cate: she did not need to make vows and record them with blood. (Oh, Cate, she thought, what if I stood up now and told about the vow you made this morning and how you broke it this afternoon?) Cate was looking at her, as she thought this, so sweet, the old Cate who used to comb her hair and give her baths; but Em turned away from her; she didn't want to start depending on people again.

"Now, Mr. Conboy," Mrs. Thompson said, tossing her little gray head like a spirited pony, "don't deny us the story of how that crazy man cared for that helpless piggy."

Wanda laughed. She and her mother admired each other. And her mother was such a wonderful conversationalist. And witty! All day long at home Wanda went about doing the housework, laughing. Sometimes she would have to sink down, wherever she was, she got so out of breath laughing. Finally, she would take off her glasses, steamed up with mirthful tears, clean them and say, "Mama, spare me now for a few minutes until I finish the dusting."

Wanda's laugh took Cate's attention momentarily from Christie. When she was visting the Thompsons she would be surprised at all the talk and laughter between Wanda and her mother: surprised but pleased. The Thompson women had high voices, and their words came out as if through little yellow clicking beaks. Cate would stand in the downstairs hall at the Thompsons', listening and admiring; and planning to go home and institute this trilling and laughing with Lib; but Lib was no triller (she either, for that matter), and such plans always came to nothing.

"Now don't you laugh at me, daughter," Mrs. Thompson called across the room to Wanda and, Wanda silenced, she bade Link, "Go on, Mr. Conboy. I want to hear every word about the rescue of that starving little piggy."

A kind of grunt escaped Lib, and Wanda decided that Mrs.

Conboy was mad at her husband for talking about a sow—and birth—on a Sunday evening. It wasn't a very nice subject, she agreed; but Mr. Conboy wanted to talk about it, and her mother was the only one in the room with enough gumption to ask him the right questions. The Conboys were funny people—not Dandie, of course, but all the rest of them. Cate was, certainly; she wasn't pretty, with her square face, short hair, and no-colored eyes, but there was something about Cate, something probably not very nice which always made her the center of a crowd, the girl at a party the boys always clustered around. She remembered one party. Cate had taken off her shoes and hoisted her skirts so that she could kick, higher and higher, at a suspension lamp which the boys, each time she touched it, raised another notch. Finally she was kicking higher than her head, an unladylike display, if ever she saw one. On the way home she told Ferris, "Cate certainly showed everything she had tonight." And Ferris had replied vulgarly, "Cate's got something to show." Well, Ferris' time with Cate had been beaten by this Indianapolis boy and she was glad of it. Ferris needed some of the conceit taken out of him.

"Manlief kept his pig alive by feeding it with a baby bottle—one of Fessler Creagan's. He'd get up three and four times a night to feed it. It's fatter right now than any of the pigs left with their mother."

"Didn't do the room any good, did it," Ferris asked, "making a pig sty of it?"

"No," Link said, "it didn't. I'll grant you that. But it did John Manlief some good. And Neddy Oates stealing it did the final good."

"So it was Neddy who did the stealing?" Dandie asked, aware suddenly that neither he nor Nory had joined in the conversation since suppertime.

Wanda explained it to him, laughter smothering her words, "*Ned, Ned the piper's son, Stole a pig and away he run.*"

Oh God, Dandie thought, oh, Sunday afternoons at home. Oh, evenings with the folks. Cooped up here, the roses crawling on the wallpaper and the air resounding with this talk of a stolen pig and Wanda steaming big-eyed at him from behind her magnifying specs. There had been a faint fresh smell of spring in the parlor when they had first entered it, but now the stove was going and the smell was dry and hot and talky. Talk, talk, talk. Why was it so important to be able to talk? Maybe John Manlief was already regretting the quiet world he left behind, cursing the pig and the theft alike now. Mrs. Thompson, duck feet at a duck's angle on the stool; Ferris oggling Cate; Cate burning to be with Christie; Em in some other world; Lib, hating the Thompsons; Link preening himself on Manlief's recovery. Only Nory, quiet, fresh, blooming as a flower in the dry hot room.

Oh, Nory, Nory, why did you do it? Why did you look at another before I came, and why do you look back, now we're together? There were times, and this was one of them, when not to act cut into him like a vise. If he didn't have to drive Christie into town he would leave now, get back to The Junction, walk the streets, ask every man he met, "Tell me, were you ever with her?"

"What I can't understand, Mr. Conboy," said Mrs. Thompson, "is why a man who wouldn't talk to human beings would talk to a pig."

"Human beings were connected with his sorrow," Link said, "pigs weren't."

"What sorrow?" Mrs. Thompson, who liked a specific grief, asked. "Did he lose a wife? Or a child?"

"I can't do more than hazard a guess," Link began, then stopped.

We're in no position to understand sorrow here tonight, he thought. It wouldn't surprise me if there was more happiness in this room tonight than in any other room in Indiana: kind neighbors, young people in love, a bright little girl, tasty food, pleasant furnishings. Comforts and pleasures. We've had them all so long we begin to think them our due. But he could remember times when he had not taken them as his due: times hard in money matters and otherwise. Nights when Lib never came to bed but stayed outdoors, beside herself with jealousy, unwilling to put a foot inside the same house with him. Nights when he'd fed the children and himself on bread and milk. Nights when he hadn't known whether Dandie'd be coming in drunk or sober. Nights of his own self-disgust. The night of Doss' call for help and the unforgettable scene in that room . . . but all past now. The lamplight falling on faces steady and calm. He had never, in his life, seen a play; but it came pleasurably to him that they were all well enough dressed and gracefully enough grouped to be sitting on a stage and speaking for an audience's benefit. Talk about pigs, he supposed, was hardly suitable for the theater, but a pig had brought about the resurrection of a man: a subject good enough for any play.

He took up once more his explanation of Manlief, and Mrs. Thompson nodded in time to his sentences. "Yes, yes indeed. There's no doubt about it. . . . I see. . . . Well, I'll declare. . . . To be sure." And when he came to a full pause, she kneaded her footstool as if it were the matter under consideration and focused her glasses on him. "So taking care of a pig is a cure for dumbness!"

Cate drew a long trembling breath so that everyone in the room turned toward her. "Oh, no, Mrs. Thompson, *that's* not what cured Mr. Manlief." She rose to her feet. "Is it, Papa?" Link said nothing and Cate pressed her hand to her heart. "The answer's so plain you can't see it, Mrs. Thompson. Love cured Mr. Manlief. Love made him speak in the first place—and then today, to save what he loved, why he could've flown, Mrs. Thompson, or walked on water. Love, Mrs. Thompson," she concluded, as if she were the speaker in the closing-day exercises at Bleeding Creek School, "can do anything."

She was aware of the absolute silence in the parlor, and she waited for her father to say, "Yes, that's right. Love made John Manlief speak"; but he said nothing, and she began to feel the nakedness of that word—love—in the parlor and all the family to hear. Em was looking at her, head on one side, something birdlike, bright—and surprised—in her eye. Lib showed astonishment, Thompsons disgust, Dandie boredom. She couldn't bear to look at Christie. "Papa," she said again, because he was the authority, the one who could justify her, "Papa? That is the answer, isn't it? Papa?"

"I doubt," Link said, "it's possible to say absolutely what caused Manlief to speak. He hadn't been in his right mind for some time. It's more'n likely he couldn't say himself what made him speak today." But, as he continued to talk, Link asked himself suspiciously, When did this happen before? What other time did someone say "love" and you fail? But it wasn't until he had finished his explanation of Manlief that the answer came to him: Dandie—that day in church and Dandie standing, as Cate stood now, saying, "Love. God is love."

Mrs. Thompson, with her usual tact, turned to Cate, when Link had finished and said, "A real Madame Modjeska in our midst. Such a carrying voice, Cate. Perhaps you should consider Chautauqua work."

Mrs. Thompson was trying to build a bridge back to some more suitable subject of conversation than love. Lib gave this bridge a blow. "Cate," she said unexpectedly, with a dab for the beauless Wanda and her piano-playing aspirations, "will not have to depend upon Chautauqua work. She is going to be married, you know."

Dandie got to his feet. "Christie," he said, "I don't want to rush you, but I've got to get back to town."

At that, the evening broke up; the Thompsons left; Cate and Christie went outside to say their farewells, while Dandie and Nory waited in the buggy; Em disappeared; only Link and Lib were left in the room. The lamps burned as steadily as before; one rocker still moved; but the evening itself was finished, gone— gone, never to be recovered. Link stood doubtfully, then seated himself in the chair he had occupied earlier, his eyes wide open, searching the room's vacancies. Opposite him, Lib, sleepily hunched, beginning already to undo buttons. Everything he had catalogued before with such satisfaction was still there: the pleasant room, the nice furniture, the warm fire, the well-dressed couple. What was missing? What had hovered at the entrance of the room and departed? What had asked for a welcome and never received it? What? What? What went on, in the play he had imagined, when all the chairs but two were vacated? He dropped his face into his hands and moved face, not hands, back and forth until his beard rasped in the silence.

"Well, Link," Lib asked, on the tail of a yawn, "well, Link?"

"One more failure to chalk up," Link said, lifting his face to her.

VII

WHEN Em came into the bedroom, Cate was already in bed; but she had left the light burning low for Em. She was wide awake,

Em saw, on her back, arms behind her head, cheeks bright. Em looked at her for a second without speaking, then began to undress. The minute she undid her belt Lily Bias' letter fell to the floor.

"You dropped something," Cate said.

Em picked up the letter without a word, opened the casket, and put it inside. Then she took out a pencil and two pieces of paper. On the first she wrote, "I dug for the first time today." On the second, "I saw Cate and Christie making love." These she folded neatly and put with the others like them in the growing heap beneath the silk sham which had been intended as a cover for the dead baby's pillow. Then she closed the casket.

"Do you write notes to yourself?" Cate asked.

"Don't you ever look at them?"

"No. I told you I wouldn't."

"Did you take a vow not to?"

"No."

"They are kind of notes to myself," Em said. She blew out the lamp and finished undressing in the dark.

Long after Em was asleep Cate lay, arms still akimbo, wide awake. Oh, Papa, she thought, the answer *was* love. Why didn't you say so? And she was troubled by his refusal to speak and lay sleepless until Manlief's image came into her mind. With his new-found powers of speech he reassured her: "You are right, Cate. The answer *is* love." His voice (which actually she had never heard) was in her ears as she went to sleep.

10

*B*ECAUSE she'd spent the whole day in dreaming of Christie, Cate elected at the end of the next afternoon, as a sort of punishment for her laziness, to carry some needed buckets of lime to the women's privy. She was bringing out her second bucketful when she was softly hailed, "Cate, oh, Cate."

She couldn't, at first, make out who was calling her or from where. She put down her bucket and walked around behind the privy and there, coming up through the apple orchard in the late and slanting light, was Nory. Nory, usually so neat, was in disorder, hair straggling and a dirty kitchen apron still tied about her waist.

"What's the matter, Nory?" she asked.

"Nothing," Nory said. "But would you stay all night with me?"

Cate noticed that Nory said me, not us. "Why, I guess so," she said. "Come on in the house while I ask Mama and change my dress."

"Do you have to?" Nory asked. "Couldn't you come the way you are—and not say anything to your mother?" Nory's face was drawn close together, as if to protect it from some threat; her usually wide-open eyes were narrowed and her usually soft smiling mouth thin and pale. "Please, Cate," she urged.

Cate always imagined herself doing well in a crisis—it was her solace in her many failures of ordinary living—and this, she thought, from Nory's strange manner, might be a crisis. "All right," she said, "I'll come." She untied her own apron and hung it over a low branch. "That will tell them where I was last, anyway. In case we disappear and they want to track me."

Nory, in spite of the fact that she had said nothing was wrong, contradicted her words by her silence and her swift walk. Cate, with her longer legs, followed at her heels. The day had been a weather breeder, clear, silent, a little warm; now a change was due. The sky was beginning to cloud up and though the air was still mild, sharp little breezes occasionally ruffled the waxy spring leaves. It was as if the day, like a sick man, was having its evening chills and fever before settling down for the night. Cate, as she tramped along a little behind Nory, thought that she knew well enough what was wrong. It was Dandie. It had come out at last —his caring about Nory's baby. And when Dandie cared about anything, he acted. She doubted there was anything in the world Dandie wouldn't or couldn't do: violence or craziness. An act another man would hesitate to perform because it would make a fool of him, Dandie would perform and dignify, because he was Dandie. Dandie could be wrong and wicked, but never foolish. He was capable of all the extremes: of love, and hence of death. The person who would take the risks in the one would take the risks in the other.

"Nory," she called, "is Dandie at home?"

"No," Nory answered, without pausing or turning.

"Where is he?"

"I don't know."

Nory, so round and domestic with her apron and bun of soft womanly hair, looked, in the raw open fields, like a china teacup, left out by a forgetful picnicker. Beside her, Cate felt manly, as if she should lift fence rails for Nory and kick stones out of her way. If I lived with Nory, she thought, I'd soon be wearing pants and chewing tobacco. Yet it would all be false for she knew that finally, Nory, like Em, in time of trouble would be the rock, while she would be trembling and shaking—no matter what she wore or chewed. What did that prove? That men were the tremblers? Or that she was the womanly one, after all? Whatever it proved she hastened to catch up with Nory at the fence and to take down the top rail for her.

Nory, as she stepped over, said, "I told Dandie who the baby's father was."

Cate, replacing the rail, said, "I didn't know you knew."

Nory stopped, stockstill. "Why did you think I didn't know?"

"You didn't marry him."

"Cate," Nory said, "what do you know about babies?"

"Well," Cate answered, "I'm the oldest. I took care of—"

"I mean—where they come from."

"Nothing," Cate said. "Nothing at all." She was ignorant, completely, and proud of it, her mother's own well-taught girl—proud, aloof, and ignorant as a stone. "If you knew," she asked, "why didn't you tell Dandie before?"

"I didn't tell him because it was all over and I didn't want us ever to think about it again. That was what Dandie wanted, too. Then he began to think about it and to be jealous. You saw how he was, yourself, that day at our house."

"Like Mama," Cate said.

"No," said Nory. "Not like that at all. Dandie's not like your mother. He had some reason to be jealous and your mother didn't. Your father never had children with any other woman, did he?"

Her father love and kiss another woman? Have other children, somewhere? The idea made her sick at her stomach. She understood what Lib had meant when she said Nory had a common streak. "Don't talk about Papa that way."

"I'm not talking about him, I'm talking about me. I did have a baby and Dandie thought he had something to be jealous over."

"Didn't he?"

"No."

When they reached The Junction it was completely dark. Nory had walked faster and faster until by the time she reached her own yard she was running. She threw open the door and stood, calling into the dark house, "Dandie, Dandie. Oh, Dandie." But there was no answer and she went inside without another word and threw herself across the bed.

"Shall I light a lamp, Nory?" Cate asked.

"Do what you want to," Nory said.

Cate went to the kitchen and felt her way to a lamp. With it lit, she saw that the noon table still stood uncleared. She started a fire in the cook-stove, put on the tea-kettle, righted an overturned chair and cleared the table. Then she carried the lamp into the front room. Nory was at the window, twisting the curtains like one of the old men at The Farm. "I expect you know Dandie better than I do," she said.

Cate put the lamp down on the center table. "No," she said, though a few minutes before she would've said yes. "I don't know Dandie at all. I don't know anybody." At the moment this struck her as being the one sure fact of her life.

"What would Dandie be doing now, do you think?"

"I don't know. I don't know what he's already done. Or what you've already done." She sat down in the rocker and began nervously to rock and found the loud squeak of the chair soothing.

"Do you have to do that, Cate?" Nory asked, and Cate stopped, dead still. "I told you what I did. I told Dandie about the baby. At noon Mr. Korby came in for a piece of pie and some coffee. And he told us that my uncle . . . had the girl who works for him now . . . in the family way."

"The uncle you lived with?"

"Yes."

"How did Mr. Korby know?"

"I don't know. Maybe she told him. He seems to hear everything."

"At funerals," Cate said, "people don't care what they say."

Nory had no answer to this. She went back to the bed, sat down, and leaned forward so that the lamplight fell full on her face and it was, Cate thought, a face not made for trouble; not like Lib's, big enough and strong enough for sorrow and anger.

"After Mr. Korby left," Nory said, "I decided I should tell Dandie. I decided it would be better for us, and that it was my duty anyway because of Alphy."

"Alphy?" Cate asked.

"The girl at my uncle's. She's only fifteen. I thought I had to tell Dandie because of her—and that Dandie'd be better off, not jealous any longer when he found out who it was. How could he be jealous then, or anything but sorry for me? Knowing who it was and how terrible it was! So I told him."

Cate's mind went forward, brushed at the edges of the meaning in Nory's words and quickly retreated. Such a thing could not be —my mind must like horrors, she told herself, and dirtiness and evil, to even—it could not be. Uncles, no. Not old men. It could not be. Uncles and nieces? Brothers and sisters? Anybody and anybody? Fathers—and daughters? Oh, no. It was her mind. It couldn't be. It was against nature, God wouldn't permit it. It spoiled every kiss. Or was it the other way around, every kiss just a step toward *that*, part and parcel of it, really. Was *that* behind every—fatherly—kiss by an uncle? Uncle Mort's kisses? Uncle Sloane's? Was there no perfect circle of goodness made up of relatives, within which you could look out, knowing you were safe from the world? Could the circle itself turn in upon you, threaten you? Without knowing when she had started doing so, she was following an arch in the design of Nory's new rug, a body Brussels, with a pattern of overlapping horseshoes topped by a cluster of cabbage roses, a pattern so intricate that really to figure it out you needed a pencil and paper.

"I told him," Nory said, "it was my uncle. I told him—" Just then the lid on the tea-kettle began to lift and fall and Cate said, "The kettle's boiling. I have to go. I have to see to the kettle." She had never known how pleasant dish-washing was; how satisfactory it was to put all the scraps together in one bucket, to fit saucers and plates together in stacks of a matching size. She did everything very thoroughly, using the hottest water and the thickest suds. She polished everyday glasses like cut glass, re-arranged cupboards and was starting on the stove when Nory came to the door. "What in the world are you doing all this time?" she asked.

"I'm just going to brush up now," Cate told her, and reached for the broom which hung between two nails on the back of the outside door.

Nory took hold of her arm. "Stop all this working." Cate stood, without moving, looking beyond Nory. "Are you thinking it was all my fault? That I didn't hate him and wish he would die? And wish I would die?"

Wish, wish, Cate thought. I would've killed myself. Or would she only have vowed to kill herself?

Nory flung Cate's arm aside. "I can't talk to you; it's like talking to a child, you don't understand anything—and you never will, because you think you know everything already. Besides, I don't care what you think. Only Dandie." She went back into the sitting-room and Cate followed her and stood facing her, the center table between them. The supper hour was over, the streets empty, except for an occasional passerby bound for a saloon or an evening visit.

Finally Cate said, "What did Dandie do when you told him?"
"He left."

[295]

"Didn't he say where he was going?"

"He didn't say anything and I couldn't find anyone in town who knew where he was. Don't think I didn't look everywhere before I came to get you." Nory went to the clothes-press, got out a jacket, and put it on.

"What are you going to do now?" Cate asked.

"I'm going to find him."

Cate knew she would have to go too, and it seemed to her, in that minute, that she was always being expected to do what was beyond her, to perform acts which half killed her. Why couldn't she, that being the case, refuse? Because something compelled her to be whatever anyone expected her to be. "Fly to the moon, Cate," was all anyone needed to say to have her start flapping her arms and aiming moonward at once. But she would flap and resent simultaneously.

"Take off that apron, Nory," she ordered, trying to prove to herself that she had a will of her own. "I'm not going any place with you wearing that." She began trying to undo the apron-strings.

"Let me alone," Nory said. "No one asked you to go with me." She turned down the lamp and without a backward look for Cate, left the room.

Cate slowly got a coat of Dandie's and put it on. When she caught up with Nory she asked, "Where are you going to look?"

"Out toward my uncle's."

11

WHEN Cate opened her eyes it was daylight. The sulphur taste at the back of her throat which had come after the hard running was still there. The birds were singing as loudly as on any morning; she listened in surprise for a few seconds. Her whole body ached, but that was perhaps as much the sleeping in her clothes, as the running. It was strange that stockings, so soft and comfortable when worn with your shoes, snubbed your toes like iron bands when you wore them without shoes in bed. She pushed the quilts back carefully, as if uncovering something injured, and slowly, inch by inch, muscle by muscle, got out of bed.

Without opening her eyes, Em asked, "Is it time to get up?"

"No. Go back to sleep."

She went out just as she was, shoeless and unwashed, into the dark unaired hall, with its smell of night and the beginning of the morning's fires. In the kitchen Link looked up from the stove, then set the lid down on the flame he had started.

"What's the matter with you, Cate?" he asked. "Are you sick?" And as she came farther into the room, "What's happened to your dress?"

Cate brushed at the mud and wrinkles. "There was water at the bottom of the ditch."

"I should've known last night, something was amiss."

Cate wondered why. All she had said, when she had opened her father's and mother's door last night, was, "I've been at Nory's." Her chief reason for coming home had been to tell everything, but once there she had not been able to speak; she had been overcome by sleepiness and heaviness; the walls of her own room and the covers of her own bed had seemed to reach out and enfold her. And once enfolded and covered she had slept the night through without dreaming or moving.

Lib, who had been out back, came in, still in her nightgown and wrapper. "What on earth's happened to Cate?" she asked Link, as if Cate herself might be beyond speech.

Cate brushed again, apologetically, at the mud. "We didn't know there was mud in the ditch when we got in it."

Lib took her arm. "Cate, listen to me. What were you doing in a ditch?"

"We were hiding. There wasn't any other place."

"Who were you hiding from?" This was Link.

"The men," she said. It seemed a strange question. Who else would they hide from?

"Come on into the bedroom before Mag and the folks get out here," Lib ordered. In the bedroom she gave Cate's arm an impatient shake and said, "Now, Cate, what men are you talking about?"

"I never saw them, except one."

Link, who had followed them into the room, said anxiously,

"Begin at the beginning of this. I understood you to say you were at Nory's last night. Where'd you run into these men?"

"On the way to Nory's uncle's."

"Nory ran away from her uncle's," Lib said. "What's she up to, traipsing back there now?"

"We were hunting Dandie."

It had been dark as a pocket, dark and gusty, when they set out. The air smelled of running water, damp earth, and the woods. They couldn't see the woods at first, they could only smell them —and hear them. The small sounds were the worst—the rustlings and creakings—though even the loud, ordinary sounds, a cow browsing by the roadside, a dog barking, had startled her: she recognized them a second too late for comfort. The road was so badly rutted that her ankles continually turned. She walked about half the time, it seemed, on the sides of her feet. A cold still air, like something holding its breath until it could pounce upon them, waited for them at the bottoms of the draws. Streams ran through these draws which they had to ford without knowing where the stepping-stones were, and, as often as not, they missed them. Nory said, "Stop pinching me," which, without knowing, she had been doing, for her fingers, when she took them from Nory's arm, were bent like claws and stiff.

They reached a better stretch of road at the summit of a climb, open fields on each side and no woods—which they had come to recognize as a blacker black—until some distance ahead. Already exploring that darkness imaginatively for horrors, she saw through the interstices of the trees the bobbings of lanterns and heard voices, not loud, but pitched at some level other than that natural to men out for an ordinary night's pleasure, possum hunting or shivareeing.

"At that open place on the top of a hill—" she began to tell her father and mother.

"Dall's," Link said.

"There isn't any house there," she said, remembering.

"Dall's place," Link repeated. "The house burned, some time back."

"It was there we saw the lights up ahead in the woods, and the man screamed."

"Screamed," Lib said reprovingly, as if she'd never heard of such a thing.

"Twice. To begin with."

When she heard the first scream she felt transfixed—as if the scream were a bull's horn that had gored her. She seemed to rise with it as it ascended, then, as it died away, to fall; as if, after goring her, the bull had tossed her and let her drop. The second scream roused her and she began to run. She climbed the fence at the left as if it were nothing, crossed the field where last year's stubble was still stiff enough to make itself felt, and somewhere at about the middle of the field, she threw herself into a little ditch, not even noticing at first the trickle of water that ran through it. She pushed her face into the old leaves and new grass there; and kept flat to the ground, without moving, even after she felt Nory crowding in close to her.

"Are they coming after us?" she whispered to Nory.

"They don't even know we're here," Nory said.

"Why was he screaming?" Link asked severely, as if a wrong answer would prove the scream could not have been.

"I don't know why—then—we couldn't see—we ran across the field and got into a ditch."

"Was that all?"

"No. The men came over into our field."

But she hadn't looked up—couldn't; though it would've been better, perhaps, if she had. Perhaps what was happening sounded worse than it really was. Her ears had been traitors; they had been eager to hear whatever in the sounds was most terrible. She couldn't control them, as she did her eyes, by hiding them. Part of the terribleness was that, except for the screams, the sounds the other men made were pleasant and cheerful. They laughed the way men do the minute before the meat is taken off the coals at a barbecue, or the minute before the ringer is tossed in a horseshoe game: all the sounds were of the minute before something happens, the laughter thick and curving like the coils of a black snake, lazy in the sun. Then suddenly above the coils, the scream, like fangs.

"The men? What men?"
"I didn't look. I hid my eyes."
"You heard, though? You know?"
"Yes, I heard. I know. I heard Dandie."

"I've got to have more light," Dandie said, "if I'm going to make a neat job of this."
"You ain't bound by oath to make a neat job of it."
"A slip or two won't be held against you."
"Fix him a fire to see by, if he wants it. It'll keep us warm, to boot."
"Use the fence rails."
"I gotta an ax in the buggy."
"Douse a little kerosene on the rails."
"Douse a little on the old coot."
"This is an operation—not a cremation."
"Cremation's too good for the old bastard."
"Strip the old buzzard."
"Take a long last look at it."
"Look your belly full."
"Belly full's right."
"You've filled your last belly."
"Bid 'em good-by."
"Boys, you ain't got a shred of proof. Boys, boys, boys. . . ."
Then the scream again—the screams again.
"Are they going to torture him?" she whispered to Nory.
If Nory answered, the screams drowned out whatever it was she said.

"They tortured him," she said. "Dandie tortured him."

With eyes still closed she had begun to get up. She couldn't let anyone be hurt that way, not an animal, no, not if they shot her for it. She was on her elbow, eyes still closed, when Nory slammed her down, pushed her with all her might, hurt her, scrounged her face around in the gravel. "Be quiet," Nory said, "this is none of your business."

The sound the man was making was like the sawmill scream: it began strong, as the saw does when the log being cut is thick, and it thinned down, as the sawmill scream does, when the log is almost cut through. The worst was the final mosquito drone, hanging in air like smoke; she couldn't tell when it was real and when it was only an echo inside her own head. The scream was beginning again then, and inside her head the sound, exploding, burst something—her eardrums evidently—for she could hear no more. She did not go to sleep, nor faint; only thought of something else—Christie and herself on the banks of the creek, the water glinting beneath them; and she resisted being taken away from there by Nory.

"Cate, Cate," Nory said, "they're gone. Wake up. Get up."

"If they're gone," Cate asked, "what is that noise?"

"Him," Nory told her. "They left him here."

Her mouth was full of grass and dirt—because Nory had pushed her; or because like Nebuchadnezzar she had come to be a grass-eater. She lay there, shaking, listening to that groan or snore, whatever it was, until Nory, taking her hand, pulled her to her feet.

"Tortured who?" Link asked.

Looking up, Cate saw that her father was speaking. "Nory's uncle."

"Are you sure?"

"I saw him, after the men were gone," she answered, and waited for her father to say, "Wake up, Cate, you've had a bad dream." But he said nothing.

He had been on the other side of the embers, a white hoop, facing them, knees drawn toward his chest, as still as if an unseen bow-string held him taut. She began to tiptoe down the ditch thinking, Now it is over, now there's nothing between me and my own room but time—just minutes. But there was more than that: there was his voice.

"Help," the man said. "Help." He spoke the words quickly, as if he had only so much breath to use; they were more like barks or grunts than words. She didn't move until she heard, behind her, Nory's retreating footsteps. Then she turned to look.

Nory stood directly over that hoop. "Uncle," she said in a cold, still voice, like the air that had threatened them at the bottom of the draws.

"Nory." The man's bark was more human than it had been before. "Help."

"No," Nory said.

"Doctor." The word was spoken as if it were two words: doc tor.

"No."

"Beg."

"No."

"Bleed—to death."

"I don't care."

"Freeze."

"Freeze, then."

"Nory."

She was walking away from him. Then she turned back. "If Dandie wants you to have a doctor, he'll send you one," she said.

"Help," the man barked faintly once more, and before Nory could stop her, Cate ran to him.

"You can have my coat," she said. She tried not to look but her eyes took their innings then. He was an old man with gray stubble on his face and when he opened his eyes it was as if stove-lids had been taken from a fire. And there was blood—where he held himself.

"Hurt," he whispered. "I hurt."

She dropped the coat across his shoulders and began to run. When Nory caught up with her she asked, "Will he die?"

"I don't know," Nory answered. "I don't care."

"Did Dandie do it?"

"Yes."

Lib had wound her wrapper tightly about her waist, as if she needed its support. "Why?" she asked. "Why? That harmless—" She stopped speaking and turned to Link: Cate filling in the pause said, "Mr. Korby said—he wasn't harmless."

"Korby?" Link asked. "Was Korby mixed up in this?"

"He told them about the other girl." For a minute Cate thought

[302]

she could use Nory's own words, but she couldn't bring herself to it, and added, "That's why Nory told Dandie about herself."

"Told him what," Link asked harshly, "about herself?"

"About herself and her uncle."

Lib sat down on the bed and leaned her head against the footboard. "Link," she groaned, "did you have any notion?"

"It seems now I must've." He turned to Cate. "And you knew all this last night and didn't tell us?"

"I tried to. I ran all the way home to tell."

"Don't you know you may have made your brother a murderer?"

"I couldn't tell," she insisted. "Something happened—" But there seemed no way in which she could describe what had happened, the manner in which sleep and blankness had enwrapped her in spite of her intention. "I wanted to tell—" No, what she wanted, above everything, was not to tell—not to remember. "I couldn't," she repeated, "something—"

But they were no longer listening to her. "Anything," Link was saying. "A cup of coffee. And ask Bob to hitch."

Her father came to her, took her by the elbow. "Cate, I understand that was a terrible thing, last night. But it's over. You didn't do what you should last night about telling us. Try to do better this morning. Eat, take care of yourself. We're going to have enough on our minds worrying about Dandie, without any added burden of worrying about you."

He bent, he was bending, Cate saw, to kiss her; with a kindness and lovingness such as arrivals and departures had never before, though she had longed for them, brought forth; but at the last second she could not meet his lips, could not offer him as much as an inch of cheek or forehead. All of Nory's words, and all of her thoughts about those words, separated her from him. Wrenching free, she ran into the parlor, stretched herself out, muddy and disheveled, on the sofa and went on from there with her survey of the old world with her new eyes. Lib's sewing basket was on the floor beside her, and from it she picked up a thimble and examined it with great intentness. She turned it over and over again until it became a form she had never before seen or at least not appreciated and she wondered what metals were in it and how it had been made, and who had made it. The morning went by. Rain began to fall. The clock struck the hours. Outside the parlor she could hear the usual clatter of work, the usual tangle of voices.

III

SHE WAS still examining the thimble (trying to make her world no larger than it) at noon, when Lib came in. Lib was still in her nightgown and wrapper. Her hair still hung in its uncombed, night-before braid. The sight of Cate, stretched motionless, in her mud-caked dress and playing with a thimble exasperated her. "For heaven's sake, Cate," she said, "put up that thimble."

She knew Cate had been through a lot and she felt concern as well as exasperation; dismay, too. Why couldn't Cate have told them last night? If that man died? Thank God, Link was a lawyer and could take care of the legal ins-and-outs of the matter in case Dandie was hailed into the courts—as she supposed he would be.

"Have you had anything to eat yet?" For all of her concern she couldn't keep the sharpness and exasperation out of her voice.

Cate said, "No," and Lib brought her from the kitchen a bowl of steaming navy beans, warm light bread, a plate of chopped onions, and a glass of fresh buttermilk. She pushed a footstool to Cate's side and put the tray on it. "Now sit up and eat, Cate," she said, "before we have you on our hands too."

Without a word Cate turned away from the food, as if even the smell were too much for her. "Well," Lib said, "you can lead a horse to water but you can't make him drink," and she took the tray over to the center table and sat down before it herself. She was trembling with hunger and not until the bowl of beans was half empty did her hands stop shaking. You are not so far gone in sorrow as you thought, she told herself, relishing your food this way.

"Mama," Cate asked, "where did Papa go?"

"He went to get that man a doctor—if he's still alive, which is doubtful."

"Did Dandie want to kill him?"

Lib looked sharply at her daughter. Cate was still toying with that thimble, eyes downcast, cheeks burning. "Cate," she said, "get rid of that thimble."

Cate dropped the thimble in the open work-basket. "What was it," she asked, "Dandie wanted to do?"

"Don't ask me. I wasn't the one who was there." Lib drank the last of her buttermilk and set the glass on the floor with a thump. Beyond Dandie, and far beyond Cate, the person she worried about was Link. Where was he now? Had he had anything to eat? And then, suddenly, all of her concern for him was burned away in a flare of anger. Except for his mulish determination to come here in the first place, none of them would now be in their present straits: Dandie would never have seen Nory, got mixed up with Korby or have been, more than likely, at this very minute, a murderer. Let Link be hungry now, be having it out with Korby, or the officers of the law, or in jail himself. She didn't care. This was his bed: let him lie in it; his rope, let him hang himself. As her anger with Link increased, an image, which often came to her at such times, filled her mind: an image of herself shaking Link, pounding him, tugging at his hair; in fact, employing every violence (though she herself did not realize this), incapable of hurting Link and capable of giving herself pleasure. She leaned back in her chair, eyes shut, more aware at the moment of Link's body than her own, how fresh, springy and resistant his flesh was as she pommeled. Deeply engaged in this, she rested, motionless, relaxed, eyes closed. Cate, the thimble once more in her hands, looked occasionally at her mother but more often beyond her to the window, which was again spattered with rain.

Into this quiet—Lib with her eyes shut, Cate sunk into a thimble-sized world—Korby, disregarding Mag behind him, stepped belligerently. It was the first time he had been inside the superintendent's personal quarters at The Farm since Link took over and he was surprised to find them so comfortable and well furnished. And he was surprised, as always, that such a dour, slab-sided hypocrite as Link Conboy should have picked up such a good-looking woman as Lib Conboy. He looked her over silently for a few minutes, then said, "Mrs. Conboy, I hate to wake you up, but I've got a few things to say to you."

Lib opened her eyes without being startled or upset. The instantaneous suited her far more than the anticipated. Little wet sop of a man, she thought, recognizing Korby, what's he been up to? He was as muddy as Cate and battered in the bargain.

"Mr. Conboy's not here," she told him coldly, "and I don't know when he'll be back."

"I know he's not here," Korby said. "I was figuring on that and I don't want to see him. One meeting a day with Lord Jesus Conboy is all I've got stomach for. I've had that and what I've got to say now I'd like to say without somebody twice my size trying to knock me down."

Trying, Lib thought, looking more closely. You've been knocked hell west and crooked already or I miss my guess. "I expect Mr. Conboy back briefly," she said, changing her tune. "If you don't want to see Link you'd better speak your piece at once."

"Better send the girl out of the room," Korby said.

"Why?" Lib asked, bridling at the idea of taking orders—from Korby—or anyone. "She has every right to sit in her own parlor."

"Suit yourself," Korby said. "I've got some ugly things to say about her father. If you want her to hear them, that's your lookout."

"I doubt Link Conboy's ever done anything he'd be ashamed to have his children hear." She believed this; but at the same time thought, remembering old jealousies and antagonisms, if he's made a misstep let Cate hear about it. She has always been for her father and against me, never able to see the slightest flaw in Link.

"Very well, madam," Korby said.

That "Very well, madam" set Lib's teeth on edge. What's he think I am? she wondered. A new widow he's got to smooth down? "Go on," she said. "If you've got anything to say, say it."

Korby rubbed his hands together, as Lib had seen him do at the graveside. "Go on," she said, "go on. We've all got work to do here at The Farm. We don't have to wait for someone to die."

"Very well, ma'am. But this is no skim-milk story, believe me. I've stomached your husband about as long as I can. He's set himself up in this county as being just a little better than anybody else. The smart lawyer. The big-hearted Poor House superintendent. Too damned fine-haired for us common folks. Can smell right from wrong a mile off. Wouldn't touch a case with a ten-foot pole if it didn't smell just right to him. Wouldn't touch mine. Wherever you go, there's Link Conboy, head up and tail over the dashboard, not wasting his breath on talk, too damn good to spill out a word on us ordinary folks, too damn fine-haired to have a drink with us, too damn sanctimonious to listen to a funny story. But not too damn good for some things. Oh, no. He's the friend of the orphan and the protector of the pauper—if you take his word for it. But if you don't take his word for it, what's he got to be so proud of? Not one God-damn thing. And I'll say it to you first. I'd scorn not to. You're the wife. You've earned the right."

"Get out of this house," Lib said.

"Not until I've had my say."

"Say it outside."

"You'll want to hear this. Ever hear of Mrs. Ashley Dukes? Ashy Dukes? I can see you have. Ever hear anything from Link about her? Did Link turn up unaccountably missing for a few days in April a couple of years back? You'd be surprised to learn you was on a little trip with him, wouldn't you? The two of you down at Madison. Man and wife, or so it says."

Lib didn't say she didn't believe it—she did. It was a knowledge she'd been advancing toward since the day she'd married Link, since before that—since the first time he'd kissed her. Half the pressure of her lips, at that moment, had been love; the other half had been a fighting against this hour and this knowledge. The minute you love, the minute you lap your arms about a man and go to bed with him, you lay yourself open to word of this kind, you invite it. It's a thing—like death—that all the rest of your life leads up to, and knowing this, you prepare yourself, steel yourself. You're not the world's most beautiful woman, are you? Or the smartest? Or the most religious? Oh, God knows, not. And for a man like Link, women gaping at him at every turn, who more likely than Ashy Dukes, a woman who could take her pick of men? And she herself a slommacky woman sitting here in mid-afternoon in her nightgown when the news comes. That would be the way of it, the way she—

"If you doubt my word," Korby said, "run your eye over this. Night of April 17th and so forth. Lincoln Conboy and wife." He held the sheet toward Lib and when she made no motion to take it he put it on the stand-table in his delicate way, motions as tender and pitiful as when he lifted a coffin-lid. "There's the evidence in black and white." Well, now Missus, he thought, say something.

The years of waiting at night for the sound of Link's buggy turning in the driveway, of watching him give a woman at an upping-block his hand, of seeing him gather up a woman's fallen napkin and spread it, touching, as he did that courteous job, her thigh—of noting even so small a thing as the inclination of his head in listening to a woman speak. Feeding on his movements, words, looks; making bitter bread of those sights and chewing that bread, swallowing it down to the last gagging mouthful. Why? As an antidote to this? So she would be prepared, the way a man who eats a little poison every day can finally swallow a tubful without taking harm? The way a soldier pictures every kind of death to himself so that finally not a one of its ways can scare him? Ashy Dukes? Yes, that was one of the ways she'd seen it. Well, she'd fought against it, pictured it, swallowed it.

She got up. She was half a head taller than Korby. "Have you any more to say, Mr. Korby?"

"More?" Korby asked. "More? You understand your husband wasn't taking Mrs. Dukes to Madison for her health, don't you?"

"Understand?" Lib cried. She stood staring at Korby, her big green eyes, he thought, like a wildcat's—or like fox fire, cold on top and underneath their glass, the burning. "Understand?"

The woman'd 'bout as well be naked, Korby told himself; that sleezy material hides nothing.

"Oh, I understand," she said. "My husband got in bed with another woman."

"Yes," said Korby, "yes. That's the gist of it, madam. That's about the size of it." Lib saw he was flustered. He wasn't prepared to rehearse the event, step by step.

"He got in bed with Ashy," Lib said. "He—" But in God's name, what then? And in God's name, what of it? This was another of her events, the nearer she came to it the smaller she saw it to be. The Christmas arrived, never the Christmas imagined. The newcomers, blown up in her mind to the size of dukes and duchesses, when she called on them nothing more than some hain'ting-ain'ting couple with a farm heired off an old childless uncle and she, sitting in their parlor, her feet on their dirty in-grain, dressed up as if for a White House call. This news, which she'd feared and dreaded, spent her life preparing for, fighting against and driving Link to (oh, yes, she had), and now, faced with it, her nose rubbed in it—what *was* it? What *was* it? An act any man was asleep five minutes after. An act—why deny it—that might've been her own and she unable to remember the name—his name—a month later. And to her and Link, what was it? To *her* and *Link*. The thing met, not imagined, was so little it was like marching up to death and losing your burdens, going into that river and coming out washed clean and new on the other side. And free.

Korby wanted to hurt Link, do him as much harm as possible, but he wasn't prepared to drive his wife clean out of her mind. "Can I fetch you a glass of water, ma'am?" he asked. "Or maybe your smelling salts? It's been a blow. Don't think I don't appreciate it. The more so because your husband's been such a two-faced old scamp, if you'll excuse my saying so. But no use not facing it, is there? In time you'll come to thank me."

"In time?" Lib said, advancing on him, her full nightgown switching from side to side in the exuberance of her motion. "Why, Mr. Korby, I don't need time. I can thank you, now. Compared with what you've done for me today, nobody's ever yet done me a hand's turn of kindness in my whole lifetime."

"Well," Korby said doubtfully, "it hurt me to the quick to be the one to bring the news. Don't think it didn't. But when a husband starts running after women—"

"Running after," Lib said shortly. "Link don't have to run after women. They run after him."

"Sleep with," Korby said, putting a plainer face on it.

"What is that, Mr. Korby? I ask you? You're a man."

Korby looked modest, felt modest: it was something certainly, but while he had a respectable vocabulary assembled with which to speak to women of death, he had no decent words for this other catastrophe which came to them.

"Name me any rememberance of your own of the ten thousand times—"

"Ten thousand?" asked Mr. Korby, startled.

"Ten hundred. Name me any rememberance."

"Well now," Korby protested, "that's hardly a subject to discuss."

"I'm doing the discussing now, and when I've finished you get out of here. Link Conboy's a man like any other man—in that regard. Otherwise he's not to be compared to a shite-poke like you. Now you go. He's too good for me, and when I'm in my right mind I know it. And in my right mind or wrong, I know he's too good for you."

Mr. Korby hesitated. "I notice you don't say son Dandie's too good for me."

"Get out," said Lib.

"I'll thank you for my little document first."

"Get out," Lib said. "I've got a whole household here at my beck and call, half of them out of their minds. You want me to sick them on you?"

"I'm a commissioner here—"

"Tell them that and there'll be no stopping them," she warned him, backing him out of the room as she spoke. "Go bury someone else, Mr. Korby. Link Conboy's not ready yet for your services."

"I'll have to go bury the man your son cut up last night, like as not."

"And you right there whetting the knives, I don't misdoubt. You must be hard pressed for business, Mr. Korby."

She shut the door in his face, walked back to the stand-table and stood looking down at that sheet with those names. It's a fact, she told herself, and nothing to imagine; and understanding this, her heart slowed down to a more regular beating. She did not notice that Cate, white-faced, had left the room.

Lib was still there—Korby's document on the table beside her— when Link came in at three, miserable, wet, and tired. He knocked the water from his hat, hung it on the knob of a rocker, and took off his coat.

"Aren't you cold in here without a fire?" he asked. Lib's nightgown and wrapper, at this hour of the day, didn't surprise him; especially after the kind of day she'd been through.

"The old coot'll pull through, I guess," he said wearily, knowing what news she'd want first. "He's too mean to die. Laying there in the rain all night would've killed any honest man—without that other. I saw Dandie—and Korby. Fact of the business, I had a little run-in with Korby."

"I know. He was here," Lib said.

"Here? What was he doing here?" The very mention of Korby's name made him feel restless, uncertain—too kind-hearted to thoroughly whip the man the way he ought to have been whipped; too uncontrolled to forbear all together. He put one hand on Lib's shoulder; its softness was a poultice to his fingers, it drew Korby's poison out of his body. With his other hand he lifted the sheet from the stand-table—saw at once and knew at once.

Lib, meeting his eyes, witnessed a darkening and deepening, a look she never forgot, the nakedest pain: his knowledge that she knew; and his own final acceptance of the fact that he had fallen from the one mark he had set up for himself in this world, to be her true husband.

"It don't matter, Link," Lib said.

"Elizabeth."

It was the first time, to her knowledge, that Link had used that name since he'd said, "I, Lincoln, take thee, Elizabeth."

He drew her to her feet and led her across to the sofa where Cate had spent her day; he brushed aside, without knowing what he did, the mud she had left there and seated first Lib, then himself. He started to speak, could not control himself sufficiently to do so and covered his face with his hands. Lib began to kiss his hands. "Link, Link, forgive yourself."

11

*L*YING wide awake in the rented hotel room, in the middle of her bed and the middle of the night, Cate told herself, You had as well admit it, there is something bad in you, some rotten spot which you don't see but which is plain as day to everyone else. Mr. Schilling saw it, that is why he acted the way he did. He is an elderly, fatherly man, and he would never have tried to kiss and hug a good girl. There is something in you that is exactly like the bad aunts, and like Em, stripping naked, and like Dandie and like—and now she saw what she had been running away from —like the nastiness in your own father and mother.

Then the scene in the parlor, which running away to Madison had kept out of her mind, came back to her; with added sharpness and pain, for she understood its meaning for her. She turned and turned in her bed, but whichever way she turned she heard all those words, over and over again. "Mr. Conboy took a little trip without you. . . . Ashy Dukes. . . . I see the name's familiar. . . . Link Conboy . . . the old two-faced scamp. . . ."

And Lib's voice, "I ask you, Mr. Korby. . . . What did he do? Nothing not natural to man. . . . Nothing but get into bed. . . . How many times, Mr. Korby . . . and never remember. . . . A man like any other, Mr. Korby."

Then the voices would cease, and she would see Em going up those stairs and stripping there, and Doss Whitt's eyes, worse than hands, on her.

And Em's body would become that white naked hoop, naked and bleeding, and Dandie with a knife in his hand standing over him.

And the hoop, the curving, would become Christie, arms about her, holding her and kissing her on the banks of Bleeding Creek.

And Christie's kiss would become Mr. Schilling's, who last night had seen all this in her and had not scrupled, because of it, to try to make love to her.

On the wall next her bed was a loud knocking, "Hush up in there. Shut up that bawling. We came here to sleep. Dry up or we'll call the manager."

She got out of bed, clamped her teeth together so that no sound could escape and walked from wall to wall of the tan cube, pausing occasionally to rest her head against the rough plastering and whisper, "Help me, help me."

It seemed to her, as she walked, that the worst of all was Lib's acceptance of Korby's words. Why hadn't she fought back, denied? Once a long time ago when Em, wading, had stepped off a sand-bar into a deep hole, Lib, though she couldn't swim a stroke, had plunged in over her head and dragged Em to safety.

Link, when he had heard of this, had said, "Lib, that was a foolhardy thing to do. Nothing but luck kept you from sinking like a stone." "It wasn't luck," Lib had answered him. "Whatever I've got to do, I can do. Swim or, if necessary, fly."

And Cate had believed this, had banked on her mother's power to resist and defy. Now that power was no more. She had heard with her own ears Lib accept and excuse what she knew her mother considered the worst thing in the world. What was left?

The pounding began once more. "This is the last warning you'll get."

She lay down on her bed and was quiet, too, for she shoved the corner of the pillow into her mouth.

11

SHE HAD "run off" to Madison the day after Korby had called on her mother. She did not have a moment's hesitation about doing so. One act after another had suggested itself to her without any willing or thinking on her part; and at their conclusion she felt a kind of satisfying mechanical jolt, almost heard a sound of the kind the lamp chimney makes as it slides into place after passing the first withholding tightness of the prongs.

All that was hard was the starting. She had never gone anywhere alone, before; never bought a railroad ticket, never entertained the idea of being by herself in a city. She thought the fact that she was running away from home and was alone must "show" on her; that everyone who saw her would know: "There goes a runaway girl, alone, not a soul to turn to." Thinking of this, the trip had seemed impossible to her: to buy a ticket, pretend to be a traveler; but buying a ticket she had become a traveler. What you did, you were. And the mechanics of the action provided her with suitable words and gestures. Though her hand shook, the ticket was put into it; though she stumbled going up the steps to the train, the train itself remained solid; though her heart seemed, at the moment of leave-taking, to be bound to the Poor Farm, the train moved away from The Junction easily and smoothly, unaware that it was breaking (as she thought) the ties which held her to her family.

The thought of registering at a hotel had frightened her too. What did you say? "Please do you have a spare room?" "Do you provide inexpensive accommodations for women traveling alone?" "Have you a bed-chamber to rent for the night?" She had gone over and over these matters in her mind on the way down to Madison, only to find at the hotel that she did not need to say a word. "Want a room, miss?" Nod. "Be with us long?" Nod. "Dollar about right?" Nod.

She had written her letters to Christie and to her father and mother that first night. She had used the bad hotel pen like a gun —to kill what had to be killed.

"Our engagement is broken. I will never marry you. You know some of the reasons. The others are the same. I hope I never see you again." This was what she wrote Christie.

She saw what her life with Christie would be like, where it would lead. With a stroke of her pen she put an end to that threat.

To her father and mother she wrote: "There is no use coming to look for me or to get me because I will never come back. I am going to stay here and work. I am not engaged to Christie Fraser any more. If he should come there trying to find me, don't help him—" She had written then, "—unless you want me to lead a life like yours"—but this she had scratched out. She could not bear to mention their life.

That first night she ate the crackers and cheese she had bought for her supper. After supper she picked up the straight-backed chair to wedge under the doorknob of the already locked door. But she put it down again. What was the use? What more could happen to her?

When she woke up on the first morning in her room, the sun was shining in yellow pin-points through the cracks in the green window-blind. She had no way of judging time except by that light, by the sounds in the street outside and by her own feeling that the night had passed. She got up, raised the blind, and saw people passing beneath her window, unconcernedly as fish in a stream: men with dinner-pails; a darky man sweeping the sidewalk in front of the hotel; three darky women, perfectly silent and in step like soldiers; a little boy, running so fast that the carpet rag (it looked like) which he held aloft was extended behind him, level and stiff as a gun barrel; a young man with a tilted straw hat, a lock of straw-colored hair on his forehead: he looked up at her, took off his hat, and pouted his lips in a make-believe kiss.

She backed away from the window; even a make-believe kiss was something she wanted never again to encounter; she washed and dressed carefully, but scarcely looked in the mirror, except for a glance at the hemline and belt of her skirt; she avoided her eyes because she was afraid she would catch sight in them of faces and words she wanted to forget.

She ate her breakfast: crackers and cheese once more; later she would have a cup of coffee in a restaurant. Eating this way, saving her money (she had only her hired girl money—a dollar and a half a week was what Link had paid her) made her feel strong, in charge of things: a feeling she needed. The mechanism which the night with Nory and the afternoon in the parlor with Lib and Korby had set in motion, and which told her what to do without her having to take thought, was still working; but there were none of those satisfying clicks, as of yesterday; though the room itself, in its faded impersonal orderliness, almost gave her that feeling. It was so unreal, so truly square, and completely tan; it was like the picture of a cube in a Normal School geometry book, so strange and inhuman in its exactitude that it excited her like a poem.

She had brought four books with her, the Bible, *Lena Rivers*, Emerson's *Essays*, and the poems of Edgar A. Poe. She was ready to leave the room for her coffee and had unlocked the door when she turned back and without premeditation, seized *Lena Rivers* and read the first chapter as if it contained the last word she would ever receive of the known world and the human race.

Outside, on the street, she missed the covering of her tan cube. She was a runaway girl again, alone. She pretended an interest in shop windows, the hang of her skirt; she was involved every second in the terrible effort of simulating the unself-conscious and spontaneous; her lips painstakingly smiled every smile, her eyes sparkled every sparkle. Every step, look, and breath was a disguise put on to hide the fact that she was alone, alone, unknown, lost. A tall dog, a hound of some kind, came to her and nudged upward against her arm, rescuing her from pretense. Oh, he was wonderful, an island to rest on. She was accompanied now, need not avoid glances, had someone she could turn to, naturally. "Doggy, doggy," she said. She whistled under her breath, patted the dog's head, and finally tried to hold him by the scruff of the neck when, at the end of the square, he turned the corner and trotted away from her: an independent dog, at home in the city, able at will to take up with strangers and part from them.

Alone again she picked out a restaurant with a cat in the window; she felt more at home with animals than human beings. But beyond the cat were strange men eating, and she went hurriedly past them to a table in the corner. Out to save money and buy only a cup of coffee, she ordered the entire breakfast, not because she wasn't hungry—she was—but because she was self-conscious and the waiter frightened her. In a hoarse faltering voice she asked, "Can you tell me where I can get a morning paper?" She was going to look for work.

At the table next her a black-haired young man with talc on his plum-colored jaws, fast, she could tell at a glance, said, "I'll be glad to let you see mine, miss."

"Thank you," she replied, "I wouldn't think of troubling you."

As she was finishing her fried potatoes and ham, the man from the table beyond the young one brought his paper to leave with her, and because he was older, gray-haired and fatherly, she took it and thanked him for it. Back in her room she read it carefully; but there was no one that day in the whole city of Madison advertising for female help. Outside the city a number of business concerns wanted agents and she copied down their addresses.

A. D. Worthington, Hartford, Conn. Looking for agents to sell Mary A. Livermore's, *My Story of The War—In Hospital and on the Battlefield*. Selling like wildfire. No Competition. Distance no hindrance, as we pay freight.

Larkin Soap Co., 120 Main, Columbus, O. Needs representatives to sell Sweet Home Soap and Napoleon Shaving Sticks. Payment to be made in percentage and premiums.

Madame Rowley, 1164 Broadway, N. Y., offers exceptional opportunities to a selected group of young women. Sell her new Face Glove, a mask which physicians recommend as a substitute for injurious cosmetics and to which innumerable actresses, women of fashion, etc., owe their beauty and charm.

F. I. Whitney, Box 173, St. Paul, Minn. Do you want money? Work? Health? Write him saying just what you desire and an answer, together with maps and publications will be sent free.

She decided that Madame Rowley offered the best opportunity (just as she said she did) for money-making and began at once a letter to her. "Madame Rowley, 1164 Broadway, N. Y. Dear Madam; I should like to become an agent for your new Face Glove. I am eighteen years old and though I have had no experience in selling merchandise I am convinced—."

She threw down her pen; she was convinced of only one thing and that was that she could never sell anything, not a book, nor a bar of soap, let alone a Face Glove. Something was running down, there were no more clicks and fewer and fewer automatic commands to "do this, do that." She had carefully and purposefully shut out the past, refused to think of it; now there began, also, to be no future; she was stranded, left alone in the center of the present minute, with its single eye regarding her; alone in the center of the perfect cube with all its equal walls edging in upon her. Hurriedly she took *Lena Rivers*, lay down with it and read it straight through without once lifting her eyes from its pages. When she finished, and without actually emerging from that world, she ate the last of her crackers and cheese; then fully dressed, lay down again and slept.

It was twilight when she awakened. She had slept heavily with her mouth open, and there was a small damp spot on the pillow where, face down, her mouth had pressed. Her dress was wrinkled, her hair tangled; there were cracker crumbs on the floor; the blind was crooked and the stand-table was covered with the disarray of scattered envelopes and paper. She was disgusted with herself and the room, and cleaned both. She looked herself, as she recombed her hair in front of the mirror, defiantly in the eye. People come to the city, she told the clean, neat girl in the mirror, to learn, to have pleasure, to make their fortunes. I would scorn, if I were you, to lurk in a hotel bedroom like a criminal. She put her sailor hat on at an angle, wore it like a chip on her shoulder; she threw her ulster on as if ulsters were forbidden by law. At the door she hesitated, went back and completed her letter to Madame Rowley. Underlining *"convinced,"* she continued swiftly, "—that I have considerable talent for canvassing. Please let me know at *once* what your proposition is. I am prepared to devote my *entire* time to selling your Face Glove and feel certain that it is what ladies everywhere have been seeking. I have a clear complexion so I will be a good advertisement for it and will certainly wear it myself three times a week as you suggest. Sincerely yours, Miss Catherine Conboy, Madison Hotel, Madison, Ind."

She mailed her letter and went out on to the street, once more, lost and alone in the spring twilight in the city she did not know.

The waiter at the restaurant recognized her and took her to the table where the fatherly man who had given her his morning paper sat; and because he *was* fatherly and because she was so lost, she was glad to see him.

"Well, well," he exclaimed, rising most courteously and helping her with her chair, "if it isn't my little morning friend again." And when Cate hesitated over the menu he said, "May I take the liberty of advising the roast lamb? It's real lamb, not mutton, and I think you'll find it very tasty."

Cate, accustomed to salt pork, boiled beans, and ham bone, was flattered by this belief that she could tell the two apart and followed his advice. While she waited for her order to be served he said, "I think if we introduce ourselves it would be a little more homey, don't you? I'm George H. Schilling. I'm the Singer Sewing Machine representative for these parts, and I live in Indianapolis. Now you tell me your name and where you live and we won't have to be calling each other 'See here' and 'Say.'"

This ease and playfulness delighted Cate as much as Mr.

Schilling's plump benign face reassured her. "My name's Catherine Conboy."

"Is Madison your home town?"

"Oh, no. I'm living at the Madison Hotel for the present, however."

"That's a pleasant coincidence," Mr. Schilling said, "since I'm putting up at that hostelry myself. But I must say I haven't had the pleasure of seeing you about the place."

"This is my first day. I just arrived yesterday."

"From where, may I ask?"

"The Junction."

Mr. Schilling gave a low and surprising whistle. "I would never've guessed that pokey little town was capable of turning out as trig and intelligent a looking young lady as you, Miss Conboy. I can see I'm going to have to amend my ideas of that little burg. Are there any more like you at home?"

This was a little too much for Cate, and Mr. Schilling, as if recognizing it, went on in a businesslike way, "And what are you doing in Madison? Shopping? Visiting friends?"

Reassured, Cate answered, "Oh, no. I'm here looking for work. I've left The Junction forever."

"Well," Mr. Schilling said, "I can't say that I blame you. People can rot and die in these little backwater towns without ever knowing they were alive. What kind of work do you have in mind?"

Cate told him about the Face Glove and Mr. Schilling strongly advised against it. "Selling's a hard and risky game for anyone and particularly a young girl; even if you've got a reputable product. Which, to be frank with you, this Face Glove isn't. And even if it was, how many women are there, with money enough or time enough, to guarantee any future for a thing like that?"

"What do you advise me to do then?" Cate asked with the feeling of a well-established career being ruined.

"I'll tell you what," Mr. Schilling said, snapping his white fingers. "The Singer people are thinking about lady demonstrators. How would you like to be a lady demonstrator, Miss Conboy? Can you sew?"

"On the machine, you mean?"

"Yes."

"I can, but I'm not very good. My seams are pretty crooked sometimes."

"A little practice would take care of that. And you've got naturally what practice can never teach, and what a sewing demonstrator must have."

Cate's eyes asked the question she was too timid to voice, and Mr. Schilling answered it. "You look nice in your clothes, dear."

They discussed the matter on the way back to the hotel, and in the lobby Mr. Schilling said, "If you're really interested in this opportunity, Miss Conboy, I'd like to come up to your room and talk it over with you."

Cate was pleased and flattered: look what happened when you took your courage in your hands and acted. She had not been in Madison much more than twenty-four hours and already she had a friend and possibly also the beginning of a career.

"I'd be very pleased, Mr. Schilling, to talk to you."

"Good," Mr. Schilling told her. "I have some business to attend to first, then I'll be up to see you. What's your room number, Miss Conboy?"

"Twenty," Cate said, "that'll be easy to remember, won't it?"

"Yes," Mr. Schilling said, "it will."

When she awakened it was full and sunny daylight. The pillow had slipped from her mouth but the taste of it, feathers and starch, was still there. And the scent of Mr. Schilling's hair oil, rubbed onto her when he had held her, trying to kiss her and before she had been able to push him, slapping and kicking in her anger and disgust, out of the door, was there too. That she had been able to get rid of him almost at once did not matter so much as the fact that she had been the kind of girl who had made him think of doing what he did. He had made for her without any talk; opened the door and recognized her for what she was: her father's daughter; Em's and Dandie's sister; Christie's easily loved sweetheart. He had recognized her before that: while she sat in the restaurant he had seen the looseness in her, the bad blood. He had seen how love-making could carry her away into forgetfulness.

She got out of bed and sat for a long time on the floor by the window, her head on the window-sill; but not looking out; scarcely aware that there was any "out" to look to. What was she to do? Where was there a safe place for a girl like her? After a while she washed and dressed. She would have to buy more crackers and cheese. She loathed her hungriness, too. Surely a truly good girl would not be thinking of food so soon after the terrible happenings of the past days. But she accepted her hunger as she accepted the rest of her nature, sorrowfully but honestly.

When she went downstairs the clerk at the desk said, "There's a young man to see you, miss."

She said, "Christie," involuntarily. That taught her how much there was yet to overcome.

III

FOUR hours earlier, Ferris Thompson had stood outside the Madison Hotel gazing at its closed doors. He had never been in a hotel; and though reason told him that a hotel was a public building on the order of a church or depot and could be entered without knocking, still he had hesitated to do so. He had on his Sunday suit, bought two years ago when he weighed a hundred and thirty instead of a hundred and fifty, and to the discomfort of his uncertainty about knocking was added the discomfort of blue serge cutting sharply into him at armhole and crotch. He wished he hadn't started so early, but then, he'd had no idea that there was so much difference between rising time in the city and in the country. Cate herself might still be in bed. He had continued to stand and stare. Finally feeling it both noticeable and unmanly to do so any longer, he had shot the door open with such force that the old colored man, polishing the door's inside hardware, was half upset. Embarrassed, Ferris had asked severely, "Why don't you watch what you're doing?" The old fellow went back to work without replying and Ferris said, "I'm hunting Miss Catherine Conboy." The Negro had nodded toward the desk, and Ferris had caught the amused eye of the clerk there and understood his mistake. He had repeated his question and got a respectful enough answer. "Miss Conboy's stopping with us, but she's not down yet this morning. Want me to call her?"

He did, he wanted to see Cate at once; but he had been uncertain as to whether it would be considered proper for him to have a young woman roused from her bed. "Let her sleep," he had said. "I'll wait for her."

He had seated himself in one of the rockers lined up before the front window, removed his hat, and wiped the dust from his shoes with his handkerchief. Time had passed slowly. After his early breakfast he was already hungry again; he was uninterested in the people outside on their way to work; and above all he was nervous about his meeting with Cate. When he had suggested the trip to Madison to Link, it had seemed to him, not only a chance to show the Conboys how helpful he could be, but an opportune time to begin his courting of Cate. With her engagement broken, and her brother in the scrape he was, he had believed she would welcome some kind of respectful attention; she ought to be glad, after all the Conboy didoes—the fights and the bad marriages and the cutting scrapes—of a little sense and reason. She ought to, but the trouble was, he admitted, that Cate wasn't always so sensible herself. She was a Conboy too, and quite capable, he felt uneasily, of walking into the lobby, giving him one unfriendly toss of the head, and walking on out. The idea made him sweat. His real trouble was, he admitted, that he was in love with the girl. That was his trouble and he leaned back in his rocker and gave himself up to it. He was in love with her, he was afraid of her, and he intended to marry her. And he didn't care what means he had to use to badger her into it. He considered himself a good catch, more than presentable in looks, prospects, and intentions. He was uncertain of himself in one respect only: he had been a pretty, spindly, curly-haired mama's boy and cry-baby; and occasionally, with fellows like Dandie, he felt that he would never be able to outgrow these drawbacks. He was no longer spindly; the curls and good looks he did not now consider a hardship, and as for tears, he couldn't imagine the happening which would ever again make him cry. Still, he was constantly aware of a need to prove his manliness and strength of character. He had an ideal, after which he patterned himself—a man hard, strong, self-contained, and in his relations with the ladies, delicate-minded and protective. The most appealing and romantic situation he could imagine, involving himself and a girl, was one in which he saved her from a team of runaway horses; or perhaps knocked down a bully who was annoying her. That would certainly prove something about himself to her. And to him.

The men he disliked most were the loud-mouthed showoffs: the fellows who were in evidence at every box supper or strawberry festival, singing, strumming mandolins, or breaking into uncalled-for cakewalks. Dandie Conboy was a good example of this kind of cut-up, and he himself always showed his superiority to such childishness by simply walking away from it. Cate, too, as in that lamp-kicking business, was capable of just such capers as Dandie; but she did such things less often and besides, in a girl, they were more attractive.

He had given himself up, he believed, to thoughts about Cate; though so far he had not quite reached her, being more concerned with his disapproval of Dandie and with that mixture of approval and uncertainty which constituted his attitude toward himself. Reaching Cate, his mind left words behind and he saw her, quite featureless, it is true, devoid of hair, eyes, lips, figure or any detail of figure; but luminous, a warm hazel-colored outline, capable of exciting him, and of reassuring him where he most needed reassurance. Images of Cate so filled his mind that he missed seeing her enter the lobby or hearing the clerk say, "There's a gent waiting for you, miss."

He did hear and recognize her voice as she said, "Christie." He got up at once to put a quietus to her fears.

"Don't worry about that fellow's hanging around, Cate. I'll take care of him. Everything's going to be all right now. I've come to take you home."

She appeared to be about to cry—as who could blame her after what her brother had pulled her through, and added to that, her present fear that that Indianapolis fellow had come back to hound her.

"Did my folks send you for me?"

"Send me?" He flared up a little at that. "No, of course not. They were glad to have me come, but it was my own idea. I've been worried about you down here by yourself."

"Have you, Ferris?" She said his name so softly that Ferris took heart. Perhaps Fraser *had* jilted her; he didn't care.

"Yes, I did, Cate. The city's no place for a girl alone." With sudden boldness he seized Cate's hand; and when she did not attempt to take it away he thought, Perhaps all her going with Fraser was no more than a trick to make me sit up and take notice. Girls were capable of such things, he knew. Perhaps he had been stone blind for six months.

"Have you had any breakfast?" he asked.

"No," Cate said, "have you?"

"I did, but so long ago I've forgotten it. Let's go eat."

IV

HE HAD proposed, but not been accepted, when they left Madison at three o'clock; and since thoughtfulness, not reluctance, had appeared to make Cate hesitate, Ferris was not cast down. Marriage was a serious matter and he wouldn't care for a girl who would be heedless about it.

Spring seethed about them as they drove homeward, spun out in whorls of blossoms, eddied in drifts of fragrance. Everything but the fenceposts was in leaf, and the fenceposts sprouted birds: blackbirds, redbirds, woodpeckers, yellow-hammers, peewees, orioles. They were all there and all, even at that late hour for birds, were singing; except for the jay who would not let spring itself jar him from his program of defiance and screaming. Far back in the hazel clumps, out of sight, the thrushes sang; so sweet, Cate felt her ears cringing a little at the sound. Wasn't there a limit to the melody ears could accept? Crab-apple trees bloomed by the roadside. They drove by so slowly she saw in their china pink centers the bees and May flies at work. Above them on the hillsides, the redbud was already fading; but higher still, on the crests of the hills, hawthorne and service-berry foamed in full tide.

Guineas cried in the farmyards; and in the spring meadows, where the little branches rippled and glinted, ganders, lifting their snowy wings, courted their willing wives. The leaves were still so new they all shone as if waxed, and all still so yellow they lit up the woods with a spangling like sunlight. Somewhere ahead of them an afternoon shower had stirred up and heightened the scents of earth and blossoming, and this sweetness was borne to them on the light warm air. They drove toward the center of this fragrance as if it, not the Poor House, were their goal; and Cate, thinking of this, thought too, it could be so.

Ferris asked, "Do you mind if I stop and put down the top? I hate tin-horn sports who go parading around with the top down, just to show off. But out here in the country where we do it to see, not be seen, well, it puts a different light on it, don't you think?"

Cate said, "Yes, I do," and she had the pleasant feeling of giving permission. A wifely feeling, she decided, and one, she realized, she'd never had with Christie. She had never with Christie thought anything at all but, He makes me happy. And Christie, no doubt, had had no better or less selfish reason for wanting to be with her. No wonder that together they had come to such a sorry pass—and no wonder that they didn't belong together.

She turned about in the seat to help Ferris; the joints of the top had rusted a little and were hard to bend. Ferris' buggy—it wasn't his but his father's—was another sign of the difference between him and Christie. Christie, the minute he'd gotten a few dollars ahead, had spent it all on a showy horse and an even more showy buggy: rubber tires, red spokes, and lamps big enough to light up a church. How silly that had been, and how silly she had been to admire it *and* Christie. But she was growing up, gaining in wisdom; she was able to understand now how much more sensible Ferris was to use the family buggy, even if it wasn't new and fashionable and to drive a horse who could pull a plow as well as a buggy.

As Ferris picked up the reins and clucked to Fanny—who preferred the roadside grass to travel—she saw she'd been mistaken in another thing: in preferring Christie's looks to Ferris'. She had been on the point, she saw, of marrying Christie for the same reason that men marry unsuitable women, because their looks stir them, move them in physical ways. Ferris was just as good-looking as Christie, even better, because his features were neater and fairer; but what was fine and wholesome about Ferris was that she could look at him without the least desire to touch him. How sweet it was—and free—to sit beside Ferris, able to see his good points, but not be upset or excited; not trembling if even so much as the edge of his sleeve touched her arm.

Ferris said, "If you were willing to marry me I had thought the twenty-fifth would be a good day for the wedding."

"Of this month?"

"Yes. It's the folks' wedding anniversary. They always have a nice celebration party and we could celebrate with them in the future."

Cate began to see those years of celebrating stretching ahead, the May afternoons when the two Mrs. Thompsons would sit together at a tea-table and pass out loaf cake of the finest grain and China tea so delicate and pale the eye could scarcely detect it in the cup.

Ferris' mother would say, "My thirty-fifth and our daughter's tenth anniversary. We always celebrate together." Cate could feel Mrs. Thompson's light hand on her shoulder as she said that and see the sheen of her silver head, lovingly inclined toward her, and the rustle of her own silk mull as she rose to fetch more hot water. Wanda, who had never married, was playing the *May Flowers Waltz* in honor of the occasion.

When she came back with the water Mother Thompson was saying, "The dear girl was up at dawn. Twenty glasses of strawberry preserves cooling on the window-sill at this minute. But who would guess it, to look at her now?" That was because of the pink silk mull and the gray kid slippers and every hair in shining order. "Five hundred quarts of fruit put up last year, if you'll believe it."

She bent to touch her lips to Mother Thompson's roseleaf cheek. "It was nothing." But nothing, or not, it was true. Five hundred quarts and the cellar when you went down with a lighted lamp gleaming like Aladdin's cave. Currant jelly, quince honey, piccalilli, watermelon preserves, corn relish, plum conserve.

Driving along, beside Ferris, she thought of the smell of blackberries coming to a boil in the middle of a July morning, when the shadows on the velvet grass are still untarnished and the starched curtains at the dining-room windows rustle in the warming but still fresh air. And she thought of evenings, when the young Mrs. Thompson, after canning blackberries, would have a berry cobbler for supper, and she could see the wonderful pattern she'd prick out, in its crust, of wild roses or birds on the wing.

She could see the evenness of all the years ahead, if she married Ferris, in the Thompson house, so white and solid—and sensible, beneath its maples. It had a little upstairs porch and she saw herself step out onto it, into the earliest light of some October morning and listen there to the soft fall of leaves and the heavier thud of persimmons dropping after the night's hard frost. She could see herself in the evening, sitting with Mother Thompson and Wanda—braiding rugs, were they? Or crocheting edging for pillow-shams? Busy and calm, anyway. And when the clock struck ten they said their good nights, for the hours in that house were planned and had meaning.

The days had meaning, too. Calendars were marked with holidays and anniversaries. Birthdays were regularly noted and kept. Church days, prayer-meeting days, and Ladies' Aid days were remembered and observed. There was nothing haphazard even about washdays or ironing-days. Wednesdays they cleaned. Oh, the wonderful sunny order which she saw in the years ahead in that neat white house, a sunniness which made, by contrast, the Poor House and all that had happened there darker and uglier than they had ever been before. As they rode toward the center of that far-off sweetness, stirred up by the storm (fading a little perhaps as they neared it), she seemed to sit heavier in the buggy seat; the imagined years of orderly content had already begun their job of thickening and quieting her body.

It had grown dusky; a whippoorwill called; a late dogwood blossom flared up in the green twilight with the tremulous shine of a lit candle. Ferris put his arm about her waist recalling her from her dream of the long, beautifully precise, housekeeping years ahead, but not arousing in her any other feeling than that of a slight discomfort since his arm prevented her from leaning back easily.

"Cate, you haven't said yet you'll marry me."

Since she felt nothing, since Ferris did not awaken in her that darkness which it was her duty to control and deny and which marriage and life with the Thompsons would ensure never again arising, she said, "I'll be very glad to marry you, Ferris."

Ferris then kissed her, and this was still more reassuring since she felt real pleasure when he had finished. She could feel marriage already at work upon her, changing her character; or rather giving her character, an object which up to this time she was afraid she had not really possessed. Ferris tipped her head over on to his shoulder and wry-necked, she let it lie there, filled with wifely kindness and consideration.

V

WELL then, for God's sake, he told himself, swallow it and don't go whining back to her saying, change your mind, saying, think twice, saying, remember how I kissed you? You've been thrown over, you've been given the mitten and the gate and the back of her hand. You've been jilted. But so have ten thousand before you, and they've gone on and lived and been the better for it and thanked God for saving them from the wrong girl. Who is she, anyway? Cleopatra or the Queen of Sheba or Lillian Russell? She's a girl named Cate Conboy, got rusty hair, freckles, and a big mouth. She's a poor little Poor House girl, blows hot, blows cold, loves you, doesn't love you, wants to kiss you, does kiss you, kiss, kiss, kiss until you've got fever blisters on your mouth, and then she'll cry, cry, cry because good girls don't kiss and have to be kissed all over again to keep her from worrying. Hurls herself at you, twines herself around you until you can't breathe and don't want to think, and crawls inside your pocket and lives there like a loving mouse and bites you to the bone the first time you put your hand in your pocket for a little fondling. What did you think was ahead of you, with her? Cosy little bite and squeak? Yes, she will and no, she won't, and maybe, sometime, now, forever; and all three so mixed all the time you can't tell tonight from yesterday or anytime from tomorrow. Except when she hits you, which is now, you're pretty sure, because she won't do it at all except it hurts her more than you. Which it does and so she can and that is now, isn't it? Which leads to self-defense and so a life with nothing missing but somebody to ring the bells for rounds.

"Oh, ring around the racoon's tail—
The possum's tail is bare!
A lady's got no tail at all,
And I don't care."

"Never heard it sung that way."
"I'm not singing."
"Won't argue about that—never heard it that way."
"I make it up as I go."
"What are you? A poet?"

He thought of Em. Me and Em. "We are two poets—me and the girl who was to've been my sister-in-law."

"Was to've been."

"She jilted me."

"Your sister-in-law-to-be?"

"No. My wife-to-be. Wrote me a letter. Told me she never wanted to see me again as long as she lived."

"Bub, you just escaped by the skin of your teeth. You've had a close call. The noose was around your neck and the knot behind your ear. The next thing you know the trap would've been sprung. You've had a lucky miss. The next drink's on me to celebrate."

He's drunk, Christie thought. He squinted between columns of smoke and veils of something, alcohol vaporizing, maybe, trying to see his companion's face. It hung like a blossom on a moonvine, limp and pale in the dark, and the moon itself gone down. He reached a hand across the table to try with his fingers if it was really there and really was blossoming, but it retreated, silently. He scraped about in the sawdust underfoot and couldn't find bottom. Soon he was singing:

> "Cover me up with sawdust,
> Bury me in a good saloon.
> My girl has got a thirty-six bust—
> It'll be forty soon."

The new drinks arrived and the face across the table was behind both glasses.

"Your girl was fat?"

"Don't call her fat. She had the most beautiful shape and the most beautiful mind and the most beautiful soul of any girl in Rock County."

"Rock County's so small the prettiest face here might win the booby-prize any place else."

"Say that again."

He said it. Christie hit him and the white face swayed, and Christie thought, High wind in the moonvine and the blossoms breaking loose. The blossom came toward him, the wind, moving it, and hit him; but he felt nothing, too sodden to do anything but splash. Finally he could feel when he was hit and fought back for the pleasure of having a different kind of pain than the one he'd been suffering. Then all of his pains vanished together and he was sound asleep, unjilted.

Awake, he was jilted again and that pained him more than his broken hand and swollen eyes and cut mouth. Why, Cate, why? He asked it as if she were at hand and could give him an answer. Didn't you love me? When we planned our life together, were you lying to me? When you kissed me, was it just the pleasure of touch and not a way of saying our lives belonged together?

Then his questions would cease and his resolutions begin: If that is what you want, Cate Conboy, never to see me again, I'll grant you your wish. I'll never see you or write you. You can come to me begging but it will be too late. I can't run my life on "yes" today and "no" tomorrow.

In this frame of mind he headed, without any decision in the matter, toward Stony Creek. He arrived in the May dusk and sat for a while in the buggy, smelling the apple blossoms and listening to the frogs along the creek bank celebrating spring. The lamps had already been lit in the house and he could see Sylvy moving about in the kitchen. Without bothering either to unhitch or tie Ajax, he went up the path toward the back door. Though he had not made a sound, Sylvy came out onto the back porch and said his name. "Christie?"

"Sylvy," he answered, and held out both hands.

She took his hands and, since even in that light his damaged face could be seen, said, "What happened to your face, Christie?"

"I was in a fight."

"Fight?"

"I was drunk," he said. "I was out of my mind. Cate's thrown me over."

She tightened her grip and his bruised hand pained him but he didn't withdraw it. "Come on in, Christie," she said. "Let me do something for you."

12

THE MORE Link encountered setbacks in other lines the more determined he was to push forward the work on The Farm. The more he grieved over Dandie's crime, Cate's change of heart, and his own failures, the more fixed he became in his resolve that The Farm itself should succeed. The corn planting had been delayed by heavy rains and in the sudden burst of good weather at the first of May he kept all the able-bodied men in the fields from dark to dark getting the seed into the ground.

At the same time he didn't neglect the kitchen gardens. He had Mag and her helpers, as soon as the breakfast work was cleared away, cutting potatoes for Em and the Creagan girls to place, eye up, in what seemed to Em, endless rows. "If every eye makes one plant," she figured, "and every plant has ten potatoes we'll have about ten million potatoes next year."

Dexter, who was hoeing the potatoes under, said, "If you don't hurry up you won't have any heels next year at all. You stop all of a sudden like that again and I'll slice one off."

"Maybe it'd grow like the dragon's teeth into another me."

"Not so long's I've got a hoe and can hoe it up, it won't," Dexter said.

Even Lib, who had no relish for outside work, had to turn her hand to it. She picked worms from cabbage plants, made soft soap, set hens, and at dusk when the press of daylight activities let up, walked along the creek bank hunting for nests stolen out there in the thickets by the geese.

Link, in the midst of all this activity, worked longer hours than anyone else. He was out of the house by sunrise; and after everyone else was in bed, he would sit in the kitchen bringing his accounts up to date and trying to figure some way to better his herd of hogs.

"So long's his hogs prosper he don't care what comes of us," James Abel complained.

The men were waiting breakfast, clustered around the wash-bench and giving the May sun a chance to melt the last splinters of winter ice from their bones.

"Before I come over here," Josh Stout told Abel, and anyone else who cared to listen, "my daughter said, 'Pa, you're facing the sundown of life. And I want you, in an easy chair and rocking when the sun goes down.' So she fetched me over here and here I ain't seen a thing but sun-ups and them over a hog trough."

"Hogs," James Abel said, "are Link Conboy's whole faith and creed. If his mind ever rises higher than a hog's hock I ain't seen the sign."

"We're building us up as fine a bunch of shoats as they've got in the county," old Marvin Dilk said.

"Shoats!" Abel spat the word out as if it were dirty. "I aim higher."

"How much higher?" Neddy Oates asked and they all laughed.

John Manlief, his face washed, continued for a minute to lean over the basin listening to the talk. He had forgotten the things men say to each other while waiting breakfast. He straightened up and noted the beauty of sunlight sparkling along the edge of the tin wash-basin and the intricacy of a whorl in the grain of the pine wash-bench, brought out clear as a thumb-print by the splashed water. He moved aside to let Abel, who was pushing in behind him, at the basin. He buried his face in the huck towel, felt the outline of nose and brow lingeringly, as if his face were something precious, miraculously restored to him from the grave and still liable to crumble under rough handling.

He was returning to life slowly, using the small and the close-together for stepping-stones. He compared his condition to that of a starved man afraid to venture on a full meal. He thought anything heaped up or running over would turn him dauncy. But heaped up? Who wanted that? What kind of glutton would ask for anything more than this sunshine and a clean wet face and a piece of dry huck cloth to wipe the water away with? He took the towel from his face and watched a dragonfly point its quivering purple needle toward Nigger Bob's blossoming wool; watched

James Abel's face, beet red and ridged as a clenched fist, go into the basin of water without any of the hissing and steam you'd expect from such a meeting. And watched it lifted from the basin, still red, still ridged, needing something cooler than water to whiten it and smooth it.

Abel came over, took the towel from his hands. "You still a hog-lover?" he asked.

"Yes, yes, I reckon you could say that."

"Hog or man," Abel told him from back of the towel, like a veiled prophet, "you have to choose."

"Why?" John Manlief asked.

Abel took the towel down so that he could explain it face to face. "They're the opposites—swine and men. Set up to show the two different ways of living. If you love the one you can't love the other."

"I can," Manlief said. He saw Abel open his mouth to contradict him, then think better of it, decide to forgive a little hog love in a prospective digger.

"Come join us," Abel said, "now you've woke up, come to yourself, so to speak. Come dig with us."

"Us?" Manlief repeated.

"Me and Mary and Emma."

"You oughtn't to have a child digging."

"She don't hurt herself. But she's seen the light. Come be a witness too, Manlief. I want you to share the blessing."

"I got so many blessings now I doubt I could support one more."

"Blessings?" Abel asked. "What blessings you got?"

Manlief thrust his hands out wide in a gesture which included the men about the wash-bench, and beyond them the summerhouse, privies, barns, hogs rooting the earth and dragonfly, still hovering in mid-air: the world and its contents, no less; and whatever enveloped both, a May breath of joy or love, a luminosity visible to a man just come alive.

"Listen," Abel said. "Before you start counting your blessings, cock your ear to that. That sound like a blessing to you, that talk?"

The men around the wash-bench had got their teeth in the coming wedding. They were chewing it so fine the juices ran clear down their chins and hung in loops of nastiness. The happenings of the past month had worked them up to it: the peeper caught peeping; Dandie's runaway marriage and his wonderful night-time party for old man Wade; Link's set-to with Korby, and now, as a pretty cap to it all, Cate's sudden switch in husbands-to-be, young Thompson in place of the Indianapolis fellow and the wedding only two weeks off. Why the change? Why all the hurry? Who couldn't wait? The girl? The man? Or somebody yet to be?

"You think that's pretty talk?"

"No," Manlief said, "I don't."

"They need rectification."

Under the cloudless May-blue sky, the scent from honeysuckle arbor and pigsties mingling, a mixture so thick John Manlief wondered how his eye could miss it, the talk went on; the young were bringing to the coming joining of a man and a woman all their imaginings, the old all their memories.

"Something's been lost," Abel said. "Gone from them and the world."

"What?" Manlief asked, flatly.

"If I knew, would I spend my life hunting? If I knew—" He broke off and Manlief saw that he had caught sight of Link coming up from the barn.

"Abel," Link said without preliminaries, "you get on back to the barn. You scamped your work there. Make tracks. And stay there till things are done right. A hog's a smart animal but it can't handle a shovel yet."

"I've just washed up for breakfast."

"You can wash up again. Water's not what we're short on here, but elbow grease. Now get."

Manlief watched Abel's face. It seemed to puff outward as if even bones and teeth were swelling.

"Go on," Link said again. "Make tracks."

11

EM WAS calling her name, "Cate, Cate."

Cate, who was wide awake but had her eyes closed, opened them.

"Stop it, Cate," Em said.

[334]

Cate turned in her bed until she faced Em. "Stop what?"

"Breathing that way."

"Breathing what way?"

"Like you were running."

Well, she had been running. And if Em had stopped her too soon she would have to run again. Running was a part of a discovery she had made. Whenever there began to be re-enacted in her mind anything she couldn't bear to see or hear, she'd found she could stop it by burying it—then running. It was strange, almost unbelievable, but it worked. She would take the whole scene—Lib talking to Korby, Dandie's voice that night, that white hoop, barking, whatever it was—roll it into a tight bundle, and then, having dug a deep hole, bury the whole of it; stamp the earth in solidly over it, and finally, and here was the trick, run: run like a flash, and never look back. Sometimes, if she didn't work at lightning speed—for while she was throwing the dirt in on the bundle, the bundle itself was stirring, heaving and jerking, trying to break the cords that bound it—the scene would rise from its burial place and get back into her mind. But if she worked fast, ran hard, never looked back, then, often as not, she was free. And it was the only way. She couldn't just command herself, "Stop thinking about those things." She had really to run away from them.

She wondered if she could tell Em about it. "I was pretending to run," she said, saying at the same time, Em, please try to understand this.

"Why?" Em asked. "You could really run if you wanted to."

"Don't you ever pretend, Em?"

"No," Em said. "Not anything I can really do, like running. If I wanted to run, I'd run."

Could she tell her about the bundle? What she put in it?

"Running isn't all I pretend."

"It's all I ever hear you do."

"First, I dig."

Em said, "I really dig."

Cate lifted herself on her elbow so that she looked down at Em, lying comfortably on her pillow. Em's face seemed to have changed recently; her lips were fuller, her straight eyebrows had begun to curve and her horsetail black hair was softer. "Em, I want to ask you a favor. Don't go out digging with the Abels, any more. Not until after the wedding, anyway. I don't know why Mama and Papa let you do it at all, it's so terrible and silly."

"Why is it terrible and silly?"

"People stare at you. You're getting to be a laughing-stock."

"That don't hurt me any."

"People'll think you're crazy as the witch diggers."

"Maybe they aren't crazy."

"Oh, Em, they're crazy as bedbugs and you know it. Digging for what was lost years ago—they don't even know *what* themselves. You don't believe in any of that craziness, do you?"

"I don't know. James Abel's spade-handle wiggles so hard he can't hardly hold on to it when he gets a strong lead."

"Any water-witcher can do that."

"Mr. Abel don't witch water though, you know that. And Mary Abel loves me."

"Loves you!" Cate said pityingly, dropping back onto her pillow. "Oh, Emmy, she'd love anyone who'd dig for her. She'd love a woodchuck if it dug a hole for her."

"She wouldn't hug a woodchuck though, or rock it, or call it lovey."

"Em, that's disgusting. I wouldn't let that woman touch me with a ten-foot pole."

"I know you wouldn't. She says I'm her lost baby."

"Lost baby! You're a pretty big lost baby." Em said nothing. "Is that what you want, Em? People going round rocking you and hugging you and calling you a lost baby?"

"Not people."

"Me?"

"No, because you *don't* love me."

"Em," Cate said, "I love you now, and I've always loved you." She thought for a second, remembered the self she hated and said, "I love you better than myself."

"You mean—greater love hath no man than this?"

"Yes," Cate said, for that was the truth of what she felt.

Em considered this, then answered, "Yes, I expect you'd die for me all right, burn up or drown for me; but not because you loved me."

"Why then? Why would I do it?"

Em was staring out into space. "You'd do it for Cate Conboy," she said.

Cate didn't answer. In her mind, it was true, she'd been seeing not the rescued Em alive, but herself dead, surrounded by lilies and praised to the skies. "The brave, wonderful girl."

She got out of bed, poured water from the pitcher to the basin, and began to wash. "Em, I want you to be my bridesmaid when I'm married. You will, won't you?"

"Even if I go on digging?"

"Yes."

Mrs. Thompson had wanted the wedding to be at their place. "You young folks don't care now where you're married and that's the way young love should be—headlong. But in later years you're going to be put out of countenance, having to admit to being married in a Poor House. There's nothing wrong with a Poor House, mind you. Except it's not the place for a wedding."

But Cate wouldn't be budged. The proper place for a wedding was the bride's home and this was her home, and here she would be married. Not, certainly, because she loved the place (she hated it) but because she wanted to be finished with it in a proper and orderly way. She wanted the next two weeks to pass as quickly as possible. She had not been able, since her return from Madison, to look her father and mother in the face; how could she, knowing what she did about them? But there had not been much occasion for looking. She was so busy. She'd taken to carrying a list—like Mrs. Thompson's—with her. The do-this, do-that of Madison was written down now, scheduled. She kept a diary. She hemmed pillow-shams and crocheted edging for wash-cloths. She was calm, orderly, content. She'd get through the next two weeks as quickly as possible, have the prettiest, best-arranged wedding these parts had ever seen—a credit to the Thompsons—and after that she'd *be* a Thompson.

One thing occasionally troubled her. What if Christie should come, sometime before the wedding? She didn't think he would. She remembered his saying once that he had no patience with a man who, if given his walking papers, didn't walk. And there was nothing to be upset about even if he did come. Except that his turning up might be embarrassing for Ferris. *She* had no doubts, no hesitancies. When she thought of Christie at all, which was not often, she thought only, I woke up just in time.

"Em," she asked, "do you know what I think would be pretty?"

Em had dressed while she'd been day-dreaming and was now fussing with the contents of her casket, rearranging the treasures she kept there. Em didn't answer and Cate didn't care. All she was doing, really, was planning out loud.

"I think a wedding bell made of white lilac with a clapper of purple lilac would be pretty. Hanging between sitting-room and parlor."

Em had been listening after all. "Tie an invisible string to it and pull," she suggested. "At the same time outside I'll ring the dinner-bell. It'll give people a start."

A month ago Cate would've said, "How crazy." Now, out of her new-found reasonableness all she said was, "Well, we can think about it."

III

LIB WATCHED Link for a second as he stood by the wash-bench talking to John Manlief, then she rapped on the dining-room window-pane to call him in to breakfast. On the afternoon Korby had set all her fears at rest by saying, yes, yes, all you feared, and more, is true, she'd accepted Link in a new way, as her committed husband. She had never done so before. There were losses as well as gains. Before, every gesture of Link's toward her was doubly rich, containing as it did not only love for her but repudiation of every other woman in the world. This was no longer so. A husband has not quite the stature of a free agent. When his eye stops its roving (even though the roving has been imagined) his circumference, for his wife, shrinks a little.

But there were great gains. She turned away from the window at the sound of Link's step behind her, advanced to meet him, took his hand, pressed her head to his shoulder, and with her free hand touched first the swelling, well-covered jut of his Adam's apple, then the up-thrust prow of his shapely nose.

"You've got a nice nose, Link."

She'd always admired it, was glad that Dandie and Cate had inherited it instead of her own too big and rambling structure.

Link bent to kiss her.

"Now, now," she said finally. "They can see us in here."

Link took his mouth from hers, turned and looked outside. Abel was already back from the barn, talking again to Manlief.

"You'd ought to get shut of those two," Lib said. "Manlief's able to work now and that Abel's too mixed up to be left here."

"Manlief's leaving in a week or two of his own accord, soon's he gets his bearings a little better."

IV

CHRISTIE came the night of the "wedding-party supper." Not a one of the Conboys, Cate included, had ever heard of such an affair until Mrs. Thompson spoke of it. It was, it seemed, as necessary a part of getting married as the ceremony itself.

"What night do you plan for the wedding-party supper, Catherine?" Mrs. Thompson asked.

"We're going to have refreshments after the wedding," Cate told her. "Is that what you mean?"

"Oh, no. I mean the supper for the wedding party. For the preacher, the bridesmaids, the best man, the parents of the bride and groom. A kind of get-acquainted jollification. About four or five days before the wedding is usual."

"For a minute," Cate said, "I thought you were just talking about the party after the wedding, not the wedding-party supper. Mama hasn't decided yet on the exact date."

"I thought I'd better let you know, dear, that Monday night wouldn't be a good date for me. That's the twenty-first, and we have our annual Mission Society Supper that night. I'm president and couldn't very well miss it. On the other hand I know how Ferris'd feel, and you too, if I couldn't be present for the wedding-party supper. The best plan's to have it on Tuesday. That's the twenty-second and with the wedding on the twenty-fifth, well, it's a little close but I don't believe anybody'd find it at all out of the way. Just the natural tight squeeze of circumstances now and then, plan as best you may. Sunday the twentieth is out of the question, being the day it is. And Saturday'd leave the party back in the previous week. That far away it'd appear to be just another social gathering, I'm afraid, not the wedding-party supper. The chief

[339]

point of that party is the kind of—hovering, so to speak. The being right on the brink, a bride and yet not a bride. You may not believe me but I've been to wedding-party suppers where a kind of, well I won't say halo—that's confined to the Trinity, though the Romans I understand give it to all their members who die for the church or are virgins, to the last, I mean—well, I've been to wedding-party suppers, Catherine, where the bride had this, not halo, but circle of light around her. It's the nearness does it, the hanging on the brink that lights her up. Tuesday'd be the most suitable date. I'll bring Father and Mother Thompson. They're staying the wedding week at our place and Aunt Iola—but you're already counting on her I expect."

"Yes," Cate said. "It wouldn't be complete without Aunt Iola."

"She's been a second mother to Ferris. He was raised *at* my breast but *on* her lap I always say. It's a picture to see him lift her up now. She's so weensy and Ferris is so powerful; though you're just the very last one I need sing Ferris' praises to, I'm sure. But you're such a big chunky girl yourself I doubt he can swing you around the way he does us slighter ones. We'll come early. Five at the latest. Now you're going to be a Thompson, we want to make the acquaintance of your folks. Your mother's a little stand-offish, isn't she? She's got no call to feel backward with me now. We're just two out-dated ones together, at this point, both just starting to learn to play second fiddle. Could I loan you anything for the party? Silver? Dishes? Nobody knows better than me what a drain a big elaborate affair like this puts on the china-closet. How're you fixed for salad plates? I've got a new set, hand-painted. Moss Rose. You're welcome to them. See that the help don't handle them though, will you? Or eat off them? There's all kinds here I expect, and we don't want any carry-over of germs, do we? That'd be a sorry start to say the least."

Lib listened in silence as Cate broke the news of the second party but Link spoke up. "They can come and sit," he said, "and welcome. And have a glass of lemonade too, I reckon, if the weather merits it. But any more big parties are out of the question. First of all, nobody here's got time for the preparation. Everything's been thrown out of kilter enough as it is with the wedding coming Friday, without any kind of practice wedding on Tuesday. And if that wasn't so, there's no money for another big affair. Those hand-painted salad plates are all very well, but I reckon Mrs. Thompson figures on having them filled with something edible. And pineapple! Do you have any idea how much pineapple costs, Cate?"

"That was just an idea," Cate said. "Pineapple's not required."

"Food of some kind is required," Link said.

"A little chicken'd go a long ways in a pie," Lib suggested.

"No," Link said, "I can't do it. First, chicken enough for a salad for fifty at the wedding supper. Now, more chicken for I don't know how many at another supper. I can't do it. I can't cut into my flock that way. My first duty's to The Farm. What with one thing and another I've already been far too slack here as it is. Let us all unite now in putting our lives in order."

"My life's in order," Cate said. "All I need's a little food for a party."

"You would think that what you and Ferris were starting out on was a period of starvation, not marriage, from all this talk of food."

"Maybe we could make do with what's on hand, Cate," said Lib. "Just our regular supper served up extra nice."

"Boiled beans with sow belly? Fried potatoes with lard gravy? No thank you. I'll do this right or not at all."

So the matter stood as late as Sunday night: the Thompsons coming to a wedding-party supper which no Conboy, except Cate, knew anything about. And the party was growing. Mrs. Thompson sent word by Ferris that in addition to herself and Mr. Thompson, Wanda, Aunt Iola, Ferris' best man, Ocie Davis, Ferris' grandparents, the Fount Thompsons, she had asked their minister and his wife, the Reverend and Mrs. Press Childs. The Thompsons were Methodists, not Baptists, and the Reverend Childs, Mrs. Thompson said, had been hurt at being left out of the wedding ceremony. An invitation to the wedding-party supper would smooth him down, she thought. Ten in all, that is, she would be bringing.

Sunday was a fine day, a sample of what summer could be like before it started overdoing things. Up to noon the weather was a little ketchy with a light skim of clouds across the sky. Link thought it was fixing to rain, but it faired off a little after midday, and the sky arched up higher and higher, bluer and bluer, until it threatened to crack open revealing some further glory of summer beyond. They all went to church in the morning, riding under the full-leafed trees. The roadsides sparkled with flowers and birds cut the air with their wings and their singing. After dinner Em went out, as usual, with the Abels; Lib broke the Sabbath to help Cate with her sewing, and Link first mended the cistern pump, then wrote a long letter to Fred. When he finished his letter he went down to the creek bank for a stroll.

The beauty of the day filled him with a desire to say, "Look" to someone; and without premeditation he climbed the bank and seeing Cate at her bedroom window called, "Come on outside, Cate. It's too fine an evening to waste indoors."

Cate, sewing a popcorn pattern crochet edging onto her wedding shimmy, came outside, the shimmy rolled up about one hand like a summer muff. She swam out into the twilight leaving the day behind her like a dream, leaving years behind her. It was like being a little girl again, to have Link call her to look at the evening's beauties; like the time he had carried her a quarter of a mile to show her snow wreaths hanging from a clump of pines, or had held her up in his arms to see the reds and golds, clashing together like swords, in the center of a sun-struck icicle. She came to him without a word, and followed him back to the creek. Water and light were about the same color now, color of the German silver butter dish when it began to tarnish. It was very still. The creek appeared to be a living thing, motionless inside its smooth, tight skin.

Link said, "We can't take it in, Cate, our children growing up and marrying."

A light wind marred the smooth skin of the stream, ruffled it up like a piece of flimsy goods.

"I want you to be happy, Cate."

"I am happy."

"It struck me you might've changed your mind. Might've come to feel Christie was the one after all. In which case I wouldn't want you to think there wasn't time yet to change your plans. I could easy—"

"It's settled," Cate said, "settled, settled. Can't one thing be done in this family in an ordinary way without a commotion being stirred up?"

Link stretched out a hand toward her, but Cate moved beyond his reach.

"How can I help you, Cate?"

"Help me with this supper Tuesday."

"Cate, whatever's on hand is yours. But I can't slaughter farm stock for you."

"Won't," Cate said, stubbornly.

"I've no choice. It's not mine."

"You could give me some money."

"I haven't got it."

"You paid those doctor bills for Dandie."

"I did. I didn't have any choice about that either."

The sun had gone down while they talked and for a minute the sundown colors, reflected in the water, made the day brighter than it had been earlier. Cate picked up a stone and sent it skipping to the farther side, mingling the water's reds and golds as it traveled.

"All right," she said. "I'll do it by myself. You don't forbid my using the house, do you?"

"Oh, Cate," Link said, "I don't forbid you anything. Nothing I've got but's yours."

Without a word Cate turned and walked away from him.

v

AT THREE o'clock on the afternoon of the wedding-party supper Cate was in the kitchen ironing the best napkins. She had discovered, only half an hour before, that they had been put away hit or miss and were too rumpled to be offered to any Thompson. So now at three, with the guests due at five and Mag needing every inch of the stove space for her cooking, she had to have her irons spread out there to heat. She changed irons and started on her sixth napkin. She was beginning to find it harder and harder to keep the days before her wedding as she had wanted them, quiet, peaceful, and even, she had hoped, holy. In addition to days of quiet, she had longed for a dignified wedding, one which would follow patterns handed down from old times and be worthy of Thompson traditions. Such a wedding, she thought, would do much to blot out memories (in her own mind as well as others') of previous Conboy disorders. But she had had no idea of the effort it took to achieve a little quiet and order; or at what a price of fighting and rampaging peace and dignity were bought. All the hub-bub in the kitchen now—and the room rang with noise—was the price she was paying for them and for her wedding-party supper.

The women had taken over her wedding. She occasionally felt that it had been arranged by them and for their pleasure and that it was on the order of a quilting-bee or barn-raising in their minds, only more exciting. She and Ferris would have to be there, of course, but only because it suited the women's plans. She tried not to hear their talk, but if she asked them to be quiet, they whispered their words into her ear or stroked their meanings into her arm with remembering fingers. Sometimes, looking back into their own lives, they seemed to regard a wedding as a side-splitting matter, and they laughed then until the tears ran down their cheeks; at other times they remembered it as a day of sadness, pitied her from the bottoms of their hearts and shed tears of real grief at the thought of what lay ahead of her. She was embarrassed by it all, the crying or laughing, and she tried to avoid their whisperings and to slide out from under their patting, consoling hands. But she had to listen to some words and accept some pats. She was beholden to them, and especially to Mag, for this supper; without them she would never have been able to arrange it.

She had been able to decide to sacrifice the gander—but she could not, herself, kill him. Mag had done that with her own hands, and had stuffed him and put him into the oven (where he now was), and Mag's cronies who weren't helping her with the cooking, were busy with the cleaning and polishing. Even Mary Abel, who usually shied off work as fast as Brother James, had been roped in by Mag for a little silver-polishing.

Cate, looking up from her ironing, protested their working so hard. "You're all being too good to me," she said.

Mag pooh-poohed this. "Honey-bunch," she said, "we just want to see that you have one last final good meal. Like the man before they hang him."

There was really so much of this in the way they treated her, she felt uneasy. They saved her every hardship, fondled her, and doted on her. They might've been preparing themselves to say afterwards, "We made her last days happy and easy." They treated her like a missionary bound for the foreign field and pretty sure to end up in a cannibal's pot. And their only concern was, not to help her to escape, but to see that she reached the pot well-fed and in good heart.

Leathy Wade passed her, bringing in a pan of milk from the milk-house. "Don't work yourself to a frazzle, honey," she said. "Save yourself for your groom."

Cate slapped her iron down onto another napkin without replying.

"Napkin or no napkin, ironed or un-ironed, he won't notice the difference," Leathy said.

"Trouble with a girl like Cate," Mag told her helpers, "she's too young to appreciate what she's getting."

"I was married at fifteen," Leathy said, "and I don't recollect a smidgin of it being wasted on me."

"I was thirty-seven," Mrs. Goforth remembered, "before Mr. Goforth wore down my last scruple."

"Wore down your last what, Lodema?" Mag yelled and Grandma Mercer unexpectedly remarked, "It is better to marry than burn."

"Marrying at fifteen's a skim-milk story," said Lily dreamily. She was pitting canned cherries, had a mouthful of pits and spoke with a sound of gravel against a window-pane.

"Going to be a spilt-milk story with you, Lily, you wait much longer," said Mag, lifting her steaming face from the bird she was basting. "No, no, Fessler," she warned, "mustn't touch. Hot." Then as the child lurched away from the stove toward Cate she said, "Give him a hard slap, Cate. It's the only way to learn him."

Leathy, coming over to inspect the gander before the oven was closed, said, "How'd you ever come to kill that old feller of yours, Cate? You've had him since time begun."

Cate, in a low voice, face down to the ironing-board, replied, "I had to have something for the Thompsons to eat."

"Roast Ferris, marry old Samson," Mag said. "Your old gander was more of a man than he is. Why, I'd rather get in bed with a good stout mullen stalk than that winchy boy."

"Sour grapes, sour grapes," said Lily around and through her cherrystones. "Foxes with chopped off tails. Mad because Ferris never looked at them. Don't you pay any attention to Mag, Cate. Eaten alive by envy, that's her ailment."

"I don't," Cate said. The more Mag ran down Ferris and praised Christie, the better satisfied she was with her choice. Look at the men Mag had chosen.

Mag shut the oven door and looked about her kitchen. The old women, faded and soft in their worn calicoes, like flowers broken by rain and ready to shatter. The light coming through the Early Harvest apple-tree outside the window and covering the floor with its leaf-shaped trembling pieces. A redbird singing in the maple. The doors and windows wide open and the cooking smells drawing the flies like a poultice. The cat winding itself around Mary Abel's ankles and Mary kicking out at it, like a touchy old horse. Fessler, picking it up and staggering beneath its sagging weight. Lily, at the calendar, counting up something, her cherry-stained lips keeping track. Cate, careful with her ironing, turning the napkin both ways, looking for the wrong side so's to bring out the pattern.

Fessler dropped the cat and came to her, leaned against her, dragged down on her skirt. Mag gave him the basting-spoon to lick and its rich juices stopped his whining. Here we all are, she thought, and not a one of us willing or able to tell the poor girl a thing. It looks as if we all grit our teeth and say, Nobody's going to have it easier than me. It's like a lodge secret. Can't know the secret till you're initiated and by that time it's too late to draw back. What secrets do you know, Mag Creagan? she asked herself. I know a few, she thought triumphantly, my time ain't been wholly wasted. I've learned a thing or two in my day. I could tell her the key, she hummed under her breath:

> "I got the key,
> You got the lock,
> I can trade back,
> And you can not."

But give Cate the key and she'd like as not throw it out the window, she's so dead set on going her own way. Fessler dropped his spoon, and she picked it up and kept time to her humming with it, beat an insolent sweep or two, disturbing the flies. I can command a thing or two, she thought, and have.

>"I went up the slippery steeple—
>Met me there a nest of people;
>Some were white and some were black
>But the best was the color of a ginger-snap."

I can't tell the girl she's picked the wrong man, baked the wrong bird, but I can do what's better. And I have. Brought the right one here to speak his own piece to her.

She went to the kitchen door and looked out, impatient to see Christie's buggy coming around the curve of the driveway. She had walked to The Junction to send him the letter so that the Poor House busybodies would know nothing of it; and had walked back again for the answer, and this was the day he had set for his coming. She had been willing his arrival since breakfast and she willed it very strongly now; though let him arrive later with the Thompsons, if chance would have it that way; nothing should be more convincing to Cate than the sight of the two of them together, that priss-prat boy and Christie, tall and goldy-brown and ready to enwrap her in his strong arms. Her secret kept her smiling, made her feel bubbles in her veins, prickles in her feet. She came back from the door and leaned her face, red from the oven, over Cate's ironing-board, tapped Cate herself, in no gentle fashion, with the basting-spoon and began to prepare her for the visit.

"What's your idea of being married, Cate Conboy? Ironing napkins? Entertaining the Missionary Society? I ask you!"

Cate half-whispered her reply, ashamed of it before it was spoken, "I didn't know you'd ever been married."

Fessler came to his mother, and Mag snatched him up and turned her apron back across his bare legs, as if the two of them had been caught together out in a storm.

"All right," she said, "all right. Throw that up at me. Say I missed one-half the marriage deal. You're settling for half too, and it ain't the best half, either."

Cate made a motion of backing away from Mag and her talk but Mag, with her free hand, reached out and caught Cate by the wrist and drew her back to the ironing-board. "Put down that iron," she ordered. "You've ironed that napkin to a fare-ye-well as it is, and hear me out. Marriage ain't the dainty tea-cup and saucer affair you think it is."

"Don't be dirty," Cate said.

"Marriage has got its dirty side like anything else and you'd better face it right now and gradual, not all of a sudden with that gimpy little Thompson boy to teach you. That sorry little piss-ant."

Every word Mag said endeared Ferris to Cate. She had never received a better sign of his worth than Mag's running him down. She wrenched herself free of Mag's hand and said, "Don't dare to talk about Ferris like that. I suppose you would've had me marry Christie Fraser?" she asked. "Which shows how much you know about him."

"Yes to both," answered Mag, undaunted. "I may not know much about him but I know enough to know he was the man for you to marry." She made another of her restless swinging loops to the door, then hurried back into the room. "Get," she ordered her helpers. "Shoo. Stay clear of here 'til I order you back."

"What're we to do?" Mrs. Goforth asked.

"Do?" Mag repeated. "What you do, Lodema, don't matter in the least. Cut your throat and it would hardly be noticed. Now clear out, one and all."

She drove the old ladies before her, flapped her apron at them as if they were so many broody hens. At the door to the hall she turned to Cate. "Keep your eye on old Samson. You've killed him, no use burning him to death in the bargain." Then Cate was alone and the porch door opening.

She held the iron in her hand, above the board, until a muscle jumped in her arm, and she put the iron down on the trivet with a harsh clang, let it fall there, really. And the minute it was down, she picked it up again and spread out the last ironed napkin and began once more to press it with furious, determined strokes.

"Cate," Christie said, "oh, Cate."

She did not trust herself to look up. She had had her sight of him as he stood in the doorway, the sight she had so longed for in Madison; so that every sound there had been Christie's step or Christie's voice. The sight she had prayed she would not have, and every minute, not praying, desired. It was no matter of good looks or bad, dark hair or light, it went clear beyond looks; beyond "goodness" or "badness"; beyond everything but the blood's twinning and because she was contradictory and longed for it, she resisted. Because she wanted to be overwhelmed, she resisted. Because her pride had been hurt, she resisted. Because she loved the image in her own mind of "good Cate, reasonable Cate, calm Cate"—she whose every breath and thought were tempestuous, she resisted.

"Cate," he said again, still the room's width between them. "Cate with a C."

"Christie," she answered.

"Your father told me I'd find you here," he said in a low voice, as if needing in some way to justify his presence.

"Yes," Cate answered, bending her head lower over the napkin. "Yes, here I am."

Outside, the redbird still sang and in the absolute silence of the kitchen the murmur of the creek was clear and steady. Christie crossed the room, leaned toward Cate over the ironing-board, his eyes searching her face.

"Cate," he said finally, "what happened? What came over you?"

"Nothing," Cate said.

"Nothing?" he asked.

"I told you," she replied desperately. "I wrote you."

"Do you call it nothing, Cate, to marry someone else, after all our plans?"

"It is nothing for you to be excited about, now. I told you I had changed my mind and that our engagement was broken. I told you I was going to marry Ferris."

"You chose him instead of me." With the tip of his finger, delicately, he touched Ferris' ring. "You are wearing his ring."

Cate held up her hand so that the little red dot of Ferris' ruby could be better seen. "You never did give me a ring," she said— as if that had made all the difference—and waited for his hand to touch hers. It did not. He had been spurned once too often. I will go to her, he had promised himself, but he had also promised himself, I will not beg. A woman can't love a man who begs, he thought; and he wanted Cate to love him. A better way, the way of commanding, had not occurred to him.

He had never seen her more beautiful. What she had suffered, and he didn't doubt she had, had fined down the school-girl plumpness of her face to a lovely tautness so that her cheeks curved away from her high cheekbones and her lips, full and red, lifted themselves with a new and passionate invitation from that new sunkenness. The heat from iron and oven made her rosy, and the natural hazel of her eyes was darkened into something nearer brown, as was always the case when her feelings were intense. She wore an old faded pink wrapper, more in the style of Lib than he had ever seen her before; and looked better than when in her fixy best, her curves were flattened by buckram and whalebone. He saw what their life together could be, its variations, its ups and downs; but its eternal freshness, too. And he felt the need to touch her, to push over the ironing-board, scatter the napkins like leaves and then, with no barriers left, bury his face in that branching softness which began at the base of her throat. But as he would not beg so he would not, uninvited, touch. Besides, it was this, the touching (though Cate was so responsive then, returning touch for touch and kiss for kiss) which afterwards she would regret and berate herself for.

He took his finger from the ring, carefully, and said, "I didn't know you wanted a ring, Cate."

"I didn't, either," she replied sadly.

So they stood, separated, each waiting for the other, entombed in pride, in wariness and hurt, each waiting for another hand to roll away the imprisoning stone; he, spurned, jilted, refusing to chance it again without help; she, overwhelmed by the image of woman retreating and woman seized in spite of her retreat. It was an image she had been able, in this very room at Christmastime, to ignore; to reach out her hand to Christie, admitting that without pursuit or begging a woman could love. And her hand moved a little toward Christie now, leaving iron and napkin.

"When Mag wrote me—" he began, and Cate's hand flew back to the iron.

"Did you come because Mag asked you?"

"I came because of you. But Mag's writing—"

"Don't tell me. I don't want to hear a word." Christie, a gift from Mag, brought here by some tale of her crying or mourning; and untrue, untrue, because she had chosen the best and was wonderfully happy. Unable to remain still any longer, she walked around the ironing-board and kneeling, opened the oven door. Blindly, she began to baste the roasting gander.

"That is a big bird," Christie said.

"It is Samson," she answered tonelessly.

At that Christie knelt beside her; then, as if in the plucked and roasting animal, skin crackling and juices oozing, he easily recognized the lordly bird who, with a lifting of white wings had placed himself like love incarnate between the shafts of their sleigh at Christmastime, he said, "You killed him, Cate Conboy. You could do that. You killed Eros."

"I forgot you called him that."

"You did not forget."

"No. I only tried to forget."

"How could you kill him?"

"I couldn't. Mag did it."

"She only did what you told her."

"We had to have something to eat."

"Eat bread and milk."

"We couldn't—the Thompsons are coming."

"You killed him for Ferris—that fool." Christie walked away from her and she said, "Calling names changes nothing."

"No, it does not." He came back to her, and as she still knelt, gazing into the oven, he saw about her neck the locket he had given her at Christmas, and with one wrench he broke the thin gold chain.

Cate jumped to her feet. "Take it," she cried, "take it, I don't know why I've kept it. It chokes me. Take it back to the jeweler's and get your money back. It has nothing to do with me any more."

Christie held the locket aloft by one end of the chain, the heart swinging forward and backward like a pendulum. He agreed. "It has nothing to do with you." Then he took the wooden basting-spoon from her hand and after he had thrown the heart into the pan with the roasting bird he smeared it with the bird's juices, smashed it and stirred it so that bird and heart were thoroughly mixed. "Now," he said, "it is back where it started and you killed both."

"I did right," Cate said.

He didn't answer her but put the spoon on the table and walked toward the door.

She said in a whisper, "Christie, Christie."

If he heard her he gave no sign, and in a second there was the sound of his buggy leaving the yard.

Mag came in, at that. "Where is he?" she asked.

"Gone. I sent him away." She added defiantly, "He shouldn't have come here."

Mag closed the oven door gently, as if old Samson had suffered enough without any further rough handling. "Now," she told Cate, "you have really ruined your life."

13

On the morning of the wedding-day Em, returning from digging, lagged far behind the Abels; and finally stopped completely to wipe the dew from her scratched legs with her skirt-tail. Continuing to bend over she inspected the grass blades, each of which carried a crystal bead of dew at its tip, like a green sentence signed with a diamond period. The grass was topheavy with these drops, and she relieved a few blades of their burdens and, under her eyes, they began to straighten. In spite of the dew it was a morning without any freshness to it, very sober and quiet. If you didn't know that east was where the sun was, you could easily think it was evening. Birds were tweeting very sensibly as if they knew that singing before breakfast brought crying before supper. She knew it too, and she wasn't singing, either. The sky was a flat gray-blue, with a light skim of clouds across it. There was no wind and trees stood steady, clouds didn't move, leaves rested; even the creek, for a change, was silent. A redbird, perched on a fencepost, lifted its wings as if preparing to scratch —or fly—but lowered them without doing either. Three or four sycamore leaves started a little twirling of their own but gave it up suddenly, as if embarrassed at the show they had made of themselves.

Jake Devlin said that weather like this in California was earthquake weather, but that here in Indiana nothing would come of it. In California, after broody spells like this, the earth would, like as not, heave and split open; but the best they could expect here, Devlin said, would be either heat lightning or unseasonable hail. The corn crop spoiled—or a touch of hog cholera—that was what they called a disaster in Indiana. She bent over, wrapping her skirt about first one leg then the other, and tried to believe she felt some tilt or lurch; saw some crack squirming its snakelike way across the green of the pasture. But nothing stirred, nothing split. Whatever the earth did in California on a morning like this, here it rolled on steady as a meeting-house, bearing its ponds and hills and weddings and graveyards without a quiver. Dive off it, dig into it, marry on it: the earth in Indiana didn't care.

Still bent over, she saw between her spread legs Mr. Manlief approaching, and she watched as he came nearer the odd, plantlike way in which he seemed to shoot up out of the ground. "Happy wedding day," she said, and straightened up to face him.

"So you're happy," he said, "to have sister Cate getting married?"

"I didn't say that," she told him.

"Are you?" he asked.

Actually, she didn't know, her mind kept changing so much concerning it. All she could do was tell him what she had felt, and was feeling.

"At first I was happy."

"And then?"

"And then I didn't care one way or another."

"And now?"

"Now I'm just beginning to think, she'll be gone."

"And you won't like that?"

"I won't be used to it." She saw she had never really thought of Cate as having a life separate from her own. Sometimes she hadn't liked Cate—about as often as she hadn't liked herself; but with Cate gone there'd be an emptiness. Cate filled things up with her goings on, her crying and singing, her making vows and pretending in dreams. Cate was always planning something. "Let's memorize a poem a day for a month." "Let's surprise Mama, and clean up the house." "Let's brush our hair one hundred strokes every night."

"Cate was a great planner," she told Mr. Manlief.

"Was?" asked Mr. Manlief. "Marriage don't put an end to planning." But Em shook her head. Who was Cate going to plan with over at the Thompsons'? And what?

"She'll miss me too," she said.

"Well," said Mr. Manlief, "you'll be getting married yourself one of these days soon."

Since he was the one who kept harping on the subject of marriage Em told him a fancy she'd had. "If you ever got married," she said, "it would be funny if you'd marry a lady named 'Womanflower'. I'd like to see that in the paper. 'Mr. Manlief marries Miss Womanflower.' It sounds like a fairy-tale, doesn't it? Rose Red and Snow White. Like that."

"I am married," Mr. Manlief said.

"I don't suppose?" Em suggested.

"No," said Mr. Manlief, "no. Her name was Cleghorn. Miss Hortense Cleghorn."

"Oh," said Em. "If it had've been the other way, Manlief and Womanflower, it would've been interesting to speak of the fruits of your marriage, wouldn't it? More interesting," she amended courteously, out of respect for possible fruits with Miss Cleghorn, "than if—"

But Mr. Manlief stopped her before she could pursue this fancy further. "No, my marriage with Miss Cleghorn was not fruitful."

"I'm sorry," Em said.

"Thank you," Mr. Manlief said, "but it's probably just as well as it is." And he added quickly, "I suppose you've been out digging with the Abels as usual this morning?"

"Yes."

"What is it you expect to find?"

"Happiness for the whole world, Mr. Abel says."

"That's quite an order. You expect that too?"

"I'll wait and see."

"If it's not, you'll 've turned over a lot of earth for nothing."

"We all do, one way or another," she said, quoting James. Then she quoted Mary, "Mary says I'm her lost baby."

"Well," Manlief asked, "what do you think?"

"No," Em said. But she added, "I don't feel very much like a Conboy either."

"Where does that leave you?"

"That leaves me an orphan I guess, Mr. Manlief. And a bridesmaid," she said to cheer him up, since he was looking so downcast. "I've got to go up to the house and put on my buttermilk mask. It's about the last thing I can do for Cate."

She ran on ahead of him to the house, disturbing the dew, and as Manlief watched her long scissoring legs, he thought, I've crossed the divide. I've progressed from things to people. He hadn't "come back" to himself again, in the old sense; perhaps he never would. But to the other human beings in the world he *had* returned. On them he doted; like a man returned from a desert island, his heart was wrung by the sight of small domestic activities. A woman pushing a broom across a back porch with little careless swoops, singing as she worked, not caring if she missed a little dirt there—that was to his mind, a sight to behold. And a woman hanging out clothes! Stoop to the basket, stretch to the line, and behind her, her whole flaunting, windstruck household, more alive than when animated by legs and arms. When would he have his fill of sights of that kind? Poor old Doss, he thought, remembering his lost roommate. What condemned you to the night scenes? Reduced you to stolen peeps, when there was on every hand this other richness free for the taking?

When he entered the kitchen, the wedding-day tide engulfed him. The women flocked to him. They felt in him his emptiness of self and his openness to them; and to them as living human beings, not as females. It was a change and a treat to be so considered. It expanded their natures. But at the same time some mulishness in their make-up, some never completely satisfied female vanity made them try to reduce him to a simple maleness: an eye for breasts and hips; a pleasure in their endearing qualities of dependence and unreliability. It was the wedding-day; and for the minute he was the universal groom, every woman's husband. Their imaginations had played with the wedding, but it was a solitary feat without the help of a man; now, if he would elect to a little make-believe, they had a partner for their playing.

Mag who could, single-handed, boost a bull out of a bull-pen said, "John, toss this cat out for me. A cat's one too many in this kitchen this morning."

Lily skipped to him and lifted Mister from his arms as if he had been their first-born. "Precious," she said, "precious old Mister," and carried the tom-cat like a breakable to the door and set him down outside. She came back and whispered to Manlief, "Happy returns of the day." She rose on tiptoe. "Wish me happiness."

Grandma Mercer, caught in the center of her wrinkles, like a fly in a web, was pumicing coffee-stains from the cups. "Good as new," she said.

Mrs. Goforth took Manlief's arm. Amidst the foolery she had a serious question to ask. "Mr. Manlief, don't a night-time wedding strike you as being impatient? From the man's standpoint, that is?"

Before he could answer, Icey, stopping her churning, asked, "Is the bride the boy?"

"No, pet," said Leathy, "the bride's the other one."

Mag, who commanded the food, had the power in the midst of all the talk to recall Manlief to her. "John, breakfast is catch-as-catch-can here this morning. Everything's on the stove. Take what you want. I've got the Thompsons to feed today, and the rest of you'll have to fend for yourselves."

Manlief ate his breakfast: the mush was salty, the milk skimmed to the quick, and he had to keep his teeth shut when he drank his coffee to strain the grounds out. When he carried his dishes back to the kitchen, there was Link displaying a crockful of strawberries. He held them out toward Manlief.

"First of the season. I've hoped for the past week these might color up in time for the wedding. Cate'll be pleasurably surprised. Have one. How's it taste?"

Link tried one himself. "Delicious." His hand hovered above the second. "No," he said, "mustn't rob the wedding."

Lib came into the kitchen. "Link," she asked, "have you got plans for Mr. Manlief for the day? I need a helper I can depend on. I've got that altar to build. And the bells to make and hang. It's beyond my power, alone."

"I've given up all idea of getting anything done here today except the wedding," Link said. "If John don't have any objections to the job, I don't."

Lib took Manlief, first of all, to the parlor, and there he watched her as she leaned, silent, against the mantel, sizing up the job that lay ahead of them. In the morning a parlor rests, is somnolent; not damp, perhaps, but with some signs of having been raised up from under sea depths. Lib, with her pale face, green eyes, and pink lips, fitted it. Her colors were sea colors rather than land colors. Her hair was kelp-colored, her lips coral. She stood, measuring heights and distances with her eye, covering the what-not and the stand-table with lilacs and maidenhair fern, making a wedding scene at six-thirty in the morning. She had on an old white skirt, rust-stained and lapped about her small waist and fastened securely with a safety-pin. Her white shirtwaist was almost clean and most of the tail was tucked under her skirtband. On one shoulder she sported a rosette of faded blue satin in the center of which was a tin button saying, TIPPECANOE AND TYLER, TOO. She saw Manlief's eyes on it, touched it self-consciously and said, "A relic." She appeared to be at home with men, not punishing them for any early slights at their hands. She felt along the mantel figuring out the marriage altar plan.

"Lib," he said.

She looked up politely. "What was that, Mr. Manlief? I was thinking about this altar."

"Nothing," he said. "It was nothing," and in a sense it was true. It was nothing more than his wondering, "Who are you?" risen to the surface of speaking.

"Cate wants pillars on each side here, decorated with smilax and the wedding party standing between them. Do you think you can manage them? And she wants banked flowers on the mantel, garlands over the windows and a lilac bell with a pull rope of smilax. It's a tall order."

He agreed. "It's none too early to start."

"No," she said. And changed the subject. "Do you have any children, Mr. Manlief?"

"No, and just as well, probably. I wouldn't've made a very good father, I'm afraid."

"If whether we'd make good fathers or mothers was the test for children, the race'd die out, I expect. It's a thing we learn by practice on our children, especially the first. Cate bore the brunt of my learning. She's got the marks on her. In the beginning it don't come to you that you've got the power to mark anyone. At eighteen, nineteen, how could you think that? All you're trying to do then is keep your own head above water. I was Link's wife, them days, not Cate's mother."

"I doubt she took harm from that," he said and believed it.

But Lib was not reassured. "She's took harm from something, I'm afraid."

11

WHEN he had finished making the framework for the lilac bell, Lib asked Manlief to show it to Cate. "If it don't suit we'd better find it out now instead of later. Cate's in her room, packing to leave. In her mind she's already living at the Thompsons'."

He knocked on Cate's door, and Cate called out for him to come in, in a voice that seemed to say he had just arrived in the nick of time. When he opened the door he saw why. Cate stood in the middle of the room and at her feet, kneeling, with his head buried in her skirts and his arms clasping her was Dexter Bemis. Cate looked at Manlief, embarrassment and excitement mingling on her face.

"He came to bring me his wedding present," she said; she was still holding it, a knife and fork box: "Then this."

She made a move to step away from Dexter, and Manlief saw the boy's arms tighten. At the same time he lifted his head and turned to speak to Manlief; and Manlief saw that since last he had noticed him, Dexter's mouth had firmed up and his down had hardened into whiskers, and his neck, with its two back tendons standing out, had become a man's neck, broad and muscular.

"I never will love anyone else," he told Manlief. "If I'd been two years older Ferris would never of dared look at her." He faced Cate once more. "Run off with me."

Cate's flecked eyes implored Manlief, over the boy's head.

"How old are you, Dexter?" he asked.

"Almost sixteen, but I can pass for eighteen anywhere. I could take care of her like a man."

He buried his face once more in Cate's skirts and she swayed, off-balance for a second. "Please, Dexter," she said.

Manlief said, "Dexter, you know boys of fifteen can't marry."

"Wait for me," Dexter said. "Wait for me two years."

Manlief went to the boy and helped him to his feet. "Dexter, you go down to the creek. Wash your face and cool off a little, and wait for me there. I'll have something to tell you when I come out."

When Manlief had closed the door on Dexter, Cate asked, "What have you got to tell him?"

"I don't know yet."

[359]

Cate stood in the midst of her packing, boxes marked Clothes, Household Ornaments, and Personal Effects.

"This is a pity," Manlief said, "on your wedding day. Pitiful for the boy too."

She nodded, apparently too near crying to trust herself to speak. "Upsetting to be broken in on this way," he sympathized.

She denied that, clasping the knife and fork box to her bosom. "That's not the trouble," she said in a low voice.

"What's the trouble then?"

"The trouble is"—and he could scarcely hear her—"I liked it."

"That's not a trouble. Nobody's to be blamed for liking to hear he's loved."

"I don't mean hearing—I mean the feel."

"The feel?"

"Of his arms. I liked that. I saw he was handsome, too. Oh, I'm weak, weak."

"We are all weak," he said, "that way. We all like handsomeness and the feel of arms."

She backed away from him suspiciously. "I expect you're another Doss Whitt."

"No, whatever else I am, I am not that."

"Don't preach wickedness then," she said. "I know what's right and what's wrong. And I'm marrying a man who does. I'll be all right with Ferris, he's rescued me. You don't know how thankful I am. And I'm proud of myself for recognizing Ferris, too. He came along at just the right time; but if I hadn't recognized him, what good would it have done? You've no idea, Mr. Manlief, how I'm going to change once I leave this place. Tonight's my last night here, and after that I'll be married and at the Thompsons'. Things like this can't happen then. Like Dexter, I mean. I won't be exposed to such feelings then."

She put the knife and fork box down and examined the bell seriously. "I had planned on something bigger," she said, "but don't change now. And thank you for helping me with Dexter."

III

AT DUSK Cate went out to say good-by to the Poor House. The day that had begun close and quiet was ending the same way.

The stars were not out yet but fireflies were already turning their little shuddering lights on and off and the whippoorwills were sounding their lonesome evening notes. You could tell from the outside of the house that something was afoot, so many lamps lit, so many women passing and repassing the windows. She, who was the center of all the to-do, felt far from it. How easy it would be to walk off down the road into an unknown world and life. Not that she would. (Let Link come out and say, "I forbid this wedding," and she would fight tooth and toenail for it.) But it was something to think about, the many lives she was turning her back on: walk off down the road, that was one of them; run off with Dexter was another. Working in Madison, marrying Christie —these were lives she'd already said good-by to. These, the lives she would never live, made her feel solemn; but not sorry, for she'd chosen the best. Especially she was not sorry to be leaving the Poor House, big and black in the dusk as a prison. Triumph was her feeling, rather. I have got the best of you, she thought: trading mournful cedars and woe-begone, weathered bricks for silver maples and the white clapboard house with its pretty trim and little lacey balcony.

Some of the relatives from far away had already arrived and were pacing up and down the side yard or resting in the summerhouse. Cate kept to the creek side of the house to miss them and in doing so she came upon still others: Dandie, Nory, Frances and Orinda McFadden, cousins from Peru, and a Mr. Herschell Nightwine, the beau of one of the McFadden girls.

"Well, Cate," Mr. Nightwine called, "are you figuring on attending this wedding or not?" Nory and Dandie, the McFadden girls, and Mr. Nightwine were all in their best and aware of their grandeur, while she had on a housedress, too old and faded to pack to take to the Thompsons'.

"Nory," Mr. Nightwine asked, "what were you doing the last two hours before your wedding? My understanding was a girl spent that time either praying or primping. One of the two. Or both."

Dandie answered for Nory. "Nory's so good and pretty she don't have to do either."

Mr. Nightwine, who was a dark thin young man with long

sideburns and a high bridged nose, said, "Conboy, that kind of talk's plain indecent coming from a married man. What's the use getting married, if it don't cure you of feelings like that? Nory, you still bit by love-sickness too?"

"Me too," Nory said.

Mr. Nightwine shook his head. "Good thing you two married each other then. No use spoiling two families with that kind of softness."

"Cate," Orinda said, "I could beat you for picking gray to be married in. Gray! What kind of a wedding is it going to be with the bride in gray?"

"Mother Thompson and I decided a soft gray wool would be more practical for year-round wear."

Mr. Nightwine, who had caught a handful of fireflies, offered them to Cate. "Carry these instead of a bouquet. Keep your hands warm for the coming winter." When Cate refused them he dropped them like sparks about her head and shoulders.

Dandie, who had one arm about Nory, pulled Cate to him with the other. "Come on, Catey. Me and Nory want to have a little heart-to-heart talk with you. We want to tell you what the young bride should know." When they had walked upstream a way, he said, "I just wanted to tell you, Cate, how sorry I was that you and Nory—were where you were that night. I'd give my right hand to undo that."

Nory pulled away from Dandie. "Don't say that. What you did needed doing."

"I wasn't talking about what I did, but about you girls being there."

"It turned out for the best," Cate told him, "my being there."

"Well, you don't always act like it," Dandie said, giving her a strong hug. Then he turned and faced her, a hand on each shoulder. "Cheer up, sis. Marriage ain't the end of the world, you know. It ain't doom. You have yourself a good happy time being married. There's nothing wrong with Ferris you can't cure if you're a mind to. Liven him up a little. Don't let him get nasty-nice. You can do it. You're the girl for the job. And cheer up now. A wedding's a party you know. No call to be hang-dog about it."

IV

CATE had asked Wanda to be a bridesmaid (Orinda could play the wedding-march on the organ), and Mrs. Thompson was set on giving the three girls in the wedding party like hair-do's, a pompadour with Psyche knot, like Wanda's. Wanda and Em were finished and Mrs. Thompson sent them out of the bedroom while she worked on Cate. "Space is at a premium here," she told them, "and I need elbow-room when I work on Cate. Em, keep right side up, please. You're a little top-heavy as it is."

Em's hair-do transformed her: she looked like a Chinese princess, Cate thought, with the complicated blue-black tower rising above her thin, buttermilk-bleached face.

"I'm going to show Mary Abel," Em said, going out stiff-necked and stately.

"Well, Catherine," said Mrs. Thompson frankly, drawing the comb through Cate's short hair, "you're another proposition entirely, and I can't guarantee success. No length here. I surely never realized how crop-headed you were or I'd had this growing out long ago. If I were you, one of the first things I'd do after I was married would be to have Ferris buy me a switch. He'll be sympathetic to the idea—he's a great admirer of long hair. Seems only yesterday he gave up combing mine. He'd stand on a footstool to do it when he was little. A switch'll tide you over until you can grow a little hair of your own—and I wish to goodness I had it right now. What I'm going to use for a knot for you is a mystery to me, and without one you'll look out of place with the other two girls."

Lib opened the door and Mrs. Thompson paused in her combing. "Come back in ten minutes, Mrs. Conboy, and I'll have her ready." Lib answered smoothly, "Take as long as you want, Mrs. Thompson, we're not pressed for time." But Cate saw her mother's head go up, and the look of pain or disappointment which came on her face, made her say, as Lib, with her fast jaunty step was leaving, "Stay, Mama, if you want to."

"I'll wait until Mrs. Thompson's finished," Lib answered and closed the door firmly on them.

"That's the best I can do," Mrs. Thompson announced finally and Cate, after one look in the mirror, said, "Mother Thompson,

I promise you that by Christmastime I'll have hair long enough to do something with."

"I grant you there isn't much to work on at present. Now, Catherine, I'll leave you. I know you want a few minutes to yourself. This is a sacred moment in a girl's life, the hour before she puts herself and all her future hopes into the hands of the man who's chosen her as his helpmeet. Since the man in this case happens to be my son, I'm more than usually interested that you be a good helpmeet to him. And I want you to know that I'm turning Ferris over to you just as clean and sweet as any girl and just as full of hopes, and when you say your before-wedding prayers, Catherine, remember to ask that you don't disappoint those hopes." She bent (Cate was still sitting), kissed her quickly on the forehead, and went out.

Cate loved talk like this—it enhanced and elevated what occasionally seemed to her a little flat: her marrying Ferris and going to live at the Thompsons'. She thought about Mrs. Thompson's words as she dressed, and they gave her a feeling of great tenderness and responsibility—as if she held all Ferris' dreams and hopes in her two hands and could easily, by an awkward movement, shatter them. Her dressing didn't take long, the gray wool was very simple. For once, she thought with satisfaction, I'm dressed in good taste. But the results of good taste somehow disappointed her, and for a second she regretted the lace and white satin in which she had always imagined herself being married. But only for a second. I'd 've overdone it, she assured herself, and ended up looking like I'd decked myself out in the parlor curtains. Good taste is something you have to get used to, and I'm just not used to it yet.

She was still at the mirror when Lib came back, and Lib exclaimed, without thought, "Cate, what's that woman done to you? You look like someone just out of an orphan asylum. You're surely not thinking of standing up there like that and being married?"

"A wedding is a religious ceremony," Cate answered. "I haven't any ambition to be decked out like a Christmas-tree."

"You have certainly succeeded in your ambition," Lib said, started to add something sharp, and thought better of it. I won't quarrel with the girl on her wedding night. "Catey," she said, "you've got such pretty hair, your hair's your glory, don't stand up there in front of everybody looking like you're scalped. What's the sense hiding your curls? Let me comb it out for you."

"You never did like to comb my hair, Mama."

"No," Lib said, "in the press of other things I didn't."

"And besides Mother Thompson knows what's suitable."

"Yes," Lib said, "I suppose she does." When she had found Mrs. Thompson established in Cate's room and taking over the task of helping the bride she had felt a great pang, first of jealousy and anger, and finally sorrow. And the sorrow was the heavier because she knew she had brought it on herself. It came to her then that the only real pleasures of life resulted from a feeling of success in relationships with others: in being daughter, wife, mother. And she knew she had not succeeded very well in any of these lines. With both Cate and her mother she had reckoned on there being more time, years when the day's emergencies and limitations and vexations would vanish and the real love get expressed. But her mother had died—and Cate was getting married—just at the moment when some understanding of what being daughter—and mother—was about to come to her. With Link, please God, there would still be time; but she saw clearly enough what she had done to him, and through him to others, in her early years of marriage.

Cate, with her usual craze for fresh air, had her windows wide open and Lib noted, in a manner unusual to her, the fresh May evening scents: the monthly rose already blooming, the beauty-bush at its height and, binding all the fragrances, known and unknown, together, the mint which grew so lavishly by the creek and which the wedding guests had trampled. She turned back to Cate—her daughter and Link's—dressed for her wedding in a get-up which would put an old-maid school-teacher to shame, more like a girl about to enter a nunnery than marriage; and while she knew this to be a pity, the greatest pity of all, she recognized, was that there had been something in Cate's upbringing for which she, as mother, was responsible and which had made Cate choose such an outfit and hair-do tonight. And there was no way to call to her, call from back in the lost years. Return; return, Cate, to a happiness suitable to a girl. Return to naturalness, return to ease and pleasure. Cate had fallen into the habit of not listening to her. She had said things to Cate which had closed her ears to anything she could say now.

"Cate," she said earnestly, "I've got a present for you." She had gone without a new wedding-dress herself in order to save a small sum of money which Cate could use for pocket money at the Thompsons'. She had the feeling that there might be some closeness in money matters over there. She pulled the folded ten-dollar bill from the neck of her red bombazine and held it toward Cate. "I wish it was more, Cate, but it was all I could get together." Secretly, she considered ten dollars a very large sum and thought that Cate would marvel that she had ever been able to save that much. "I want you to have a little pocket-money to call your own when you go over there. The best men in the world, Link sometimes, even, forget to give their wives money and it's not always easy to ask."

Cate made no motion to take the bill. When Lib mentioned a gift she had supposed her mother had in mind something appropriate—a pin which had belonged to Grandmother McFadden or a new white leather-bound Bible which she could hold during the ceremony. But a dirty ten-dollar bill! How like Lib and how different from Mother Thompson, with her thoughts about the hopes and ideals of marriage.

"I'm not going to carry money to my wedding."

Lib tucked the bill under the scarf on the bureau. "You remember this is here, Cate, and get it before you leave tomorrow."

"You had money enough all the time for a proper wedding-party supper," Cate said accusingly.

"Yes, I did," Lib admitted. "And I didn't intend then, and I don't now, for that money to go on buying anything for the Thompsons. I didn't set ducks and bug cabbages for that. I scrimped and saved so you could get yourself some little treat, sister, just when you wanted it."

The words of her childhood—"treat," and "sister"—melted Cate's heart. She was a little girl again, and her greatest desire was to please Lib and be accepted by her. In spite of herself she began to cry. "Mama, Mama," she said.

Lib, for the first time since Cate was three or four, put her arms around her daughter. "Now, now, Cate. No crying. You've got you a nice boy and you ought to be rejoicing. Spunk up, now.

You don't want to be an old maid, do you? Dry up on the vine like Wanda, do you?"

"No," Cate said, though none of these things or their reverse caused her tears.

"I didn't think so." Lib couldn't quite bring herself to kiss Cate, but she did hug her—and in doing so managed to loosen up a little Mrs. Thompson's severe hair-do, so that a tendril or two from Cate's curls fell free.

"Come on, now," she said, as Cate continued to cry, "it's the bride's mother, not the bride, who cries at weddings. Don't you know that?"

Something in Lib's voice made Cate look up, and for the first time in her life she saw tears on her mother's cheeks. "Now that I'm doing my part," Lib said, "you can stop." She lifted her lace jabot and dried her eyes on it. "Link's ready to give you away. Let's not keep him waiting."

v

THE WEDDING was over. The last guest had either left the house or gone to bed. Cate was in her bridal chamber and Ferris, outside, was bidding his family good-by. In the sitting-room Link and Lib talked things over, Lib on the sofa, Link moving about trying to restore a little order.

"Let things go for tonight," Lib urged.

"No use leaving these cake crumbs to be tramped into the carpet."

"Why doesn't that boy finish his farewells?" Lib asked impatiently. She wanted to get out of her shoes and corset, take down her hair, and go to bed. But Ferris was still too new a member of the family to be treated like one. Link put the crumbs in the grate and drew a chair up to the sofa. "Before you sit down," Lib said, "turn that light down a little. I'm so tired it hurts my eyes."

Link did so, then sat down and sighed. "Were you satisfied with the way things went off, Lib?"

"Cate never looked worse in her life."

"I thought she looked nice."

"You mean she had a nice look out of her eyes."

"Maybe I do," Link said.

From the kitchen, where Mag was still busy with the dishes, came Neddy Oates' high cackle and Devlin's lower-pitched snorts.

"Mag's got help tonight, I see," Link said.

"You can call it help if you want to."

Outside, wheels began to turn, then stopped again. Lib asked scornfully, "Who's that boy think he's married to anyway?"

Once more the wheels turned and this time kept on going. Lib sat up, the hall door closed and Ferris came into the sitting-room. He wore a dark blue serge suit, white shirt, and had a white rose bud in his buttonhole. The other lapel of his coat was decorated with a half-dollar-sized pin imprinted with a picture of Cate. Such pins, he had told them, were all the go in Indianapolis, and his wedding present to Cate had been a similar pin bearing his picture, which Cate had worn fastened to the belt of her wedding-dress like a buckle. A queer idea, Lib thought, and it was queer now to have Cate staring down at her from Ferris' shoulder. But it's all a matter of fashion, she reminded herself. When you were a girl, you went around wearing a hair brooch.

"Your folks get off all right?" she asked Ferris. "Finally?"

It was lost on him. "Why, I think so," he said, with a slight tone of surprise. "I don't see why not." He pulled a chair up beside Link's and sat down companionably. "I expect you've had quite a day of it," he sympathized.

"We had our work cut out for us," Lib agreed.

"Mother admired the decorations. I was a little too nervous at the time to notice them very much myself. I reckon I'd better look at them tonight if I want to see them before they wilt?"

Lib nodded in assent. "If you're interested in them." What night did the boy think this was? And why in creation had he and Cate elected to spend their first night here, anyway, instead of going to Madison or even The Junction? If any other girl beside her own daughter had been waiting in the spare bedroom she would've said, Get on in there to your bride, now. How do you think she's feeling, waiting for you—wondering what's keeping you? Just when she thought the long silence was beginning to suggest to him that this was no hour for visiting, Link kind-heartedly gave the conversation a new lease on life; and with this help

Ferris was off again. In the first lull, and after giving Link a meaningful look, she rose and said, "It's long past my bedtime. If you men'll be kind enough to excuse me I'll leave you to your talk."

In her room she put on her nightgown and took down her hair, and still from the sitting-room came the drone of Ferris' voice. She went to the open window and without knowing what she was doing began to pinch off the tender honeysuckle shoots that had pushed themselves up to, and even over, the sill. She imagined Cate in her room, wondering what had happened to Ferris, but too bashful to come out and ask. Was he afraid, before his in-laws, of appearing over-eager? She tried to excuse him on these grounds—but couldn't. Didn't he know over-eagerness was the bridegroom's nature? What else did he have to offer? In time, concern for his in-laws' opinions might be a nice enough trait, but on his wedding night it wasn't called for. Dandie, for all his mistakes, hadn't, on his wedding night, she'd wager, made the mistake of sitting around talking crops and the weather. And Link—Link was perhaps the cause of her belief that marriage for Cate would arrange itself naturally. Link came to me so naturally, when I was still so young a girl, and without taking thought I knew he was the man for me, and with him I have had the best there is. A woman's wedding night might easily miss a number of pleasures—and all of these she could forgive and forget—all but one, that the man didn't play a man's part. Whether, as a result of that, she had pain or pleasure, happiness or disappointment, didn't matter much, but let him be with her in love.

She heard Ferris laugh, easy and loud, as if he were enjoying himself. Nervous or self-conscious, she could've forgiven him; but enjoying himself was another matter. She half understood that she was trying to make up to Cate, in the person of Ferris, for some of her own omissions and misunderstandings. She would extend her new conception of being a good mother clear to the point of providing Cate, willy-nilly, with a good husband. She buttoned the red bombazine basque on over her nightgown and with bare feet, and full skirt swinging, she went angrily out to the sitting-room.

At first, she beat the devil about the bush, in the person of Link, an operation to which Link was accustomed. "Link," she said, "have you lost all sense of time? It's past midnight, and if you have any idea of working tomorrow you'd better be coming to bed." But she couldn't forbear, having launched into the subject, a swipe at the devil himself. "And, Ferris, if you expect to cut any kind of a figure at that shivaree tomorrow night, you'd better be getting some sleep, too."

"Thank you for reminding me of it," Ferris said (as if she cared a hoot whether he had a wink of sleep, now or ever), "but with all this shivareeing and so forth in mind, I've been getting a few extra winks these last few days. So an hour or two less tonight won't hurt me, I guess."

Lib considered restraining herself. It was within her power. But she chose not. "Ferris," she said, "stop thinking and talking about yourself. And about us, too. What're we to you? And begin thinking about Cate. It's her you've married. I never in my life saw or heard of a man spending his wedding night talking with his in-laws. If that was what you had in mind in marrying Cate, say so and I'll take her the news and you can go on home. And we'll give you a standing invitation to supper every Sunday night."

Lib's voice wasn't loud, but it carried. Mr. Manlief had told her once, "You have the voice of an actress." "I can yell if that's what you mean," she had answered. "You don't have to yell," he had said. And she hadn't been yelling now, but it had carried to Cate; and Lib, who had advanced, in the earnestness of her speaking, nearer and nearer Ferris, turned to Cate in the doorway and asked, "What are you doing here, Cate?"

"That's what I came to ask you," Cate said.

She stood there, thin and tall in the stark plainness of her gray dress. When had Cate lost her buxomness? Lib wondered. Her young girl plumpness? It left her when I wasn't noticing. She's got a woman's broad-across, thin-through-shoulders now, and a woman's narrow waist and full bust. But her face, it's still a girl's face, the face that had been ardent about Shakespeare and curious about trains. A child's face, full of ideas and empty of knowledge. Lib yearned toward her daughter—not without reminding herself, however, that the yearning was simultaneous with the leave-taking.

"What are you doing, Mama?" Cate asked again.

"Reminding these two men it's bedtime," Lib said, drawing

Link into it—trying to make out, for Cate's sake, that the night was no different for the two of them.

Cate said, "It is really too nice a night to go to bed; what I came out for was to ask Ferris if he didn't want to take a little stroll before bedtime."

A gentle breeze, as if hastening to bear out Cate's words, sprang up at that, lifting the curtains and starting up that old whispered rustle about the eaves which she—and Dandie too, Lib remembered—had loved so well.

"Wouldn't you like a little walk, Ferris?" Cate asked; and Lib watched her daughter taking charge of Ferris and of her marriage, doing what she knew was no woman's inclination, at any time—and certainly not on her wedding night.

Back in their own room, with Link beside her, Lib cried again, the second time that day and this time not lightly. They had been in bed some time, and still they heard from outside, Cate's and Ferris' voices: Ferris doing most of the talking, Cate responding with unconvincing party-laughter. Lib suddenly cursed, not one of her occasional half-dirty, half-funny swear words, but a real taking of the Lord's name in vain, something Link had never heard her do before.

"I hate you too, Link Conboy," she said, replying to his exclamation of surprise. "You paved the way for this. You made me expect too much of men."

The first grayness was already in the room when she asked, "You asleep yet, Link?"

"No," he answered. "Not yet."

Lib gave a little dry laugh. "You'd think we were the bride and bridegroom—we're so wakeful," she said.

But there were no more sounds of talk from outside and soon Link heard Lib breathing with the even slowness of sleep.

14

On the morning of the Fourth the sun came up shortly before five. This hour, for children who'd been awake half the night anticipating firecrackers, seemed late; for their parents, awake half of the night because of the heat, the sun seemed scarcely to have gone down before it was up again and blazing. But the grown-ups, like the children, had anticipated the day. No one in Rock County in 1900 unless drunk, dying or giving birth, awakened forgetful of it. Even the newly married, or those gone to bed without such sanction, did not forget it and awakened and made holiday love because of it.

In some ways the Fourth was a better holiday than Christmas: there was no responsibility for presents; no need to face ten miles of snow banks and blustery winds in order to spend the day with a pack of relatives you'd ordinarily walk around the square to miss. And if things got a little rowdy, that was nothing to be cut up about. No Christmas holiness was required of you on the Fourth: nothing on that day but a lot of eating, setting off of fireworks and rejoicing in the fine, steamy growing weather. And perhaps a little listening to patriotic oratory. In The Junction the bandstand, already draped in red, white, and blue bunting, awaited the day's orator: Clate Newby, born on a hill farm over Sandusky way, and now a big Indianapolis lawyer. "Are we, like those glorious heroes of '76, '61 and '98, willing to offer up our lives on the altar of our country's need?"

Hell, yes! And just to prove it, a punch or two would be thrown at neighbor or kinsman. For the Fourth belonged to the men, as Christmas belonged to the women. But all holidays alike belong to the children, and hours before sun-up children's hands were going out to chairs pulled up the night before to the bedside: two Roman candles, one sky-rocket, six torpedoes, six giant crackers, four packages ordinary crackers, one catharine-wheel, six punk sticks. Nothing missing, and so back to sleep for another thirty minutes before counting again.

II

BEFORE sun-up a water wagon made the rounds in The Junction, trying to lay a little of the dust on the main streets before the crowds began to arrive. As it went up Sycamore past the back of the Flat-Iron Building, the jangle of its chain traces and the creak of its wheels awakened Dandie. He had been sleeping on his back while Nory, facing him, pillowed her head on his outstretched arm. He rolled toward her, sliding his arm, which was numb, out from under her head.

The movement awakened her. "Is it raining?" she asked.

"No, that's the water wagon." He put his arm across her. "Go on back to sleep."

"Is it the Fourth?"

"It was the Fourth before we went to bed," he reminded her.

She was quiet for a minute, then she asked, "Will firecrackers be bad for the baby?"

"No," he said, a yawn cutting his throat in two. "Be good for it."

"Anything that'll let you go back to sleep you think's good," she chided softly. He didn't deny it. Nory took his hand and put it on her stomach, which was warm, smooth, and still flat. "There he is," she said.

Dandie gave a few gentle pats. "Sh," he said, "you'll wake him up."

III

TOWARD morning it seemed to get a little cooler, and Lib fell asleep. Then, resist it as she would, some sound kept lifting her nearer and nearer consciousness. Without opening her eyes she said, "Link, what're you doing, fumbling around out there in the dark?"

"It's not dark," Link answered, "and I'm not fumbling."

"Can't see my hand before my face."

[373]

"Open your eyes," Link said, "and you can. Be full daylight before you know it."

"Nothing's going to happen before I know it, with all your noise."

Something fell to the floor. "What'n the Sam Scratch is this?" Link asked.

"I told you it was too dark to see."

"Flags," Link said.

Lib sat up. "Now you put them right back where you got them, Link Conboy. They're none of your business."

"What're they for?"

"I'm going to use them for a decoration. Put one on each dish of ice-cream."

Link sniffed, but returned them to their box. "How much did you pay for them?"

"Ten cents. They were six for a penny and I thought it'd be nice to have a few extra on hand."

"What for?"

She didn't know. "For celebrations," she said and hurried on before he could comment. "What're you up this time of day for, anyway?"

"This time of day? It's after four. And with all the rampaging there'll be here today, I'll have to look after most of the work myself. Dilk and Manlief are the only ones here I can halfway depend on. And with Fair time coming I don't want any slip-ups with the animals."

Lib lay back again. "Those pigs," she said. "I wish you were half as worried about your wife and children."

"If I had you entered in the County Fair I would be."

Though it was against all Poor House rules James Abel went into his sister's and Leathy Wade's room. Holidays powerfully affected him. They were a kind of sign left upon present times by those gone before, and he believed in signs and took strength from them. The Fourth was a particularly good day, connected as it was with the pursuit of happiness, and he had had a strong lead about the day's digging and wanted to take no chances on Mary's sleeping late and being delayed in starting for the gravel pits by unfinished kitchen chores.

[374]

He had stepped out of bed, imagining the world as it might be. He was filled with love like a cloud with rain, swelled tight with conviction and election, justified, sanctified, and ordained by invisible powers. He crossed the room to Mary's bed and felt the warm floorboards of the uncarpeted floor supporting him like the approving palms of the Fourth's founders. He put a hand on Mary's shoulder, and she sat up, a sudden rigid angle.

"James," she whispered.

He reassured her. "I wanted to be sure you were awake, Mary. I want us to get up and out early. I've got a strong lead for today."

"It's the Fourth," she exclaimed, remembering.

He nodded. "The day's got a sign on it. I feel myself being led." He extended his opened hand, as if each finger had a wire in it.

Leathy Wade, awakening, said, "Wires in his hands, bats in his belfry," but he ignored her.

Mary asked, "Is it early?"

"The hog-tender is up and about." He motioned toward the window where Link could be seen crossing the yard to the barn. "Shall we be less faithful?"

At the door he turned back. "Get Emma up early, too. We'll need all hands today."

He was brimming with conviction and happiness. He carried his chin like a hatchet, prepared to cleave the world's secret wide open with it. He closed the door behind him without any quietness. He was up, wasn't he? And with that the day started, didn't it?

The banging door awakened Em. She dressed with one hand, fished her giant firecracker from the coffin with the other, then left the house on the run, determined to be the first person at the farm to set off any fireworks. There had been some set off the night before; but they didn't count any more than a firecracker lighted last Thanksgiving would count as first. She rounded the summerhouse and crashed into Mr. Dilk, and ran on leaving him tottering. "Excuse the awkwardness," she called back over her shoulder.

She got an enamel chamber pot, left back of the privy to air, and brought it to the side yard. There she turned it upside down over the lighted cracker. Even expecting the blast, she was startled. When the echoes died away she put her ankles together, drew herself up straight, and sang, "My Country, 'Tis of Thee," all four verses.

Before she had finished there were heads out of windows. Mary called when she stopped, "Beautiful, Emma. Beautiful, beautiful."

From another window Mag yelled, "Beautiful? What that was, was loud. Loudest singing I ever heard in my life. Cracked my eardrums."

Satisfied, Em carried the chamber pot back to the privy. Opinions might differ as to whether it had been loud or beautiful, but it had certainly been first.

The faculty of day-dreaming was not lost to Lily, but she was old and words instead of pictures raced through her mind. To calm herself she tried to change the words to images: to see Christie instead of saying his name; feel his arms instead of saying the word, love. Oh, but that was just the trouble, with his letter resting under her pillow. If she saw him now she saw him with this other person, this girl he said he was going to marry. And she would like that to stay as it was in the letter: words only. That girl, his cousin, got him on the rebound, she thought. It won't last. His pride was hurt, and he grabbed whatever was nearest just to show he could. She took his letter from under her pillow. In spite of what it said she couldn't help loving it; it was his, wasn't it? His hand had rested on the paper and written the words. There was no need to read it. She knew every word by heart. But she liked to look at it:

Dear Friend Lily,

I appreciated your writing me all the news. I'm glad the wedding went off all right. And speaking of weddings I'm engaged to be married myself—to my cousin Carmen Sylva Cope. I was in love with her a year ago but didn't have sense enough at the time to know it. We plan to be married in September and go to New York on our honeymoon. I won a trip there as a prize for selling the most insurance in this district. Remember, you told me I would?

Sylva joins me in sending best regards to you and she hopes that you will come pay us a visit after we are married.

I still have the whiskbroom-holder you gave me at Christmas-time and still find it highly useful.

I hope you are enjoying your usual good health.
Please remember me to Mr. and Mrs. Conboy and Em. Tell Mr. Conboy I hope his pigs are doing as well as he thought they would. I never had any idea that animals could be interesting till I talked to him about them when I was there last year. This year really, I guess, but it seems a long time ago.
Looking forward to your next letter, I am
Most sincerely yours,
Christian J. Fraser

Mrs. Goforth, from the bed next Lily's, watched Lily fondle Christie's letter and said, "I'm glad Herschell can't see me living in a room with a woman lovesick about a boy young enough to be her grandson."

Lily just patted her letter. "The boy I'm in love with ain't any relation to me—anyway," she said.

When the breakfast bell rang, Link and John Manlief left the barn together, Link continuing his talk of the County Fair and the blue ribbons he hoped to win there with his hogs and with Hoxie's rugs. When he had finished and while they were waiting their turn at the wash-basin, Manlief said, "I'd like to get an extension of my time to stay here if it's possible. What I'd like to do is to stay on through July. I know the county can't go on paying for my keep indefinitely and I don't expect it to. I can pay any amount you like, and if you can arrange for it, I'll stay here until I get my bearings a little better."

Link said, "There's no provision for my taking boarders here, but I tell you what we can do. I have to hire extra help each year at harvest time. If you're willing to work as a hand then it would be a real favor to me."

"You think I could do the work?"

"I wouldn't be asking you if I didn't," Link said heartily; though the heartiness was an expression of his pleasure in Manlief's staying rather than any conviction concerning his ability as a harvest hand. Manlief was one of the few men (since he'd recovered from his apathies) to whom he could talk freely. Another of my life's failures, he thought, is my lack of friends—a failure he could never understand, since inside himself he felt he had great stores of friendliness. But beside Fred and Lib who was there? And Fred was so much less than a friend in many ways and Lib so much more, they scarcely counted. He kept waiting (himself silent) for someone to make a sign, give him the password: someone he could open his heart to, say this is how things stand with me.

Happy as he was with Lib, he felt her limitations when it came to any talk of general ideas. General ideas riled Lib. He had only to mention the county's duty to its poor, for instance, to have her flare up and say, "How're we going to keep Lily from throwing herself at some man," or "How're we going to keep Hoxie busy at that loom?" Don't start speculating about the county, was Lib's policy, as long as you have unsolved problems right under your nose. He knew he was a family man, more satisfied than most with the pleasure he found inside his home; yet there were times when he longed for the friend he had never made.

He remembered Emerson's saying that his whole life had been nothing but a search for a suitable companion. His chin lifted involuntarily—as if he were speaking to Emerson—so strange a saying did that seem to him coming from a man, surrounded and befriended as Emerson had been by those wonderful ones: Thoreau and Hawthorne and Bronson Alcott and that old aunt of Emerson's, and the woman writer who talked like a man. Every scholar and poet and preacher and traveler in the country had been at Emerson's hearthside. What of me, Emerson? he asked. What of Link Conboy? I've got some good ideas. But no, he answered himself, I guess not. Otherwise the scholars and poets would be here.

"Wonder what Emerson would think of me?" he asked Manlief. That was why he hated to lose Manlief. Who else in the county could he say that to? "What would Emerson think of this place?"

"He'd like it better than Brook Farm anyway."

Link remembered that there had been an asylum near Emerson's home, near enough so that Emerson spoke of hearing a crazy woman yelling all one afternoon. But of the keeper of that asylum, the man who had charge of the crazy woman, Emerson never spoke. That ought to answer my question, "What would Emerson think of me?" Link asked himself.

"I've never understood," Manlief said, "how you happened to come here in the first place."

"I wasn't a very successful lawyer—and this guaranteed my family a roof over their heads, at the least."

Manlief said nothing and Link thought, You say you have no one to open your heart to: perhaps the trouble is that you have no heart to open. "I didn't have an easy conscience," he added. "I'd come to the age of stock-taking and I decided I had some amends to make to society."

He would've said more perhaps, but James Abel and his sister stalked up at that minute in their graceless way.

"We wanted to tell you we wouldn't be to the picnic," said Abel. "We're leaving to dig soon as breakfast's over."

"No," Link told him, "not today you're not. No one's leaving the place today. You don't have to come to the picnic, if you don't want to, but there'll be no traipsing off digging today."

"This is a legal holiday," Abel said, "and I've done all the hog-tending the law requires for one day."

"You'll do your regular feeding tonight and between now and then there'll be no digging, unless you want to do it right here on the place. The countryside's going to be swarming with picnickers today, and I won't have you and your sister out making public spectacles of yourself. I'm not running any three-ring circus here for the entertainment of county riff-raff."

"We're doing our duty, and if people stare it's nothing we're going to be held to account for."

"Well, I'm held to account for it. We've got three hundred acres here and if you're set on digging, pick out a spot here and dig."

"I've got no lead to dig here."

"Take the day off then. Have a rest from digging."

Mary Abel stepped closer to Link. "Think twice, Mr. Conboy," she advised, "before you come between my brother and his work."

"I don't need to think twice about this, Mary. On ordinary days when you and James have finished your work, you can dig to your heart's content. But if either one of you leaves the farm today I'll lock you up."

And he's got a suitable place for it, too, Manlief thought, remembering that wash-house room with its barred window and padlocked door which had been strong enough to withstand all Doss Whitt's batterings on the night he waited the Sheriff there.

"You are going against unseen powers," Mary Abel warned.

Link laughed shortly. "I don't suppose it's the first time."

He and Manlief washed without further talk, but at the kitchen door Manlief said, "I think you ought to keep your eye on that pair."

Link made no reply but there was some humorous alteration in his expression which made Manlief, guessing at its meaning, say, "You think I'm the last one to say that? After the state I was in? Well, set a thief to catch a thief, they say."

IV

NEDDY OATES looked up at the sun and told himself: Make up your mind, crawl or fry. But he couldn't crawl, not with his leg broken between the knee and hip-joint. The best he could do was to drag himself along, using his arms as crutches. Even that way, and going backwards, he was continually jarring the broken leg—and that started up the puking all over again. And he couldn't stand much more of that; not and keep his stomach inside his body.

He was in the pasture, midway between the new cornfield and the big poplar. If he had been anyways near the cornfield he thought he would've just crawled deep to that greenness and never come out. He would just as lief die as go down to the house and explain what had happened to him—though to fry to death while waiting for his leg to kill him was a kind of double dying he hadn't figured on. The pasture was already jumping and shimmering with heat-waves; beginning to float, double-decked, one pasture about a foot above the other; and both decks mighty hot and he between the two like the fried egg in a sandwich. He hauled himself another two or three lurches nearer the shade of the poplar, then fell back, sick and sweating, and took from the grasses that brushed his lips an experimental nibble, as a sick dog does. The sour damp taste seemed to settle his stomach, and he dragged on for another painful hitch, then lay back with his heart thundering so that he felt the earth rising up in solid swells to wallop him in the small of the back. He put his arm across his face to keep out the sun, but it kept out the air too and his head began to steam like a cabbage boiling in a pot with the lid clamped on. He took his arm down and there at the end of the pasture, her nose in the watering trough, was the cause of his troubles. If he had a gun he'd shoot her. Or hang a medal on her, he wasn't sure which. A mule that could fool him the way she had for two years needed some kind of special recognition.

After supper last night, hoping to cool off a little before bedtime, he had gone out to the pasture. He couldn't say it was cooler, but it had been a change, the cornfield smell dry and sweet, and overhead the Milky Way running as thick and rich as Jersey cream. Below him the house lamps had twinkled and about his knees the fireflies had gone on and off like cigars in the mouths of uncertain smokers. The heat had made him sweat, but it had limbered him up, too. If nobody'd ever told me my age, he'd thought, I could be twenty-three now not sixty-three. Same old gism, same old piss and vinegar. He had run a few paces, leaped straight up, clapped his feet together once, and come down breathing hard. Out of practice, he had admitted, shut up down there with them old fellows, half of them with one foot in the grave; and all of them either born simple or made simple by a lifetime of walking up one furrow and down another, locked between a pair of plow handles and no more idea of the world than you can get from peering over a mule's back. Me, he had said, that's been where I've been and done what I've done. He had pitied himself. He had lifted his head and stared at the stars and they had blinked back at him like the eyes that rise to the top of a crock of ripe batter. He had walked up the hill, fireflies breaking around his knees like the surf on the beach at St. Petersburg; and then he hadn't walked, but ridden, up on Foxy Buttons, and the spread of Foxy's saddle in his crotch and her shifting muscles against his thighs. And he had been able to smell the sweet spice from the carnation horseshoe they had hung over Foxy's neck and feel the sweet twitch of the feather boas across his face as the lily-shaped ladies had caught the flavor of his looks and sidled up to him with their silly questions and the restless weaving of their little gloved hands. He had crossed the pasture, up on Foxy Buttons, and had stopped at the fence along the cornfield and there the cornfield rustling had been the ladies' taffety petticoats, and the creek sliding over its stones their merry ha-ha's, and the whippoorwills calling, the whistle of kids anxious for his salute so they could go home and say, "Neddy Oates waved at me."

But old Maude had been at the fence, hanging her head over the top rail to get at the corn, and he had either (standing beside her) to admit he was afoot, or that Foxy Buttons had shrunk to the size of a cottontail. He hadn't been ready to admit a thing so up he went on Maude, he still twenty-three, and Maude, the minute he straddled her, Foxy Buttons herself. He had dug his heels into her flanks and hit her over the head with his hat (he wished to God he still had it). He had electrified Maude so that she had taken off like a bolt of greased lightning, and about half way down the pasture, the grease came into play. She had lifted her hind-quarters like a flag and waved them, and he had risen in salute and was up in the air and still climbing when Maude passed him several feet below.

He had been sixty-three when he lit; though for a while he had thought he had gone clean out of time and it was the sweet by-and-by and the lights he saw were the blaze of pearly gates and golden streets. When the lights had died down and he had been able to think with his cracked skull, he saw that his leg was broken. But worse than the cracked skull, the broken leg and the wavering stomach, was the matter of explaining back at the house how he'd got in his present fix. If he died for it, he wasn't going back to the house to admit that he'd been bucked off a twelve-year-old mule: not him, not Neddy the jockey, who'd been where he'd been and done what he'd done, not if he died in the cow-pasture and the buzzards picked his bones so clean nobody'd bother to gather them up for burial in one of Link's pine boxes.

What was he going to say then when they found him? Was he kicked by a horse? Had a cow butted him? A tree fallen on him? He dragged on, inch by inch, aiming, without realizing it, for the gate in the center of the pasture, and when he got there he had to crawl around it because he couldn't reach the latch. The base of the poplar was covered with cow pads and he couldn't miss them all and could only be thankful for old ones. Down below him Maude was still at the watering trough and beyond her Link was calling his pigs, "Sooey, sooey, sooey." He sank back against the exposed tree roots, a cow pad for a pillow, and damned all hogs, mules, and cows everywhere.

V

DANDIE had asked Cate and Ferris to ride to The Farm with him and Nory, for Lib's Fourth of July celebration, but Ferris had said no. "One or the other of us would be almost sure to have to wait this evening. It'd be better if we had two rigs."

They had started out together, but Dandie, with his new horse and buggy, had soon out-distanced them. "Darned fools," Ferris said when Dandie, in passing, had tossed an exploding firecracker in the air. "He's liable to cause a runaway, doing that."

"I don't think you could make Fanny run away, could you? I wish you would cluck her up a little, though."

"If you wanted to travel fast, you should've gone with Brother Dandie."

"I don't want to travel fast. It's only that the dust's so thick."

"I told you to wear a duster."

"I know you did." Cate touched the sleeve of Ferris' duster. "You're going to be clean and tidy when we get there, and I'll be a mess."

"You'll be dirty," Ferris admitted.

Cate had wanted to ride with Dandie and Nory, to make a holiday lark of it, an expedition of young married couples, singing songs and waving to their friends, but Ferris had not, and she was determined now not to be pouty. This was their first trip home and she knew the critical looks Ferris would receive from Lib, and she started planning means of getting him to The Farm in a good humor. She began to pry tentatively at the fingers of his right hand, outspread on his thigh. For a while he held his hand pressed down and stiff, then, little by little, he relaxed it so that her fingers slipped into the little cave between his thigh and the arch of his palm. And at last, after some minutes of stroking and caressing Cate felt the resistance leave his fingers altogether, and they rode, as she had planned, united, hand in hand.

"Oh, Ferris," she said, "let us be one."

"Who's keeping us apart?"

Am I? she asked herself. She watched the passing summer fields: corn with more yellow now than blue in its greenness; wheat, toast-colored, looking not only ripe but cooked; clover, fresh and fluid as running water. Am I? The leaves of sumach and horseweed and elderberry were thick and glossy. Am I? Blackberries, not yet fully ripe, shone like red eyes in the midst of all the greenness. Am I? Garden flowers were at their height; they paid no attention to picket fences, but crawled under and through and over: Cana, lantana, cabbage roses, monthly roses, snowballs, pretty-by-nights, lilies, white, orange and mixed sweetpeas, sweet-williams, stock, petunia, phlox, flags, honeysuckle. She drew a deep breath, tempted by scents she imagined, rather than smelled, and got more dust than fragrance—for the road was filled with rigs all headed the opposite direction, bound for The Junction and the celebration there.

In the earnestness of her desire to answer Ferris' question truthfully, she turned squarely about to face him. "If I keep us apart, I don't want to, Ferris."

Em was waiting for them at the top of the last hill before they reached The Farm. Ferris pulled up for her and she climbed in and made her announcement as she climbed. "Nory and Dandie are going to have a baby."

"That's not a thing nice little girls talk about," Ferris told her.

"Why not?" Em asked. "What's wrong with babies?"

"There isn't any baby yet," Ferris reminded her.

"A baby that isn't, can't be worse than a baby that is? Can it?"

Ferris changed the subject. "You seem to have picked up a good deal of information in a hurry."

Em denied it. "Dandie and Nory've got here a long time ago. We thought you'n Cate'd never come."

"I'm not driving a racehorse like Brother Dandie."

Em didn't contradict this and Cate leaned back thankfully and looked at the Poor Farm buildings, warm and red in the morning sunlight.

VI

THE FOURTH was one of Lib's days. Such days, like cyclones, rise up out of nowhere and like cyclones, can be accounted for but not predicted. They overtook Lib on the most unlikely occasions. A time she had either dreaded, or given no thought to, became, quite suddenly, as this day was becoming, purest joy. In the midst of worry and hard work suddenly she would feel, and be, strong enough to accomplish anything: strong and loving and loved, and just to cap the climax, side-splittingly funny besides. Taking up the potatoes, now—they had been boiled with their jackets on for the potato salad—she lifted them from the deep iron kettle in a way that had everyone in the kitchen laughing. And in the matter of clowning she had plenty of competition. The kitchen was filled with gifted comedians; Mag, Dandie, Leathy, artists and show-offs all three, and all three a lot noisier than Lib. But not a one of them could've made the lifting of a boiled potato from an iron pot to a stone crock the side-splitting thing Lib made it. Were those potatoes wild animals? Would they open their eyes and lunge at her? She handled them that way and used her big spoon like a ringmaster's whip and wore her faded pink sleeveless dressing-sack, lashed to her petticoat (she hadn't had time to put on a skirt yet) with a blue checked apron, like a ringmaster's red Prince Albert. It was a three-ring circus in the kitchen, but Lib was in the center ring and commanding the show.

It was ten o'clock, the entire house hot; but the kitchen, which faced east and had had the range roaring away in it since sun-up, was a furnace. Lib who relished heat was only agreeably flushed; the others were fanning and complaining. Over by the open door, Lodema and Lily were taking the jackets off the first batch of boiled potatoes. Next them, Leathy was dicing the peeled potatoes into a dishpan. Mag, in the center of the room was chopping onions and keeping an eye on Icey and Airey, making jelly sandwiches. At the kitchen cabinet Nory was deviling eggs. Dandie and Fessler, doing nothing, were about equal nuisances; Fessler noisier but more easily controlled: slap him and he stopped whatever meanness he was up to. Nothing stopped Dandie. He snatched up a dib of this and a dab of that; at the minute he was making what he called potato sandwiches, slices of boiled potato with a filling of deviled egg yolk and a sprinkling of chopped onions.

"Dandie," Lib cried, "stop that piecing. You're going to ruin your appetite for dinner that way."

"Not me," Dandie said. "I'm eating for two nowadays," and he clapped one potato sandwich into his mouth and started another.

Lib took a swipe at him with her long-handled spoon; but Dandie was too quick for her. "Let's not have any loose talk," Lib said, and threatened him with a hot potato.

"Aim at me," Dandie said, "and I'll be safe."

"I'll aim, never fear of that," Lib answered and did; Dandie caught the potato, then got rid of it in a hurry. "Hell's fires," he yelled. "What're you trying to do? Blister me?"

Leathy scooped up the broken potato and dropped the pieces into her dishpan of cubes. "Give it flavor," she said and no one contradicted her. Everyone in the kitchen that morning was feeling strong enough to eat poison and survive: kings and commanders, every one of them, all able to pull swords out of stones and part the waters with words. What was a little dirt? A piece of potato peeling? Not a thing. Let it stay in the salad. When somebody said, as somebody would, "Best potato salad I ever ate, can't remember anything so tasty in a month of Sundays," they would have a fine joke. "It's the special flavoring," they would say. "We've got a patent on it."

Cate, running up the walk, heard the clatter and confusion before she reached the door. Why, it sounds like a party, she thought. She had jumped out of the buggy while the wheels were still turning. "I didn't know you were homesick," Ferris had said.

"I didn't know it, either," she replied.

Dandie saw her first. "Have a potato sandwich," he yelled.

She walked past him. Mag said, "Well, Cate, still able to stomach the smell of chopped onions so early in the morning?" She went by Mag. Lib put down her spoon, turned her hands palms outward to protect Cate from their dirt and drew Cate's face down and kissed her on the cheekbone, the first kiss Cate could remember ever having received from her mother. Tears came to her eyes.

Lib rescued her from crying by saying, "What've you done to yourself, Cate?" Then she stepped back for further inspection and said, "What's happened to your pretty hair, Cate?"

Cate put her hand to her head. "My switch, you mean?"

[386]

"Switch?" Lib demanded. "What in the name of time are you doing with a switch?"

"I'm just wearing it till my own hair grows out."

Dandie took a swipe at her knot, wobbly at best.

"Don't, Dandie. You'll knock it off. It's human hair. Ferris bought it for me for a wedding present."

"Human hair!" Mag snorted. "Why don't he buy something human for himself while he's at it?"

"It's expensive," Cate defended her switch. "It's imported."

"Imported from a horse's tail," said Mag, "and the horse was a sorrel and you're a bay."

"Blood bay," said Dandie.

"Don't be a martyr to hair," Lib advised. "That wad at the back of your neck will give you a headache."

"I'll rescue her," Dandie said, "I'll save her from hair." He made a big struggle of it, careful to give Cate every opportunity to save her switch and escape if she wanted to. But she didn't want to; Dandie was tickling her, holding her wrists in one hand and playing a tattoo on her ribs with the other and she leaned back against him, laughing as first the hairpins and finally the knot itself fell to the floor.

Dandie picked up the switch, uncoiled it and held it aloft. "Hang the thing on your butt," Mag advised, "and you can enter the trotting races at the Fair."

The idea pleased Dandie and with the switch arching upwards from the base of his spine he cantered in circles about the kitchen neighing and prancing, nuzzling the old ladies and nibbling at Fessler. It was little wonder that in the midst of this racket no one paid any attention to Ferris, standing in the doorway waiting to be recognized and welcomed. He saw in a twinkling what had happened to Cate. She was back in the heart of her family, at home with her show-off brother and the paupers and half-wits who thought it was funny for a grown man to act like a horse. And who, except Brother Dandie, would care for the applause of an audience like that? And what was so side-splitting about that vulgar display? They were mighty hard put for entertainment to find the ruining of an expensive switch funny. He was alone and unnoticed. He hunted justification—and if not justification at least some employment—which would bring him into relationship, positive and telling, with these people who ignored him. See me! Watch me! Hear me! Laugh at me! Admire me! Inside himself this cry was as strong as it was in anyone else; stronger because so seldom satisfied. Stronger than ever now, because of Cate and because Cate was where she was. But he was cautious, too, a burnt child, accustomed to failure. If he commanded Cate, "Put that switch back on," would she do it? He didn't know. And even if she did, his in-laws would laugh at him, consider him a bossy husband and make him the butt of new jokes.

Unhappily, he stared down at the dishpan of diced potatoes at his feet and seeing the fragments of the potato Lib had tossed at Dandie, he tapped Leathy's shoulder. "You've got some dirt in there," he said.

Leathy gave the dishpan a sharp shake or two so that the dirty pieces and the clean ones were thoroughly mixed. "We're leaving it in for the flavor," she told him, lifting her puckered old face to him with the smile he got everywhere: insolent.

The picnic was to be held where all Poor House picnics were held, on a grassy shelf which ran along the creek a little upstream from the house. As soon as the food was ready, a little before noon, the folks set forth with it, Dandie supervising the loading activities. The more he piled on them, the happier they were. He had on a peak-billed railroader's hat, a pair of ramshackle highwater pants and a shirt with the two top buttons missing so that the spring of black hairs on his chest spilled into sight. He whistled *Nita, Juanita* low and a little off-key and occasionally snapped his fingers impatiently.

Link watched the boy with some wonderment. Everybody wanted to help him. Why? Mrs. Goforth, ordinarily besmirched by Poor House activities, couldn't carry enough. Nigger Bob, with a dishpan of salad on his head, showed Dandie his empty left arm. They staggered off creekwards proud to have been selected for burdens beyond their strength. What was the explanation? What was the grace Dandie shed? Nothing connected with goodness, anyway. Was it some other virtue, that of being fully alive, so that they crowded around him to soak up like sunlight that unaccustomed warmth and brightness? Dandie, who'd done none of the work of preparation, was the one who parceled out the food and they moved away from him, as if he was the fount of all picnics, the source from which all jelly sandwiches, deviled eggs, giant firecrackers, and squeezed lemon juice flowed. They sang, as they marched, *"Bring the good old bugle, boys, We'll sing another song"*; not a song very appropriate to the day, and Link speculated as to what meaning the Fourth could have for men like Hoxie and James Abel. For women like Lily and Leathy? Was the Fourth, whether they understood it or not, somehow a sign to them, in spite of a lifetime of disappointments and a Poor House ending, that they were connected with one successful enterprise? Ignorant or not of the day, he couldn't help feeling that they were enlarged by it, that they marched toward the creek singing, "Hurray, hurray, the flag that makes us free," with some of the imprint of the document Jefferson wrote, and Hancock signed, on them.

Lib, however, was not dwelling on the past or any generality, past or present. "I think you ought to go have another look for Neddy," she told Link.

"He's likely laying off drunk somewheres."

"He'll get a sunstroke in this weather, if he is."

"Fools and drunkards," Link quoted, but finally gave in. "I've been out twice, but I'll go again, if you'll keep your eye on the Abels. They've been told they're not to leave the place, and I don't want them sneaking off the minute my back's turned."

"Aren't you pulling them up pretty sharp?"

"If I am, it's for their own good. No telling what harm they'd come to out digging today with all the celebrating that'll be going on."

"I'd count on James Abel to look after himself."

"Maybe, but that digging of his is giving us all a bad name here. People are getting the idea we've got a pack of lunatics here."

Lib asked dryly, "What do you call them, Link?"

"Notionate," Link said. "Notionate. Now you keep your eye on them while I go out and have another look for Ned."

VII

AT THE creek the picnic at once divided itself into three parts. Upstream, at a cleared-off spot, the men pitched horseshoes; downstream, Cate and Ferris, Cate with her back against a big sycamore and Ferris stretched full length with his head in her lap, talked; between the horseshoe-pitchers and the talkers were the workers, the women, spreading the red tablecloths and setting forth the food. In the water below the three groups and weaving back and forth like bobbins to unite them were Em, Airey, and Icey. Airey and Icey, their feelings hurt by Em, stayed close to the far bank but paralleled in their navigations, upstream and down, Em's movements.

Airey had been excited by the picnic and had wanted to talk. She had felt speculative. "How long will it be before Nory has her baby?" No answer from Em. "Why do they call a switch a switch? Because it looks like a whip?" No answer. "Do you think Dandie'll let me set off a Roman candle?" No answer. "Let's practise belching under water."

"No," Em had said.

"Are you mad?"

"No. But when I'm in the water I feel silent. Like a fish."

Airey had submerged and belched a big bubble to show what she thought of this. When she came up she said, "I guess when you climb a tree you sing like a bird."

Em had said, "Next time I climb a tree listen and find out."

That had done it. Airey's feelings had been hurt. "Come on, Icey," she had said, "Miss Bird wants to be alone." But before leaving she had given Em a chance to say a reconciling word. She had stood sidewise in the stream and Em had looked at her meager shape and her skin, green-white between the blue-brown freckles and her wrinkled fingers flabby as worms. She had known exactly what she meant to Airey and knowing this she had turned her back on her. Wanting to be quiet, she acknowledged to herself, moving upstream her hands on the creek bottom, was only half of it. The littlest half. The biggest half had been that she had wanted to indulge herself in a meanness. These meannesses always disgusted her, but if she never gave way to them, how would she ever know who she was? Now she knew one thing, anyway. She was the girl who could be unkind to the poor and the fatherless on the Fourth of July. Digesting this knowledge, which had the metallic taste in her mouth of a captive lightning-bug—held there so that the lightning-bug could see what a mouth looked like, and for no personal pleasure—she plied along the creek bank. She stared at the three groups of people above her as if they were actors on a stage. She had been opposite the horseshoe-pitchers when Ferris left them. There'd been an argument and Ferris wouldn't argue. He just left. She had followed him to the women setting out lunch. Here he'd taken Cate by the arm and had led her to the sycamore and seated her and made a pillow of her lap. Anchored by her arms, her body floating fish-like, gently undulating on the water, Em lingered opposite them, observing and wondering. Why was it that the love-making of married people made you more uncomfortable than the love-making of people who weren't married? Married people, she thought (watching Ferris' hand), were like between-meal piecers. Though Cate, she had to admit, might've been in church she was so dignified—in spite of what was going on.

"Go on away from here, Em," Cate called. "There's miles and miles of creek. You don't have to stand right there in front of us staring."

"I'm not standing," Em said.

Ferris lifted his head from Cate's lap, smoothed down his pompadour, then turned to face Em. "The point is, you're staring," he told her.

"There's no law against staring."

"Can't you tell when you're not wanted?"

"Yes," Em said, "I can." But the knowledge didn't move her an inch. Ferris burrowed his head in Cate's lap again. Like an ostrich into a sand pile, Em thought, gently waving her waterborne legs and continuing silently to observe.

The eating had started by the time Link got back from his search for Neddy. The first thing he did was to locate the Abels. Seeing them a little removed from the main body of picnickers, their plates heaped, he filled his own plate and sat down beside Lib.

"Any sight of Neddy?" she asked.

Link shook his head. "He must've slipped off to The Junction last night sometime."

The picnic, to the eye, he thought, was laid out like a flower: the red tablecloths, its center; the dishes of food its pollen; the picnickers, its bright ragged petals. To the ear the picnic was less than flowerlike, nothing near so delicate. Dandie had passed out firecrackers to the young people, and the explosions came without any pattern so that there was never a chance to warn yourself of what was about to happen.

"Watch out how you throw that!" Link warned Dandie. "We want to leave here with our full quota of arms and legs."

No one heard a word he said. Dandie's giant cracker had exploded as he opened his mouth; and who cared about arms and legs anyway? They were Fourth of July heroes, every one of them, and could all grow a new set by morning. There were sycamore leaves in the lemonade bucket. Mud-daubers tested the potato salad. The knife that had been used to chop the onions was now being used to cut the cake.

"Cate, this cake you made has a mighty smooth grain."

"I didn't make it. Mother Thompson did."

"Mighty tasty, whoever made it."

The lids were off the freezers and a cold sweet, vanilla scented vapor rose from them. Em and the Creagan girls—out of the water Em was willing to talk—carried the dishes around to the folks. When the ice-cream was finished Dandie, his back to the creek, lit the rest of the giant crackers, holding them aloft where he couldn't see them and at the last possible second before they exploded sending them arching upward and creekward. Only once did he miscalculate, throwing a cracker so soon that it hit the water before it went off. A miscalculation the other way would lose him a finger or two, possibly a hand.

"The poor fool," Ferris said and looked at Cate. Surely she felt as much scorn for this show-off business as he did? Even if it was Brother Dandie who was showing off? He had his hand on Cate's thigh, less at the minute from fondness than because the gesture gave him a feeling of power. It was a very ambiguous caress. Cate, as if aware of this, lifted his hand, but continued to hold it.

"Love me?" Ferris asked.

Cate nodded.

"Say it," he commanded.
"I love you."
"Who?"
"You."
"Who am I?"
"My husband."

Cautiously, he lifted the edge of Cate's skirt and carefully, inch at a time, moved his hand upward until he touched the slight bulge of soft flesh above her gartered stocking-top. With his hand there he watched Dandie with considerable pity—busy with firecrackers like any grade-school boy.

"Don't, Ferris."
"Don't what?" he asked innocently.
"You know."
"Why not?"
"People can see."
"Whose wife are you?" When she didn't answer, he took a little roll of flesh between thumb and forefinger. "Whose?" he insisted.
"Yours."
"Well, then?" he asked.

After Devlin had spoken—"Three cheers for California," was the gist of *his* speech—and Dilk had answered some of Link's questions about Chancellorsville, Dandie threw his last firecracker over his head and made an announcement. "Everybody else making a speech, I'd about as well make mine. It's short and sweet. 'Vote for me.'"

Ferris felt his gorge rising, but the folks loved it. "We sure will, Dandie boy. What job do you want?"

"The Sheriff's. Elect me Sheriff this year, and I'll get all your friends and relatives out of the pen. I'll make things easier for you here at The Farm, too. I understand your superintendent here is a mighty hard man to work for. News has reached me by the grapevine that he's a man can't tell dark from daylight when it comes to working and can't tell whisky from pot lye any time of day. Elect me Sheriff and I'll see if I can't bring him to reason. Or get you a more reasonable man for the job."

"Anybody who'd kick about this place would kick about being hung," Devlin said.

"What's the difference?" Abel asked.

"It's a free country, Abel," Dandie said. "You tell us."

"No," Abel replied, "there's been too much talk here already. It's up to somebody to do something. Somebody's got to do the work while the rest of you blab. That job's for me and Mary. And Emma." Without another word, Mary and Emma following him, he headed for the house.

Link got slowly to his feet, brushing off cake crumbs as he rose. "You'll keep in mind what I told you this morning, Abel? No going off the place."

Abel, at that, turned around and came back to the creek bank. He was a medium-sized man, not bad looking, if you left the redness and rigidity out of the account, and he drew himself up now and looked down on the picnickers as if they were a prairie-dog colony come out for a sunning.

"I wish you could all see yourselves," he said, "the way I can." He paused and ran his eyes over them one by one, his face, as he did so, settling into long, down-curving lines of dislike. "Squatting there in the wreckage of your food and fireworks. A nasty sight if I ever saw one. Pussy with food and full of suffering, but not a one of you with gumption enough to do anything about it. You been talking about the day it is and the country it is, and elect me Sheriff and the kingdom of heaven'll be at hand. It won't be. You ain't happy and no Fourth, sixth or seventh of July will turn the trick. No new Sheriff, no go west or no stay home either, no new wars or old battles. Something's been lost out of the world and until it's found everything else had 'bout as well stop. But cheer up, friends. My leads are getting stronger every day. Every day I'm a step nearer finding it. Maybe not today or tomorrow, but you hold yourselves in readiness, and I'll work."

He stood looking at them for a few seconds and as he did so the lines of disapproval in his face softened. "Poor people," he said. "Poor misguided fools. Full of laughter. But trust me. I'll make it possible for you to cry. You won't be afraid to cry when the lost's found. The danger will be gone from it."

Having reassured them he turned cheerfully about and went up the hill with stiff-backed zeal.

Link called after him, "Where are you heading, Abel?"

Abel, without stopping, called over his shoulder, "I don't know the answer to that myself."

"I can give you the answer: not off this Farm."

Abel, at that, broke into a run. Link, already on his feet, followed him, first at a rapid walk, then, as Abel drew away from him, sprinting. The path Abel was following lay uphill over loose stones and depressions which the grass hid. Neither man was a natural runner and both were past the age of easy running. Link turned finally and called Dandie. "Give me a hand here, Dandie."

Dandie quickly overhauled his father. "What's your plan?"

"Catch him first," Link wheezed, slackening speed and motioning Dandie on. Dandie had Abel by the arm when Link drew abreast them. "What's next on the program?" Dandie asked, holding the plunging, threshing Abel like a fish hooked, but still full of fight. "I don't want to keep this up all day."

Ferris, arriving at that minute, hunted for another available handhold on Abel. "I'll help you with him, Dandie," he volunteered.

"You go on back to the picnic, Ferris," Link told him. "Dandie and me can handle him all right."

Ferris went back faster than he'd come. "You put somebody's nose out of joint then," Dandie told his father.

"We got more important noses than his to consider just now. I don't want any crowd gathering on this. Abel, you heard me tell you this morning you weren't to leave the place. Didn't you?"

Still bucking and rearing, Abel said, "I heard you."

"You willing to abide by it?"

"No. I hear voices that drown yours out."

"That being the case, I've got no choice but to lock you up. For your own good."

"Everybody so unselfish," Dandie observed. "Abel digging for your good, and you locking him up for his good and neither one liking it. I just work for Dandie, say so, and everybody's happy."

"Don't preen yourself too soon," Link advised. "You ain't working for yourself now, and Abel don't like it. Abel, I'm running this Farm, and no matter how many other voices you hear you're going to listen to mine. I'm going to put you where you can cool off overnight, and by morning I hope you'll have come to your senses. Now you can walk back up to the house like a gentleman or you can keep up what you're doing and we'll drag you. You can have your choice."

He didn't, actually, have any choice. Dandie had taken a turn on his arm which made anything but gentlemanly walking out of the question.

Link, when he came back from the job of locking up Abel, had brought with him the thermometer which usually hung beside the kitchen door. It had stood at 96 degrees when, at three o'clock, he put it in the crotch of the sycamore that shaded the picnic ground. At four, Ferris, who had nothing better to do, went over to see if it had fallen any. It had, the temperature was now 92 degrees.

Em and the Creagan girls were back in the water again. Upstream, where you could swim without barking your knees on the creek's bottom, Dandie and the other young bucks were cooling off. Nothing had been said to Ferris about joining them, and he didn't care about Dandie's company anyway. Link and Manlief, after some wading, sat on the foot-bridge, their pants still rolled up, talking. Pigs, no doubt, Ferris thought. Nory was stretched out (Dandie had put his hat over her eyes before he went swimming), sound asleep at the very edge of the tablecloth, undisturbed by the cackle of the old ladies all about her. The older men had gone back to their horseshoe-pitching. Ferris listened to the clang of ringers and the shouts that followed with some longing; but after what had happened that morning he couldn't very well join them. On the other side of the stream—they had crossed the foot-bridge when the clearing-up was over—Lib and Cate sat at the foot of a clump of willows, talking.

Ferris thought for a minute of calling to Cate and asking her if she wasn't about ready to go home. The entire day, as far as he was concerned, was a failure, one unpleasantness after another. Though, he supposed if he were to suggest to Cate now that they go home, there'd be one further unpleasantness: the whole Conboy clan yelling at him that he was spoiling Cate's visit. Cate was over there now talking to her mother as if totally forgetful that she had a husband. One thing this day had taught him: he had a jealous mother-in-law. Lib certainly resented it if Cate paid any attention to him.

He threw a twig he'd been peeling into the creek. Em threw it out, back at his feet as if anything touched by him would pollute Conboy water. His first thought was to ignore it, but he decided that this would be weak. Who was to determine what he could and could not throw into creeks! Himself or a twelve-year-old girl? He tossed it back in the water and walked hurriedly off determined not to get involved in an undignified twig-throwing duel with a child. All he asked in the world was so little: to be accepted and valued, not as something unusual or heroic—he didn't claim that—but in and for himself, for his own virtues and merits and here and now; today, before Cate's eyes and in her own home.

Without knowing it, he was half-way to the house. Mag, bringing an installment of supper supplies to the creek, paused to advise him. "Better take that collar off before you have a stroke, boy. You'll blow up, you leave that on much longer, and make your bride a widow."

Ferris felt the prospect pleased her. "I'm used to wearing a collar," he told her.

Arrived at the house he didn't know what to do and went into the summerhouse and sat there, half smothered by the heat and the nasty, thick honeysuckle scent. He kept hoping that Cate would miss him and would come this way looking for him. He thought he heard her call once or twice and didn't answer, picturing her disappointment and concern. But the sounds he had heard were not Cate; and from enjoying the idea of repulsing her he was swept into repulsions opposite, great longing, a longing so overwhelming that he felt he could, by will alone, conjure up the sounds of her approach out of the windmill's creaking or Abel's muttering from his lock-up room. The summerhouse was half dark, and on the benches that ran its length he and Cate could make love, right in the midst of all the Conboys, and never be detected. He was leaning back, lost in this dream, when a hen wandered in, one suspicious step at a time, her head shooting backward and forward like a snake's. He shooed her out, but his dream went with her and he went outside too and, hearing Abel once more, had a kind thought. He had seen him, as he came up from the creek, standing, red face close to the barred door of the wash-house, gazing at the summer world from which he was excluded.

There wasn't, in the Poor House kitchen stripped of victuals for the picnic, much choice as to what he could fix in the way of a snack for Abel. But what there was, he fixed in an appetizing manner: two neatly spread apple-butter sandwiches and a glass of cool buttermilk. He set the glass on the ground, while he poked the sandwiches through the bars. "I had an idea everybody else'd forget your supper. All that excitement down at the creek."

"All that celebrating," Abel said, taking a sandwich in each hand.

Ferris agreed. "They're pretty much taken up with themselves down there, all right."

"Fireworks down there," Abel said, "and apple butter here. And it's all one."

He lifted his hands, a sandwich in each, and with precisely timed movements sent both flying edgewise between the bars. They landed rolling, then fell apart and lay still, four slices of bread, the apple butter glistening in the sun and the glass of buttermilk near enough to look as if a picnic were being spread there in the dust of the back yard. While Ferris gazed at the ruins of his sandwiches, the hen who had disturbed his summerhouse dream came flying, wings outspread, to the feast.

"Why did you do that?" Ferris asked Abel.

Abel said, "You're a fool. I don't want anything from you."

Another hen appeared and Ferris kicked at her and missed; and aimed again and lifted the slice the hen had been after, and had been scared away from, high in the air. Then he ran back down to the creek and went directly to Lib who, with Mag, was spreading out the supper things.

"Where's my wife?" he demanded.

"Cate?" Lib asked, and as if he might have more than one wife.

He wouldn't accommodate her. "My wife," he repeated obstinately.

"Cate," Lib said, not budging either, "went for a little walk upstream."

He followed the path which was narrow and wound between the trees. Fox grapes garlanded it and wild blackberries hedged it and heat, without air, flowed along its curves. He felt as if Mag's prediction about blowing up were about to come true. He took off his collar and threw it, with a momentary flick of amusement as to what Em would think when it came floating past her, into the creek. He unbuttoned the first two or three buttons of his shirt, mopped his wet chest and face with his tie, then threw his tie after his collar.

"Cate," he called, "Cate."

To his surprise she answered from near at hand. "Cate," he called again, and in a minute or two he came on her, seated calmly on a stump, facing the creek and watching—she didn't lift her eyes—the flow of the water. Her lavender skirt billowed out over the stump with a kind of exasperating party elegance—as if she were superior to all the day's mishaps. The heat had done nothing to her but make her cheeks pinker and her hair curlier. With her switch off and her hair standing on end in this tomboy way she was the Cate he had seen kick higher and higher until her frilled drawers and the curve of her thigh showed plainly. The purpose of the switch had not been to do away with that Cate—only to hide her from outsiders. He could not understand how he had ever been able to capture that girl—or this one. He felt the same wonder, married to Cate, he had felt as a boy when he had captured a fox and semi-tamed it; the same desire to fondle and the same fear. Soft, soft, but wild and not to be depended on.

"Cate?" he asked again, but Cate had nothing to say. Not "Poor Ferris, are you hot?" or "Let's go home," or "I have missed you."

His lips started to form an often-spoken question: "Cate, do you love me?" but he choked it down. Oh, always asking, he rebuked himself, always asking permission of somebody, even your wife. You know she loves you. And these words, though he spoke them to himself, sounded in his ears with a nerve-fluttering conviction. She loves you and she is your wife.

He looked at Cate more closely, seeing more exactly what kind of person she was, this girl who loved him and belonged to him. Looking, he became breathless. His heart-beat jarred him. It was a good thing he had thrown away his collar. Why had he been so worked up, earlier, about horseshoe-pitching? And Em's throwing twigs out of the creek? And locked-up crazy men? He was the crazy man himself, with a wife like Cate, to be concerned about such things. He went unsteadily, lurching over an unevenness in the ground which his eyes told him wasn't there, toward her. At the back of his throat, at the very roots of his tongue, he felt a tingling and fluttering which threatened to choke him and which kept him swallowing and swallowing. At last his hands touched her and he steadied himself leaning against her; then this unsteadiness overcome, he began to unbutton Cate's bodice.

Cate protested and he had expected her to: the struggle was a pleasurable part of what he had anticipated.

"Ferris," she whispered. "It's broad daylight. There are people all around. You mustn't. Please stop."

It was not broad daylight; the sun was either down or soon would be—the creek had already turned yellow—and as for people, what person had once that day thought of him? But the day's meannesses and slights were slipping from him and he pulled Cate up off her stump and out of her water-gazing and meditating.

"Ferris, what's the matter with you?"

Let her struggle, protest, scream. Under the circumstances—he admitted to himself that it wasn't dark—it was to be expected. She protested, she struggled, but she didn't scream. "Don't, Ferris, don't. Someone will see us." But Cate was a strong girl. She could get away, he felt sure, if she wanted to; and all this, "Don't, Ferris, don't, Ferris" was no more than what she thought was required of her. Then, all at once, as if she had carefully protected herself from the knowledge of what was happening until it was just too late, she began really to try to get away. He knew her heart wasn't in it though, and he held her, lying full length on the ground, where all her efforts were useless. And all her "Don'ts" and "Stops" were useless, and finally her crying. Her dress was in the way, but he was feeding on difficulties now and could take care of that, too. She was quiet finally and her face, slippery with tears, was unmoving when his hands touched it. He hadn't intended to ask the question he did, but it was wrung from him. "Cate, do you love me?"

He awaited the answer—but with no uncertainty: she always said yes.

She said, "I hate you, Ferris Thompson. I hate everything about you and wish you were dead."

Ferris went away but Cate stayed where she was. No one called her to supper and she thought that Ferris had perhaps told them that she had gone to the house. After a while she saw that the sun had gone down because the creek was red. A little later the creek was the same color as the tree trunks, and she knew that the day was over. The next time she opened her eyes the creek carried on its moving surface a sprinkling of early starlight.

She told herself, You could have stopped him. There was no reply to this. After a while she asked herself, Why didn't you? Her mind ran away from this question and she saw a bird flash low over the surface of the water as if picking up crumbs of light, the last shining unharvested seeds. But the question was asked again, "Why didn't you?"

I said no in every way.

"Except fight, except scream."

That was too humiliating.

"There's nothing humiliating about saying no."

Humiliating to him. The worst thing, I should think, that could happen to anyone. And I am like Papa. It is easier to kill than to hurt.

"There wasn't any question of killing—you know that. There was some question of dying, though."

Dying?

"You died some this afternoon."

My mind is alive and free, that's all that counts. What happens to my body doesn't matter.

"It matters."

It doesn't. If I had fought and struggled I would've been a part of what happened. But I didn't. I went away and now I am not a part of it.

"You are a part of it."

But he was in the wrong.

"Yes, he was in the wrong. He will almost always be in the wrong. Is that any satisfaction to you?"

I hate him.

"How can you hate your own husband?"

Oh, how can I? But I do. I hate the shape of his face and the sound of his voice and the babylike way he puckers up his mouth when he wants a kiss. And all his rubbings. And rubbery kisses and damp palaverings.

"You should've found this out before you married him."

I thought marriage would change it.

"You aren't perfect yourself, you know."

That hasn't anything to do with love or hate.

"You, such an expert on love and hate, why did you marry him then, a person you hate?"

Because I didn't know I hated him. Because he was the opposite of all the terrible things that had happened. Because I thought he would help me to be good.

"And loving and being good don't go together?"

That's what I thought.

"But hating and being good go together?"

I don't know.

"You used to know."

Used to?

"With Christie."

But oh, no, no. She wouldn't listen to that or think of it. She turned onto her face and laid her cheek against the earth and was ready once more to bleed and make vows. She explained herself, justified herself, to Christie now. I married for the best reasons, I thought.

"You knew better than that."

Oh, no, I didn't. I swear I didn't.

"Mag told you."

Was that what Mag was saying?

"I told you."

She scooped up sand and earth and rubbed her face with it. Christie, Christie. She sat up, resting her face against her updrawn knees and began to cry. She saw Christie again, the olive cheeks and the dark precise eyebrows. Her hands relaxed, letting the sand and gravel slide away and she rested quietly, humped over against her supporting knees. She saw how Christie walked, the strange little up-spring at the end of each stride. And how he sat, ankle on knee outlining with his crossed legs a kite-shaped space. And she remembered how he had come to her—was it less than a year ago?—when no one else had noticed her, and had taken her cape and asked her to dance. And had learned to dance so quickly, shouting and singing, much better before the evening was over than boys who'd been going to play-parties all their lives. Christie, Christie. In the weeks when she had not let herself think of him, memories and images had piled up and they rained down on her now so that she was more sensible of Christie than of herself or where she was.

After a long time she was aware, through her closed lids, of light. She opened her eyes and saw the first of Dandie's fireworks gushing upward; fountains red and gold rose above the trees, then fell and faded toward them. Streamers of sparks; sky-rockets with rainbow colors, leaping and resting and leaping. The sky above the trees was veined with lights, cobwebbed. A catharine-wheel went off and she could see it now and then through the trees, turning like a flight of trained lightning-bugs. A Mount Vesuvius erupted, blew its head off and dropped, hissing into the creek.

When next she opened her eyes, she thought it was deep into the night. The fireworks were over and the picnickers gone back to the house. She got up very slowly and felt her way through the trees to the creek. She wanted to wash herself and tidy up before she saw anyone. At the creek's edge she heard a sound which stopped her in her tracks. She leaned against a tree, her mind, which didn't want to explore the sound, busying itself with deciding by the feel what the tree was: her hand slid up and down the trunk while her mind said; sycamore, willow, poplar, alder, beech. But it recognized the sound and named it. It was a human sound, the sound of a man who was sick, a moan.

"Who's there?" she whispered.

The sound stopped.

"Who is there?" she repeated.

"Cate?" the voice asked.

"Yes," she said, "who are you?"

"Ned. Come on down here."

"Ned? What's the matter? Are you sick?"

The groans broke forth again, and guided by their sound she felt her way toward him. She touched him before she saw him, then knelt beside him. "What's the matter, Neddy. Are you sick?"

He groaned for a while before answering. "Broken, broken," he said finally.

She touched his forehead, it was burning beneath her hand, and asked, "Are you drunk, Neddy?"

He controlled his groans enough to say, "I wish to God I was."

"They've been looking for you all day."

"I just got here. My leg's broke. I fell off a cliff upstream and I've been crawling toward help ever since."

Cate said, "I'll run get Papa."

"Splash me," Neddy said, "splash me first."

She dipped up handfuls of water from the creek and let them trickle over his face and chest. By the time she had finished with him she was soaking herself; but she didn't care, her dress was already ruined and she couldn't imagine ever again being interested in what anyone thought of her looks.

Neddy asked, "What's the matter with you? What you down here for this time of the night?"

She couldn't think of any answer except the true one, and after a few more groans Neddy asked, "You sick too?"

She told him the truth then. "I hate my husband."

Neddy said, "That's one of the worst sicknesses all right. But you won't die of it."

"No," she said. "That's the trouble. I have to go on living."

Up at the house she found Link, Lib, and Ferris sitting in the kitchen. Nory and Dandie had gone on home. Ferris, after one glance at her, kept his eyes on the floor.

Link said, "I was just getting ready to send out a search-party for you, but your husband here said you were all right."

She said, "Yes, I'm all right."

"What's happened to your dress?" Lib asked. "You fall in the creek?"

Ferris lifted his head and gave her a momentary beseeching look. "No," she answered. "I've been helping Neddy. He's down at the creek with a broken leg. I've been dipping water on him."

Link rousted out Manlief and Hoxie to help him with carrying Neddy up to the house. "Ferris," he said, while those two were dressing, "would you mind driving into The Junction for the doctor? I hate to ask you, but except for Manlief there's no one else on the place to ask to go—and I may need his help here."

Ferris went quickly, eyes still downcast. Link stepped back into the kitchen after Manlief and Hoxie had left for the creek. "It's a pity to have to start up a fire on a night like this, Lib, but I reckon we ought to have some hot water on hand when the doctor gets here."

Cate sat huddled in her chair watching her mother start the fire and fill the kettles. Ordinarily she would've helped, but tonight she felt too broken, too sorrowful to move. Lib, not usually very sensitive to people's physical states, evidently understood her tiredness. "Why don't you stay here tonight, Cate? There's no sense your driving on back to the Thompsons' tonight. You can go to bed right away, not wait for Ferris to get back."

"Has Em gone to bed yet?" Cate asked.

"I don't know," Lib said. "I've got an idea she and Mary are still out talking to that old rip of a James. I let them take some supper out to him. He'd ought, by rights, be kept on bread and water for a week or so, defying Link the way he did."

"Could I sleep in my old room? With Em?"

Lib, who had been moving about the kitchen setting things to rights, stopped and gave Cate a long look. Cate said nothing and didn't care what her mother thought. Lib went over and poured herself a glass of new milk from a bucket still sitting unstrained on the table. She took a drink before replying, then said, "It would be a good idea to sleep there. Ferris won't be waking you up when he comes in that way."

Em, coming into her room after her talk with the Abels, perplexed and heavy with knowledge, was surprised and happy to see Cate. Cate diverted her mind from the decision she had to make. She sat down on her bed, pulled up her knees and rested her face against them. Cate was at the table, writing; and except that she looked half-drowned, and a little crazy too with her hair dried in spikes and her dress dirty and torn, it might've been last year and Cate unmarried.

"Are you going to stay here all night?"

"Yes," Cate said.

"Here, in this room?"

"Do you care?"

"Oh, no. You're welcome. It'll be like old times." Cate paused in her writing and Em asked, "Cate, did you ever miss me?"

"Yes," she said. "Yes, Em, I missed you terribly."

Em was shaken and astounded by that "terribly." "Terribly," she repeated, seeing pictures of Cate's life at the Thompsons' she had never seen before. "Cate, is marriage quite a trial sometimes? Especially with Ferris?"

Cate gave her a look that opened momentarily to places Em did not care to see, and she said hurriedly, "I expect I'm interrupting your writing?"

"No," Cate said. "I've got all night to write. It's going to be too hot to sleep."

"Did you get the pen and paper out of my casket?"

"Yes. But I didn't look at any of your things. I told you I wouldn't and I won't."

"Maybe you'd ought to've looked," Em said in a low voice. "Maybe it's your duty."

"If it's my duty to read anything in there you'll have to tell me," Cate said, and went back to her writing.

Em thought about doing that, about telling Cate what she knew and letting her decide what should be done. Or just tell her, to have someone to share the burden of knowing with. Then the memory of the last time she'd told Cate anything came to her, and she buried her face against her knees so that she couldn't see Cate's face. But shutting out Cate's face wasn't enough to shut out what Cate had brought upon her and upon Doss. And closing her eyes only made the pictures she saw clearer: Doss in the kitchen, shame-faced, while his pictures were burned; Link upstairs while she stood there, her coat on the floor at her feet. And afterwards Lib taking hold of her coat, shaking her and saying, "Take that coat off, miss, and let us see what you're so proud of." And Doss dragged off to the jail room. All that from Cate's telling.

Her heart hardened against them all, especially her father and mother; but it had started with Cate, with telling her what she knew. Never tell anything, she had decided then. Not vowed, because she could remember how things had gone without that. Now, she told herself, you know exactly what is going to happen. It's not anything very good, but at least you know what it is, not the worst thing in the world anyway. And if you tell? Who knows what'll happen? You know exactly what Mary'll do. And she trusts you and they don't, and tells you everything and they don't, and loves you and they don't. If you told you'd be the worst traitor in the world.

With her decision made, she opened her eyes, dropped her legs flat to the bed and watched Cate write.

"Are you writing to Christie?" she asked.

"What makes you think I'm writing to Christie?" Cate asked in a very low voice, a frightened voice, Em thought.

"The way you look." She waited for Cate to ask her how that was, but all Cate said was, "Yes, I'm writing to Christie."

Cate bent her head again to her tablet and Em watched silently. Presently she heard Ferris' buggy turn into the driveway and a little later the doctor's. She got off the bed. "I'm going out to watch Neddy have his leg set," she told Cate. "It's broken in two places. Why don't you come? It might be the only chance you'll ever have to see a leg set."

"No," Cate said. "I'm too tired."

"You look dead," Em said truthfully. "Loan me the pen and a piece of paper, will you?"

Using the casket as a desk she wrote, "Mary is going to do away with the pigs." She lifted the casket lid and put the folded sheet with the other communications of a similar nature—the facts and opinions with which she would not trust her family, a considerable stack by this time. Then she closed the lid and handed the pen back to Cate.

"Thanks," she said.

Cate said nothing and still Em lingered, in spite of the inviting sounds in the kitchen. Poor Cate, bent over the table, her small square face resting between her hands as if her neck alone wasn't strong enough to hold her head up. It would've been better, it came to Em, if I could've been the big sister and Cate the little one—as it was, she didn't know what to do or say.

"I'll call you," she suggested, "if it's real interesting."

"No, I'm going to bed."

"Well, give Christie my love."

Cate looked as if she was about to cry. "Do you mean that?"

"Oh, yes. Christie was always real brotherly to me."

Cate, as soon as Em left, finished her letter quickly. When she put the writing materials back in the casket she saw Em's latest note to herself, the newly folded sheet half open so that she read, in spite of herself, the word "Mary." For a second, remembering Em's "Maybe it's your duty to read them," her hand hovered over the sheet. Then quickly she closed the lid of the casket. It would be weak and dishonorable to read a word. And strong, honorable Cate Conboy was an image which just now greatly needed strengthening in her mind.

She blew out the lamp and got ready for bed in the dark. She stood at the window for a while looking at the stars; it seemed a long time since she had seen them. Then she said, "Christie, Christie," and lay down in the room she had left so happily two months ago.

15

CATE's letter was forwarded from Indianapolis to Uncle Wes, where Christie was taking a vacation from his insurance selling. The mail arrived each morning between ten and twelve, depending upon the amount of business and gossip encountered by the rural delivery man en route. On the morning of the ninth he was held up by a lot of stamp selling and C.O.D.'s and it was almost noon before he reached the farm at Stony Brook. He put Uncle Wes' *Farm and Fireside,* and a redirected letter for the Copes' visitor, Mr. Christian Fraser, in the mailbox, waved to the Copes, who were playing croquet on their front lawn, then clucked up his horse, hopeful of making Bentonville in time for a hot dinner with his sister who lived there.

"I'll go get the mail," Christie said, but Uncle Wes, who resented any lack of enthusiasm for croquet, told him, "Let the mail wait. It's your shot. You're not expecting anything special, are you?"

"Not me. I don't expect a thing, special or otherwise. You're the one who's always hot-footing it down after the mail."

"It's your *Farm and Fireside* day, Papa," Sylvy said. "Have you forgotten that?"

"I know what day it is," Uncle Wes told his daughter. "Now you be quiet while Christie makes this shot. You're dead on me, Christie, so no use eyeing my ball."

Uncle Wes' liking for croquet was genuine. Sometimes he wondered what he had done all of his youth without this clean, cheerful, healthful game. What had they all done in the hours before dinner and after supper without croquet? And he was good at it; he could beat Sylvy and Christie with one hand tied behind his back. But beyond his skill and the pleasure he took in the clack of the balls and their pretty brightness as they rolled across the smooth grass was the opportunity the game gave him to be with Christie and Sylvy. He basked in their happiness, especially Sylvy's. For a number of years he had been afraid that Sylvy would never marry, and he believed in marriage. He had been happily married himself, and the unmarried state seemed completely unnatural to him, a kind of half-living, about equal to spending your life in a strait jacket. He would've rejoiced, for Sylvy, if she had found herself nothing better for a husband than a middle-aged widower with a houseful of children; but she had found someone much better. Christie, for all his didoes, all the uncertainties of his job and his lack of any knowledge of farming, was, he thought, the right husband for Sylvy. Sylvy was a quiet girl—and though he knew well enough that quiet waters don't always run deep, he felt Sylvy had depths that the widower and his children might never have plumbed. Christie, for all he was five years younger than Sylvy, and for all his high spirits and flapdoodle, had in him some quality which was not going to be fooled by quietness or content with surfaces. He would want for a wife all the Sylvy there was: not just the fine housekeeper and the dutiful church-worker and the pretty woman. Though Sylvy's looks reassured him concerning the marriage. Sylvy was a woman like her mother who, at twelve, had passed for sixteen and was, in her fifties, still as dark and glowing as she had been in her handsome thirties. She would not be saddling the boy, Christie, with a middle-aged wife. He looked up thinking this and surprised them in a kiss.

"Come on, you two," he said, "and play croquet. You've got all the rest of the day for courting."

"No time like the present," Christie said, but he left Sylvy, made his shot and missed the wicket.

Uncle Wes, in spite of his sympathy for love, didn't believe that it should interfere with croquet. "Look what you've done," he told Christie, "not keeping your mind on the game."

"Well, you rushed me," Christie complained. "Come on, Sylvy. It's up to you, now. You get a whack at the old man and don't let his gray hairs soften your heart the way they did mine. Knock him clear to kingdom come."

As she crossed the grass, Christie watched Sylvy, a summer picture in her white skirt and white shirtwaist with a pink bow in her dark hair and a matching pink rose in her belt. Or, not a summer picture, but summer itself, he thought. Sylvy has summer's bloom and warmth, its ripeness and flowering. She is August, he thought, the sultry month, the month when corn is in the milk and the wheat is shocked. Was it her dark hair put him in mind of Damson plums? Of swallows in August and their flutterings in the dusty, midday shadow of the peaked barn roof? And the first yellow willow leaves on the streams?

"Hurry up, August," he called.

Sylvy turned around inquiringly. "Yes, I'm talking to you," Christie told her, "and don't look so startled."

"August?" she asked.

"My harvest home, my summer's bounty."

Sylvy came toward him, trailing her mallet in the grass.

"Christie, what're you talking about?"

"Come on, come on," Uncle Wes called to them. "Either give up, or play. And talk up so's I can hear you, if you're going to talk at all. You want to give up?"

"No," Christie said, "we don't. Sylvy's going to put you clear out in the driveway. Go on, Sylvy."

How was it possible, he asked himself, that two months ago he had been on the point of marrying another girl? Now Sylvy seemed destined to be his wife. And Cate destined to be no more than a girl he had loved unhappily and, happily, not married. What had happened appeared to be the result of chance, since, if Cate hadn't jilted him, he would surely have married her. Still, he couldn't help feeling that chance was working with something which would've been demonstrated anyway, in a short time, without its help; all that had been needed, he felt, was a little more time, and tendencies and inclinations deep in his make-up would have drawn him to Sylvy. Only Sylvy had not needed time nor required events outside herself to open her eyes, as he had—and as Cate had. Sylvy had known, she had told him, that she loved him and would marry him and no one else on that very first afternoon when they had stayed in the dining-room talking. "I knew then that I would marry you—that night, if you asked me. Or whenever you did ask me. Or love you without being married to you. By the time I found that cut-glass pitcher I was looking for I had forgotten what to do with it, I had traveled such a long ways from lemonade. All I could think of was, I love him. I love him so much."

How different from Cate. It didn't seem strange to him that Cate was often in his mind or that he often compared and contrasted her with Sylvy. Poor Cate! Without knowing her, how would he ever have been able to appreciate Sylvy? Cate, with her spring blow-warm, blow-cold, that made the calm, settled bitterness of winter seem preferable.

But his love now for Sylvy didn't mean he hadn't suffered when Cate threw him over. After he'd seen her for the last time, that evening in the Poor House, he must've been out of his mind. He had whipped up Ajax in the hope that a runaway would put an end to his misery, and that failing, he'd sat in a saloon drinking whisky he wasn't accustomed to, and didn't want, until he was drunk. And had found some relief finally by picking a quarrel so that he had finished the evening in peaceful calm, knocked clear beyond any memory of, or sorrow concerning, who had or had not jilted him.

In spite of all this he didn't consider himself as having been caught "on the rebound," as they said. His love for Sylvy had been there before he ever saw Cate, hidden by the nearness of his mother's death, by the fact that Sylvy was his cousin, was older than he was—even by the fact that she had loved him before he knew that he loved her. Fool that he was then—was it only a year ago?—he had had some feeling that love easily come by weighed light in the scales. (Thank you, Cate, for teaching me the contrary lesson.) He had believed then that a girl ready to declare her love, at the first asking, or even unasked, was like a windfall apple—nothing much to offer but a kind of bruised over-ripeness. Now he saw that windfalls, resulting from the luck of a perfect joining of weather and readiness, had a sweetness that tree-picked fruit could never equal.

Uncle Wes' exclamation, as Sylvy's shot went wide, recalled him to the game. "Good-by, children," Uncle Wes said. "I'll roll on home now."

"You'd think he could be content with winning—without having to crow about it too," Christie said.

"Can you learn to put up with a father-in-law like that, Christie?"

"You'll have to be awfully good to me and awfully loving to make up to me for him. Look at the girls I could've married who were orphans. Or whose fathers don't know a croquet mallet from a pump-handle. And with all that to choose from I have to fall heir to this old croquet fiend for a father-in-law. This lucky old croquet fiend."

"Don't think I don't hear you," Uncle Wes said, lining himself up for the two final wickets. "I hear you and luck don't play any part in it. Croquet's a game of skill."

"It's going to take an awful lot of hugging and kissing to reconcile me to a father-in-law like that," Christie said. "Boasting how good he is."

Sylvy dropped her mallet and came to him. "I will kiss you and hug you. Now," she asked later, "are you reconciled?"

"No," he said, "it'll take a little more."

Up ahead, unaware that behind him the croquet game had fallen to pieces, Uncle Wes rolled smoothly on toward the victory he had predicted.

Afterwards, at dinner, Uncle Wes looked up from his peach-pie. "I handed you your letter, didn't I, Christie?"

"Letter?" Christie repeated. "I didn't see any letter."

"You don't half know what's going on these days, Christie. Look in your pockets."

Christie looked, but found no letter.

"I gave it to you. I distinctly remember. Did you leave it out in the lawn swing when you and Sylvy were there?"

"Maybe," Christie said, "I did."

After dinner he and Sylvy went out once more to the lawn swing. The swing, so large it could easily hold six, was a kind of cross between a land-locked boat and a sea-going stage-coach. There were sounds and motions reminiscent of both in its swaying and squeaking. A couple in it was just as visible as though they sat in the center of the open lawn, but either the floor beneath their feet or the roof over their heads always succeeded in convincing them that they were as hidden as in any parlor—and safer from intrusions: for they were traveling, weren't they?

Sylvy and Christie shared this illusion—and though Christie's letter lay on the floor of the swing, plain as day, they felt no hurry to get to it, but turned toward each other the minute they were seated; eyes first searching and exploring, asking and promising so much that the kiss itself, when it came, was almost a recession from the look. Almost but not quite.

"Stop, Christie," Sylvy said. Sometimes she wondered what would happen if he didn't stop. Would she faint finally, swoon away with love like a romantic heroine in a book? She thought she actually would. For that was what she felt, faintness and dizziness, so that it was not coquetry which made her finally cry, "Don't, Christie, don't. I have to breathe." For she had no intention of wasting any time in swooning. She was going to be alive for every minute of the years that were left to her, alive, married to Christie, waking every morning to the unbelievable delight of another day to be with him and to love him. It *was* unbelievable. Girls who fall in love and marry at seventeen and eighteen take love and marriage for granted, she thought, the way we old maids never can. For I am an old maid, she assured herself, and soon I would've been happy for almost any husband rather than keep on with this feeling that I was missing half of life. And then Christie. To have watched him fall in love, under my very eyes with someone else, and to have had him, finally, return of his own free will to me. It was almost too much to believe. She would never have enough, she felt, even of such a simple happiness as looking at him.

It was strange in the months after he had left last summer the trouble she had had trying to recall the exact outlines of his face. She loved him so much that at times she felt she *was* Christie; but she could recall the face of a pack peddler who had stopped at the house the summer before better than she could Christie's. She knew certain facts about his face and could make a catalog of them: dark straight hair rising from a widow's peak; eyes which appeared, in a sidewise glance, to be concentric rings of deepening shades of gray; upper lip with a deep central break; scar an inch above and paralleling one jaw; two threadlike scars on the outer edge of the palm of the left hand. All these she could see and enumerate; but when she had added them up they did not make Christie, and it seemed a great misery to her in those days that since Cate had the whole man she could not at least have a distinct and living memory of his face.

It was strange about Cate, too. As things had turned out she was not sorry that Christie had had that time of thinking he was in love with her. If she and Christie had been married when he came down for his first visit after his mother's death, she might never have been sure that he hadn't turned to her for mothering as much as anything else. Now she had no such feeling. He had gone with this other girl—this tomboy kid—and she could understand that too. Cate had just that touch-me-not air which made a boy want to go with her on sight—just to see if he could. And he had discovered (Cate's discovering it first made no difference) that he and Cate weren't suited to each other. Nothing planned, she thought, planned especially, could have been a better safeguard for the happiness of their marriage, and she felt a rush of real tenderness toward Cate—for loving Christie in the first place, as well as for jilting him later.

"Read your letter, Christie," she said, "before we go to town."

She leaned back, eyes closed, and heard him tear open his letter. With the swing gently rocking and the air flowing about her face, she was reminded of a boat and began to think about the trip up the Hudson which she and Christie planned as a part of their honeymoon. The Palisades, people said, outdid the castles on the Rhine for grandeur, and the arm of the swing became the steamer rail in her imagination and behind her closed lids she saw spires and turrets half natural stone, half man-made castle.

The farm sounds brought her back from the Hudson: a door slamming up at the house, the light clatter of the windmill in a sudden lifting of air. Then, quiet again, as if in midafternoon and midsummer, the grain still erect in the field, the season briefly napped, took itself forty winks while it could, before next week's threshing began. After next week they would all look toward winter, the height of summer would have been passed. Now they were suspended at a midway point between the two—and the swing oscillated gently as if it were the very pendulum marking time's passing and summer's peak. But not love's, she thought. Time can do nothing to love, but give it an opportunity to grow and ripen. She put a hand on Christie's knee and in the midst of the general drowsy midafternoon quiet was aware of a more particularized quiet, a small core of absolute silence forming within the larger circle.

"Christie?" she asked.

"Read this," Christie said, and she opened her eyes and he put a single sheet of ruled tablet paper into her hand. "Read it," he said again, as she looked at him inquiringly. "It's from Cate."

She smoothed the sheet doubtfully for a minute, then began to read:

Dear Christie,

I am as surprised to be writing you as I expect you are to hear from me. I know I haven't any right to ask you a favor, but I can't help it. I have to. My asking doesn't mean you have to say yes. You can say no by not answering at all, or by writing me to say you can't do what I ask and that you hate and despise me. I wouldn't blame you if you did either.

The favor I want to ask you is not very big, only to see you for one hour to talk to you. I don't know anyone else to talk to. Who is there? I don't know which way to turn. Oh, I don't know. Would you come for one hour, only? You can watch the clock and leave on the minute and depend on me for no begging to stay as much as one second longer. It seems to me now you used to be very good to me. If you come I can thank you for that anyway.

I should stop writing. All I can say, I have said. I want to see you for one hour. We have had a very bad day here for everyone, not just me. Neddy Oates broke his leg in two places and James Abel, the only one here with a plan for helping people, is locked up in the jail room for defying Papa. This is the way we celebrated the Fourth. I hope you had a happier day. Please come. CATE. Please.

Sylvy said at once, "You must go, Christie. It would weigh on your conscience not to go. She has a right to call on you. You loved her once." She re-read a few lines. "Why, she sounds like a child."

"A married child," Christie said.

"Is there anything?" Sylvy faltered.

"No. There is nothing."

"It doesn't matter one way or the other. I shouldn't have asked that. You must go to see her. For a while you were sure you did love her. Six weeks can't have changed things so you wouldn't be willing to see her for one hour."

"They have, though."

"Then go because it's right and kind." It *was* right and kind that he go, but she had other reasons for urging him. Go to prove

I'm not jealous. Go to prove to me that you can see her and return.

"By the time I get there she's liable to have changed her mind and not want to see me at all. She doesn't know her own mind from one minute to the next."

"Well, then all you will have lost is a little time on the trip. And your conscience will be clear."

"I could write her, tell her I'm about to be married."

"What does that have to do with it? She's married herself. She's not expecting to throw herself into your arms, is she?"

"Not as long as I can run, she won't, whatever she's expecting."

"And she's not expecting you to propose to her."

"No."

"Then you should go. If you don't, what can I think? Nothing but that you don't trust yourself with her. If you can't go for one hour to answer whatever questions she has to ask, it will surely look to me, Christie, as if you didn't dare to step into her presence." She spoke passionately and was open to a passionate contradiction from Christie.

He replied reasonably, "What questions can she possibly have to ask me that I can help her with in any way? Even if she has a sensible question in the first place. Which I doubt."

"It will help her just to know there isn't any answer. Christie, you mustn't fail her in this. It isn't Cate you'd be saying no to if you don't go, but love. Don't you see? You'd be saying love didn't have any obligations. Oh, Christie, I beg you to go. I don't think I could marry you happily if you didn't." Now, she had said all she was required to say. If Christie refused to go now, it was his own affair.

Christie said, "You think I really ought to go? You think it's my duty?"

"Yes. How could I count on your love if I thought there wasn't enough kindness in it to make you do a small thing like this for a girl you were once engaged to? You do feel some kindness toward Cate, don't you?"

"I suppose so."

"The thing to do is go at once and get it over with."

"You think so?"

[417]

"I do. I think you should catch the three o'clock train. We were going into town anyway. We can go a little earlier."

"How do I get back?"

"Why, on the first train tomorrow morning. I'll meet you. You don't think I want you staying over in that neighborhood any longer than you have to, do you?" She tried to be light, for she was beginning to feel a heaviness in her chest. "Maybe you could even sell a policy or two while you were over there."

"I feel more like taking one out."

He was going to go, then. She put out a hand to stop the swing. "I'll help you pack a bag."

They went together, slowly, toward the house and stopped to tell Uncle Wes, who was on the front porch, feet on the railing, reading his *Farm and Fireside*, about the trip. Uncle Wes closed his paper and slapped his extended legs with it. "The craziest wild-goose chase I ever heard of. Running off, clear across the county, just because some girl crooks her finger at you."

"Cate's not just some girl, Papa," Sylvy said.

"No, she's not and that makes matters all the worse. She's no girl at all. She's a married woman and Christie's one-time sweetheart. No, no," he said, as Sylvy tried to interrupt him, "you can't tell me anything about it. I know the full story down to the last comma. And I seen the girl, too. Don't forget that."

"What do her looks have to do with it? She wants to talk to Christie for one hour only. To ask his advice."

Uncle Wes let his chair down with a bang. "Advice! Is that what she calls it? If I'd had any inkling what was in that letter, I'd of burned it without thinking twice. Advice! If advice is what that girl's after she'd better see me. I can tell her a thing or two and in no uncertain terms."

"Now, Papa," Sylvy said, "no use getting on your high horse. Christie's only trying to do what's right."

"If that's his aim, he don't need to try so hard. Let him stay right here."

"Don't think I don't want to," Christie told him.

"What's to hinder, then?"

"My duty."

Uncle Wes exploded. "Duty! You poor addled boy. I can tell you to a T what's happened. This Conboy girl's had a falling-out with her husband. So she starts thinking about her old beau. Nobody ever appreciated me the way he did, she tells herself, and if I could just see him once more, maybe I could reconcile myself to the mistake I've made. Either that, or she tells herself, I'll just let hubby see what I could've had and that'll bring him to time. That's the size of the business, Christie, I tell you. You go over there and you'll just get yourself mixed up in a family ruckus, do that girl no good and yourself harm."

"I can't just think of myself."

"What's that husband of hers going to think, you coming to see her?"

"It don't matter."

Uncle Wes got up and sent *Farm and Fireside* skimming across the lawn. "What's got into you two? Are you both set on ruining your marriage?"

Sylvy said, "If Christie's seeing for one hour a girl he was once engaged to is going to ruin our marriage, why, it'd better be ruined now than later."

"Seeing for one hour a girl he was once engaged to! Running after a married woman was what we called it in my day."

Christie, who'd been sitting on the porch railing, stood. "I don't know about your day, Uncle Wes. Maybe your intentions with married women weren't all they ought to be. Which doesn't change the fact that all I intend with Cate Conboy is a little common courtesy."

"Mighty common," Uncle Wes agreed. "Mighty, mighty common."

They parted in anger and silence.

And in silence for the first half of the trip, Sylvy and Christie rode into town. When finally they did begin to speak it was not of Cate or the impending parting but of their wedding, the trip to New York and their life after they returned. Presently they were able to laugh and to pretend that, after some shopping, they would be driving back together.

When they reached the mustard-colored depot, which was on the outskirts of town, she walked with Christie to the tracks to await the train. The depot yard was empty, except for a woman in black and a spindly boy sitting at her feet on a roped and bulging telescope.

"Is this train usually on time, do you know?" the woman asked. "If it's going to be late, I'd better take Teddy into the depot out of this sun. He's just come through typhoid."

"It's usually on time in summer," Sylvy told her.

"Is that it, whistling now?"

Sylvy listened but could hear nothing but the hot wind twanging in the telegraph wires overhead. "I think it's just the wires humming," she said.

Christie took her arm and walked her across the yard to the shade of the depot. A few rusty hollyhocks were growing along the depot wall and bumblebees, at work in the purplish blossoms, kept the thin unhealthy plants bending and bobbing. While they watched, Sylvy heard first the whistle of the train as it entered the cut above town, then its long, re-echoing whimper as the banks of the cut tossed the sound back and forth. She waited for herself to say the words that were in her mind: Don't go. Father's right. It's a wild-goose chase, going down there. Stay here. Let's go to the ice-cream parlor, and have a soda, then drive on home. What're *we* doing here anyway? We two, who love each other? How did we ever get started on this, this parting?

But she said nothing and turning around she saw a plume of smoke rise above the trees, transparent, barely visible, like the bloom on a grape.

Christie took her in his arms. "You'll meet the train in the morning?"

"Yes," she said, her face against his chest. "I'll be here. I'll be waiting." She heard the train pulling in but Christie still held her close. The woman called to them, "If you're planning on catching this train, you'll have to come on. It's not going to wait."

"You must go," Sylvy said, and Christie took down his arms. The woman in black stood on the top step of the car gazing anxiously at them. "Do you want to miss it?" she called.

"Do I?" Christie asked.

"You must decide," Sylvy said.

Christie kissed her once more. "I can count on your being here in the morning?"

"You can count on me."

He left her and went directly up the steps and into the car without once looking back. But the woman, as if hungry for someone to love and say good-by to, stood in the vestibule and waved to Sylvy as the train pulled out. Then, as if it had never been there, the train was gone, the plumes of smoke vanished, the telegraph wires humming quietly in the hot wind.

Sylvy walked past the hollyhocks and the little wooden depot to the hitching rack. She sat in the buggy awhile, listening to hear a final train whistle. There was none and finally she unwound the reins from the whip and started on home alone.

11

CATE had the house to herself that day. She put her foot out of bed into the milk-warm air and felt the house's emptiness before she remembered it as fact. She had been ailing, "down in the mouth," Mrs. Thompson called it, since the Fourth, and because of this had been excused from going with Wanda and her mother-in-law to help with the cooking for threshers at their neighbors', the Fawcetts. Ferris and his father were exchanging work with Mr. Fawcett, so the day and the house were hers from sun-up to sundown. Since the Fourth she had been inert and silent, passive as a rock in a stream with time sliding past like water, unregarded. "Let it pass, let it pass," she had heard, like the refrain from a song.

But awakening in this summer morning's heat, alone in the house, the figure changed; the rock came to life and she began to move with time. She stepped from her bed, dropped a dress over her naked body and so, without underclothes or shoes, walked through the house she had dreamed about so much before her marriage, saying, "Summer at the Thompsons'," as if it were a finished thing.

She supposed she had said those words a hundred times in the days before her marriage. She could remember stopping her work at The Farm and seeing this house more plainly than the broom or dust-cloth in her hand; she had seen it, blue-white under the big billowing clouds of midmorning; silvery-white in the evening with the lamplight streaming from its windows onto the delicate-leafed maples. Summer at the Thompsons', she had thought, would be more flowery-smelling than any place else. The summer storms would be fiercer and the quiet afterwards, when she and Wanda and Mrs. Thompson sat in the parlor sipping the cold, greeny-yellow lemonade, would be more noticeable.

And, in that way, it had been really the summer she had imagined; the blazing noons with the sweat trickling with flylike feet; the roads, tunnels of green lit by flowers as big and flaming as winter lanterns. She had gone out to the cornfields, after dark, to listen to the corn growing, to hear the soft thunder of the unfolding leaves. On those nights she had seen heat-lightning tremble at the dark edge of the sky, as if the earth, though cooling, still smoldered a little. And the thunder-storms! Sudden gusty winds would rattle the screens and set the windmill to whining. The hand-shaped leaves on the maples would flutter and cry at the same time; they were the tree's mouths in spite of their shape. The wheat, midway between gold and rust, would be flattened like a carpet. She and Wanda and Mother Thompson would speed to close the windows. They would run from room to room, get two or three loose watery drops on the bosoms of their dresses as the last window was banged down and stand then, with that sign on them of the power outside, listening to the downpour. In ten minutes the storm would be past and steam would rise from the drenched roofs and soaking roads. In these alternations of rain and sun, flowers blossomed with jungle lushness; tiger lilies and sweet sultana and Turk's-caps. Snow-on-the-mountain was the garden's only coolness.

"RECORD-BREAKING HEAT IN THE OHIO VALLEY," the papers said, and she rejoiced that her private pleasure was really great, and publicly recognized. Who wanted tame weather? Blazing summers, freezing winters, great storms, that was how it should be. Full of contradictions, she stood at the bottom of the stairs and longed for climatic disturbances which ask leave of no one, which seize and toss, which engage wholly, leaving no part free, able to assess and calculate.

In the sitting-room the shades had already been pulled against the day's heat; but even in this gloomy light the highly polished furniture gave off a few subdued twinkles. The Thompson house, like the Thompson summer, was all she had imagined—shining, a house without corners, it almost seemed, though of course it was only that the corners were so clean. Or had the little bellows finally blown some of the angle out of the corners, along with the dust? With Lib as a yardstick to measure herself by she had considered herself a housekeeper. Here, she had felt she was no more than a cavedweller, jerked up from the midst of her well-ordered stacks of bones and stones and set down among civilized people. This had suited her. She was of a nature to learn. Besides discovering that she was no housekeeper, by Thompson standards, she had discovered something else and more important: that under new circumstances a new person emerges; one not dreamed of before. This, she saw, was what made travel valuable; not the new places, but the new person you became there. The trouble was, she thought, that this made planning difficult, or even useless. The person you had made your plans for was not the person who arrived.

It was because of this, which she hadn't anticipated, that it had been so useless for her to plan about marriage beforehand. It wasn't only that she hadn't known about marriage; that didn't matter so much. What mattered was that she had been planning for a *person* she didn't know anything about, either—her married self: a person, though, with whom she was becoming day by day more familiar—and liking less and less. Liking less and less, and, she thought, as she ate her breakfast of three saucer peaches and a glass of lukewarm milk, leaving behind. Oh, yes, leaving behind. The knowledge came to her suddenly and joyously, and she went to the kitchen door and gave the peach seeds a far fling and watched where they fell—in Mrs. Thompson's well-tended bed of portulacas. They will be the only things left here in after years as a remembrance of me, she thought, for of course she and Christie were running away together.

As she went back through the empty house she saw that the feeling she had had for it earlier was truly one of good-by. Good-by, good-by. Good-by, dining-room and the butcherman's cuffs of woven straw which Mrs. Thompson made her husband and son wear at meals to spare the tablecloth; good-by, parlor with the piano over which Wanda wept her laughing tears; good-by, sitting-room where Mr. Thompson sat behind the paper whose pages he never turned. And especially, good-by, stairs up which she walked at night with Ferris. Good-by, whole Thompson house, blown clean by a miniature bellows, and good-by, Thompson summer.

Oh, and good-by, Cate Thompson, good-by to the girl who had never existed: Christie is coming.

With that knowledge she ran upstairs as if lifted and wafted. Christie, oh my darling Christie. Her heart, which had been a stone, clenched, closed, untouchable, had opened, was fluid as water; was as easy and sure as a stream running bank to bank down a steady incline to the sea. Her mouth went in smiles, her feet in dancing. My darling, my darling. She admitted everything to herself. It was not advice she had wanted of Christie, or talk. It was Christie himself. She knew quite well that once he came, no words except "Cate," except "Christie," need be spoken. She began to pack, feeling as if she had walked out on the far side of a spell; as if the old witch were melted and the mirror cracked and the princess set free forever.

It never occurred to her that this might not be the day of his coming, any more than it occurred to her to think that he might not come at all. They were one, she and Christie, and this, the earliest day he *could* come after receiving her letter, would bring him to her. For the first time in her life she permitted herself to dwell in a reverie of love-making without self-chastisement. She packed, with Christie's mouth on hers, his arms about her. It was not until midafternoon, with the last small article she owned boxed and ready to go, that the enormity of what she was doing came to her. She was in front of the bureau, taking off her wedding ring and the little ruby engagement ring, when she caught sight of herself in the mirror. What she thought then was not, "You are a married woman planning to run off with another man," for Christie was not another man to her but only Christie, her love; what she thought was, "How can you leave Ferris?" and she went over and touched his pillow with the feeling of a mother abandoning a child. For a while all her earlier happiness left her, and she could not bring herself to write the note telling Ferris what she was doing. She sat at the window looking out across the varicolored summer fields and orchards and remembered the dream she had had, coming home with Ferris that day from Madison, the dream of everlasting contentment in this house. But how could I know? she asked herself. She wrote the note, crying, and put it under Ferris' pillow; and that done, it was as if the parting were over and the elation she had felt when she threw the peach seeds away, came back to her: I am leaving here forever! Christie is coming!

III

JEFFERSON AMES kept Christie company for the last fifteen minutes of his trip to The Junction. "Haven't seen you for some little time."

"No," Christie said.

"Fixed you up with a ride, didn't I, on your first trip?"

"That's right."

"Hear your girl out at the Poor Farm gave you the mitten?"

"That's right. She did."

"Maybe coming down to collect the engagement ring?"

"No," Christie said. "I never got around to giving her a ring."

"I hear she's married the Thompson boy from over Brush Creek way."

"So I've heard."

"You don't appear to be much cut up about it. Figure there are still plenty of good fish in the ocean, eh?"

"Better, probably. I'm going to be married in a couple of months myself."

"I've noticed that once a man gets the fever to marry he don't let any one girl's no stand in the way. Don't seem to matter much to him who the girl is. If he can't get one he'll make do with another. My wife was the third I asked, and all in a month's time. And it sure was God's mercy the first two said no. I can promise you I wouldn't be where I am today if either of the first two'd said yes. You can't tell me there ain't a plan behind it all. Looks like chance maybe, but the Good Book says the hairs of our head are all numbered and if the Lord numbered our hairs, you don't think the women have been skipped over, do you? No, this was all planned out for you and you'll profit by it. Much as you likely took on over the Conboy girl's jilting you, you'll see the time when you'll thank her for it."

"I don't doubt it."

"When was it you first came down this way?"

"Christmas Eve."

"I thought so. Six months makes a big change, don't it?" He motioned toward the green cornfields and the full-leafed orchards, and Christie remembered the wintry desolation of these fields on his first visit to Cate. But he said nothing.

"What's eating you this evening, boy? You got something on your mind?"

"Been wondering when this hot spell would break."

The whistle sounded for The Junction and Mr. Ames got to his feet. "Well, I'm sorry I can't fix you up for a ride again today. This weather surely merits it as much as snow."

"I'm just as happy not to have another ride like that."

"Old Kissing Korby! Well, he got you there, didn't he?"

"Me and the coffin. This time I'd just as lief make the trip without it."

"Visiting The Farm again?"

"No."

"Not planning on heading out Brush Creek way, are you?" When Christie didn't answer Mr. Ames said, "Married women ain't got a thing a girl don't have. Only difference is, it comes a sight higher with them."

No one else got off at The Junction. Christie stepped from the train into a yellow sundown light. People walked the streets with ponderous underwater motions, struggling against heat and twilight like swimmers against a river current. Or sat, or lay, as if water-logged and would never move again unless fiercer tides than those that flowed through The Junction hit them. Two Negroes, with a little spotted dog at their feet, dozed on the baggage car. The dog lifted an ear—to a sound dreamed, for the depot yard was silent—then let it collapse, like a picked dock leaf in the sun. Christie watched the sleepers for a while then told himself to get on to the livery stable. Arrived there, he said, "I'd like to hire a good horse and buggy for about three hours."

The livery stable man was reading, sitting in a tip-tilted chair. He marked his place with a match and said, "Can't accommodate you at the minute. I've got a rig ought to be back in a half hour or so. Nice little chestnut mare. Want me to hold her for you?"

Christie didn't say yes and he didn't say no. He idled back toward the depot where the sleepers still slept. He felt sleepy himself and entertained the idea of lying down by the black men and their dog, sinking beyond the pains of decisions and farewells. He leaned against the baggage car for a minute with eyes shut and when he opened them the sky had grown empty and peaked; the clouds had slipped down to the horizon and from them, or through them, more and more yellow light streamed onto The Junction so that store windows were deep in color, as alive as skins, and the railroad tracks, running away from The Junction— and toward each other—were shining gold. Even the wooden ties were light-soaked. Yellowness filled the air—as if summer had suddenly gone to seed and the pod had broken open and was throwing its bright riches across the town. This is the color of the end of the world, he thought suddenly, a brassiness like judgment trumpets.

One of the Negroes sat up suddenly, thin and right-angled as a blade from a jack-knife. "What's the time, boss?"

Christie touched his pocket. "I've forgotten my watch."

The Negro lifted his eyes, the whites clear and shiny as fresh clabber, to the sky. "It's getting late," he said, vaulted off the baggage car, and walked swiftly away. The dog opened one eye, then shut it. The second Negro never stirred. Christie hoisted himself and sat beside him. "Oh, Cate," he said.

The Negro said, "You say something?"

"No," Christie told him, and the Negro was at once asleep again. Christie gazed into his face which the yellow light turned a little green. But there weren't any answers there.

"I love you, Sylvy," he said, jumped down and began to walk rapidly in the direction of Brush Creek.

A mile out of town Christie reached the turn-off for the Poor Farm. Why not visit Link? he asked himself. See Link, talk to Link. And afterwards borrow a horse and rig of him and drive over to Cate's? He took a tentative step in Cate's direction. Why postpone seeing her? Why not go to her at once, tell her he was about to be married, but that this didn't keep him from wishing her well? Or from wanting to help her in any way he could? It should be easy to see her. A quick walk through the summer dusk would bring him to her. His back was to The Farm, his feet picking up the dust of the Brush Creek road. Cate, Cate. Sylvy was all summer, all warmth and openness. But Cate was warm, too, the warmth of a skyful of spring rain hissing down with the wind behind it upon the unprotected body. Oh, Cate. He opened his arms to that tender violence, then in painful indecision stooped and gathered up a double handful of dust and rubbed it between his palms and threw it finally against the wind so that it came back into his nose and throat and remained to begrime his sweating hands and face.

Behind him was the smudge of light that marked The Junction and he turned toward it imagining the women washing their supper dishes and the children playing one more game of Run Sheep Run in the warm dark before going to bed. He thought of returning there. Sleep on the baggage train and catch the first train in the morning back to Sylvy.

Then, Cate waiting, Sylvy waiting, he began to walk furiously toward The Farm and Link, Link's goodness and reasonableness drawing him on. He skirted a cornfield, the stalks erect and fragrant in the downpour of starlight; kicked through bind-weed and wild morning-glory creepers and stained his shoes with the juices of ripe roadside blackberries, in his hurry to reach The Farm and hear the words of sense Link would speak to him.

IV

CATE had expected Christie at dusk. The Thompsons would not be home until eight or nine. The men intended working again after supper for as long as the light held, while the women would do up the dishes and set the tables for the four o'clock breakfast. She had volunteered to do the evening chores—but the hired man would come home from Fawcetts' for that, and her only responsibility was to set him out a cold snack for his supper.

She spent the last two hours of the afternoon bathing and dressing, decking herself with all the pleasure which had been absent from her wedding-night preparations. When she went down to the porch, the two cows, already milked, were moving back toward the pasture, bags comfortably slack, tails rhythmically slashing at flies. The sun was down, but light still flooded up from behind the rim of earth, golden and warm. She sat in the porch swing for a while, deep in her reverie of Christie's coming, the first words and the first touch and the first kiss. She was content to be there inside that dream without any conjecture as to where Christie really was at that minute or when he would really arrive. But a sudden diminishing in the shrilling cries of katydids and crickets brought her out of her imaginings into a world visibly darkening. Night was coming on and where was Christie?

For the first time it occurred to her that he might not come and she had no more ease. There was, in her chest, a pain as heavy and sharp as though her heart were actually breaking; being torn or crushed. Now that this fear had come to her, nothing could take it away—except the sight of him. She hurried across the lawn and stood by the mailbox where she could see the road in both directions. It was empty; after a while she saw a cloud of dust off to the south, not the direction from which Christie would be expected to come, but a direction from which he *could* come. She willed Christie and Ajax to be in the center of that dust cloud; she shut her eyes until she heard the crunch of wheels and clap of hooves opposite her, then opened them to see Clem Brewster and his girl, arms twined about each other's necks and their horse picking his own gait and possibly his own direction.

After the dust had cleared away she followed the buggy until she reached the spot where the road curved around Fawcetts' wood lot, a dark stand in the fading light, of hardwood, black walnut and hickory and beech. She had made herself walk there slowly. Go slowly, she told herself, and you'll get there at the same time he does. It was a bargain she was making with somebody, and she kept her half of it, she went slowly. But somebody was no bargainer, and there was no sign of Christie. She stayed there as long as she could see. The stars were out and fireflies alight when she got back to the house. Except as pain, she did not exist. She went up to her room and sat on the floor with her elbows on the window-sill gazing out into the deepening darkness.

v

THEY had been threshing all that day at The Farm and a good many of the folks went right from the supper-table to bed, too tired for even a game of checkers. Old Josh Stout, who had had no hand in the threshing, was one of the first to drag off bedward, complaining of his rheumatism. Josh had what Link called "grain" rheumatism, since it always hit him at planting and harvest seasons. As soon as the grain was in the ground, or out of it, Josh limbered up mighty fast.

Hoxie and Nigger Bob, too tough to be tired by a moderate fourteen hours' work and both too simple to pretend that they were, sat in the men's sitting-room playing their own version of checkers.

"You don't care if you win or lose," Bob complained. He stood up and looked at Hoxie morosely. "Your heart ain't in it," he accused him.

"No," Hoxie admitted, "I guess it ain't."

"I'm going to bed then," Bob said.

After Bob left, Manlief, who had been watching the game, said, "Want to play me, Hoxie? My heart ain't in it, either."

"No," Hoxie said, "I'm going to visit Neddy."

"You visit him pretty often, don't you?"

"He tells me stories."

"What kind of stories?"

"Horse stories." Nothing a horse did ever puzzled Hoxie. With two more legs he could've lived in their world, honored and respected, playing for the fun of it and no danger of picking up bad diseases. He was homesick for the world Neddy told him about, and he hurried off toward it.

Left alone in the room, Manlief rose to put away the checkers. He had been riding a rake all day and the muscles of his right leg, the one used to release the catch, twittered up and down his thigh like a flock of birds dying of bruises. He leaned over, clutching and kneading, but that was like trying to cure a wound by patting it. He stood upright and went groaning to the table. He brushed the checkers off the table and into their box like crumbs. After he had blown out the lamp he noticed a final streak of light in the western sky, a curl of yellow like a lemon peel. Before he knew it just such a curl would be twisting up over the eastern hills and he would be hobbling down the stairs again and climbing up onto the rake. For once he wished he had a downstairs room, with the old and infirm. He thought he had enough infirmities tonight to merit it.

✦

All the women except three had gone to bed. In the women's sitting-room Lily Bias, Mary Abel and a newcomer, Nancy Sharon, waited out the day. Lily was at the table scratching out a letter with spidery pen-strokes; Mary sat by the window, motionless, watching the dark come down; Nancy Sharon rocked and nursed her baby and, when she wasn't coughing, sang to it. Overtaken by a cough she appeared to try to disguise it to her own ears by finishing it up as a tune. Her cough was low and soft and before her listeners knew it she would have it changed into a low soft song. *"Oh, my darling Nellie Grey, They have taken you away, And I'll never see my darling any more."* The cough itself, when it returned, seemed to keep time with a kind of muffled drum beat to *Nellie Grey*—and under the song was, always, the threat of the raw lungs. Nancy's breast, full and blue veined, showed through the opening of her brown calico as surprising as a peony growing on a fencepost. Where, on what was so straight up and down and lean as Nancy, could so much bounty be hidden—so much floweriness?

Lily watched her for a while, then said as the baby sucked noisily, "That baby is eating you alive, Nancy Sharon. He's swelling and you're dwindling. You'd ought to wean him."

Nancy rocked and patted. "It rests me to nurse him. I get so hot these summer days and baby seems to draw the heat out when he nurses." She began to cough then, turned the cough into *Rock of Ages.*

"You're killing yourself for him," Lily told her.

Nancy stopped her singing, but before she could speak Mary Abel said, "She's got the right to choose."

"Choosing to die," Lily said, "is what she's doing."

"She's got the right," Mary said and added to herself, Die or kill. You have to do what's best for the most people. Lily went back to her writing, Nancy to her singing, and Mary to her watching. She saw everything, could name everything: rocking, singing, nursing, letter-writing. They existed out there in that other world, but were important only as they helped or hindered James and his mission. As far as she could tell they were unimportant to James, didn't matter one way or the other, and so she watched Lily and Nancy as pleasurably as though they were moths or hummingbirds.

Besides James' mission and James himself, only Em was important to her. Em was her own little lost child. Oh, not born to her and lost, but lost even more completely, lost before she'd had a chance to be born to her. She didn't tell James any of this, and she had no doubts about not telling him. She had to do what was best for him in every way. She sat, quiet and patient, untroubled by uncertainties, waiting for complete darkness when she would prove to James himself just how much he and his mission did mean to her. She contemplated the women's sitting-room and its equipment with a bemused tenderness she had not experienced since she was ten years old and had owned a doll's playhouse: lamp, table, chairs, baby, mother, all so lifelike, so exactly duplicating real things, *but not* real. She could not help smiling a little at the exactness of the similarity. *She* knew it was only make-believe, Lily scratching away at a make-believe letter and Nancy making believe she nursed her baby. The way she did with Em, sometimes. It was pitiful in a way, how no one else saw through the pretense, and somehow sweet and funny, too. Exactly like a doll playhouse. And her knowledge of its real nature gave her a sense of power. Oh, yes, she had power tonight, power to see through some of the world's simplicities, and to do some simplifying of her own. Weed out some of the excess of the world, open the way for James and teach his jailers a needed lesson.

When Em entered, barefoot, none of the women looked up, Lily from her letter, Nancy from her baby, Mary from her dream. Em had been wandering from room to room, testing them like ovens for heat. All the rooms were warm and most of them empty. Everyone had gone to bed early. Mag had left the kitchen for bed as she looked in. Her father, a paper over his eyes to keep out the lamplight, was sound asleep on the sitting-room sofa. She passed Manlief in the hall, his eyes already half shut. It was strange, all this noonday heat and midnight sleepiness—like a bright apple with a dark core.

Lily looked up and beckoned to her. "Tell me how to spell these words," she said.

"What words?"

"Eternal, wait, matrimony."

Em wrote, "Eternel, wait, matrimony."

"Thank you. Bad spelling ruins a letter, I think."

Em saw the first sheet of Lily's letter headed, "My darling Christie."

"Everybody is writing him," she said.

"Everybody loves him," Lily answered, matter-of-factly. She put eternel, wait, and matrimony into the spaces she had left for them. Matrimony was bigger than she had counted on and had to be crowded a little. "He is planning marriage again," she told Em. With pride, Em thought, as her father spoke of a rosebush which bloomed and bloomed.

"Who to this time?"

"His cousin."

"Does it make you sad?"

"He will never marry her."

"How can you tell?"

Lily lifted her old, played-out eyes, the color of oak-leaves that fall in a branch and stay under water for a month or two. Her long ears hung down in soft colorless lobes. Eyebrows on her soft forehead were surprising, like hairs in a pudding. Her face, Em thought, is like an old piece of velvet with needle-holes in it to show how much it has been used.

"I don't know how I can tell. But I can tell. He is coming toward me and away from his cousin."

"Is he going to marry you?" she asked, and felt guilty. Lily was in earnest and she was joking.

But Lily had her dignity. She would not be fooled with. "That's not for the woman to say nor for children to think about."

"I think about it sometimes."

"You're too young for such thoughts."

"Except for marriage, I wouldn't be."

"Let's not blame marriage," said Lily tartly.

Em laughed. Then she was serious. "All around me everybody married and getting married. And still I don't know what it is."

"Like air."

"Nothing gets born of air."

"Thunderstorms," said Lily shrewdly. "Cloudbursts. Cyclones."

"I never thought of that."

"Love gives me strange thoughts sometimes. I surprise myself with what I know."

"What do you know?" Em asked.

Lily rose, holding the letter close to her chest. "I know about death." She walked to the door, then turned again to Em. "I know it is near."

"Near who?" Em called after her, but Lily was through with talk. Love and death. Being alive was enough for Em and gave her more strange thoughts than she knew what to do with. She went past Nancy Sharon and her nursing baby, imagining the effort which it must take to raise milk along that whole network of tubes which in her mind's eye she saw branching like the roots of a jimson weed clear to the ends of Nancy's toes. By the time she reached Mary Abel, Mary had changed to a rocking-chair.

"Sit on my lap," Mary said, "and I'll rock you."

"It's too hot."

Mary paid no attention to this but pulled her down on to her lap. "Poor tired baby," she said. "Poor tired baby." She rocked and stroked with warm firm fingers. "Mary's poor tired baby." Her hand moved about Em's hair and forehead with the bewitchment of that which cannot be quite depended upon, with the magic of irregularity.

Nancy left the room. Beneath stroking and endearment Em changed. The foolishness of her long, dirty legs (she hadn't washed yet for bed) sticking out, grasshopper-like, beyond Mary's lap, and her head lolling back, as babyish as Tommy Sharon's, against Mary's big bosom, was lost on her. She had become as little as Tommy Sharon, as dependent, as loved. Mary rocked and hummed and stroked and sometimes talked. The sitting-room was all love, all contentment. The lost found. The lamp burned steadily, its yellow flame rising tulip-shaped and with the clear sharp smell of all country evenings when, work over, the words which daylight won't countenance, may be spoken.

"Petty," Mary whispered, "are you awake? Tonight's the night I'm going to do it, petty."

Em went to her room almost at once. First she confided the news to her casket. "Mary is going to do it tonight." Then she stretched out on top of her bed, not trying nor expecting to sleep but just lying and listening and waiting in the hot dark evening.

VI

THE HOGS were what Mary wanted to destroy, not the barn; but to kill the hogs she was willing to burn the barn. She had all the best ones penned there, together with such of the cows and horses as she had been able to lock up without trouble. She had had the corncobs soaking in coal-oil since morning, and she went about the job of distributing them in a calm, housewifely way, as if she were sprinkling clothes, or feeding chickens. She enjoyed the work, imagining James' pleasure when he woke next morning to find himself forever rid of that circle of pink eyes and hairy snouts shoving and snuffling at him, keeping him day and night from his real business of digging. She would run them all over the cliff—like the swine. She would set James free. She would teach Link Conboy a needed lesson.

She paused for a moment when she had placed the last cob, like a careful housewife inspecting effects, looking for a book out of place or a pillow dented. The guest was coming, and the guest was fire and she wanted it to feel at home. It was now the first hour of what could be called the real night. She had worked without a lantern, lit only by the speckling light of the stars and guided by her will to destroy. The hogs, packed in the stalls, had come to her as she put the cobs in the mangers. As she began to light them she said, "Eat your fill, now. Have yourselves a bellyful of burning."

As the fire began to catch she gathered up a pick and shovel—not hers or James'—but it was a pity for such good digging implements to be destroyed, and carried them outside. Supported between them she rested meditatively, waiting for the light, which already showed red through the barn's cracks, to lick its way into the open—and for the first hog to scream.

Out at Brush Creek Cate stayed at her window until the sky in the west had lost its meaning, was as dark as north or south, without the remnants even of an afterglow to show that the sun had once been there. The katydids were quieter, the maples were stirring in the night wind. When at last she rose, Cate had passed from the conviction that Christie was not coming tonight, to the conviction that he was not coming at all, not ever.

She took the note from under Ferris' pillow and tore it into minute pieces; then, that done, began slowly and heavily to unpack her clothes. As she moved from packing-box to closet she noticed off in the direction of what she still thought of as "home" an arc of red against the sky, and for a moment she had a fear unconnected with Christie. What if some of the buildings at The Farm were burning? But it was a second's pang only, a passing flicker, incapable of silencing her unceasing cry of Christie, Christie, Christie.

Christie, being outdoors, saw the flames first; but Em lying there, the responsibility for death heavy upon her, heard the first hog scream, a high, piercing cry, almost birdlike to come from throats so heavy and fat. She began running later than Christie, but he had farther to go, even coming slaunchwise, as he was, through the apple orchard. He was crossing the barnyard as she left the kitchen door and the glow from the barn was strong enough now for her to recognize him, and she called his name: "Christie, Christie!"

If he heard her, he made no sign; but it made no difference. She saw that he was going to do, anyway, what she wanted him to do, get into the barn and try to put out the fire. He paid no attention to Mary, menacing him with her shovel, but ran past her to the door of the barn and stood there fumbling with the latch. Em, while Christie worked at the lock, was seized without a word by Mary, enfolded and half-smothered in the soft depths of her bosom.

She struggled to free herself, cried, with her mouth full of calico and buttons, "Let me go, let me go." But Mary, without a word, only enwrapped her more closely. When finally she had wrenched her head about so that she could once more see, the barn door had been opened and Christie was gone from sight. Two horses ran screaming through the door, one with its mane on fire so that it shed sparks like a locomotive plunging through the night. The horses, blind or mad with fright, would have run them down and Mary let Em go while they both sprang back to escape. But she regained her hold at once and paid no attention to Em's struggles to get away.

Em's concern for the animals had changed to fear for Christie, but in trying to get away from Mary she only pulled the knot of Mary's clasping tighter. "Let me go, let me go," she cried, turning and twisting. "Let me go to Christie."

Mary held her with stubborn love. "It is too late, petty," she said and, as she spoke, the floor of the hay mow gave way, dropping into the barn the mass of hay which, igniting as it fell, roared upward in an enormous swirl of flame. Flames and screams: they mounted together, and Em, no longer trying to escape, burrowed deeper and deeper into the hiding-place of Mary's bosom.

16

Link and Cate drove into The Junction together and together saw Christie's body put onto the train for return to his uncle and cousin. Cate thought she might never shed another tear as long as she lived, or smile again either. An old bleached bone, she thought, could not be more free of feeling. There had been rain earlier in the afternoon, and the sky had not yet cleared. Link drove, leaning forward, head down, reins held in one hand which lay loosely and brokenly across his knee. The buggy rolled steadily on past the new fields of wheat stubble and the green cornfields and the apple orchards where Summer Sweetings and Early Harvests were already taking on color. Neither Cate nor Link had spoken since they left town, but when they reached the first hilltop from which the Poor Farm buildings could be seen, Cate said the words which had so intolerably filled her mind since Christie's death.

"I killed him."

She did not expect any reply from her father, certainly no contradiction. He knew she had written the letter which had brought Christie. He had read it, even. But he did speak and, in a way, he did contradict her.

"We all killed Christie," he said.

Cate turned to look at her father and saw the shiny glazed tear tracks running down his cheeks. "We?" she asked.

"I," he said. "I killed Christie. I'm the responsible one."

"I wrote the letter," Cate said. "I brought him here."

"None of us would've been here except for me. I killed the boy the day I set my mind on coming here."

"No," Cate said, "we could've lived here a hundred years and Christie still be alive if I hadn't written the letter."

"And Em killed him," Link went on, as if she hadn't spoken.

[438]

"So she thinks. She knew and she didn't tell. And your mother killed him."

"Mama?"

"What kept you from marrying Christie in the first place?"

Cate put her hands across her face.

"We all killed him, we all had a hand in it. We began preparing it a long time ago. And finally," he said, "Christie killed himself. He chose to die."

Cate, who had believed herself wrung dry of tears, began once more to cry. "He is dead," she said. "He is dead. He is dead forever and I'll never see him again." At that minute Christie's death seemed to her to have grown out of all their plans. Link's plan to come to the Poor House and Lib's plan to have pure daughters and Em's plan to lead a secret life and the Abels' plan to make everyone happy. All planning and no trust. All scheming and arranging. She took her hands down from her face and said, "We planned. The trouble was we all schemed and planned."

Link said, "That was not the trouble. The trouble was, our plans were bad. We didn't plan well enough."

She didn't believe it. All the planning in the world would not have saved Christie, but love would. Love would have kept him alive and she had denied love.

At the top of the last downgrade before making the turn into the grounds, they saw Lib and Em with Manlief between them, walking out to meet them. Link pulled up to await their coming, gazed toward them as if assuagement for what had happened could be found in the upright stance of their firm bodies against the clearing sky; assurance for the future in their steady oncoming: Lib, in her undiminished eagerness, forging ahead of the other two; Manlief, even at that distance, with his air of a man newly awake and taking stock of wonders he had half forgotten; Em, neither eager nor wondering but marching forward, each minute manufacturing for her whatever the minute needed. Clouds, remnants of the morning's storm, crossed the sky, momentarily darkening them, and at the bottom of the hill they appeared too frail for the climb ahead of them; and on the slope itself they were not very graceful in their climbing. But they came on; eagerly, wonderingly, calmly; and in their various ways, they made it.

When they reached the buggy, Link put the lines into Cate's

hand and got out. "I'm going to walk back to the house with your mother," he said. "You girls, and Manlief too, if he'd like to ride, go on ahead."

Manlief got in on one side, Em on the other. Cate sat in the middle, the reins loose in her slack hands, not attempting to drive. Lib and Link passed them and still they sat.

At last Cate said, "I can't drive."

"Why?" Manlief asked.

Cate looked down at the reins lying loose across her open hands. "I can't close my hands," she said. "I can't drive because I don't care if we move or stand still. I am dead. I am as dead as Lily or Christie. Lily died because she loved Christie. So did I."

"No," Manlief said, "you did not die."

"I am dead," Cate repeated.

"You are not dead because you have never been alive. What hasn't been alive can't die. Your time for dying is not yet."

Cate, whose eyes had been on the dust of the road, was caught by the authority in Manlief's voice and she turned to look at him. "Tomorrow," Manlief told her, "we bury Lily. Then we are through here with death for a while."

Cate shook her head. "I can never be through with it. I was responsible for it."

She felt the impatient movement of Manlief's arm. "It was chance," he said, "and you are through with it." He started up the horse and, out of habit as the wheels began to turn, Cate's hands closed on the reins. "I will help you," Manlief said.

Cate took her eyes from Manlief's face. That statement, "I will help you," was the first thing she had encountered since Christie's death that had any reality for her. How Manlief or anyone else could help her, she didn't know; still his voice and manner were convincing.

"I loved Christie," she said in a very low voice as if confessing a sin.

"That is nothing to be ashamed of," Manlief told her.

Ashamed! But she understood, with his words, that she had been and, understanding, the shame left her. The only shame would have been to have lived in the same world with Christie and not to have loved him. The only shame she had now was that she had not known the right way to love him. What is the right way to love? The question, as it formed itself in her mind, was addressed to Manlief. It was a question she could not ask him now; someday, she thought, I will ask him.

On Cate's side of the buggy, as they proceeded down the final hill, was one of the Abels' empty, abandoned pits, a little rainwater, stained red with clay, covering its bottom. Cate stared at it, the old lunacy still asserting itself: if they had dug another inch, say, would they have discovered the word, the answer? Whatever it was they were digging for? Was there a ready-made answer, like that, available to all who sought and equally good for all?

Manlief, as if reading her mind, said, "Don't stare at that, Cate. It's a blot on the landscape. Hoxie and I will fill it in tomorrow."

It was behind them as he spoke, and though they had proceeded so slowly, the horse putting down his hooves as if reluctant to disturb the dust, crusted over by the storm, they soon caught up with, then passed Lib and Link. Cate, as they went by, lifted the hand which only a few minutes before she had felt powerless to move, in a gesture both of greeting and good-by. Then, as they distanced the walkers, there was nothing visible ahead of the three in the buggy but the empty road and the summer world.